Praise for Domin

"I don't normally recommend novels on my website, but I'm making an exception for The Reiki Man by Dominic C. James. It's an action packed thriller with lots of spiritual information woven through it, and as the title suggests, lots of Reiki too – I couldn't put it down!"
Penelope Quest, Best-selling Reiki author

"The Reiki Man combines the spiritual world with the physical and tests both to the limit. James creates a believable narrative and I felt totally drawn into the mystery of Reiki. However, what is clever about this story is that it is a murder mystery with more to it than the usual 'whodunnit'. The ending made me desperate to read the second part of the trilogy! Fans of Dan Brown will love this book."
Victoria Watson, Young Reviewer of the Year

"All in all a good fun read – and first in a trilogy. With its surprise ending, The Reiki Man will leave you ready for more."
Beth Lowell, Reiki Digest

"I really enjoyed it. And perhaps enjoyed it all the more as it is not normally the genre of book that I would read. So, it started out as a duty and definitely ended up a pleasure. I enjoyed learning about Reiki and fell totally in love with Titan. It's a fascinating book, and holds the attention throughout, which is no mean feat. An unusual subject that's written about in a fascinating way...well done!"
Laura Lockington, Author *Cupboard Love* and *Stargazy Pie*

"It's about time there was a novel about Reiki. And as an added bonus it is a suspense/mystery story. This is a great read and I recommend the book to all."
Steve Murray, Best-selling author of *Reiki: The Ultimate Guide*

"The book is fantastic and a service to mankind I think as it's so accessible for 'non-spiritual' folk."
Heather Mackenzie, UK Reiki Federation

"WOW! A fantastic paranormal thriller that left me stuck for words (and there's not much that can do that, I can tell you!). If you like a book that's full of thrills, mystery and excitement with a plot that is forever twisting and turning, then go and buy this book – NOW!"
Kim the Bookworm

A
SACRED
STORM

Part III of The Reiki Man Trilogy

A
SACRED
STORM

Part III of The Reiki Man Trilogy

Dominic C. James

Winchester, UK
Washington, USA

First published by Roundfire Books, 2012
Roundfire Books is an imprint of John Hunt Publishing Ltd., Laurel House, Station Approach, Alresford, Hants, SO24 9JH, UK
office1@jhpbooks.net
www.johnhuntpublishing.com
www.roundfire-books.com

For distributor details and how to order please visit the 'Ordering' section on our website.

ISBN: 978 1 78099 580 9

Design: Stuart Davies

Printed in the USA by Edwards Brothers Malloy

We operate a distinctive and ethical publishing philosophy in all areas of our business, from our global network of authors to production and worldwide distribution.

For Angela

Acknowledgements

Once again, thanks to all my friends and family for their support over the three books; everyone at John Hunt Publishing for making the trilogy possible; Jim, Karen, Peter, Amelia and especially Angela for bringing me back to the light; everyone at JT's.

Prologue

Ali Hussein hobbled out of his mother's house and began the agonizing walk towards the marketplace. Fortunately, the sun was only just climbing, and the dusty streets and alleys were still cool. With his weight on his battered old crutch he limped slowly through the outskirts of the city, stopping frequently either to rest his leg or converse with friends on the familiar route. Ali's easy going nature, and resolute determination in the face of disability, had earned him many allies and admirers, and it was difficult to go more than a hundred yards without at least one person stopping him for a chat. His popularity sustained his will and served as a palliative for his pain.

Halfway between his home and the bazaar, a low wall broke the stream of buildings. From here Ali could see right the way down into the heart of Mecca. Every morning he would lift himself up and sit with his legs dangling over the side, at once overawed and inspired by the breathtaking expanse. At the centre of this magnificent vista was the Masjid al-Haram, the Grand Mosque, built around the Kaaba – the cuboid structure that was the most sacred site in Islam. Ali knew that whatever life had thrown at him, and it had thrown a lot, he was more than fortunate to live in such a wondrous city; the place that Allah himself had singled out as the centre of the earth.

Invigorated by his five-minute break he continued the laborious journey to work, hobbling as quickly as he could so as not to be late. His boss, Farouk, was a kindly man, and had employed Ali when no-one else would give him a second thought, so Ali was loathe to let him down with tardiness. He was lucky to have a job and did everything in his power to keep it.

When he eventually reached the square he was surprised to find it already heaving with activity. In the centre of the market-place a large group of people had formed a circle, and were clamouring around an unseen trader. On the outskirts of the throng he could see Farouk jumping up and down to get a good view.

He hopped over and tugged at his employer's shirt. "Farouk!" he shouted. "What is going on?"

"Ali! You are here at last!" he yelled, ecstatically. "I have been waiting for you. Come, we must cut through the crowd and bring you to him."

"Bring me to who?"

"You will see!" Farouk grabbed his arm and pulled him through the melee, shovelling bodies out of the way like a human snowplough.

"Over here, Master!" Farouk shouted as they reached the middle, waving his hands furiously to attract attention. "Over here!"

The man at the centre of the furore heard Farouk's pleas and walked over to them. He was tall and bearded and dressed in a white robe. "What would you ask of me, friend?" he said kindly.

"This boy is crippled, oh Master," said Farouk excitedly. "Please, show him some mercy and heal his leg!"

The man they called Master knelt down before Ali and took his leg in his hands. Ali felt a brief chill in his limb, followed by a soothing warmth like the desert wind. There was an audible crack as his mangled muscles and bones started to reform into their intended shape. The sound made him wince, but he felt no pain. It was over in less than ten seconds.

The Master stood up and smiled. "Throw away your crutch my child," he said. "You need it no longer."

Ali did as he was told, casting his prop aside and tentatively allowing some weight onto his leg. His confidence growing, he began to jump lightly from foot to foot, until eventually he was leaping up and down in a full-blown dance. The crowd whooped and cheered working themselves into a febrile frenzy.

"Who are you, Master?!" Ali shouted in the middle of the

tumult.

The Master placed his palm on Ali's head. "I am the Mahdi. I am the Hand of Allah," he said. "I have been sent to carry out his bidding. Come with me, young Ali. Come with me to the Kaaba where I shall reveal myself."

And so they walked, side by side through the streets, down into the heart of Mecca, followed by an ever-increasing multitude. Euphoric cries echoed round the city walls, bringing happiness and hope to all that heard them. It was time for great rejoicing; it was time to rise up and display devotion; it was time to show the world the true meaning of faith. They were strong; they were invincible. The Hand of Allah was among them.

Chapter 1

It was nearing midday in the far reaches of the jungle, and a lone kite hovered above the trees searching for prey. The air was still and throttling, and the sun crackled in the heavens, piercing the canopy with acute shards of brilliant yellow radiation. In a hidden clearing surrounded by banyan trees stood a large wooden hut. Inside, an old Indian monk sat beside the sick man's bed and tended to his fever. For over two weeks the virus had raged on unabated, but now, on the sixteenth day, it looked as though it might finally be breaking. The monk recited a small prayer and forced the man's head up to take on more water.

Majami, as the monk was known, had never encountered such an illness in his long life. He was well-practised in all aspects of healing: from a small cut to a broken limb; and from a mild cold to malaria, cholera, typhoid, and even cancer. But this latest malady was beyond his wisdom. He had tried everything from basic herbal remedies to complex elixirs, and drawn inordinate power from the cosmos, yet he had still failed to lower the man's temperature by so much as a degree. Whatever was afflicting him it was something that humankind had never previously been exposed to.

The man briefly opened his sweaty eyes, uttered something unintelligible, then closed them again. These fits had been a sustained punctuation of his incapacity, causing Majami to jump each time one occurred. They were becoming less frequent, but continued to hold their power of surprise. If the man was speaking an accepted language, then it was not one that the multilingual monk recognized.

The afternoon drew on without remorse, bringing with it a swathe of insects. Majami ignored the persistent barrage and continued to administer waves of pure energy into his patient. He was tired and hungry, his white robes drenched in sweat, but his will refused to give up lest his charge relapse into the darkness once more.

And then, just before sundown, it happened. Majami's hands, hovering two inches above the man's head, were suddenly overcome by a searing cold; followed rapidly by a blinding heat that shot through his body and knocked him backwards to the ground. A mighty wind blew through the room, shaking the walls and sending the primitive furniture flying up and around in a mini cyclone. For an instant Majami thought he was going to be swept away; but then the gale died, the furniture clattered to the floor, and stone quiet enveloped the room.

For a while Majami lay still, regulating his breath to expel the excess energy and return to an earthly plane. Only when he was fully grounded once more did he lift his head and clamber to his feet. He looked down at the man and found that he was conscious and pulling himself up to a sitting position. They stared at each other passively and then smiled simultaneously, each registering the wonder of their shared experience.

Eventually the man spoke: "Thank you," he said, clasping his hands and bowing his head. "*Namaste.*"

"*Namaste,*" said Majami, returning the gesture. "I am glad to see you well. I feared you may not return to us."

"How long have I been here?"

"Just over two weeks…Sixteen days to be precise."

The man shook his head. "Bloody hell! The last thing I remember is lying in the brush." He thought for a moment. "I'm Stratton by the way." He held out his hand in Western fashion.

Majami took his hand and introduced himself.

"Well then, Majami, perhaps you can shed some light on exactly how I got here?"

"Perhaps you should eat first, and then rest," said Majami.

"I feel fine."

"I am the healer. You are the patient. Clear your mind."

"Fair enough," Stratton conceded. "But can you at least tell me if…"

"The panther is fine," Majami interrupted. "He has been waiting for you."

Majami left without another word, and a few seconds later the familiar sleek black figure of Titan trotted in and padded up to the bed, nuzzling at Stratton's outstretched palm.

"Hello boy," said Stratton. "It's good to see you."

Titan gave a friendly growl and laid a soft paw on his friend's chest. Stratton began to relax and took in his plain surroundings. He was in a room no more than eight feet square with rough log walls and a small glassless window looking out into the jungle. On the floor, in disarray, lay: a small table; a chair; a water bowl; and the remains of a spent candle next to a pool of wax. The doorway led into a narrow passage that bore left and out of sight.

Sixteen days! he thought, running his hands through the thickening growth on his face. Where had they gone? One minute he was fading to nothing on the jungle floor, the next he was here. Save for brief flashes of colour he remembered nothing. Over two weeks of his life lost, never to return. He imagined it must be how people felt coming out of a coma.

And then there was the not inconsequential matter of his friends. He shivered as he recalled the chilling screams echoing through the jungle the night he lost consciousness. He was as sure now as he had been then that Jennings was their source. What manner of sadism had produced such an outburst he dared not think, but he knew that those cries would haunt him for a long time to come, if not forever. He hoped that wherever Jennings was, alive or dead, he was no longer suffering.

And what of Stella? Was she still out there in the jungle with Jimi the guide, or had she too been captured along with Jennings? His stomach spasmed and shivered as twisted images shot through his overactive mind. Jennings' torture would be light compared to what a group of savages would do to a woman alone in the wild. He closed his eyes tightly and shook his head to disperse the painful pictures.

At least there was a glimmer of hope for both her and Jennings. For Oggi there was none. He had met his doom on the jagged river rocks. Stratton replayed the scene in his head over and over again, wondering if maybe he could have held on a bit tighter or a bit longer. Did he really try his hardest to stop his friend from falling, or were there extra reserves he could have called upon to lift him to safety? Where was the superhuman strength that ordinary people found in such situations? Why had he not dug deeper?

His guilt-ridden musings broke as Majami returned with food. He handed Stratton a bowl of steaming vegetable stew and a flat bread similar to a naan.

Stratton thanked him and began to eat, dipping the bread tentatively and forcing a slow mouthful. But the meal was delicious, restoring his appetite as he ate, and it wasn't long before he was finished and sitting back with a full belly.

"That was fantastic," said Stratton. "I didn't think I was hungry. What's in it?"

"It is a special recipe," said Majami. "Made to stimulate the appetite and strengthen resolve. I use traditional vegetables and also rare jungle plants. It has taken years of trial and error, but I think I am close to perfecting it."

"Well, it's certainly worked the oracle on me," said Stratton. "I feel much better already. So perhaps now you can tell me exactly who you are and how I got here."

"I think you should sleep first."

"I've been asleep for over two weeks."

"No," said the monk. "I mean proper sleep."

"I'll sleep better if my head isn't pounding with questions," countered Stratton.

Majami smiled. "Very well," he said. "If you must know, I am the head of an order of monks charged with protecting the secrets of life and healing. I believe you were on your way to find us."

"Yes, I was…well we were – I was part of a group."

"Indeed. You were being guided by my young friends Jimi and Tali."

"Yes. I'm afraid Tali is dead though."

"Yes," said Majami. "It is most unfortunate. And even more unfortunate that Jimi too has joined him."

Stratton bowed his head. "I'm sorry to hear that. He was a good man."

"Yes, a very good man."

A horrible thought entered Stratton's mind and he looked up earnestly to Majami. "Jimi was looking after one of our party – a girl. Do you know anything of her?"

"No, no girl. We came across Jimi's body on the jungle path – he was alone."

Stratton breathed a respectfully internal sigh of relief, and continued to probe. "So how did you come to be that far out in the jungle? I was led to believe that your temple was right in the very heart of the forest."

"It is, and we would not normally venture so far, but one of my brothers had a terrible vision and it was decided that two of us should come and aid your party. Unfortunately we were too late to save Jimi, but we found you and brought you here to heal."

"Where is here?" asked Stratton. "Surely you didn't carry me all the way back to your temple."

"No, of course not. This is one of our way-houses. It is not at all far from where we found you. But it is off the beaten track and extremely well-hidden."

"Is it?" said Stratton. "The men who were tracking us seemed to know all about Jimi's little hiding places."

"Not this one," Majami said assuredly.

Stratton wasn't convinced, but decided to take the monk's word for it. He was about to ask about Jennings when the monk interrupted him.

"No more questions," he said.

"But I just wanted to know…"

Majami repeated himself. "No more questions. It is time for sleep – for you, and for me also." He got up and bowed and bade Stratton a goodnight.

Stratton lay for a while, stroking Titan's head absentmindedly as he went through different scenarios in his head, each one becoming progressively worse. But then Majami's words floated gently into his visions and he knew it was time for sleep. He closed his eyes and vacated his mind, hoping that tomorrow would bring some much-needed answers.

Chapter 2

Cardinal Miguel Desayer was troubled. He leant back in his chair and ran a weary hand down his weathered face. For thirty years and more he had been dreading this moment, ever since the day his mentor, Gabriel, had let he and Abdullah in on the secret. Over four decades of subterfuge and searching had followed: pretending to be the perfect holy man; obeying doctrines that he knew to be false; pedantically toeing the line to keep his cover. It had been torture at times, but he had kept his composure and held his tongue throughout so that his promise to Gabriel would be honoured. If the rumours coming out of Mecca were true, though, then it had all been for nothing.

Opening his desk drawer he drew out an old silver-framed photo and reminisced. The two boys in the black and white picture were barely into their teens, but both were strong and vital. They were barefoot and dressed in raggedy kit ready for a game of soccer. The boy on the left, the darker of the two, held the ball under his right arm. They were locked together and grinning like Cheshire Cats, their whole lives ahead to do with what they wished, or so they thought. But that was then. Now Abdullah was gone, and all that remained of him were fading memories.

A knock on the door stopped him dwelling. He put the photograph back in the drawer and beckoned his visitor to enter, hoping it would be Father Patrick Cronin with fresh news. He wasn't disappointed.

Cronin hobbled in on his crutches, greeted the Cardinal formally, then sat down and faced him across the desk. His boss tried to appear calm but the lines etched on his face gave away his concern.

"Well then, Father," said Desayer. "What do we know?"

Cronin cleared his throat and proceeded. "It doesn't look good I'm afraid, Your Eminence. Our sources in Mecca have confirmed it – there is a man there claiming to be the Hand of Allah. He has been healing all manner of illnesses and deformities: curing cancers; restoring vision; remobilizing the crippled – the list goes on."

Desayer's fists tightened as he tried to control his breathing. "Then they have found the sacred knowledge. They must have."

"I can't be sure, Your Eminence, but it appears that way. Our sources have witnessed this man's healing powers for themselves, he's definitely the real thing."

"So how have they come by it? I thought that the box and the parchment were safely on their way to Majami."

"So did I, Your Eminence. And as far as I knew everything was going to plan. Kandinsky's man dropped them at the beach and they were last seen heading off with their guides."

"But you've had no word since?"

"No. But then I didn't expect to until they came back out of the jungle."

"Didn't they have a satellite phone?" the Cardinal asked.

"No. It would have been too dangerous for them to have contact with anybody once they were in the jungle. It doesn't matter how careful you are nowadays – there's always someone listening. And it only takes a few seconds to pinpoint someone's position from their phone signal."

"Of course," said Desayer. "You must think me terribly outdated."

"Not at all, Your Eminence. Most people don't realize how vulnerable technology has made us."

"Yes, indeed. Soon there will be no secrets left." He gazed thoughtfully out of the window. "What about Kandinsky? Are you sure he was telling you the truth? Perhaps he took the box and sold it to the highest bidder."

"With respect, I think that's highly unlikely, Your Eminence. I've known Kandinsky for a number of years and, although he wouldn't be first in line for canonization, I've always found him to be a man of his word. He has never been anything but honest with us from the start, and he wants to see the sacred knowledge safe just as much as we do. And besides, even if he had taken the box it would be useless without the key to the symbols; and they were taken by a different route."

"Yes, yes, of course they were. Sorry, Father, I am just not thinking logically at the moment." He took a sip of water and a deep breath. "So, Father, have you any ideas as to what has actually happened?"

Cronin shrugged. "To be honest, Your Eminence, I'm as in the dark as you are. I can only really hypothesize."

"Well then – go ahead."

"We have to assume that the Muslims have managed to acquire both the box and the symbols – it's the only way this man could have gained his power. Therefore it stands to reason that they waylaid both our parties in the jungle. I don't know how they did it, but it's the only explanation I can think of."

Desayer raised his eyebrows. "But the box and the parchment were taken by separate paths."

"Yes, they were. And I didn't for one minute think that both would be found, but I guess that whoever took them was one step ahead of us. I suspect treachery somewhere along the line."

Desayer digested the information for a moment. "What about this man who took your place? What was his name again – Brady or something?"

"Grady, Your Eminence. Scott Grady."

"Yes, that was it, Grady. Well, is there not a chance that he may have betrayed us?"

Cronin looked to the floor awkwardly. Grady had been a gamble on his part, a big gamble. Stratton and Stella seemed to trust him which is what had swung it for him in the end – well, that and the fact that there was nobody else available – but he'd had reservations about the guy from the start. It wasn't anything personal, it was just an inbuilt mistrust of anyone from American intelligence. He'd experienced first hand how they operated, and it certainly wasn't on an ethical basis. On the outset Grady appeared to have seen a brighter light, but the temptation to make a small fortune from what was effectively just a piece of paper may have proved too much.

Cronin looked back up to the Cardinal and decided to keep his concerns to himself. "Theoretically he could have done, Your Eminence, but I doubt it – he didn't seem the type. Anyway, with respect, I think we're getting away from the main issue. It doesn't matter how they got hold of the artefacts, the point is that they did. We've got to figure out what to do about it."

"You are absolutely right, Father. You must forgive me. Like I said before – I am not thinking logically at the moment. Have you got any immediate suggestions?"

Cronin sighed. "I'm not sure what we can do at the moment. According to our sources this man – the Hand of Allah – has already built up a massive following in Mecca. It won't be long before his legend spreads right across the world."

"Is there no way of getting to him?" asked Desayer.

Cronin raised his eyebrows. "You mean an assassination?"

Desayer nodded.

Cronin shook his head. "Not really, Your Eminence. But even if we did manage to get to him they'd just replace him with someone else wouldn't they? Or bring him back to life. Then they really would have a Messiah on their hands. The only thing we can do is watch and wait, and hope that a solution presents itself."

"Yes, I think you are right, Father. Although I fear we are fighting a losing battle. As soon as they got their hands on the symbols we were beaten. It will not be long before Islam has conquered the globe. And I do not believe for one minute that it will happen peacefully."

"Don't despair, Your Eminence, nothing's happened yet. There's always hope."

"Yes, hope..." He said the word reflectively. "There is always hope."

Preceded by a quick rap on the door a young priest walked in with a message for Desayer.

"Cardinal Vittori requests your presence at an urgent meeting, Your Eminence," he stated.

"Right this minute?" asked Desayer.

"Yes, Your Eminence, it is a matter of some importance."

"Very well, tell him I shall be along directly."

"Thank you, Your Eminence." He bowed his head deferentially and exited the room quickly.

"Well then," said Desayer. "I suppose I must go and see what this is all about."

"Of course, Your Eminence," said Cronin. "I shall return to my office and make some more enquiries." He struggled to his feet and shuffled out of the Cardinal's chambers.

As he turned into the corridor, his mind elsewhere, he was knocked back into the wall. His head jerked in confusion and his left crutch clattered to the floor. He was about to follow it down when a firm hand steadied him.

"I am very sorry, Father," said a voice. "Are you okay?"

Cronin looked up and stared at the man. He was a civilian with sharp features and looked very familiar.

"Yes, I'm fine," said Cronin. "If you could just pass me my crutch."

The man obliged and Cronin thanked him, brushing off more apologies politely, and trying to place his accent. He watched him head down the corridor accompanied by Cardinal Vittori's messenger. As they moved out of sight he furrowed his brow in contemplation and started back to his office. Just where had he seen him before?

Chapter 3

Stella stared up at the ceiling and traced imaginary faces in the elaborate mouldings. It was something she did at home; trying to pick out shapes in the stippled paintwork, or maybe animal forms in the clouds. If you looked hard enough at something it would invariably distort and reveal a hidden treasure, a bit like the 'magic eye' pictures that had been so popular in the nineties. Perhaps if she focused all her energy into one point she could create a hole from which to escape through, but even her imagination she felt would not extend that far. She was trapped, and no amount of dreaming or wishing was going to free her.

Of course, there were worse places to be held captive, and she shuddered as she remembered the cold cellar within which Augustus Jeremy had incarcerated her and Stratton, but a prison was a prison, mink-lined or not.

Having grown tired, and with her eyes beginning to strain, she shuffled across the substantial bed and sat on the edge with her toes dangling on the cool marble floor. She stretched her arms and yawned, blinking a couple of times to restore her blurry sight, and then allowed herself a brief smile as she took in the wondrous surroundings. She didn't know how long she'd been there – a week, maybe longer – but she still couldn't help but be impressed by the sheer unadulterated luxury of the place. With the finest furniture, hand-woven silks and original art on the walls, and solid-gold fittings in the almost cavernous bathroom she felt like a storybook princess. And the ornate, probably priceless, porcelain just added to the indulgence. But if she was a princess then she was one locked in a tower awaiting her Prince Charming to come to the rescue.

It seemed like a lifetime since she had been captured in the jungle. If only she hadn't been so bloody stupid. Jimi had told her to stay quiet and still in the undergrowth, but as soon as she heard the horrific howls of pain she knew she couldn't just lie there. But what had her rash actions achieved? Nothing.

The image was etched in her brain now, an indelible tattoo of her sorrow. She hoped that Jennings had died quickly, and that his pain was short-lived, but she knew the reality would probably be very different.

Beginning to dwell, she forced herself from the bed and took a walk around the room, bending and stretching her legs with exaggeration as she moved to shake off the stiffness. After a couple of small circuits she went to the bathroom and refreshed her face with cold water. The woman staring back at her in the mirror looked, unsurprisingly, pale and drawn. A close inspection of her hair revealed a few strands of grey creeping through into the black as well. When she returned to civilization she would do have to do something about it. But for now it could wait, because despite the fact that cosmetics, including hair-dye, had been made available to her, she was determined to look her worst. She wasn't going to give her jailer the satisfaction of her beauty.

The mere thought of him angered her to the point of explosion. His false smile; his creepy, clammy, wandering hands; his foul breath that mingled noxiously with the smell of frankincense on his clothes; and most of all his unwillingness to accept that what he was doing was wrong. His constant referral to her as a guest was infuriating, not only because it was a million miles from the truth, but because he actually believed it. The reality was, though, that she was a prisoner, a white slave, and it wouldn't be long before his advances became more pressing and brutal, until eventually he would go ahead and take what he wanted without her consent. And so it would go on, day after day, week after week, maybe allowing his friends and business associates to have a go as well. Any resistance on her part would probably just make it more fun for them.

She took a determined look in the mirror, pursing her lips resolutely, and promised herself that she would escape or die trying. She then returned to the main room and started her daily workout. With nothing but time on her hands it had been easy to get back into a fitness regime. After an initial bout of cramps her body had accustomed itself and each day since had been a progression. She was starting to feel strong again, like she had been at her peak in the Met. Every strained press-up and sit-up was accompanied by a grunt and a burning likeness of her keeper and the men that sold her to him.

And what of Stratton? What the hell had happened to him? One minute they were racing along the track, and the next he and Jennings had disappeared. She had been trying so hard to keep up with Jimi that she hadn't noticed them falling behind. He had been in a bad way, so if Jennings was captured why wasn't he? He certainly wasn't the guy hanging next to Jennings on the branch – that, although she couldn't figure how, appeared to be Grady.

So where was Stratton now?

Many scenarios streamed through her head, but the one that pleased her most was the idea that he had survived and was at this very minute planning a rescue mission. She pictured him crossing the desert with a group of crack mercenaries, each one ready to do battle with the sheik and his cadre of bodyguards. They would scale the walls and Stratton would come bursting through the barred window in a cloud of explosives to save her from peril. She smiled at the thought, but knew in her heart that no such thing was going to happen. If she wanted saving she was going to have to do it herself.

Chapter 4

Stratton woke to the sound of jungle chatter. It was some time after dawn, but light was only just beginning to filter through the thick canopy. He yawned loudly and stretched his arms wide, accidently hitting Titan's head as he did so. The panther paid little attention and continued to snooze happily by the side of the bed.

Stratton strained to see in the gloom. He reached out to the small table and fumbled for the water bowl, being careful not to upset it. His throat was burning dry and he drained the vessel in several prolonged gulps. Thirst quenched, he propped his back against the wall and closed his eyes for a brief meditation.

The fever that had held him for so long seemed all but gone, and for the first time in ages he could feel blood and energy coursing once more. He tried to remember when he had first started to ebb, and figured that it must have been just after he and Oggi had arrived at the motel. From then on it had been a downward spiral until his resolve completely gave way that night in the undergrowth. Technically speaking, however, it wasn't actually *his* resolve that had capitulated.

His mind drifted back to his time in between worlds, after Jeremy had killed him, and before Oggi had brought him back. He recalled the improbably vivid colours, the almost unbearable light, and the constant current of the cosmos pulsating through his soul like a climax without end. He also recalled the choice he had been given, and the conditions attached when he decided to forego his ascent and return. There could only be two explanations for his recovery: either the world had suddenly become a better place, or Majami had somehow managed to override the limitations imposed upon him by the universe. Neither seemed very likely.

Suddenly feeling a presence in the room he opened his eyes. Majami was standing next to the bed holding a candle. He bent down and lit the one on the table from his own.

"Did you have a good sleep?" asked the monk.

"Yes thanks. I feel a lot better. I could do with getting up and having a walk about though – if that's okay with you, Doctor?"

Majami smiled. "That is fine, as long as you feel up to it. You can join us for breakfast if you like. Unless you would like me to bring it to you?"

"No thanks. I think I've spent long enough in bed. I could do with a wash before I eat though."

"Of course," said Majami. "I can bring you some water, or there is a stream at the back of the hut."

Stratton had an urge to get out into the open air. He put on his T-shirt and trousers and followed Majami out of the hut and down a small slope to the water. His legs were surprisingly stable considering his long incapacity and, after supplying him with some leaves to act as soap, Majami appeared happy enough to leave him unsupervised. The water was cool but not unkind, and he immersed himself fully to expel the inertia. Within minutes he felt revitalized, and after a thorough scrub down he dried off on the bank and headed back up to the hut. The only thing missing had been a shave. He would have to ask Majami if he had salvaged his rucksack, which contained a blade.

The hut was divided into four rooms; two on either side separated by a small corridor. On returning Stratton found Majami in the front left section, stirring a rice dish over a small stove.

"Please, sit down," said the monk, motioning to a rustic table surrounded by four equally basic chairs. "Help yourself to some tea."

Stratton poured some hot liquid from the copper kettle into a wooden cup. A wonderful, invigorating fragrance wafted up to his nose and he savoured the scent momentarily before taking a sip. It was quite unlike any tea he'd tasted before.

"You like?" said Majami, turning from his pan.

"Yes, very much," said Stratton. "What's in it?"

"Ah, that is a secret. Special jungle herbs, similar to the ones in the stew I made you."

"Well, whatever it is, it's absolutely delicious."

Stratton relaxed back in his chair and gazed out of the window. The sun was just peeking into the clearing, lighting it up in a misty gold. In the branches of one of the banyans he spotted a curious monkey staring straight at him. He stuck his tongue out at the creature and found the gesture returned. He laughed and proceeded to make comical movements with his hands and arms, all of which were mimicked by the little simian.

"I see you have found our little friend Samson," said Majami.

"Yes. Interesting little fellow, isn't he? Does he ever come in the hut?"

"He has been known to occasionally, but he usually stays out there in his tree just watching us."

Stratton heard footsteps behind him and turned round to see another monk, similar in size and looks to Majami, come through the door. The new monk bowed his head and clasped hands in greeting. "Namaste," he said.

Stratton returned the compliment.

Majami introduced his friend. "This is Tawhali," he said. "And Tawhali, this is Stratton." Both men nodded in acknowledgement. Majami continued, "Tell me Tawhali, where are our other guests? You have not lost them I hope."

"No, they are washing down in the stream. They will be with us shortly."

"Other guests?" said Stratton.

"Yes," said Majami. "You are not the only person we picked up on our little journey."

Chapter 5

Cardinal Vittori's office was much like Desayer's own: grand, imposing and rich in religious detail and iconography. The two grave men sat opposite each other across the desk in a respectful silence. Desayer stared up at Jesus on the large rosewood crucifix and, not for the first time, wondered what he would make of the overly opulent surroundings that had been built in his name. He didn't doubt for one moment that the carpenter's son would find it grossly indulgent, and in no way a fitting testament to the message he had propagated, particularly when so many of his children were starving around the globe.

Desayer was first to break the silence. "So, Fabio, what is the matter that needs my attention so urgently?"

Vittori sat back in his chair and drummed his fingers. "We have, Miguel, what I would call 'a situation' – a rather delicate situation." He paused, then added, "Or maybe not so delicate."

Desayer raised his eyebrows. "Oh?" he said.

Vittori leant forward earnestly. "I am about to tell you something very important, Miguel. Something that very few people in this world know about. I have watched you, Miguel. I have watched you for many years. You appear to be the model of Catholicism: you say all the right things; you make all the right moves; you write the correct words. But there's something about you, Miguel, that doesn't quite add up…"

Desayer felt his chest contract but kept his composure.

Vittori continued, "…The thing is, Miguel, I believe you are different from the other cardinals. I think you see things that the others do not. I think you feel things that the others do not. I think you sense things they do not. Do you understand what I am saying?"

"I think you credit me with more than I deserve, Fabio."

"No, no. Do not be so modest, Miguel. You have vision. You can see beyond this material world. And I am sure in your heart you must know that there is some great secret out there waiting to be unearthed."

Desayer tried to look perplexed. "I am still not following you, Fabio."

"Very well," said Vittori. "I am going to let you in on this great secret of which I speak. Possibly the greatest secret ever kept from mankind."

Desayer continued to feign puzzlement, but inside he felt like a detective who had cracked the case. He had suspected Cardinal Fabio Vittori for a very long time. Like himself the man followed doctrine to the letter and was never seen to rock the ecclesiastical boat, yet from the beginning of their acquaintance Desayer had sensed that all was not as it seemed with his contemporary. There was nothing concrete for him to go on – a furtive glance here, a silent grimace there, perhaps one too many trips to obscure places – but as a whole Vittori just did not add up. Unfortunately, Vittori had obviously had exactly the same suspicions about him, a case of taking one to know one, although it was yet to be proved that this was a bad thing.

"What if I told you that Jesus did not die on the cross," said Vittori. "Or rather that he lived on for many years after."

"There have been many theories propounded along such lines," said Desayer. "But none of them backed up with hard facts."

"No, none of them backed up with hard facts," Vittori echoed quietly. And then loudly: "But it is a fact, Miguel! It is very much a fact!"

Desayer recoiled with the force of the statement.

Vittori smiled. "I am sorry, Miguel, I did not mean to startle you. I only wished to convey the importance of my words. I wish to make sure that I have your full attention, because I am about to change your life forever."

I doubt it, thought Desayer.

"Where to start," Vittori mumbled to himself. "Let me start by telling you about Jesus' missing years. There is no real record of his actions from between the ages of twelve and thirty – am I right?"

"Yes," nodded Desayer. "At a rough estimate anyway."

"Well, during this time he was travelling in the East – in India and beyond. He was learning how to heal. He was given knowledge handed down from the ancients. When he returned to his home country he had become the most powerful healer the world has ever known. But he was not only healing bodies, he was healing minds as well – and that proved to be his downfall. Encouraging free thought was not exactly welcome in those days.

"So then we come to the crucifixion itself. The common conception is that he rose after three days and ascended to heaven. But this is not strictly true. He did in fact come back to life, but it was the Apostles that did it."

"His disciples?!" exclaimed Desayer, playing along.

"Yes, his disciples, Miguel. Before he was crucified Jesus gave Peter instructions on how to bring him back. Peter and the other Apostles took him to the cave and performed a ritual that returned his soul."

"So he lived on after the resurrection?"

"Yes, Miguel, he did. He gave each of the Apostles their own specific mission, and then returned to India where he lived a long life. Some say he made it to 120, but we do not know for sure."

"This is amazing," said Desayer. "But how do you know all this?"

"The knowledge has been handed down from Pope to Pope right the way back to Peter."

Desayer pretended to be flustered. "So our religion is built on a lie?!"

Vittori held up his palm. "I would not call it a lie. We give billions hope. But I do not wish to get involved in that discussion. This is not a time for arguments, this is a time for pulling together. We very much need your help, Miguel; the Pope needs your help; and if you let me finish my story I would be most grateful."

"Of course, Fabio. Forgive me. It is just a bit of a revelation, that is all."

"I understand. But if I did not think you could handle this information then I would not have begun to tell you." He stood up, cleared his throat, and continued. "When Jesus eventually died he left his knowledge in the safe keeping of an order of monks in India. This knowledge was in the form of symbols that could harness the power of the universe to cure all ills. They were to be kept safe until such time as the monks deemed the human race fit to utilize them in a compassionate way. Unfortunately, we believe that this knowledge has now been compromised."

"Compromised?" said Desayer.

"We believe it has been stolen," said Vittori. "We believe that the Muslims have taken the symbols and are using them for their own purpose. We suspect their intention is to convert the entire human race to Islam."

"And how are they going to do that?"

"By producing a Messiah of course. By unleashing their very own messenger of God, or Allah as it would be. With a divine being at their head they would be absolutely uncontainable. All they have to do is give one man the knowledge and then…" He made a sweeping gesture out of the window.

"Are you saying that these symbols can give someone the same powers as Christ?" said Desayer.

"Exactly," said Vittori. "And I am afraid that the deed has already been done. We have had news from a source in Mecca that there is a man in the city claiming to be the Hand of Allah. He has been healing all manner of illnesses."

"If that is true, Fabio, then where is the problem? Surely healing is a good thing."

"Yes, yes, of course it is," Vittori said sharply. "But that is only the start of it – don't you see? The healing is just a ruse to get the world on side. Then will come the laws, the rules, the beatings for people who disobey. The world will be in eternal subjugation to them. Imagine it, Miguel: a world where thieves have their hands chopped off; a world where adulterers are beheaded; a world where women have no rights. What about forgiveness, Miguel? What about turning the other cheek? What about freedom for all men and women? It cannot be allowed to happen. We have to stop them."

Desayer stared impassively. Yes, he thought, of course you want to stop them, because if you don't this whole façade will come crashing down around you. It is not their gain that you fear the most, it is your loss.

Vittori interrupted his meditation. "Well, Miguel? What do you think?"

"I am not sure what to say, Fabio. It is all a bit of a shock. I cannot pretend to comprehend all your talk of symbols and how they work, but I think I understand what you are saying in more general terms. How can we hope to stop them though?"

Vittori sat down and faced Desayer once more. "We create our own Messiah."

Chapter 6

Stratton poured himself some more of Majami's herbal tea and sipped at it trying to contain his excitement. He had given up all hope of ever seeing Jennings again, but from Majami's expression it appeared that he was very much alive. He was, however, intrigued to know who the other 'guest' was.

"Out of bed at last then, Rip van Winkle," said a voice.

Stratton turned to see Jennings standing in the doorway grinning at him. He got up and gave his friend a spontaneous embrace. He held him briefly and then let go. "It's good to see you, mate. I thought you were a goner."

"So did I, mate," said Jennings. "To be honest there's been times over the last couple of weeks when I wish I had been."

"Have you got a hug for me too, honey?" said another voice. This one had an American twang. Scott Grady poked his head into the room.

"What the hell…?"

"It's a long story," said Grady.

Stratton laughed. "It always is where you're involved, Grady. Come on, let's sit down and have some breakfast."

Tawhali procured another chair and Majami dished up the food: rice, vegetables, and jungle herbs and spices. Stratton ate avidly, his appetite surprisingly hearty after weeks of fasting. Whatever Majami put into his cuisine was certainly working wonders. After finishing his second helping he lay down the small wooden spoon and sat back with another cup of tea.

Grady related the tale of Cronin being shot on the beach and how he'd been persuaded to take the priest's place. "…Of course, I didn't want to," he said. "I just wanted to go home to Brooke. But he laid so much guilt on me, in the end I didn't feel like I had a choice."

"I didn't think guilt was part of your psyche," said Stratton.

"It isn't," Grady replied. "Or rather, it wasn't. I'm finding my conscience growing with age. Or maybe it's love – I just don't know. Either way I wish it would shut the fuck up and let me go back to being selfish."

"Too late," said Stratton. "You're a human being now Grady – get used to it. Anyway, you make it over here – what happened then? How did you meet up with Jennings? Have you still got the box and the parchment?"

Both Grady and Jennings looked at the floor.

"That's a 'no' then," said Stratton.

"Yeah, sorry about that," said Grady. "It's my fault really. I tried to stick to the plan, but I guess my newfound humanity got in the way."

"How's that?"

"Well, I was taking the path that Cronin instructed me to when I heard gunfire in the distance. I should have ignored it, but somehow I couldn't. There was this little voice in my head telling me to check it out. Anyway, I felt confident of finding my way back to the path so I headed off in the direction of all the shooting. I was hiding in the undergrowth when I noticed this clown," he pointed to Jennings, "about to surrender. I pulled him into the brush, but eventually we got noticed. Then this crazy fool jumps on top of me and tells me I can't use my gun. Needless to say – we were captured."

"And they took the box and the parchment?" quizzed Stratton.

"Yeah," said Grady, "and that's not all they took." He looked sorrowfully down to his crotch. "Little Grady may never be the same again."

"You will be fine," said Majami. "I have already told you."

"So that was all the screaming I heard then," said Stratton.

"Yeah," said Grady, "and I'm not ashamed to admit it. They strung the pair of us up and…well, you heard." He winced. "Anyway, moving on – I blacked out and the next thing I knew we were here being tended to by these guys. And that's it really."

Stratton sighed. "Well, at least we're all alive, that's one thing I guess. I'm glad that you two are okay anyway. I don't suppose either of you knows what happened to Stella?"

"No," said Jennings, shaking his head sadly. "The last time I saw her was when we were running down the jungle path. The only saving grace is that we haven't found her body."

"What do you think in your heart?" asked Stratton.

"What do you mean?"

"What does your instinct say?"

Jennings closed his eyes briefly and thought. An image of Stella flashed through his head. "She's alive, I guess. But I don't know if that's just wishful thinking or what. You're the one with the sixth sense, mate, why don't you tell me?"

"Because I can't," said Stratton. "Everything's still a bit hazy at the moment. And besides, I think your call will be better on this one." He gave Jennings a knowing glance.

Jennings held his gaze for a moment and then looked away uncomfortably. It was as if his friend had crawled inside his head and was picking through his emotions like a worm in a hard-drive. And what was he thinking? Did it amuse Stratton that he had feelings for Stella? Did he pity his devotion to someone he could never have? Was he playing with his mind?

Majami cleared away the bowls and they all went to sit outside in the early morning sun. Titan who had been hunting, returned licking his lips. He trotted up and sprawled himself out in front of them for a post-feed nap.

"So what do we do now?" asked Grady, pointing his question at Stratton.

"I don't know. I'm not too sure what we can do. They've got over two weeks start on us. The box will be in the hands of someone who knows how to use it by now."

"So, basically, we're fucked," said Jennings.

"I wouldn't have put it quite like that, but yeah, I guess for the moment we are," said Stratton. "We really need to get back into the outside world and get some news. What do you think, Majami?"

"I think perhaps you should rest for another couple of days before you go racing back to civilization. None of you are fit for a journey yet."

"No. I suppose you're right," said Stratton. "But the longer we leave it, the worse it's going to get. And it's not only the box. If Stella's still alive then I'd hate to think what's happening to her at the moment."

"Exactly," said Jennings, echoing the sentiment. "After what they did to Grady and me it really doesn't bear thinking about at all."

For a while they sat in silence, each of them collecting their own thoughts and reflecting on the situation. Jennings knew what he wanted to do. Much as he appreciated the importance of reclaiming the box and parchment, there was only one thing on his mind – and that was finding Stella. His long recuperation had given him plenty of time to contemplate, and nearly all of that time had been devoted to her. More than anything he regretted not telling her how he felt. True, the time had never been quite right, but he'd come to realize that he could spend the rest of his days with the time not being quite right. When it came down to it he'd just been too damn scared to say anything to her, fearing rejection right to the core of his fragile soul. All he wanted to do now was put that right and, more importantly, save her from any further harm.

Grady had spent his time thinking about his wife and impending fatherhood. After too many years of travelling the world and doing the US Government's dirty work, he'd finally found himself. He knew it was a bit of a cliché, but the minute he'd laid eyes on Brooke he felt like he'd come home. Before that moment he hadn't realized that he'd spent his entire life without one. As a child his family had moved from city to city, following his father's work. One day they would be in Washington, the next they would be heading for New York or San Francisco. Although some secondments had lasted longer than others they were never in one place for more than a couple of years. Whether consciously or not, Grady had followed this pattern into adulthood, even though as a child all he had wanted was to stay in one place like all his friends (he recalled being extremely upset, bordering on traumatized, every time they upped sticks and relocated him at a new school). It was perhaps why he found it so difficult to make lasting bonds. But Brooke had heralded a new era, one where he found himself settled, not only geographically but emotionally as well. Whatever the others' goals, his personal objective was to get back to the States as soon as possible. He was, however, under no illusion that this was going to be easy. Any plan that Jennings or Stratton came up with was inevitably going to involve him, and ducking out wasn't an option.

Chapter 7

The lights came on in Stella's room, causing her to wake with a start. A servant walked towards her, head down with a tray in his hand. He set her food on a table next to the bed, then bowed and left the room. She didn't thank him.

Sliding out from the covers she slipped on her cream silk blouse and pale blue trousers and sat down to eat. It had briefly occurred to her to go on hunger strike, but that idea had soon been jettisoned. There would be no escape if she didn't have the strength to move, and more importantly, the food was just too good to waste.

Tonight's meal was a light goat's-cheese salad followed by a spiced chicken dish with couscous and vegetables. She set about it hungrily and made sure she bulked up on the fresh flatbreads that accompanied every lunch and dinner. Back home she would never dream of eating so much, but here food meant muscle, and muscle meant options.

After she'd mopped up the last of the couscous with some bread she leant back in her chair with a small cup of sticky black coffee. She was about to take a sip when the door open behind her. Her visitor was the repulsive sheik. He stood in the middle of the room smiling at her through yellowing teeth. She wondered why with all that money he couldn't afford to have them whitened.

"Good evening, my dear," he said kindly. "I hope that the food was to your satisfaction."

"It was alright," Stella grunted. "I could have done with some pudding though."

"That can be remedied. Is there anything else I can do for you?"

"Yeah, you can fucking well let me out of here!"

The sheik wagged his finger and said, "Now, now, my dear. There is no need for such language. Perhaps you would like a cigarette." He produced a gold case from his pocket and offered her a smoke.

Stella accepted without a word, but instead of letting him spark it for her she grabbed a lighter from the dressing table. After a couple of stressed drags she sat down on the edge of the bed and gazed around the room avoiding eye contact with the sheik, who in turn stood staring right at her. The stand-off continued for over a minute until she could bear it no longer.

"Have you got nothing better to do?" she said. "I mean, surely you've got some wives to attend to? Or maybe some camels?"

"You are a very humorous young lady."

"I try."

The sheik moved across the room and sat down at the dressing table. He carried on staring. "You could have a nice life here in the palace you know," he said, "if only you would let yourself go. There is no need for you to be locked up all day. I am a very generous man to those that I favour."

Stella grunted. "I'm sure you are, but to be honest I don't wish to be in favour. And if you've got any ideas about me suddenly succumbing to your nonexistent charms, then think again. You're not coming near me. Not now; not ever. Get the picture?!"

The sheik exhaled some smoke and gave a hideous tobacco-stained grin. "You are forgetting yourself, my dear. Remember this: I paid for you; I own you. You are not in the West any longer. This is my country and we play by my rules. I think perhaps you ought to consider your position a bit more carefully. It will be far less painful for you to give me what I want than for me to take it."

Stella felt her hatred welling up inside. "Listen to me," she said stonily. "YOU - ARE - NOT - GOING - TO - HAVE - ME!"

Yet again the sheik grinned. "We shall see. Perhaps it might be more fun to break you in against your will."

"Over my dead body!"

"That's the spirit," mocked the sheik. "I do like a lively one. And so, as a matter of fact, do my friends and business associates." He got up and walked to the door. "Have a think about it. Either be mine willingly or be everybody's unwillingly – it is entirely up to you. Goodnight." He gave one last leering smirk and exited her quarters.

As the door closed behind him she shivered with revulsion. After stubbing out her cigarette she immediately lit another and began to pace around the room. It appeared that the sheik was beginning to lose his patience. She wondered how long it would be until he carried out his threats. It was possible that she could hold him off for another week or so, but after that it was looking grim. First it would be him, and then all his dirty little associates. An unwanted picture entered her head and she almost vomited. Grabbing a glass of water she drank it straight down.

It occurred to her that she might have to bite her tongue and start being nice to him. The thought was almost too much to bear, but she figured it might buy her a little more time. A subtle change of mood day by day, a gradual thawing of relations, could possibly get her a month or more if she played it correctly. "I will sleep with you, but I just want it to be special," she would say. "I want to know I can trust you. It takes a woman time to trust someone you know." Yes, that was it! A protracted tease; an unspoken promise of heaven to come. It would take all of her resolve to pull it off, and hiding her true feelings might ultimately prove impossible, but she had little or no option. It was either that or…

She felt her stomach retch once again.

The servant entered the room carrying another tray. He placed its contents on the table, cleared away her dinner plates, and left quickly. Stella went over to investigate and was pleased to find that the Sheik had deferred to her request for a dessert. It was a large piece of sweet honey-cake accompanied by a light lemon sorbet. The taste was sensational, and it took her mind away from the dark thoughts that had been festering.

The flavour was reminiscent of baklava and carried her back

to her days in Oxford with Stratton. She remembered long dreamy afternoons lounging by the river with bottles of wine and assorted pastries from the local patisserie, the time passing so languorously that the earth almost stood still. She remembered making love under the willow tree, and how the sun blazed through its weeping tentacles, shimmering like a thousand jewels and embodying the sensation of pure togetherness flowing through their souls. She remembered laughing so hard that she felt like she would explode into a billion fragments of unquenchable joy. And most of all she remembered the happiness, the feeling that whatever life threw their way it could never extinguish the flame of their love for one another. A small tear began to form in the corner of her eye.

A couple of seconds later she shook her head and returned to her food. Memories weren't going to help her escape. It was going to take a steely, ruthless nerve to get out of the palace. It was no task for a simpering bimbo with unrealistic delusions of romance.

She finished her last mouthful, sat back in the chair, and sparked up another cigarette. With the hardened resolve that she had developed over the years, she banished the past from her head and focused on the job in hand. She was going free herself or die in the attempt.

Chapter 8

"We create our own Messiah?!" said Desayer, echoing Vittori's statement. His mind reeled, wondering exactly how the cardinal was going to achieve this aim without the symbols.

Vittori leant forward intently. "Yes, Miguel, we create our own Messiah."

"And how are we going to do that, Fabio? You said yourself that the Muslims have stolen the knowledge."

Vittori reclined once more and smiled. "Yes, they have, Miguel. But the last few days have brought to light new information."

Desayer looked perplexed. "New information?"

"Yes," said Vittori. "Allow me to introduce you to somebody." He pressed his intercom and asked his assistant to come through with their guest.

Desayer turned round as the door opened. A gaunt man with quick eyes entered the room behind the cardinal's assistant. His thinning, mousey hair was slicked back and he was dressed casually in grey slacks and black polo-neck jumper. He carried a large envelope in his right hand. After giving Desayer a brief but unnerving glance he took a seat next to him.

"This is Anatol," said Vittori. "I believe he has some very exciting news for us."

Desayer exchanged nods with the newcomer, but avoided prolonged eye contact.

"Anatol is one of the faithful," Vittori continued. "He believes in the Catholic Church. He has risked a great deal to bring us a precious gift today. Please show us my friend."

Anatol reached into the envelope, removed a piece of A4 paper, and laid it out on Vittori's desk. It was covered in symbols. Desayer tried to hide his astonishment as he looked at it.

"This," gestured Vittori. "Is an exact replica of the lid of a box that Christ himself carved. Each symbol is extremely powerful, and all have a different purpose. These are the icons that the Muslim 'Messiah' is using to draw power from the universe."

Desayer continued to stare, wondering exactly how they had managed to get hold of the sacred symbols. He couldn't be certain that it was the genuine article, but he recognized the four Usui Reiki characters in the four corners, and the power sign in the centre, so it matched with Cronin's description. "Forgive me if this is an ignorant question, Fabio, but how exactly do we utilize these characters?" he asked, remembering that he was supposed to be unaware of their nature.

"It is a very good question, Miguel," Vittori replied. "And one which I will try to answer as simply as I can. They are basically a link to what we would call the 'spirit world'. Tracing one of these symbols in the air or imagining it in your head draws power from the unseen universe. Each symbol performs its own unique function. For instance this one," he pointed to the bottom left corner, "is used for emotional healing."

"And how do you know that?" asked Desayer.

"Because that one and the other three corners are symbols used in a Japanese healing practice called Reiki."

"Oh," said Desayer, feigning surprise. "I think I may have heard of it. But what is the connection with Jesus?"

"These symbols have been around for many millennia. They are the basis for all healing. Jesus was not the first person to use them. We believe he was taught them when in the East."

"But what about the other symbols?" said Desayer. "There are hundreds of them."

"We believe they were of his own design. A gift given to him by the cosmos during prolonged meditations. Whereas the four basic symbols have a more general healing effect, the others are used to target specific parts of the body and diseases."

Desayer scanned the paper leisurely. "Assuming this is an exact replica, how are you supposed to tell which symbol does what?"

"There is a key. Hidden in the original box was a parchment with drawings that corresponded to each character. Unfortunately the box and parchment were separated and Anatol was unable to get hold of it."

Desayer breathed an internal sigh of relief. "Then this piece of paper is useless?" he said, sounding disappointed.

Vittori smiled. "No, not useless," he said. "Fortunately, we have a copy of the parchment from another source. It will be arriving with us tomorrow."

"Really?" said Desayer, his heart thumping faster and faster. "That is good news." He glanced at the clock on the wall behind Vittori. "However, I really must be going soon, Fabio. I have an appointment in five minutes."

"I'm sure whoever it is can wait," said Vittori. "This is much more important. Is it not?"

"Of course," said Desayer. "It is just that I do not like to keep people waiting. I pride myself on being punctual."

"I know you do, Miguel, and that is the reason that I have let you in on this. You are a shining example to all in the Church. You command the respect of everyone, from the lowliest priest to the Pope himself. If you are seen to be behind us then all will follow. In these deceitful times you are easily the most trusted of our order. Even the Pope has his detractors, as I am sure you are aware. You my friend are universally popular. If Cardinal Desayer heralds a Messiah then everybody will."

"You are too kind," said Desayer. "I really do not think that I am all you say."

"Of course you do not, and that is why you *are* all those things. You are too modest by far, Miguel."

"Thank you, Fabio, I really do not know what to say."

"Say you are with us, Miguel."

Desayer looked into Vittori's eyes and held them. "Do you really think this is the best course of action, Fabio?"

"If we wish to honour the Church and Christ's memory, then

yes."

Desayer sighed and said, "Then I must do my duty. I am with you."

Chapter 9

Night fell in the jungle. A small fire burnt brightly in the clearing by the hut. Stratton sat with his back against a log, digesting his meal. Titan lay next to him stretched out in the glow of the flames. Jennings and Grady were similarly relaxed, each idling in his own thoughts. Majami and Tawhali had gone inside to prepare an after-dinner brew.

Grady lazily grabbed some wood from the pile and flung it on the fire causing a brief crackle and spit. "It doesn't get much better than this, does it?" he said to no-one in particular.

"No," Jennings agreed. "There's something about camping out under the stars isn't there? Although I'm surprised to hear *you* say it. All you've been doing for the last few weeks is moaning about missing Brooke."

Grady shrugged. "Well, I do. But it doesn't mean I can't make the most of where I am. As Majami said, 'there is no past or future, there is only now'."

"Alright, Buddha," laughed Jennings. He lay back and gazed up to the stars shimmering in the cloudless sky and imagined himself floating among them, drifting farther and farther into the cosmos, until he was lost in a blissful sea of strikingly coloured nebulas and brilliant white streaks of dust and light. It was beautiful.

"So, Stratton," said Grady, breaking the silence and interrupting Jennings' flow. "Can you tell me why exactly I was stopped from using my gun?"

"Because I was perilously close to dying, that's why?" said Stratton.

"So what?" said Grady. "I wasn't going to shoot *you* was I? In fact it would have been better for you if Jennings and I had found you earlier."

"If you'd have used your gun and killed somebody then it would have been over for me, and maybe for you as well."

"Why?" said Grady. "I don't understand."

"Because I'm linked in with your consciousness. I'm linked to everybody's consciousness."

Grady raised an eyebrow. "Come again?"

"When I came back from the dead it wasn't without its conditions. In essence my health and energy is linked to your thoughts and actions, everybody's thoughts and actions."

"Okay," said Grady, as if humouring a madman. "Go on."

"It's like this," Stratton continued. "Mankind is at a critical point in its history. It's balanced on a fulcrum between light and oblivion. What we do now will determine our fate forever. Our spiritual consciousness is at its apex. Every choice we make now, however small, will affect the way forward. Any act of violence, or hatred, or revenge will take us into the dark. Conversely, any act of kindness, selflessness, or compassion, will take us into the light. Every day we're getting closer and closer to the point of no return."

"So you're a kind of spiritual barometer," Jennings interjected.

"It's slightly more complicated, but yeah, that's basically it. Are you with it, Grady?"

"Yeah, of course. So if Jennings and I had shot those guys then it would've taken away more of your energy."

"That's right."

"Fair enough, Obi Wan, but what about those fuckers torturing us? Isn't that worse. Why didn't that affect you?"

"Good question," said Stratton. "It's because they're already in the dark, Grady. You and Jennings are still part of the light, and to stay part of it you have to lay down your fears. It's much easier to go from light to dark than the other way round. If you react to the darkness you'll become it."

Grady grunted. "It's all very well you saying this, Stratton. But what am I supposed to do – just let myself be killed. If some mother's trying to kill me then I'm going to defend myself. It's a natural reaction."

"I know it is," said Stratton. "But you've got to unlearn it. Instead of reacting, just bow to them, just surrender."

"What if they can't be reasoned with?" said Grady. "What if I surrender and they shoot me in the head anyway? I'm not going to let that happen."

"But it might not happen. It's all about fear. You shoot them because you're afraid they're going to shoot you."

"Maybe. The bottom line is – I don't want to die. And neither does anybody in their right mind."

"So you're afraid of dying. It's fear again."

"I wouldn't say I'm afraid of dying. I'm just saying that given the choice I'd prefer to live. Some of us can't just flit between worlds at the drop of a hat you know. I've got a wife and unborn child to look after. What do you think, Jennings?"

Jennings continued to stare up to the heavens. "I don't think anything. Or I'm trying not to at least. I'm just enjoying the night sky."

"Thanks for that, buddy," said Grady.

"Listen, Grady," Stratton started. "I'm not preaching to you, I'm just telling you the way things are at the moment. It's really up to you what you do with the information. You're a free spirit like every other being on this planet. All I'm asking is that you think about it. If we want to survive as a race then we all have to think about it."

Grady threw some more wood onto the fire. "Why did you come back then, Stratton? You obviously had the choice. Is it that bad on the other side?"

"No, it's not. But it's not like that. It's not this side and that side. There's different levels...But that's a separate issue. I came back because I've got faith in human nature, because I believe we can pull things round. I didn't want to leave just as things were getting difficult."

"He is a bodhisattva," said Majami, returning with Tawhali and a pot of jungle tea.

"What's that?" asked Grady.

"It is a person who postpones their own salvation to guide others along the path of enlightenment." He poured out five cups of the hot liquid and handed them around. "Buddha was probably the most famous bodhisattva, although not many people know that in fact Jesus was one too."

"So you've come to save the day then?" said Grady.

"I wouldn't put it like that, Grady," said Stratton. He blew on his cup and took a small sip of tea. "I'm here to help out, just like you are. In fact I've got less say in what happens than you do. All I am is a manifestation of good will; if the human race wants to self-destruct then there's nothing I can do about it. I'm not a king, I'm not a president, I'm not any kind of leader, and neither do I want to be. I'm a servant of man's wishes."

"So the fact that you're alive and well is a good sign for us, right?" said Grady.

"I guess it must be," said Stratton. "Although a lot of it's down to Majami here. His unremitting patience and kindness towards me have tipped the balance for the moment, but I don't know how long it will last."

Jennings felt his legs cramping and got up to move around. Although he hadn't got too involved in the conversation, he had listened to every word. He understood now why Stratton had been so against the use of weaponry, and even though the memory of his torture still burned, he was pleased to have kept his promise. It did, however, pose many questions as to their future direction. He couldn't imagine how they were going to accomplish anything without using at least some force. And what if Stella was being held captive? How the hell were they going to liberate her?

Chapter 10

The sun was setting over St Peter's square as Cardinal Desayer paced round his chambers deep in thought. The fact that Vittori was one of the hidden enemy hadn't surprised him one bit, what had shocked him was that they had copies of both the symbols and the key. Vittori had been extremely cagey about his sources, and neither he nor the mysterious Anatol had revealed how they came by the symbols. But the how was irrelevant, what to do about it was the more pressing concern.

A few minutes later Father Cronin knocked and entered the room. Desayer motioned him to sit down. Facing his boss Cronin thought that the strain was beginning to tell. "What happened with Vittori then, Your Eminence?" he asked. "I take it the news isn't good?"

Desayer shook his head and sighed. "No, the news is not good. Not good at all. Things are far worse than we imagined. Vittori is the enemy as we suspected. But what we could not have known is that he has copies of both the symbols and the key."

"What?!" blurted a nonplussed Cronin. "How have they managed that?"

"I'm not sure about the key," said Desayer. "But the symbols were brought in by a man called Anatol. He was Eastern European I believe. Quite a tall fellow…"

"…and skinny with sharp eyes?" said Cronin, finishing the sentence.

"Yes," said Desayer. "How do you know?"

"I bumped into him outside here earlier on today. I thought I'd seen him before. Now I know where."

"Really? Where?"

"He's Arman Kandinsky's right-hand man," said Cronin. "I saw him once when I first met Arman."

Desayer banged the desk with the palm of his hand. "So!" he barked. "Kandinsky has betrayed us! Did I not tell you this would happen?!"

Cronin jerked back at the outburst. He was unused to seeing Desayer lose his temper quite so forcefully. Avoiding the cardinal's gaze he stared at the floor and collected his thoughts. After a brief silence he said, "With respect, Your Eminence, I do not believe Kandinsky has betrayed us at all. If he wanted to get hold of the actual box he could have done so quite easily. Why make a copy of the symbols? No, Kandinsky isn't our man. Anatol is obviously working by himself. He must have been left alone with the box at some point during the voyage to India and made a copy."

Desayer sat back chewing his lip. "Yes, I suppose that makes sense. Do you think he recognized you?"

"I hope not. It was a long time ago and I was in civilian gear. I only saw him briefly when he walked through the room we were in. I don't think he paid that much attention to me to be honest, although he seems the type that doesn't miss a lot."

"Well, let's hope he did miss you," said Desayer. "If he connects you to me then we are finished. How much do you think he knows about Kandinsky's dealings?"

"I don't think there's much he doesn't know," admitted Cronin. "But I have always dealt with Kandinsky personally on his private line. He knew that we required absolute anonymity so I doubt very much if he would have mentioned names."

"Maybe not," said Desayer. "But I still do not like it. Whatever he knows, it is already too much. He obviously knew exactly where to come with his information."

"Yes, that is a worry," Cronin agreed. "But there's not a lot we can do about it now. We'll just have to work on the assumption that he doesn't know about us, and carry on from there. Perhaps you should tell me exactly what happened in Vittori's chambers."

Desayer gave him a brief rundown of all that was said, including Vittori's praise.

"Mmm, interesting," said Cronin when Desayer had finished.

"So he thinks that your opinion will sway the other cardinals. I guess that's a good enough reason to let you in on the act. But it could also be a cover to keep you close. It's quite a heavy load to put upon someone who has no idea about symbols or energies."

"Yes, it is," said Desayer. "And I tried to feign as much incredulity as I could. But you are right, he could be trying to keep me close."

Cronin's phone rang. He apologized to Desayer and moved to an ante-room to take the call. Desayer turned his chair round to the window and looked into the twilight. He felt strange now that his destiny had finally caught up with him. Throughout all his years of planning and searching, deep down he never really thought that anything would come of it. It was not that he did not believe in the sacred knowledge, it was more that he felt it would be someone else who had to deal with it. Someone in a future time. When he had first entered the Church he had been exceptionally eager, looking everywhere for signs of the symbols being found, but after a while his enthusiasm had waned, until eventually he assumed that his role in the long history of the knowledge would be much like Gabriel's: that of a tutor, breaking some young light into the secrets of the universe. So when the symbols were actually recovered it had been a shock to his unprepared system. As he watched the sun disappear into the horizon, he wondered if he still had the strength to see his mission through.

He heard Cronin return and swung back to face him.

"That was Kandinsky," said the priest. "I left a message with him earlier to call me back."

"And?" said Desayer.

"And, to put it mildly, he's absolutely furious. I won't repeat exactly what he said, but needless to say it was punctuated with expletives. It appears that Anatol left the submarine a couple of days ago, citing a death in the family as his reason. When I told Kandinsky about the symbols he exploded, but he calmed down eventually and apologized profusely for Anatol's betrayal. He said that he had kept the box in the safe for Stratton, and that Anatol must have taken it from there. He said he has no idea how Anatol knew who to take the symbols to."

"Do you think he is telling the truth?" asked Desayer.

"Yes, Your Eminence, I do. And what is more, he has promised to help us in anyway he can. The first thing he's going to do is return to India to find out what's happened to Stratton and his party."

"Is it worth it?" asked Desayer. "I would imagine they will all be dead by now."

"Maybe," said Cronin. "But there's always a chance that some of them will be alive. We have to find out at least. If Stratton is still alive, his knowledge of the symbols will give us more options. And besides, we owe it to them to try."

Desayer sighed and shook his head. "Once again Father, you are absolutely right. It is you who should be sitting here making the decisions, not I. I am afraid that I am going to make a complete hash of everything. We are already in severe crisis. If I continue to make bad calls everything will be lost."

"You have done nothing wrong, Your Eminence. You have done all you could to protect the secret. All that has happened has been beyond your control. Don't start doubting yourself now. We have to see this through to the end – whatever that may be."

Desayer smiled. "I did get one thing right, Father – and that was hiring you. The best decision I ever made."

Chapter 11

There was a time when Jennings was young that an old man had come to visit. He remembered the day well. It was early in the summer holidays and his parents had popped out to do some shopping. Jennings had refused to go with them, saying that he would rather play in the garden than be stuck in a supermarket all morning, and those being more innocent days, when parents felt safe leaving a nine-year-old for half an hour, they relented and let him stay.

About five minutes after they had gone there was a ring on the doorbell. Jennings was in the middle of a game of 'keepy-uppy', and having just hit forty decided to ignore it. As he reached fifty-five it chimed once more, breaking his concentration and forcing the ball to the ground. He let out a childish grunt and went to answer the door. In his frustration he forgot all about putting the chain on and opened it fast and wide. On the threshold stood an old man. He was dressed in a grey suit and had silver hair poking out from under the brim of a battered trilby. His face was pale and worn, but his eyes were the brightest blue Jennings had ever seen.

"Hello, young Thomas," he said. "Can I come in?"

Although there was a glint of recognition, Jennings didn't know who the man was. "I'm sorry, but my parents aren't home at the moment. You'll have to come back later."

"But I've come to see you."

"I can't let strangers in. I shouldn't even be talking to you. You'd better go before I start to shout."

The old man smiled. "There's no need for that, is there? My name's Alan." He held out his hand. "Pleased to meet you. Now we're not strangers."

Jennings couldn't remember exactly what happened next, but before he knew it they were sitting on the swinging sofa in the back garden, chatting away merrily without a care. Alan told him tales of the war, and how he had been a fighter pilot in the Battle of Britain, soaring and swooping and shooting down enemy planes. He told him of his life afterwards as a doctor in a big city hospital. And he told him of his wife and the times they had shared together. Jennings had sat rapt throughout, carried away by the old man's unrestrained enthusiasm and unique gift for storytelling. He was disappointed when he eventually heard his parents coming through the front door shouting his name.

"You'd better go and see them," Alan had said.

"I'll bring them out to meet you," said Jennings.

Alan's eyes shone brighter than the stars. "Fill your life, Thomas," he said.

Jennings felt a warmth spread through him and beamed.

He raced in to find his parents, and after a lot of babbling and tugging, he coerced them outside to meet his new friend. But when they arrived at the sofa there was no-one there. Jennings looked around flummoxed. His mother and father smiled knowingly at each other and went back inside…

…"So, they thought you were imagining this guy?" said Stratton, as he and Jennings strolled down to the stream.

"Yes, they did. But that's not the end of it. I described him to them and told them all his stories, and then my dad suddenly became angry. He raced upstairs and came down two minutes later with a photograph of the old man. I got excited and said it was the same guy. My father began shouting, telling me not to lie, and that making up stories was no game."

"What did you do?" asked Stratton.

"I argued my case until I was blue in the face of course. It went on for days until he bullied me into submission, and I guess after that I just accepted that I'd been playing games and made the whole thing up. After all, Alan Jennings – my grandfather – had been dead for over ten years."

"Did your father not wonder how you knew so much about

your grandfather?"

"He said I must have been listening to stories at family gatherings and fabricated the whole thing from that. It sounded feasible so I believed him. If you're told something enough as a child it becomes your reality. I must have blanked the whole episode from my mind."

"But you remember it now?"

"I remembered it when I was hanging there in the jungle waiting to die. It all came back to me, particularly my grandfather's eyes. They seemed to contain a whole world of their own. It gave me comfort somehow. But it also made me think – I haven't filled my life at all, I've just been ambling along in an empty daze…When I think of all he'd done by the time he was my age…"

They reached the stream, stripped down to their shorts, and waded in to wash. Stratton began by clipping his beard with a pair of small scissors from his recovered rucksack, and then set to work with a razor blade, savouring every stroke of delightful depilation. Satisfied that he hadn't missed a patch, he dunked his head into the water to remove the excess foam, and then jerked back with an invigorated exhalation.

Jennings was almost dry when Stratton finally emerged from the stream. He patted himself down one last time and put his clothes back on, thankful that Massa and his men had left them behind. If they hadn't he would probably be having to wear robes like the monks, and even in the jungle it wasn't a good look.

"You shouldn't be so hard on yourself really, mate," said Stratton as he dried himself off. "You might think you've done nothing with your life, but I'm sure to other people it probably looks very exciting. I mean, I'm sure there's loads of people out there who would love to be in Special Branch. You've been the Prime Minister's personal bodyguard for Christ's sake! How cool is that?! It's better than working in a factory isn't it?"

"When you say it like that it sounds better," Jennings admitted. "I suppose when you're in a job you tend to forget how it looks to other people. The reality is never quite as glamorous though."

"Maybe it's not your job that's the problem," said Stratton.

"Maybe you're right."

Stratton put his clothes back on and slung his towel over his shoulder. "Right then mate, are you ready for this?"

"I guess so," said Jennings doubtfully.

"Well then, let's go and find Majami."

Stratton had persuaded Jennings to receive an attunement from the monk. He believed it essential in the current climate that Jennings be protected as much as possible from the negative energies that were sweeping the globe. Although a basic attunement would not give him immunity, it would give him a deeper spiritual insight and make him more aware of what was going on around him. Stratton had also tried to get Grady to agree to one, but the suggestion was met with a typically humorous dismissal, so he had let the matter lie.

When they got back to the hut Majami was waiting for them. He took them inside to his quarters and bade Jennings sit on a chair in the middle of the room. There was a lit candle in each corner, the air filled with a delicate waft of incense. Majami instructed Jennings to close his eyes and relax with his hands in the prayer position, and to think about letting positive energies flow through his body. Only six months previously Jennings would have laughed at what he was doing, but today, in the middle of the jungle with Majami, it seemed like the most natural thing in the world.

At first Jennings found it hard to imagine the energies flowing like Majami had suggested, but as soon as he felt the monk's hand touch the crown of his head he immediately felt a subtle surge of warmth travel through his body. After that he remembered little of the physical aspects save for Majami making signs on his palms. What he did recall was the sensation of floating in another dimension, a divine weightlessness that transcended the world as he knew it. It was like speeding through the cosmos at a million miles an hour and standing motionless at the same time. It was like a seismic explosion of knowledge had hit him full in the face and illuminated his entire mind, as a blind man regaining his sight after years in the dark. And most of all it was simply beautiful, like nothing his temporal existence could even begin to match.

When he finally came back to earth he could hear Majami's mellifluous voice coaxing him out of his trance. He opened his eyes slowly and found the world out of focus. The room was blanketed by a thick haze, with Majami appearing pixilated. Jennings shook his head and blinked but his vision remained fuzzy.

"Is everything alright?" Majami asked.

"I'm not sure," Jennings drawled. "I feel a bit drunk."

"Good," said Majami. "That means the attunement is strong. It will take some time to ground yourself again. Just sit there until you feel your senses return to normal. I will go and fetch some water."

Jennings leant back in the chair and enjoyed the moment. The fact that his faculties were temporarily disabled didn't matter. He'd never felt so good in his life. His body was generating energy like a nuclear reactor and his grin was so wide it threatened to engulf his entire face. Problems were a thing of the past, and had transformed into a colourful sea of opportunities. It was like entering a dream, or perhaps coming out of one, he wasn't sure which. What he was sure of though was that he'd crossed a border into another realm and his life would never be the same again.

A fuzzy dark figure appeared in front of him. "How are you doing?" said Stratton's voice.

Jennings didn't answer, he just grinned even wider.

"That good, eh?" said Stratton. "Welcome to wonderland."

It took a good half hour before Jennings finally returned to some sort of normality and even then it wasn't quite what he was used to. The world seemed somewhat sharper than it had: colours were brighter, objects more defined, sounds crisper and more melodic, fragrances were sweeter and more pungent; it was like he'd been watching an old black-and-white TV and was suddenly immersed in state-of-the-art high definition with super-stereo and ultra-smell.

Later on, as he sat outside with Stratton enjoying the evening sun and sipping jungle tea, he felt on the verge of a incredible new dawn. "Is this how you feel all the time?" he asked.

"I don't know, mate, it's difficult to tell isn't it? Only an individual can know how he or she feels. But if you feel the same way I did when I had my first attunement, then no. It's one of those moments you should savour. I think I felt supercharged for about a week – I hardly slept, then it sort of tailed off, or seemed to anyway. It was more like I grew accustomed to my new view of the world though, and that then became my normality."

"That's a shame," said Jennings. "I could quite get used to feeling like this forever."

Stratton took a sip of his brew and gazed out into the trees. "One day you will feel like that forever; everybody will. Or let's say that everybody has the chance to if they let themselves. You're at the start of a new journey. Every step you make will be accompanied by a similar reaction to the one you're feeling now. Each stage of enlightenment will produce a new wave of elation. At the moment you're dazzled by what you see, but that will pass and you'll be ready to move on to something even brighter, and so on until you're able to look directly at the ultimate light and become a part of it."

Jennings smiled into the distance. "You know what, Stratton? This is the first time I can honestly say I really know what you're talking about. Before, I kind of grasped the concepts, but now I actually understand. Does that make sense?"

"Of course it does. But I think you've always understood more than most people. You've always had the capability it's just been buried underneath years of instilled ignorance. From the moment your parents dismissed the story of your grandfather as fiction you were always going to struggle. Subconsciously you closed yourself off from anything spiritual and concentrated all your thought on the secular world around you, either to please your mother and father, or through fear of looking stupid I guess."

"Do you think my grandfather will come and see me again?"

"I don't know. He's probably moved on elsewhere. But you'll see him again one day, in some dimension, I'm sure."

Chapter 12

Anatol stood at the window of his hotel and looked out on the buzzing piazza. It was nine pm, and the outside tables of the restaurants and pizzerias were filled with hungry diners all wanting to enjoy the clement evening. Tourists wandered up and down pointing and taking photographs of everything that moved and didn't, while street artists tried to distract them with offers of intimate portraits with their loved ones. In the middle of the square, a performer sat on a unicycle juggling three firebrands, his overly glamorous assistant eliciting exaggerated donations for what was effectively a mediocre effort.

Anatol had half a mind to go out and join the party, but the day had been long, and instead he decided that room service might be a more fitting alternative. He picked up the extensive five-star menu and had a quick browse, but even with all the luxuries on offer he found it hard to work up an appetite. The magnitude of what he had done was beginning to cloy. Eventually he ordered a light selection of antipasti and, more importantly, a bottle of Smirnoff Blue Label to help calm his shattered nerves.

It wasn't guilt that was eating away at him so much as the fear of retribution. After years of working for Kandinsky he knew only too well the penalty for treachery, and a betrayal of this size would be met with an equally severe punishment. But what choice had he been given? Over the previous year Kandinsky's behaviour had become increasingly erratic. The ruthless businessman he once knew had all but disappeared, replaced by some weak-willed philanthropist hell-bent on giving away money faster than the US Treasury could print it. At his current rate of benevolence the whole lot would be gone in less than two years. And where would that leave Anatol himself? There was no way he was going to let all those years of hard work go down the pan just because his boss had seen some kind of imaginary light.

Of course, he had put plenty of money away in various accounts, but not enough to accomplish what he wanted. He envisaged himself at the head of his own organization, and with all the contacts he'd made in his years at Kandinsky's side he could easily set up networks in everything from drugs and gun running, to pornography and money laundering. It wasn't that he had anything against legitimate business, it was just that he didn't know anything about it. His background was firmly on the wrong side of the law where the big money resided, and that is where his future dealings would be. His decision hadn't been an easy one, but he was sure it was the right one. And was it really treachery anyway? All he'd done was copy a few symbols from the top of an old box. It wasn't as if he'd sold Kandinsky out to a competitor or anything like that.

Being a trusted employee had made it easy for Anatol to work out what was going on, and as soon as he knew the Catholic Church were interested in the box he smelt money.

And what a deal he had got. Twenty million dollars' worth. It would be enough to set him up in business and then some. He figured that in a couple of years he could turn it into at least a hundred million, if not more. Within a decade he would be bigger than Kandinsky, and able to support his own undersea fortress. He lay back on the bed and started to dream of the future.

Five minutes later, room service turned up with his order. Before answering the door he went to his suitcase, pulled out a Browning 9mm, and slipped it into the back of his waistband. It would have been almost impossible for Kandinsky to have tracked him down already, but there was no point in being blasé about the situation. He hadn't stayed alive in the underworld for so long by being complacent.

He opened the door slowly and invited the boy into the suite with his trolley. The kid appeared nervous under Anatol's stare and stumbled his way awkwardly inside. After checking his order with a steely eye he tipped the gangly youth and bade him leave.

The first thing Anatol did was open the bottle of chilled vodka. He poured a good measure straight into a glass and swigged it down in one go, letting a out shiver of pleasure as the liquid hit his throat. Feeling peckish he picked up a stuffed olive from the plate of antipasti. But before it reached his mouth he started to feel faint. It dropped from his hand limply as he first struggled for breath, and then seconds later fell to the floor. As he clasped his throat the world turned black.

A minute later the boy from room service re-entered the suite with his pass key. His graceless gait gone, he strode confidently across to Anatol's suitcase and rifled through, finding what he sought in the side zipper. Folding the paper delicately he placed it in his breast pocket. He took one last look at the dead man, shrugged, and left, strolling casually out of the hotel and losing himself in the crowded piazza.

Chapter 13

It was a beautiful morning and the sun pierced Cardinal Vittori's chambers like a divine spear. He unlocked his desk drawer, took out a small flask of cognac and added some to his rich dark coffee. Although his physician had warned him away from alcohol, it was part of his ritual and he believed that giving it up would do him more harm than good. And on a day like today, when everything was falling into place so very nicely, he felt it only right that he should allow himself a little indulgence. After all, lent had finished weeks ago.

He took a sip from his freshly charged drink then looked down at the piece of paper on his desk and smiled. Although he could easily have mustered together twenty million dollars, in the present financial climate he felt that taking the frugal approach had been the correct thing to do. Of course, a man had lost his life, but then – was that man really worth saving? There were too many gangsters in the world anyway. He had done mankind a favour.

Smoothing the paper with his hand he leant forward and studied it closely. Some of the symbols appeared incredibly intricate, and he wondered if the recently deceased Anatol had copied them accurately enough. Although from experience he knew there was some leeway with the four main Reiki symbols, he wasn't sure how exact one had to be with these new characters. Just one erroneous line could theoretically be quite disastrous. Unfortunately the only way to find out was to use what they had and hope for the best.

After five minutes of scrutinizing the page he sat back to give his eyes a rest. He finished the dregs of his coffee and poured himself another, again adding a little extra treat for good measure. The clock on the far wall indicated that it was coming up for ten am, telling him that it would not be long before his important guest arrived with the last piece of the puzzle. Smiling broadly he sipped his drink and let out a satisfied sigh. Years of searching were about to come to fruition.

Ten minutes later there was a knock on the door. Vittori felt a pulse of electricity shoot up his spine. For a moment he was giddy with excitement, but then remembering his position and the need to remain authoritative, he took a few deep, steady breaths and called for his guest to come in.

Due to their respective positions Cardinal Vittori had only met Jonathan Ayres in person twice before, but their correspondence dated back many years and he felt closer to his fellow conspirator than any of the Vatican flunkies he dealt with on a day-to-day basis.

"Jonathan!" Vittori beamed, rising from his chair offering an outstretched palm. "How very good to see you!"

Ayres returned the smile and took the cardinal's hand. "Fabio! It's been too long."

Vittori motioned for his assistant to leave them alone and they both sat down. He offered the British PM a coffee, which was gratefully accepted, as was the shot of cognac.

"A man after my own heart," said Ayres. "If you ask me coffee just doesn't taste right without a little snifter. I swear by it myself." He looked down at the piece of paper on Vittori's desk. "Is that what I think it is?"

"Yes," said Vittori. "This is it. Have you brought the key with you?"

"Of course," said Ayres, and reached into his jacket. He withdrew two sheets of A4 paper and unfolded them on the desk.

The two men went silent, suddenly overawed by the realization of what they now possessed.

Ayres was the first to speak again. "Takes your breath away somewhat, doesn't it?"

"Yes, indeed, Jonathan. I honestly never dared believe that it would happen in my lifetime. But here we are, after two millennia of frustration, finally about to learn Christ's secrets. I just hope that we are able to tap in to the power before the Muslims start to poison the world with their false Messiah, and messages of intolerance."

"Yes, let's hope so," said Ayres. "Have you heard any more about this 'Hand of Allah'?"

"Not a great amount. He is still containing himself in Mecca, but I'm sure it won't be long before he announces himself to the world. And when he does we have to be ready. It is shame we had to wait so long."

Ayres looked across apologetically. "Yes, it is. I'm afraid that's my fault really. Everything seemed to spiral out of control after the assassination attempt. It served its purpose in that I got assigned more men, but unfortunately they spent most of their time chasing down the assassin instead of searching for the box. It was one mistake after another. I really must get better help."

Vittori waved the apology away. "Do not worry Jonathan, these things happen as they say. The important thing is that we have the information we require. All we have to do now is find ourselves a Messiah."

"Yes," Ayres agreed. "Have you anyone in mind?"

"It is difficult," said Vittori. "I have been running it through my head for days. We really need someone without a history, an unknown who we can mould into what we want. Someone who will not question us. Someone who will not get carried away with the power."

Ayres sipped his drink thoughtfully. "You're right Fabio, it is difficult – extremely difficult. The problem being that we need someone who is devoted to the faith, and yet at the same time open enough to come to terms with the truth. We'll be asking someone to defend their beliefs after blowing them to smithereens."

"Technically, yes," said Vittori. "But I am sure we can suggest it in a way that makes sense to the person. If we handle it correctly I do not think we will have a problem. Between us I am certain we can be most persuasive. And of course we will have the Pope himself to help us sway the argument."

"Yes, I'd almost forgotten that. Is he not joining us this morning?"

"He has other engagements that were planned a long time ago I am afraid. We cannot go letting the faithful down now, can we?"

"Of course not," said Ayres. "Business as usual until we have a definite plan in place."

Chapter 14

Jennings lay on his bunk watching the ceiling and grinning like a madman. Majami had suggested that he have a small nap before dinner to allow the attunement to settle, but he was too pumped up to think about sleep. Every time he shut his eyes and tried to close his mind a new thought would suddenly pop into his head and send him off on another tangent of mental discovery. For the first time in his life he was beginning to see just how limitless the universe was.

As he floated deeper in, Stella once again came to the forefront of his thoughts. He found that if he concentrated hard enough he could picture her in minute detail, her dark hair flowing like a stream of silk and her eyes glowing like amber. He began to call her name in his head, searching the vastness of space and time for a sign as to her whereabouts, letting the energy flow as he drifted further in. Her image grew sharper and brighter until he could almost see a background forming behind. But just as it came into focus the window snapped shut and he found himself staring into a vortex once more.

Before he could get back to the vision he was disturbed by Grady craning his head round the doorframe. "Are you all right there, buddy?"

Jennings opened his eyes and blinked. "Yeah, I'm fine, I was just daydreaming that's all?"

"Oh, okay," said Grady. "It must have been a good one then – you looked like an extra from *One Flew Over the Cuckoo's Nest*. I was worried you were about to start dribbling."

Jennings pulled himself up and sat on the edge of the bed. "Yeah, it feels a bit like that to be honest. For some reason I just can't stop smiling."

"You don't say," laughed Grady. "Still, it's better than having you moping around like a lovesick puppy, I suppose. I just popped in to tell you that dinner's going to be ready in about ten minutes."

After a brief sit down to get his head together Jennings ventured outside and found Grady sitting with Stratton by the campfire. Night had not yet completely fallen, and the flames cast a long shadow over the clearing as they danced and licked under the blue-grey sky. Jennings stood for a while, hypnotized by the haunting beauty of the scene, breathing deeply the lingering smell of crackling wood.

"Are you going to join us?" Grady called.

"Yeah," said Jennings. "I was just trying to enjoy the moment."

He walked over to the woodpile and threw on a couple of logs before sitting down opposite his two friends.

"How are you feeling?" asked Stratton. "Have you come back to earth yet?"

Jennings leant back with his hands behind his neck and smiled. "No, not yet. And to be honest I hope I never do. This place is far better." He stared up to the heavens and began singing *Space Oddity* to himself. "*Ground control to Major Tom…*"

Grady raised an eyebrow then shook his head.

After dinner, which again was the ubiquitous jungle stew, they started to discuss heading back to civilization. Majami, though, was still against the idea. "I really do not think it is wise for you to be journeying quite yet," he stated. "You are all still some way off full recovery."

"I appreciate that," said Stratton. "But we really can't wait any longer. Not only do we have a friend missing, but if we don't leave soon I'm afraid it'll be too late to repair the inevitable damage that will be done if anyone should use the symbols."

"It will be worse if you hurry," said the monk. "The universe is eternal, it will not be destroyed in a matter of days."

"No," said Stratton. "But mankind might be."

"And so might Stella," Jennings interjected. "I appreciate what you're saying, Majami, but time, as they say, is of the essence. The universe may work slowly, but people don't. It only takes a second to kill somebody."

"I agree," said Grady, joining the discussion. "If we wait until we're all fully recovered then we might not have a lot to go back to. I was never a great believer in all this stuff with energies and symbols, but the last six months have really opened my eyes. And whilst I don't pretend to understand it all, I've seen enough to know that this sort of power in the wrong hands is bad news. So I'm with Jennings and Stratton on this one." He paused. "And besides, Brooke's going to be wondering what's happened to me."

Eventually, realizing that his words of wisdom were wasted, Majami agreed that they should set off early in the morning. He and Tawhali would guide them out of the jungle and into the nearest village, where they would be able to secure a guide and transport. And, if they were very lucky, perhaps a phone.

One by one the group retired for the evening until Stratton was left on his own with Titan, lazily stroking the stretched-out panther's stomach. He knew he should be getting some sleep, but he also knew that soon he would have to leave his companion behind in the jungle. It occurred to him that they may never see each other again. The moment had been inevitable of course, but Stratton had tried to cancel it from his thoughts for as long as possible. He cast his mind back to the time years ago when they had first bonded, and smiled as he remembered. A longing crept over him to return to those simple days, when they explored the moors together without a care in the world. Not for the first time he wished that he had left the box buried, hidden forever from human eyes. But he couldn't change the past, only the future. And, as he stared mistily into the dying campfire, he hoped that one day he would be able to come back and see his friend.

Chapter 15

Christiano Rossini hopped briskly onto the busy bus and secured himself a space near the front, grabbing the hand-strap tightly in anticipation of the inevitable jolt as the driver pulled away. He looked around at the familiar faces, each one with their eyes staring into space or at the floor, and wondered why they chose to avoid any contact with their fellow commuters. Occasionally there would be a nod of acknowledgement, or maybe a brief, forced grimace, but generally the journey was completed in a stuffy half-silence, with each person occupied by his or her own worries for the day ahead. He didn't take it personally of course, he guessed that it was much the same in every major city, but it didn't stop him wondering how much happier people would be if they just took the time to smile at each other, or chat on the way to work. Were the people of the world really that unhappy? Did nobody apart from him have a job that they actually liked?

Christiano was part of the maintenance team in the Vatican. He wasn't involved in the upkeep of any of the major artworks, just the general fixing, screwing and hammering of everyday objects like tables, chairs, roofs and walls. But this didn't stop him being immensely proud of his work. Without the likes of him there would be no Vatican City, merely a crumbling mass of derelict buildings. He was not only serving society, but also God himself. It gave him great satisfaction to know that his contribution to the world was good in the eyes of the Lord.

After a bumpy fifteen-minute ride the bus arrived at St Peter's Square. Christiano leapt off and made his way through the gathering crowds. It was a glorious morning without a cloud in the sky, and he whistled merrily as he strolled without a care towards the maintenance office. He guessed that it would be an ideal day to continue the repairs they were making to the dome of St Peter's Basilica, and hoped that he would be part of the team assigned to the task. The good jobs were handed out on a first-come basis, and the fact that he was nearly always the earliest to arrive wasn't going to hurt his chances.

When he reached the office he did indeed find that he was the first there, but instead of securing the plum roof job he was instructed by his foreman to go and see Cardinal Vittori.

"The cardinal wants to see me?" said Christiano in disbelief.

"Yes," said the foreman. "Apparently so. I couldn't tell you what about though. He said to send you up to his office as soon as you got in. You know where it is, don't you?"

"Yes, I do, but I'm a little confused."

The foreman shrugged. "Well, I'm sure it's nothing to worry about. You should be honoured – he's never asked to see me."

Christiano left the office and started the long trek to the wing in which the cardinal's chambers lay, his mind abuzz with conflicting emotions. It was indeed a great honour to be asked to visit the cardinal, but even though he could think of nothing he had done wrong he was racked with a sense of guilt, and couldn't quite believe himself important enough to be bothered with unless it was for a scolding.

On arrival he was welcomed by the cardinal's assistant whose unreadable face gave no indication as to the purpose of the audience. Christiano's attempts to engage him in conversation proved fruitless as well.

As the door opened the cardinal stood up and smiled. "Ah, Christiano," he said, raising his arms. "It is so good of you to come at such short notice. Please, take a seat." He gestured towards one of two chairs in front of his desk. The other was already occupied by a dark-haired gentleman in a suit who Christiano thought looked vaguely familiar.

After dismissing his assistant Vittori offered Christiano a coffee, which was accepted nervously, and then sat back down. "Well then Christiano," he said warmly. "It is good to see you again. We have met before – do you remember?"

"Of course, Your Eminence, it is not something that a man

such as myself would forget," said Christiano, casting his mind back fifteen years to when the cardinal had visited his school. They had exchanged a few words, but he couldn't for the life of him think how the cardinal remembered.

"I have a very good memory for faces, in case you were wondering," said Vittori. "And also I believe we ascertained that I had known your grandmother – a tireless devotee to the faith."

"Yes, Your Eminence. You were missionaries together in Africa."

"Indeed we were. I was sorry to hear of her passing," said Vittori. He briefly looked away in reflection, then continued, "Before we get started I'd like to introduce you to a friend of mine." He motioned to the man in the other chair. "This Christiano, is Mr Jonathan Ayres."

Something in Christiano's brain suddenly clicked and he realized that the man sitting next to him was the British premier. Ayres held out his hand and greeted him in fluent Italian. Not knowing quite how to react, Christiano took his extended palm and gave it a bewildered shake.

"Well then, Christiano," said Vittori. "I suppose you are wondering why I have called you here."

Christiano nodded nervously. The cardinal's eyes were drilling right through him.

Vittori took a sip of coffee and continued, "I can see that you are a little on edge my friend, but I want you to answer my questions honestly and openly. Do not be frightened of the truth. Do you understand?"

Again Christiano nodded.

"Good," said Vittori. "Then I shall begin." He paused briefly to make sure that the young man was suitably in awe and then started his inquisition. "I am given to understand that you are a devout Catholic, a firm adherent to the faith. Is this correct?"

"Absolutely, Your Eminence. I have been devoted all my life. My grandmother showed me the way of the Lord when I was young."

"Good, that is what I thought," said Vittori. He drummed his fingers on the desk for effect. "The thing is Christiano, I have been doing my annual check of the staff files," he lied, "and I have noticed something very disturbing on your record. It appears you have been 'dabbling' in the occult. Is this true?"

Christiano felt his chest tighten. "N-no, Your Eminence," he stammered. "I would never be involved in such a thing."

Vittori held up his hand. "It is alright Christiano, there is no need to become excited, I would just like you to answer my questions. Now, where was I? Oh yes, the occult. This particular practice that you have allegedly become involved in is called Reiki. Does this mean anything to you?"

Christiano stared open-mouthed. How did the cardinal know about his Reiki? It wasn't as if he'd broadcast it around his workmates. And why was he calling it the occult?

"Well…" Vittori pressed.

"Well, yes, Your Eminence, I do indeed have an interest in Reiki. But I had no idea it was so sinister. It is for making people better. That is good, yes?"

"The occult does not have to be sinister Christiano, it can be any supernatural practice. So you admit to being involved with it?"

"Yes, Your Eminence, I cannot lie to you. It would be the same as lying to God himself." He bowed his head in reverence and hoped that the cardinal would forgive him his transgression. Although he really didn't know what he had done wrong.

"So, tell me about this 'Reiki' Christiano. What does it involve?"

Christiano looked up to see the cardinal's expression, but it was impassive. "It is almost like the laying on of hands, Your Eminence. You transfer good energies through your body to the person you are treating, and it helps rid them of their ills."

"That is a very bold claim," said Vittori, raising an eyebrow.

"Does it actually work?"

"Yes, Your Eminence, I believe it does."

"You believe it does? Does it, or doesn't it?"

"It does."

"Can you give me an example of how it has worked?"

Christiano could feel both Vittori and Ayres staring now. He wanted to leap up and run out of the room, or better still for the ground to swallow him whole. Instead, he calmed his nerves and said, "Well, Your Eminence, one of my mother's friends recently came to me complaining of chronic stomach cramps. She had been to the doctor lots of times and he had conducted many tests, but nothing could be found. I performed Reiki on her and the next day the pain was gone. There have been many instances where friends and family have come to me and I have eased their pain."

"Really?" said Vittori. "And how does this happen?"

"Like I said, Your Eminence, it is positive energies. I draw them from the universe and channel them into the patient."

"So you were born with this talent?"

"No, no, Your Eminence," said Christiano, shaking his head. "I was taught how to do it by a Reiki Master. Anyone can do it if they learn how to. Everyone can tap in to the universal life force."

"Universal life force you say…interesting," mused Vittori. "But it does not sound very Catholic. Only Christ had the ability to heal with his hands. Are you telling me that you are like him?"

"Not at all, Your Eminence. My healings are but mere trifles compared to the miracles of the Lord."

"Maybe. But let me ask you this Christiano – how do you balance your faith with this Reiki business. Can one believe in a 'universal life force' and one true God at the same time. These tenets do not seem compatible to me. God is all powerful – it is he that heals through the word of the Church. What you seem to be suggesting is something more akin to Buddhism, and that I am afraid is no good within the Vatican. We believe in God the

Father, the Son, and the Holy Ghost."

Christiano's eyes welled up in frustration. "Yes, yes, Your Eminence, and so do I...So do I..."

"Now, now, Christiano," Vittori said kindly. "Do not work yourself into a state. All I wish to know is how you manage to harmonize these apparently different ideals in your head. So please, take a few moments and then tell me your thoughts on the matter. And remember, be honest with me."

Christiano looked first at the cardinal and then at Ayres, and noted that their faces had softened somewhat. He took a few deep breaths and attempted to drive the fear from his mind. "I believe, Your Eminence," he began nervously, "that it is okay to practice Reiki whilst maintaining a strong belief in God and Jesus. Jesus wanted us to be kind to each other and Reiki is all about being kind to other people by healing them. Jesus also said that every human being could be like him, and by healing we become as he was. As for God, I believe that it is his power that I harness when I heal people. The universal life force is just another name for the great being. Every religion has a different name for him, and every religion interprets him differently, but he looks after everyone. I do, though, believe that the Catholic way is the correct way to honour him. And by being as much like Jesus as I can I believe I am doing that."

The room fell silent as the cardinal mulled over his statement. Christiano could feel the walls closing in rapidly, drying his throat and sending beads of sweat trickling down his cheek. He said a little prayer in his head, pleading with the Lord to deliver him from the predicament he had got himself into. Promising that he would do anything as long as he could keep his job.

He was about to hyperventilate when at last Vittori spoke. "Well, Christiano, you make a very good case I must admit, albeit a very basic one. The doctrines of the Catholic Church go far deeper than your limited knowledge, but as a layman I do not expect you to understand complex theological matters. The important thing is that you believe yourself that the two ideals can go hand in hand."

Christiano nodded. "Yes, Your Eminence, I do. But I would gladly stop the Reiki if it displeased you in any way. You understand God's wishes so much more than I do. Being a good Catholic is more important to me than anything else in the world."

Vittori gave a broad smile. "That is very good to hear Christiano, you are indeed one of the faithful. But I do not wish you to give up your healing, I would like you to use it to help the Church. Would you like to do that?"

The realization that he was not in trouble sent a rush of ecstatic release through Christiano's body. His chest, arms, and head loosened instantly sending him into a slump on the chair. The relief was so great that he almost started to cry. "Yes, Your Eminence," he blurted, pulling himself straight again. "I would very much like to help, in any way I can."

Vittori looked across to Ayres who smiled and nodded his assent. "Well then, Christiano, I suppose I had better tell you what this is all about." He paused and held up a cautionary finger. "But before I say anything you must promise me that you will keep everything I tell you a secret. You must swear to me the greatest oath you could possibly make."

"I promise," said Christiano urgently. "I swear upon my mother's life and my own, may the Lord strike me down." He crossed his chest with his index finger.

"Good," said Vittori. "So be it. Now, let us start with a question. You say that you wish to become more like Jesus – how would you feel about becoming exactly like him?"

Chapter 16

Stella's appetite for a fight still smouldered, but over the last two days she had managed to curb her anger and put on a generally civil façade for the sheik's benefit. He was patently suspicious about her sudden change of heart, and still had his guard up, yet he was evidently enjoying the thawing of relations and had rewarded her compliance with a number of small, but useful, concessions.

The most welcome of these compromises was being allowed out of her room for half an hour a day. Although watched at all times by two armed guards, she could wander around the palace and enjoy the wondrous garden in the centre. There were, however, specific areas in which she was not permitted to venture, and she was also forbidden from making conversation or eye contact with anybody other than the sheik or her guards.

These restrictions had not stopped her gaining valuable information though. She had already made a map in her head of the general layout of the place, and had pinpointed areas relatively weak in security. What she needed now was access to more of the building, to complete her mental picture and formulate a viable escape plan.

She was lying on her bed thinking of ways to accomplish this when there was a knock on the door. After a ten-second pause the sheik entered the room. He smiled his sickening smile, and after containing a shiver she smiled back.

"Good morning," he said cheerfully. "I trust that you slept well, my dear."

"Yes, thank you," she said, rising to her feet.

"And your breakfast was satisfactory?"

"Yes, everything's fine. The food is excellent."

"Good, good," he said, clapping his hands. "I am so glad that you are enjoying yourself at last. It would be a pity to waste all the fine things on offer to you just because of misplaced pride. I will look after you here, you will never have to worry about anything again, as long as you live."

It may have been paranoia, but she was sure she detected a sinister undertone in his final words, and they echoed in her ears. She halted briefly, then put it out of her mind and continued to be civil. "What more could a girl want?" she laughed.

"Exactly," the sheik agreed. "All a woman needs is to be looked after." He touched her arm lightly in a show of empathy. She resisted the urge to flinch. "I have some spare time in my schedule this morning," he continued, "and I thought I might accompany you to the garden if you would not object."

Of course I object, you disgusting pervert, she thought.

"I would be delighted," she said in her very best English.

The sheik opened the door and ushered her out in gentlemanly fashion. They walked side by side through the palace with the guards two paces behind. Stella had the feeling that he wanted to link arms, so she kept a respectful distance and moved subtly sideways if he got too close.

The sheik's garden was situated in a huge central courtyard. It was about half the size of a football pitch and filled with plants from around the world. The many flower beds were intersected by veins of rich green turf which formed a lush walkway. In the middle, surrounded by tall sculpted hedgerows, a magnificent fountain imitated the one outside the Bellagio in Las Vegas, with streams of water rising and falling, and dancing and twirling in a brilliant aquatic ballet. The effect was enhanced by various pieces of classical music to suit the mood, and in the evenings a dazzling light display that took it from awesome to breathtakingly spectacular.

Stella sat down on one of the ornate marble benches and watched the water twist and turn to the graceful sound of Beethoven's Fur Elise. The sheik joined her, but for once kept a comfortable distance.

"You should see this at night," he said. "It is the most

wonderful sight to behold. If you continue to please me I shall allow you the privilege."

"That would be lovely," said Stella, resisting the temptation to be sarcastic. "I'm sure it must be absolutely amazing. I expect you have some fantastic parties out here."

"I do indeed. I have entertained many people in this garden, from businessmen and celebrities to presidents and kings and queens. I am a very influential man. I have wealth beyond most people's imagination."

"You must have," said Stella. "I can't begin to think how much all this costs." She made a sweeping gesture across the whole palace. "I suppose you must be in the oil business."

The sheik nodded. "I have made most of my money from oil, but I have branched out into many other areas like finance and technology and communications. I am also in the process of buying a football team in England. Not one of the Premiership sides, but one that I can build from the bottom into something great. It would be no fun to buy a readymade success."

"Don't you worry about people's reaction to foreign money?" she asked.

"Not at all," he replied. "They will soon change their minds once their team starts rising through the leagues. Teams need money to succeed – it matters not where it comes from. I will bring employment to the area as well, so it is a winning situation for everybody."

"I wouldn't be so sure," said Stella. "If there's one thing supporters of the smaller teams don't like, it's change. They're quite happy going along every week with their small crowds in their small stadiums. The thought of being successful appeals to them, but they want to keep the intimacy of their little clique – they'll just see you as a threat to their individuality. They'll worry that you'll turn them into a big conglomerate and take the heart right out of the club. Which of course you will."

The sheik fell briefly silent, then said, "I only wish to make things better for people. I can understand their fears, but the world is constantly changing. They must see that they cannot live in a bubble for the rest of their lives. Progress needs to be embraced, not rejected."

Stella felt her whole body gush with incandescent anger. She agreed that progress needed to be embraced, but wondered how this man could say such things and still justify his treatment of women. He talked about change eloquently and yet his attitudes were still firmly rooted in the Dark Ages. She wanted to leap up and beat him to a bloody pulp. Again though, she managed to hold her tongue.

"Progress is all very well," she said calmly. "But it shouldn't be at the expense of people's souls. The problem with you money men is that you think everybody wants the same thing as you, but they don't. Some people like small communities, they enjoy knowing everybody in the village or town. Once you start expanding things it takes away the beauty of their lives, instead of being an essential part of a group they become a faceless number in a sea of faceless numbers."

"I do not agree," said the sheik. "But I cannot expect you to understand the bigger picture."

This statement was nearly all too much for Stella. Every single one of her nerve endings began to bubble with rage. She imagined herself ripping an AK-47 from one of the guards and splattering the sheik's disgusting wiry frame with a thousand hate-filled bullets, each one penetrating deeper than the last until not even dental records could identify him. She tried to combat her wrath by focusing in on the leaping water and breathing the soothing music deep into her lungs. When this failed, however, she reached instinctively for her cigarettes. After a couple of drags the red mist had all but disappeared.

"I am afraid I must leave you on your own soon," said the sheik, oblivious to his captive's fury. "I have business to attend to, and I must prepare for this evening."

"What's happening this evening then?" asked Stella, uninterested but making conversation.

"I have a meeting with the local tribesmen. Once a year they come to me with requests for items that they need. It is traditional for me to share my wealth and grant their wishes."

"What sort of things do they ask for?"

"Anything really – cars, money, livestock, computers – they can have what they want as long as they can justify it as a necessity for their livelihoods."

"So it's a sort of begging party," said Stella.

"No," said the sheik sharply, creasing his brow. "It is not begging. I have a responsibility to my people and I offer them help. They are invited here at my bidding, they do not sit at my doorstep pulling at my conscience. It is a custom that the West could learn from." He got up and made to leave. "I must go now and attend to my business. Have a good day."

Stella remained seated and watched him hurry away. Once he was out of sight she leant back and relaxed into the bench, which for stonework was remarkably comfortable. She guessed it was all in the design.

Without the distraction of his odious presence, she enjoyed the rest of her cigarette and updated her mental map of the palace, wondering all the time what her misogynistic jailer would look like with a knife in his back.

Chapter 17

Christiano gaped at Vittori incredulously. "Exactly like Jesus?" he repeated. "Nobody could ever be exactly like Jesus, Your Eminence."

"Could they not?" said Vittori, raising his eyebrows. "You yourself pointed out that the Bible quotes Jesus as saying that we can all do what he did. That we all have it within ourselves. Have you suddenly changed your mind in the last couple of minutes?"

Christiano shuffled awkwardly in his chair under the cardinal's stern gaze. "No, of course not, Your Eminence. It is just that the statement took me quite by surprise. Please, I do not wish to upset you."

Vittori muted his glare and relaxed. "I know you do not, Christiano. I am sorry to be so serious, but this is a very serious matter. The fate of mankind depends upon it." He stopped to clear his throat. "I will now divulge to you exactly what is going on, and please leave any questions until the end. Is that okay?"

Christiano nodded.

"Good," said Vittori, "then I shall begin. You will know from the Bible that Jesus was a great healer, the greatest healer that ever lived. You will also know from the Bible that he was crucified and came back to life. These are both very much facts, as are the tales of his extreme humanity. What is not known is that Jesus was in fact using a form of Reiki to heal people, and also that it was Peter and the disciples that brought him back to life after the crucifixion – again using a form of Reiki. Not only did he survive, but he lived on for many years afterwards, journeying to the East where he remained until his death up to ninety years later. When he eventually died he left his secrets to an order of monks who were to keep them safe until such time as the human race was ready to utilize them safely. These secrets came in the form of hundreds of symbols that could be used to cure any illness. They work in exactly the same way as the regular Reiki symbols that you would use. Are you following me?"

"Yes, I think so, Your Eminence," replied a bewildered Christiano.

"Good. The thing is Christiano, these symbols have been located by some very dangerous people and I fear they are going to use them to fool the world into thinking that they are God's chosen ones. We need to stop them, and we need your help. There is obviously a lot more to the story, but I wanted to give you the salient points to start with. I know this is all a big shock, but you must try and keep your head. Now, if you have any questions, please ask."

Christiano had a million questions but his brain was too battered to assimilate them all. Yet, although shocked, a part of him was suddenly overjoyed as everything he had learned suddenly began to make sense. Jesus was a Reiki master, of course he was – the mightiest that ever lived. He had been sent by God to teach human beings the way forward, showing them how to access the power inside of each and every one of them. Christiano felt stupid for never thinking of it before. All those nights of trying to juggle his faith with his healing, when all the time they had been part of the same thing. "I really don't know what to say, Your Eminence. I am honoured that you should tell me all these things, but I don't know how someone like me could possibly help you."

"You are very humble, Christiano, it is most commendable," said Vittori. "It is one of the reasons I have chosen you. The thing is my friend, we have a very real problem facing us. The dangerous people I was telling you about are very high up in the Islamic religion. The have stolen this sacred knowledge and have given it to one of their number. At present this man has confined himself to Mecca, healing people and building his following, but soon they will unleash him on the world, and the entire population will begin to come under his sway. Within months, maybe weeks, the whole world will accept him as a new Messiah. Can you imagine what would happen then?"

"I am not sure, Your Eminence. I don't see how somebody healing people could be bad for the world. Surely healing is good – whoever does it."

A wave of anger crossed Vittori's face, but quickly passed. "Yes, Christiano, of course healing is good, but you must look at the bigger picture. Once people believe that this man has been sent by God himself, they will take to heart everything he says and follow any doctrine that he cares to teach them. You must see how dangerous that will be. Islam will take over the entire world. Sharia law will be introduced everywhere. Women will be treated like animals. No longer will there be tolerance and forgiveness, we will enter a dark age of rule by fear and violence, where any transgression, however minor, will be punished with disproportional retribution. Is that a world you wish to live in Christiano?"

"No, Your Eminence, of course not. You must forgive me, all I saw was the healing, I did not think about the consequences. It would be truly devastating if such a thing came to pass. But again, I ask you, how can I help?"

Vittori reached into a drawer and withdrew three sheets of paper. He laid one out on the surface of the desk and turned it to face Christiano. "This, Christiano, is a copy of the sacred symbols that Jesus left to mankind. I think you'll recognize some of them."

Christiano studied the paper carefully. The majority of the icons were alien to him, but he did indeed recognize the four Usui characters at each corner, and the repeated power symbol in the centre. "This is amazing," he said. "But what do they all do? I cannot possibly imagine."

Vittori held up the other two sheets. "The key to their various properties is held on these." He laid the papers out next to the first one. Christiano noted that instead of symbols there were small pictures. "You will notice that these pictures are laid out in a grid similar to that of the symbols," Vittori continued, "each picture corresponds to its relative symbol. Do you understand?"

"Yes," said Christiano. "So this symbol here," he pointed, "corresponds to this picture here." He pointed again, to a diagram of a man with fire emanating from his stomach. "And I assume that the symbol must be used for the healing of a stomach ailment."

"The boy's got it," said Jonathan Ayres, joining the conversation with a clap of his hands.

"Yes, indeed he has," said Vittori. "Well done, Christiano, that is exactly how to read it. It is very simple really, but I was afraid that it might look confusing. You are obviously a very bright lad, which will help you greatly in your task ahead."

"What is the task?" asked Christiano.

"To learn all of these symbols and their properties off by heart of course."

Christiano's mouth fell open. "That is a very great task!"

"I know," said Vittori. "But it is one that you must complete if you are to do your duty."

"And what is that, Your Eminence?" asked Christiano, suddenly feeling uncomfortable, and not really wanting an answer.

"You are to become the new Messiah."

Chapter 18

Grady hacked wearily away at the clawing foliage with his machete. It was hot and humid and humourless. Since leaving what passed for a path, the afternoon had been one long serious slog through walls of creeping plant life. Even though Majami and Tawhali were clearing the way in front, it seemed like the jungle had developed the phenomenon of instant regrowth behind them. Jennings' intermittent chirpy whistling from the back was doing nothing for his morale, and neither was his sudden popularity with the brotherhood of mosquitoes. It was fair to say that he'd had better days. "How much further, Majami?!" he shouted to the monk.

"Not far now," Majami replied brightly. "Maybe another hour, maybe two."

"Another hour," Grady muttered, slicing at a huge fern. "I could be dead in another hour."

Behind him Jennings sniggered and said, "Come on mate, I thought you were in the US Marines. A finely tuned killing machine and all that."

"I'll finely tune you in a minute!" barked Grady. "I've been bedridden for almost two weeks. It doesn't take long to lose your edge."

"Obviously not," Jennings chuckled.

"That's it," said Grady, "laugh it up while you can. We'll see who the daddy is when I've had time to recover properly."

Over the next hour the vegetation gradually began to thin, until eventually they found a track heading out towards friendlier terrain. Grady's mood became lighter, and without the constant effort of swinging his heavy knife he regained the ability to smile once again. Jennings walked beside him sharing some of his newfound wisdom, and Stratton took up the rear with Titan ambling at his flank.

As they hit the fringes of the jungle Stratton bade them stop for a while so that he could say goodbye to Titan. He had dreaded the moment, but knew that they would soon be coming upon a settlement and that a black panther, however tame, would scare the villagers, and without doubt induce a violent reaction. Fighting back the tears he knelt down beside the great cat and whispered into his ear.

Jennings, Grady and the two monks looked on from a respectful distance.

"Must be hard for him," Grady said quietly to Jennings. "He really loves that animal doesn't he."

"Yes, he does," Jennings agreed. "He'd probably take him everywhere if it were feasible. But the jungle's the right place for him – Stratton knows that."

They watched as Stratton kissed Titan's forehead for the last time. The panther turned around and trotted back into the wild, his paws bouncing effortlessly off the uneven ground, his head noble and keen and alert. Stopping briefly at the edge of the undergrowth he glanced back and gave a loud roar. And then, in the blink of an eye, he was gone, swallowed up by the impene-trable forest as he strode fearlessly into his new life.

Stratton returned to the group slowly with his head bowed, a solitary tear trickled down his left cheek. Jennings, who already had a lump in his throat, noticed this and felt his own eyes brimming up. Even Grady had a queasy sensation in his stomach, but he convinced himself it was the after-effects of Majami's jungle stew.

"I suppose we'd better get going then," said Stratton, wiping his face as he ambled up. "How far to the village, Majami?"

"Another mile or so. We should be there in twenty minutes."

They continued along the same path with the trees growing sparser at every step. The sun was sinking and dark clouds hovered in the fading light. Titan's departure hung heavily over Stratton, and the mood of the group was sombre. It was a great relief when at last they saw lights twinkling in the near distance.

The village was a small settlement of twelve solid timber constructions, six on each side of a dusty track. Having expected something far more primitive, Jennings was suitably impressed with the high level of workmanship. He was also impressed with the delicious smell of herbs and spices that filled the air, and began to salivate. A group of children playing out in the street recognized Majami and swarmed up to the band of travellers, hollering at them in friendly tones.

"What are they saying?" Jennings asked Tawhali.

"They are asking about you and your friends," said the monk. "They wish to know if you are staying and whether you have brought any gifts for them."

"Gifts?"

"Preferably money," said Tawhali. "American dollars."

"Ah," said Jennings. "How sweet. Bless their little weatherworn sandals."

When the hubbub had died down and the children realized there were no riches to be had, Majami led them through the village to a house at the far end. It was slightly bigger than the others and positioned away from the main track. Majami knocked on the door softly, and a young woman dressed in a bright green sari answered. Elegant and beautiful, she welcomed the monk graciously and invited the group to enter. They were escorted to a room at the back and greeted by a gruff-looking, thickset man seated at the head of a large table. He gestured for them to sit down and started talking to Majami in Malayalam, the language of Kerala. After a brief discussion he spoke to the group in English.

"Good evening," he said kindly, breaking into a smile. "Welcome to my home. My name is Sunil." One by one the group introduced themselves.

"Majami tells me you have had an arduous day," said Sunil. "My daughter is preparing dinner, and I would be delighted if you would join us. There is plenty to go round."

They accepted the invitation gratefully, Jennings in particular looking forward to sampling some of the local cuisine he had smelled outside. Grady was just happy to take the weight off his feet. He sat at the end of the table with his legs stretched out and started to nod off.

Sunil ordered his daughter into the room and asked her to bring their guests some beer.

"I notice that you have electricity," said Stratton, pointing to the lights on the wall. "What's your source?"

"We have a large diesel generator that supplies the entire village," Sunil explained. "We had it installed five years ago. It has certainly changed our lives for the better, although I'm not convinced that television is the best thing to expose our young children to."

"I guess not," Stratton agreed. "But the world moves on and on."

"Yes, of course," said Sunil. "And it is not all terrible. In fact, some television is quite educational. I just do not want them getting into bad habits."

Sunil's daughter returned with mugs of cold beer and went dutifully round the table handing them out. Right on cue, Grady opened his eyes and took a tentative swig. Happy it was palatable, he proceeded to drain half the contents in one go. "Now that's what I'm talking about!" he chimed, wiping his mouth with his sleeve.

Jennings followed his friend's lead and took a long quaff. After almost three drinkless weeks and a hard day's march the beer tasted nothing short of heavenly.

For a while they chatted with Sunil about his village. There were twelve families in all, and they farmed the surrounding land as a collective. Sunil dealt with the monetary side of the business, and since he had taken over six years previously it had thrived. Under his guidance they had made enough to buy new equipment and more than treble their output. It was also his financial acumen that had enabled them to obtain their generator.

"We have made centuries of progress in very little time," said Sunil.

"It's very impressive," said Stratton. "And your English is excellent."

"Thank you. I decided to learn it so that we could start exporting our crops. There is a huge international market for our produce."

"Really," said Stratton. "What sort of stuff do you grow?"

"It varies," Sunil said noncommittally. "Exotic fruits, things like that." He waved his arm casually.

Sensing that their host no longer wished to discuss business, Stratton dropped the subject and sipped at his beer. A few moments later Sunil's daughter returned once more bearing trays of food. They ate from bowls with their fingers, mopping up the fragrant dishes with freshly made chapattis. Jennings consumed far more than he needed, and by the time he was finished he had to slacken his belt a notch for comfort.

"That was quite possibly the best meal I've ever had," he said to Sunil. "Thank you very much. Your daughter is a wonderful cook."

"Yes, she is," said Sunil. "She takes after her mother – God rest her soul. I will be lost when she finally marries, which will probably be not far away. She is not short of suitors, as you can imagine."

"She's very beautiful," said Jennings. "I don't doubt that every young man in the province has got his eye on her."

"This is very true, but she is a very headstrong girl and very intelligent. It will take an exceptional man to win her affections. Much as I would miss her, I do hope that someone worthy comes along soon. I would not like her to miss out on the joys of love."

After a brief discussion it was decided that the group would spend the night as Sunil's guests. He explained that he had two spare rooms for business associates and that they were very much welcome to use them. In the morning he would take them to the nearest major town in his Jeep.

"You are very kind," said Stratton. "I just wish we could offer you something in return."

"There is no need," said Sunil. "You are a friend of Majami's and that is enough for me. It is a man's duty to help those in need if he possibly can."

Taking Sunil to his word Grady made his own request. "I hope I'm not overstepping the mark," he said apologetically, "but I don't suppose you have a phone I could use for a couple of minutes. I really want to let my wife know that I'm okay."

"Of course," said Sunil. "It is not a problem. I have a satellite phone in the other room."

After thanking Sunil many times Grady stepped outside the front door and dialled his home number. He had no idea what the exact time was in LA but he imagined it would be morning. He hoped Brooke would be in. The phone rang and rang, and he was just about to give up when a sleepy voice answered on the sixth tone. It turned out that it was in fact four o' clock in the morning in LA and a distraught Brooke had only just dropped off to sleep.

"Where have you been?!" she cried down the phone. "I've been worried sick for days."

"I told you that I'd be out of contact for a few weeks, honey."

"I know you did, but it's been nearly three now. When are you coming home?"

Grady went silent.

"Well?" she pressed.

"I don't know for sure, honey. I'm stuck in India at the moment. It's a long story and I can't go through all of it right now. Just know that I love you and I'll be home as soon as I can. If you need anything just ask Grant, he'll take care of you."

The conversation continued with much weeping from Brooke and much pacifying from Grady. He eventually managed to calm her down and promised that he would call again as soon as he could. But her voice had made him even more homesick, and he hung up with a heavy heart.

For a while he sat on the wooden steps at the front of the house, staring into the gloom. The sound of children's laughter cut through the night, filling him with both joy and longing. He imagined himself sitting in his garden back in LA, a cold beer in one hand, his other entwined with Brooke's, and a boy and a girl running round the lawn playing in the bright California sun. It was a picture he kept in his head for hope, but just now it seemed a million miles away. Before darkness overtook him he shook his head and got to his feet.

He was about to go back inside when he caught a flash of movement in the corner of his eye. Turning quickly, he leapt over the porch barrier and landed solidly at the side of the house. Without pausing to think he sprinted after the dark shape running away into the trees behind. Within seconds he was bearing down on his target, and with a mighty effort he launched himself into the air, tackling the man's waist and sending him crashing to the floor. There was a loud gasp as Grady landed on top of his prey.

Without giving him a chance to get his breath back, Grady turned the man over and sat on top of him with his hands at his throat. "What do you want, you sneaky little mother?!" he barked.

Beneath him the unfortunate man began to babble in his own language.

"Right then," said Grady. "Let's get you inside and see what Sunil makes of you." He forced the man to his feet, whipped his arm behind his back, and frogmarched him round and into the house.

"Look what I found," he said, walking triumphantly into the dining room. "He was sneaking about round the side of the house; listening in on my conversation, no doubt."

Sunil gave the unfortunate man an icy glare and grilled him in their own language.

Jennings stared for a while until it dawned on him that he had seen the captive before. "He's one of the men that tortured us, Grady!" he exclaimed. "He's one of Massa's thugs!"

Sunil took the information in and continued to question him roughly. Eventually he spoke to the group in English. "I am ashamed to say that this is one of my men. Massa came here about a month ago attempting to hire some of my workforce. He offered me a lot of money, but we were too busy with the harvest to let anybody go. It appears that Rashid here could not resist the temptation and defied my orders. I knew from his manner that Massa was up to no good."

Jennings stared at the man called Rashid and felt the pain come flooding back. He grimaced as brutal memories flashed through his mind and body, pictures of Rashid's cruel and gloating eyes blazing with hatred as he struck blow after blow with his heavy branch.

"So why was he snooping around outside the house?" asked Grady.

"When he saw you walking into the village he became scared," said Sunil. "He could not believe that you were alive. He feared that you were coming to find him."

"Well, we weren't," said Grady. "But now that we have I've a mind to give him a little bit of payback."

"That won't do any good," said Stratton.

"Maybe not," said Grady. "But it'll make me feel a whole lot better. You wouldn't understand, Stratton, you're not the one who was strung up."

Stratton opened his mouth to apologize, but before he could Jennings suddenly snapped. He leapt out of his chair and flew across the room at Rashid, his hands outstretched in a beeline for the sorry villager's throat. Caught unawares, Grady was knocked aside like a ninepin as the full weight of Jennings' body hurtled past and crunched down onto Rashid. In an instant he had pinned him to the floor, and without thought began wailing his fists vigorously, pummelling away like a jackhammer.

"Where is she, you motherfucker?!" he screamed. "Where is she?!"

Chapter 19

Sequestered in a small white room in the heart of the Vatican, Christiano sat at his desk and continued to pore over the symbols and the key. Unaware of time – he might have been in there two hours, perhaps twelve – he plugged on assiduously trying to make everything stick in his brain. In the corner a tiny stereo played Mozart and Beethoven on a loop, the music being permitted only because Vittori considered it to be a study aid. Every other possible distraction, including Christiano's watch, had been removed from the vicinity. He felt like an inmate at a mental asylum.

With icons and pictures chewing his mind and blending into one, he stood up and stretched his arms wide. Hundreds of symbols flashed in front of him, lit up in bright yellow. He rubbed his eyes and blinked a few times to restore his vision, but the illusion continued to swirl about the room following every twist of his head. Suddenly feeling very nauseous he lay down on the hard floor, closed his eyes, and began to regulate his breathing. The images slowly drifted away, but an uncomfortable queasiness remained.

Everything had happened so quickly that he had not had time to absorb his position. One minute he had been strolling in for a good day's work on the roof, the next he had been landed in the most surreal situation imaginable. Such was his respect for Cardinal Vittori he had not even thought to question what was going on, but now, as tiredness started to play with his mind, he could feel doubt and fear slithering up his spine with insidious stealth.

It wasn't that he didn't believe the cardinal's story about Jesus leaving a legacy for mankind, this seemed perfectly feasible to Christiano, it was the way in which they were approaching it that was giving him problems. He loved the Catholic Church with all his heart and would do anything to save it, but taking sacred knowledge and using it on a false premise – was that really what Jesus would have wanted? Was it really what God wanted? The Muslims may well be unleashing a fake Messiah onto the world, but did that give Vittori the right to do exactly the same? Surely it was just as bad for the Church to do it as anyone else?

As he lay there staring into a void his uneasiness grew. Vittori had been most persuasive in his argument, and had made his plan appear perfectly ethical and logical, but Christiano's inner voice was telling him something quite different. It was almost begging him to break out of his cage and run until he could run no longer. *Forget Vittori! Forget the Church!* It screamed. *This is all wrong! So terribly wrong!*

Christiano sprang up straight and scrambled to his feet. Leaping to the door he tried the handle in vain before beginning to hammer away on it, screaming to be let out. He carried on beating and hollering until his hands and lungs ached, but nobody came to his rescue. Eventually he gave up, hanging his head in despair and flopping back to his chair.

Almost instantly the door opened and Cardinal Vittori walked in. Without a word he strode over and put an avuncular hand on Christiano's shoulder, comforting him with the softest of touches. Christiano started to weep.

"I am very sorry, Christiano," said Vittori. "This is my fault entirely. I have put too much pressure on you. You are tired and emotional, and badly in need of some sleep."

"I can't do this," Christiano stammered through his tears. "It is too much for me. It is all wrong."

"Come, come, Christiano, it is surely not as bad as all that. You have been in here a long time – almost twelve hours in fact – and you just need some rest. I expect you are hungry as well, it must be at least six hours since you were last brought food."

Vittori walked round to the front of the desk and stared down at his bewildered charge. Christiano looked up and wiped away the frustration from his eyes. The cardinal gave him a benign smile and put a hand to his moistened cheek. "Come with me, Christiano, we shall go and eat together."

Vittori led the way through a maze of corridors until they arrived at his private chambers. Christiano sat down at the round dining table and accepted a goblet of red wine. The cardinal sat opposite and poured one for himself from the decanter. "This is from my own vineyard in Tuscany," he said. "It is almost twenty years old. I do hope you enjoy it."

Christiano took a small mouthful and then a larger one. He wasn't a connoisseur but he knew a good wine from a bad one, and this was one of the best he'd tasted. He immediately felt his burden ease as the liquid warmed his body. "It is a beautiful wine, Your Eminence," he said.

"I am glad you like it," said Vittori. "It is my favourite vintage. I only open it in very special company."

Christiano felt a swell of pride. "I am honoured, Your Eminence," he said. "But I fear I am not worthy."

"Of course you are," said Vittori. "You have worked hard today, and will do so again tomorrow. Unless, that is, you are still having doubts?"

Christiano looked across into the cardinal's kindly gaze and suddenly felt rather foolish. How could he question this noble and peaceful man? What madness had caused him to think that the cardinal's intentions were anything other than humanitarian? He was tired, of course he was, and his fatigue was causing paranoia. "No, I do not doubt," he said. "I am just tired as you suggested. My mind is playing tricks on me. I will be fine after some sleep."

"You are a good man, Christiano, and a wise one. It takes a wise man to understand his body and to know his limitations. My faith in you grows stronger by the minute."

Christiano had not known his father, nor the joy of paternal approval, but as he wallowed in Vittori's kindnesses he felt the esteem of a favourite son. "I will do my best to repay that faith," he said.

"I know you will," said Vittori, ringing the service bell. "Now let us eat."

Chapter 20

Jennings woke in a cloud of shame. It didn't matter what the wretched man had done, he knew he had gone too far. Dark memories of Rashid's bloodied face zipped through his mind in a never-ending slideshow. The fear in the man's eyes would haunt him for a long time to come. And all for what? What good had it done them? The poor guy was just a foot-soldier, a lowly farmer who had been given an opportunity to make a bit of extra money. He knew nothing of magical symbols and religious power struggles, and as it turned out, very little about Stella's fate. He had inflicted a savage beating for all the wrong reasons. Not that there was ever a right one.

"Don't beat yourself up about it," said Grady, sensing his friend's guilt from across the room. "The guy fucking deserved all he got. I didn't see him having any compassion when we were strung up like carcasses on that tree."

Jennings continued to stare at the ceiling. "That's not the point. He's a simple man and probably doesn't know any better. He got swept up in the mob mentality and just did what everyone else was doing. I expect they were all fed a pack of lies by Massa, making us out to be some kind of 'white devils' who had come to hurt their families."

"Who are you calling a 'white devil'?" said Grady.

"You know what I mean," said Jennings. "Anyway, the point I'm making is that the guy probably isn't evil at heart. You saw how terrified he was last night."

"Oh, for fuck's sake," said Grady rolling his eyes. "Not you as well? Am I the only person left who can see things as they are?"

Jennings turned to face his friend. "What do you mean?" he asked.

"I mean that Stratton's obviously infected you with his bleeding-heart liberality. All this 'turning the other cheek' crap. Don't get me wrong, I do understand it, but sometimes a well-aimed punch is more effective than a kind word."

"I don't know," said Jennings. "A week ago I would have agreed with you, but now I'm not so sure. Beating the guy just felt plain wrong."

"Have it your way," said Grady. "But we did get some information out of him, and I doubt he'd have said anything without your persuasion."

Grady went to search out some breakfast, leaving Jennings alone with his thoughts. The all-encompassing happiness of his attunement had been sorely tainted by his violent actions. Instead of an overwhelming joy, he was now saturated with guilt. It pervaded every last outpost of his body and soul, causing his insides to contract and ready themselves for a brutal purging. Stratton had warned him that the attunement would give him cause to question his innermost demons, but he hadn't realized that the effect would be quite so profound. Unable to contain the pressure he shot out of bed and paced around the room in his boxer shorts hoping that the physical effort would somehow help to calm him.

A minute later Stratton appeared in the doorway with a look of concern on his face. "Grady tells me your feeling bad about last night," he said.

"That's an understatement," Jennings replied. "I feel like a walking mountain of guilt. It's not like a thought I can shake off, it's taken over my whole being."

Stratton nodded sagely. "I thought it might."

Jennings sat down on the edge of his bunk and put his head in his hands. "Is there anything I can do to get rid of it?"

"It'll go in time," said Stratton. "But you could always apologize to Rashid, that might go a long way."

"Of course," said Jennings raising his face. "I'll go and find him once I'm dressed. I just wish I hadn't done it in the first place."

"We all wish that at some time or another," said Stratton. "But the good thing is that you can see your actions were wrong and you know why they were wrong. Most people in your situation would convince themselves that Rashid deserved what was coming to him, at least you have the intelligence to see beyond that."

"Yeah, I can see it, but I couldn't stop it."

"That's because you care."

"So the only way to stop reacting is to stop caring. Is that what you're saying?"

"No," said Stratton. "The only way to stop reacting is to stop being afraid. You did what you did out of fear – fear of what might happen to Stella if we don't find her."

"I'd say it was more like anger," said Jennings.

Stratton shrugged. "Anger's just a by-product of fear."

"Perhaps," said Jennings. "But I can't help the way I feel. The thought of anything happening to Stella makes me mad. I don't know how you can be so calm about the whole thing. Don't you give a damn about her any more?"

Stratton looked to the floor. "Of course I do. But it's complicated. This whole thing isn't all about one person. I've got to keep my mind on the bigger picture." He looked back up and smiled. "And besides, I think you care enough about her for everyone."

Jennings held Stratton's eyes trying to gauge the intent of his statement, but he could see nothing except genuine warmth.

"Listen," said Stratton. "You'd better get dressed and join us for some breakfast. We need to be heading off as soon as we can. I'll go and find Rashid so you can apologize to him. Okay?"

"Yeah, of course," said Jennings. "And, Stratton – thanks for helping me."

"Not a problem, mate. Not a problem."

After breakfast they gathered together outside the house next to Sunil's Jeep. Jennings had made his peace with Rashid, and although he still felt ashamed it was not nearly as bad as it had been when he woke. Majami and Tawhali waited with them to say goodbye.

"Well then, I guess this is it," said Stratton to Majami. "I can't thank you both enough for what you've done for us."

"It is nothing," smiled the monk. "We wish you the best of luck. Bring back the knowledge if you can."

"We'll try."

Sunil started up the Jeep and they headed through the tiny settlement. A group of children stood at the side of the track and waved them off enthusiastically until they turned out of sight. Stratton relaxed in the front seat and looked up into the brilliant blue, wondering what they would find when they re-entered the modern world, and how they were going to locate Stella.

After a while the trees began to thin, and before long they were driving in a dusty wilderness. Jennings suddenly felt lonely and insignificant, and started to remember the situation he'd left behind in England. Whilst they were ensconced in their own little jungle world, he hadn't really thought about anything outside apart from Stella. But as they drew nearer to civilization his predicament crept back into his thoughts once again.

"Are you okay?" asked Grady, sensing his friend's solemnity. "You're not still worrying about Rashid are you? I thought you'd sorted that out?"

Jennings stared out onto the plains. "No, it's not that," he replied. "I was just thinking about what's going to happen to me. I mean, it's all very well us going back to the real world, but where do I fit in? I'm still an outcast remember – a wanted man. My picture could have been posted all over the English-speaking world for all I know, and probably every corner of the globe."

"You're being a bit melodramatic, aren't you?" said Grady. "You're hardly likely to get recognized as soon as you set foot in the first town we come to."

"Probably not. But it's hanging over my head, and it's not going to go away any time soon. I won't even be able to get out of the country. I've got no passport – nothing."

"None of us have got passports," said Stratton.

"True," Jennings agreed. "But you two aren't wanted men. It's not so much that anyway. Where's it all going to end up? What am I going to do when this is all over? I'm never going to be able to go back to Britain, and…"

"Stop right there!" said Stratton forcefully. "Take a step back and clear your head. You're getting on a bad thought train. Just remember where you are. You're sitting in a Jeep in Kerala, and that's it. Nothing's happened yet. Don't try and visualize outcomes, it'll only bring you down."

"Don't you think I know that," said Jennings. "It's not easy though, is it? I can't just switch off at the drop of a hat."

"No. But try thinking of a happy scenario – one where you get your life back as you want it. At least it'll keep you going. Just go with the flow and trust that everything will turn out alright. You'll be no use to anyone as a negative mess."

Jennings concentrated hard on ridding his mind of the doom-laden thoughts that had begun to fester. Despite his best efforts the beating he'd given Rashid still lingered. It was taking him to places he didn't want to go, places that conjured up his innermost fears. With great force of will he closed his eyes and imagined the happiest situation he could muster. After a brief shuffle through his mental slides, inevitably his first surge of joy came when he pictured Stella. It was a simple image, just him and her walking through a golden wheat-field hand in hand heading towards a distant sun. It was cheesy but he didn't care. Within seconds a wave of happiness had overtaken him, and his post-attunement content was restored. He continued to focus until his whole body glowed, then opened his eyes and breathed in the fresh whistling air.

"Better?" asked Stratton looking back.

"Much better, thanks," Jennings beamed.

The ride continued in semi-silence with just the occasional

grunt of thanks as the water was passed round. Stratton drifted in and out of a lazy sleep until something up ahead caught his sharp eyes. "Is that a car on the side of the road?" he said to Sunil.

Sunil squinted into the distance. "I cannot tell," he said. "My eyesight is not what it used to be."

Jennings stuck his head out to the side. "I think it is," he confirmed.

As they drew closer Stratton realized it was another Jeep. Three men were hovering around the lifted bonnet, pointing and pushing each other out of the way. Sunil slowed and pulled up behind the distressed travellers. "I will go and see if I can help," he said.

He got out and ambled up to the flustered group.

"I don't like this," said Grady from the back seat. "It smells."

"No, I don't like it either," Jennings agreed. "What about you, Stratton?"

"I'm not sure. My instincts aren't that good at the moment. But if you two think it's dodgy then we'd better be wary."

Sunil chatted briefly to the men and then disappeared behind the bonnet with them. Thirty seconds later the men reappeared with rifles. Sunil followed them armed with a pistol.

"For fuck's sake!" growled Grady. "I knew this was all going too easily."

Within seconds the Jeep was surrounded with a rifle trained on each of them.

"What's this all about, Sunil?" Stratton asked calmly.

"Money, I'm afraid," Sunil replied. "Apparently your heads are worth quite a lot of it. Especially yours, Stratton."

"So you're just going to shoot us in cold blood?"

"I am afraid so," said Sunil. "At least it will be quick and painless. I have instructed my men to make one shot straight to the head." He drew out three cigarettes from his shirt pocket. "I believe it is customary for the condemned men to have one of these each."

"We don't smoke," said Stratton firmly.

"Speak for yourself," said Grady. "I'll have one thanks."

"Me too," said Jennings.

They took the cigarettes and a light, and puffed slowly away stalling for time. Having not smoked for many years Jennings had to stifle a few coughs, but he was determined to keep himself alive as long as possible. He gave Grady a furtive glance, half expecting the American to come up with a plan, but he was met with a shrug and a look of resignation. His only remaining hope was that Stratton might pull off one more miracle. That, however, was most unlikely considering his current health.

He smoked the rest of the cigarette in a state of acceptance, unable to muster any resistance to his impending doom. As he reached the butt, and threw it out into the dust, he began to laugh. The absolute pointlessness of it all hit him like a freight train of joy. He stood up and spread his arms wide and shouted, "Shoot me! Just fucking well shoot me!"

The mystified firing squad looked to Sunil for help. He ordered them to shoot immediately.

Jennings closed his eyes and continued to roar. A shot rang out, and he wondered who had bought it first – Stratton or Grady. It didn't matter anymore, nothing did. He would soon be joining them.

Chapter 21

It was cold, wet and windy as Tariq walked through the town on his way to the college. He pulled his hood up tight and braced himself against the elements. After dodging through the motionless traffic he set off down the pedestrianized high street, upping his pace as he checked his gold watch. He'd missed too much work already this term and he didn't need to fall behind even further by being late again. At the Banbury Cross he stopped briefly to adjust his rucksack and then began to run.

He skidded into the classroom bang on nine o'clock and took a seat at the back, where he divested himself of his bedraggled outer garments and attempted to regulate his laboured breath.

"Are you alright, mate?" asked Daniel Trent, sitting at the adjoining desk.

"Yeah...fine," gasped Tariq. "Just a bit...knackered."

"Up all night again?"

"Nearly."

"You should try sleeping mate."

Tariq nodded but said no more as their tutor had started to speak.

Out of his four 'A' level subjects History was his least favourite. He'd only taken it at his father's request – "we learn from the past so that we don't make the same mistakes in the future," he had said. Tariq didn't have the heart to argue with him, and for a peaceful life had agreed to add it to his curriculum. The more he did for his father the less the old man interfered in his life, and at the moment he was glad of the freedom.

As Mr Asquith rambled on about the dissolution of the monasteries, Tariq found his head nodding forward. He had to check himself straight three times before he finally shook off the weariness and regained the thread of the lecture. His attention, however, was tempered with passionate memories of the previous night.

At eleven o'clock when the lesson ended Tariq found that he had no more idea about Tudor religious politics than he had done two hours before. Thankful that he didn't have another class until one o'clock he made his way to the library for a bit of peace and quiet, and perhaps a little snooze. Finding his usual desk in the far corner unoccupied he set out his books and started to read. It wasn't long before he once again started to drift off, but this time instead of fighting it he simply let his head drop into his arms and fell asleep.

He was woken an hour later by the buzz of his mobile phone indicating an incoming text. Expecting it to be a sweet nothing from Jenna he smiled sleepily to himself and reached for the keypad. The message was not from Jenna but his friend Mo. He read it quickly: 'Phone me – now!'. He put the phone down and went back to his nap – if it was that important then why didn't Mo ring him?

Before he had a chance to switch off again the mobile buzzed once more. This time it was a call. He picked it up lazily and said, "Hi, Mo. What do you want? I'm kind of busy."

"You're not too busy for this," said Mo. "I've just heard something that'll blow you away."

Tariq sighed. Mo was forever bombarding him with calls and texts about things that were quite frankly of no interest whatsoever, but as his oldest friend he felt obliged to humour him. "Go on then mate, what is it?"

"The Mahdi! The Mahdi has come!" Mo shouted excitedly.

"The Mahdi?"

"Yes, the Mahdi! The redeemer, the bringer of justice."

"I know what he is," said Tariq. "But it's just a Sufi myth, isn't it?"

"Where are you?" asked Mo.

Tariq told him.

"I'm coming to see you."

Tariq sat up in his chair, stretched his arms, and yawned. The last thing he needed was an overzealous Mo storming into the library and disturbing the peace. Having built up an understanding with the various librarians, he didn't want it all blown apart by some loudmouth lunatic spouting religious fanaticism at over a hundred decibels. With this in mind he gathered his stuff and made his way to the entrance to halt Mo's progress.

It wasn't long before his outspoken friend came storming down the corridor. "Taz!" he shouted. "It's bloody unbelievable!"

Tariq moved swiftly towards him with a finger over his mouth. "Shush, Mo. I have to study here you know."

Mo lowered his voice. "Sorry, mate, I'm just so excited."

"Let's get out of here," said Tariq. "We'll go and get a coffee in the town."

Outside the weather had taken a turn for the better and they walked side by side in the sun, Tariq becoming mesmerized by the multicoloured light reflecting off the puddles, oblivious to Mo's incessant chatter.

"So what do you think?" said Mo loudly and pointedly.

Tariq broke from his reverie. "About what?"

"About the Mahdi, of course."

The Mahdi, thought Tariq. He'd heard the legend, but like all rational Muslims he knew it was just that. He was supposedly a spiritual and secular leader who would reveal himself before the end of the world and restore religion and justice. The idea appealed to the more unorthodox branches of Islam.

"I'm not sure what to think," said Tariq. "Where did you find this out?"

"Haven't you been listening to me at all?"

Tariq admitted he hadn't.

Mo sighed. "Oh well, I suppose I'd better go through it again."

They walked in to Costa Coffee, ordered two hot chocolates, and took them to an outside table.

"Right then," said Mo. "Have I got your full attention?"

Tariq nodded.

"Well then. Like I said before when you were dreaming of whatever, my mum's uncle's cousin knows a bloke who lives in Mecca. Apparently, about four or five days ago, this bloke in Mecca claims that he witnessed a number of miracles. He says that this guy turned up in the marketplace and started healing people. There was one bloke who'd been on crutches all his life and then suddenly – SHAZAM!" he flicked his fingers, "the guy's thrown away his crutches and he's running down the street like Usain Bolt, not a care in the world."

Tariq raised an eyebrow. "And you believe this?"

"Why not?" said Mo. "The bloke's a reliable source so my mum says."

Tariq stirred his chocolate and spooned some of the whipped cream into his mouth. "Think about it though," he said. "A marketplace in Mecca? I could take you to a marketplace in Mecca, hand you a pair of crutches, pretend to cure you. It'd be easy to fool people."

"No, no," Mo protested. "It wasn't like that at all. This bloke was a genuine cripple – a local boy who everyone knew. Unless he'd been putting it on for sixteen years then a miracle's the only explanation. I don't know why you have to be so suspicious of everything."

"I'm not suspicious of everything, just tales of miracles from faraway places, where they probably still use abacuses to count, and camels to carry messages."

"I'm telling you, Taz, this is the real thing. And you know as well as I do that Mecca's not a backward city. With all the money at their disposal it's probably more advanced than most places on earth."

"Fair enough," said Tariq. "But you're still asking me to believe a story that's come third or fourth hand. You have to admit there's a lot of scope for exaggeration."

"Maybe there is," Mo agreed. "But my mum's not the only one to have heard the rumour. There's been whispers round the mosque for days now. But you wouldn't know about that would you? Not having been there."

Tariq shrugged. "I've been busy with college."

"More like busy shagging," laughed Mo. "Don't think you can put one past me mate. I know you too well remember."

"Whatever," said Tariq.

"Anyway," Mo continued. "You'd better be free later on because there's a meeting at the mosque. The truth will be unveiled."

Chapter 22

A second shot rang out and then a third and fourth in quick succession, followed by loud screams. Jennings began to wonder why he was still alive. As the wailing grew he opened his eyes to see what was going on. To his amazement Sunil and his three accomplices were writhing around in the dust next to the Jeep, each clutching their legs. He looked about to try and get a handle on the situation. Stratton and Grady were both still alive and appeared equally perplexed.

A horn tooted behind. All three turned round to see yet another Jeep heading their way. Grady was the first to compose himself and leapt out of their vehicle to gather the weapons before Sunil and his cronies had a chance to retrieve them. As the oncoming Jeep drew up Jennings suddenly realized who it was. Standing on the passenger seat waving his shovel hands was the giant figure of Arman Kandinsky, a rifle slung over his shoulder and a grin on his face.

"Hello, my friends!" he hollered. "It is a fine day for shooting practice, yes? Ample light and very little wind."

The big man's cheerful demeanour turned Jennings' bewilderment into a broad smile. There was something about Kandinsky that would hearten the most miserable of souls. Jennings jumped out of the Jeep and walked over to greet the big Russian.

"It's very good to see you, Arman," he said, shaking his hand. "But, what the hell are you doing here?"

"I will tell you later," said Kandinsky. "First of all we must sort out this little mess. These men need medical attention." He walked over to Sunil and towered over him like an angel of doom. "You are a stupid man, Sunil. You have crossed the wrong people."

"I did not know they were your friends, Arman," Sunil whimpered. "Please forgive me. I will make it up to you."

"There is no need," said Kandinsky. "We will see to your wounds and then you can go wherever you will – I suggest the nearest hospital."

Kandinsky and his two men set about tending to the injured. Each one had been shot in or around the kneecap in a display of expert marksmanship. The bullets from the high-velocity rifle had gone straight through, leaving clean wounds. With help from Stratton, Jennings, and Grady they were soon patched up, and given painkilling injections from Kandinsky's emergency kit.

Once Sunil and his men were sorted, and before the group departed, Jennings asked him if he knew anything about what had happened to Stella. At first he said nothing, but after Kandinsky had given him a severe glare he began to talk.

"I sold her," he said.

"Who to?" demanded Jennings.

"His name is Malik."

Kandinsky stared fiercely. "You sold her to Malik?"

"Yes."

"Who is this Malik?" asked Jennings.

"He is what you would call a scumbag," said Kandinsky. "He trades in anything and everything. He will get good money for a beautiful woman like Stella. I will find out who he has sold her to when we return to the submarine. But now we must leave."

They took two Jeeps. Kandinsky in one with the three friends, and his men in the other. They left the third vehicle for Sunil.

"Are they going to be able to drive that thing?" asked Jennings.

"They'll manage," said Kandinsky. "They're lucky to be alive. A few months ago they would not have found me so forgiving. But they are only simple men, they do not understand. If they are offered money then they will take it."

Jennings should have been angry with Sunil, but he was so elated by the news of Stella being alive that nothing else mattered. "So, come on then, Arman," he pressed. "How do you know Sunil? And how did you manage to end up here?"

Kandinsky took a cigar from his breast pocket and let the steering wheel drift for a moment while he lit it. "Ah, Sunil," he said. "I have known him for many years. I used to buy his crops from him – if you know what I mean."

"I thought there was something suspicious going on there," said Jennings.

Grady rolled his eyes.

Kandinsky continued. "I stopped dealing with him about a year ago whilst I was legitimizing my business. To be honest he was becoming far too greedy anyway, and charging far too much for the quality of merchandise he was offering. I am not surprised he accepted an offer to kill you, I expect he would murder his own brother for the right amount." He took a long puff on his cigar. "And he is not the only treacherous snake in the nest I am afraid. The reason I am here is because we have been betrayed, my friends."

"How do you mean?" asked Stratton.

"I have spoken to Father Cronin in Rome. It appears that my trusted friend Anatol is a trusted friend no longer. He has turned up at the Vatican with a copy of the symbols. He must have taken the box from my safe and replicated the carvings. I am livid, to say the least. But more than that I am hurt, and a little bit ashamed. I feel like a fool for allowing him inside my private world. I feel like I have betrayed you myself."

"That's not true," said Stratton. "You weren't to know, Arman. The man had been with you for years, you had every reason to trust him."

"This is true," said Kandinsky. "But it does not make it any better. I really cannot understand it. There was no shortage of money. He knew if he ever needed anything he could come to me – whatever it was." He went briefly silent, then forced a laugh. "But come now, I am burdening you with my own sadness. We must move on and decide what we are going to do. There is much to think about. I come bearing more bad news I am afraid."

"What's happened?" asked Stratton.

"Father Cronin's sources in Mecca have informed him that there is a man there claiming to be the 'Hand of Allah'. A man performing miracles on the street. He is curing the crippled and helping the blind to see. As soon as Cronin heard about this man he knew that you had been waylaid, and he sent me to find you and see if you were still alive. He very much needs your help."

His worst fears having been realized Stratton tried to digest the information. After a brief pause he said, "The Mahdi."

"What is that?" said Kandinsky.

"It's an old Islamic legend. The Mahdi is their version of the Messiah. He's a redeemer come to restore justice to the world. Not all Muslims believe in it of course, but they soon will when they see him performing miracles before their very eyes. I don't think the situation could be worse." He paused for thought. "Although I suppose at least the Vatican can't use the symbols – they haven't got the key."

"I am afraid that they have," said Kandinsky.

"What?!"

"Yes. We do not know how, but they acquired a copy. And at this very moment they are making plans to unleash their own Messiah upon the world."

Stratton's face fell. So this was it, he thought. The two religious superpowers were about to fight out a battle for spiritual supremacy. Each would have their own miracle worker to act as a persuader, and each would claim the other to be a false Messiah. The repercussions would echo throughout the world, setting man against man in an ugly clash of faith. Previous holy conflicts would fade to nothing in comparison. This would be the war to end all wars. This would be Armageddon.

Chapter 23

Tariq and Mo walked up to the Merton Street mosque together. Mo was prattling on about a car he was thinking of buying, but Tariq wasn't listening. His mind was firmly on the matter in hand. As they rounded the bend and the mosque came into view he had a sudden sense of foreboding. People were entering the building in their droves. A crowd such as he'd never seen congregated outside, waiting patiently to join the internal gathering. He stopped walking and pulled Mo's shirt.

"What's up?" said Mo.

"I don't know, mate," said Tariq. "I've just got a really bad feeling about this. It doesn't seem right."

Mo turned and slapped his friend's shoulder. "Stop being so stupid, mate. This could be the start of something wonderful. Don't you want to find out if the rumours are true?"

Tariq shrugged his shoulders. "I guess so. I'm just getting a bad vibe from it, that's all."

"You're just paranoid, mate. All these late nights are catching up with you and fucking with your head." He pulled Tariq's arm. "Come on, let's get going or there'll be no room for us."

Unable to summon up any more resistance Tariq followed his friend through the gates, and two minutes later stood at the back of a murmuring throng.

The Imam called for hush and began to speak. "As you will have heard, there are rumours coming out of Mecca of the coming of the Mahdi – the redeemer. I know that some of you, even most of you, do not believe in this old legend. We live in an educated society that has moved beyond such folklore. We no longer give credence to these tales, designed by an elite minority to hold sway over those with little or no education. I, myself, find the idea fantastical to the point of being impossible." He paused and gazed around for effect. "And yet," he continued, "I stand in front of you now as one who has been converted. Three days ago

I received a summons to the holy city. After attending a council there and seeing with my own eyes the power of the Mahdi, I can inform you all that this is no legend, and no trick to deceive us. What I witnessed in Mecca was nothing short of miraculous. This man is a healer of the like this world has never seen before. In just thirty seconds I saw him transform a man who had been in a wheelchair for life into an able-bodied citizen without a care. Tumours have dissipated at the touch of his hand. There was a queue over a mile long just to be granted an audience with him. And if you doubt my word then just look at me." He gestured to his lower limbs. "You all know that I have been unable to walk without the aid of a stick for many years, and that at times the pain is so unbearable that I cannot stand at all. But if you will notice my brothers – I have no walking stick, and I can assure you that I am no longer in any pain whatsoever. I feel like a young man again."

Tariq, stifling a laugh, watched in amazement as the old man, whom he knew to be severely crippled, performed a little jig – hopping from leg to leg like an extra from *Riverdance*. His logical side tried to come up with a rational explanation for the transformation, but instinctively he knew that he was watching the result of something beyond the confines of convention. He was suddenly overwhelmed by a rush of adrenaline which scared and excited him at the same time.

After quieting the gasps of the audience the Imam continued to speak, "So, there you have it. I hope that my testimony has been enough to convince you that the Mahdi is no longer just a fiction." Raising himself to an imposing height he lifted his voice. "We are standing at the edge of a new world order! A new age for mankind, where peace and harmony will wash away the depravity and greed and lawlessness of our current society. The Mahdi will show the world the grace of Allah, instructing us on how we may best achieve Allah's vision for his children. He will right wrongs and convert the unbelievers. Islam will be revealed as the only true religion, to which other faiths must defer if they wish to gain salvation. We are honoured to be here for this time of change, the most pivotal moment in the history of the earth. It is our time to rise up and light the way!"

Inspired by his stirring words the whole mosque erupted into a frenzy unbecoming of a place of worship. Forgetting where they were, shouts and cheers rang out filling the building with a wall of ecstatic noise. The sound so ferocious it broke through the walls and carried more than half a mile down the road, causing the passengers at the train station to stare up in bewilderment. Even Tariq with all his preconceived doubts couldn't help but be swept away on the tide of unbridled fervour. This was it, he thought – the world was finally going to change. What a time to be alive.

Chapter 24

Arman Kandinsky's submarine, the *Marianna*, lay just off the Keralan coast. Decommissioned in the mid-nineties, it was a Soviet Akula-class nuclear sub refitted and customized to Kandinsky's own design, and in effect an underwater pleasure palace. As the powerful dinghy sped towards it under the too-hot sun, Jennings' mouth began to salivate at the thought of the excellent cuisine that would undoubtedly be waiting for them when they boarded. After an interminable drive across never-ending plains, he was looking forward to unwinding in opulent comfort. Kandinsky was a host beyond compare.

Stratton too was hoping for some relaxation. His mind was still filled with the catastrophic news that the two most powerful religions on earth were about to go head to head in a battle for ultimate supremacy. The ensuing hatred would devastate not only towns, cities and countries, but his own fragile reserves. He doubted if he would survive, let alone be able to help stop it.

"You look like you're thinking too much," said Jennings.

"I've got a lot to think about," Stratton replied.

Jennings wiped his sweaty brow with a handkerchief. "What was it you said to me – 'don't visualize outcomes, it'll bring you down' – or something like that."

"I'm not visualizing outcomes."

"Are you sure?" quizzed Jennings. "You face tells a different story."

Stratton gave a small laugh. "Alright, fair enough, you've caught me. What should I do?"

"Remember where you are," said Jennings. "You're sitting in a boat on the ocean heading towards a submarine – and that's it. Nothing's happened yet."

"You're absolutely right mate, nothing has happened yet." He smiled. "It's a good job you're here to advise me."

"I had a good teacher."

The submarine drew close and the boat slowed, skipping lightly across the water until it pulled up alongside the turret. They boarded without trouble and were immediately given their own rooms in which to wind down and shower before eating. Grady, the only one not to have been present on the journey out, was suitably impressed with his new surroundings. After showering he took full advantage of the facilities by pouring himself a large scotch from the drinks cabinet, and lighting a fat Havana. He then sat back on the bed and enjoyed the moment, feeling the stress drain out of him with every sip and puff.

An hour after boarding they were seated in the long, luxurious dining room with clear minds and fresh clothes. Kandinsky was at the head of the table with Stratton to his right and Grady and Jennings to his left.

"Well, my friends," said Kandinsky. "I have some good news, and I have some bad news. I will start with the good news, which is that our friend Stella is definitely still alive."

"And the bad?" asked Jennings.

Kandinsky took a swig of whisky. "The bad news is that she has been sold to a sheik in Yemen."

Jennings' mind immediately sprang to the worst possible scenario, imagining Stella locked up and being forced to do God knows what for this sheik and his disgusting friends. A shiver ran through his spine.

"You wouldn't think that people could get away with stuff like that in this day and age," said Stratton.

"No," said Kandinsky. "But they do. I personally never dealt in human traffic, but the option was certainly there for me if I wanted. There is no level of government that is not corrupt, and there are plenty of people who will turn a blind eye for the right amount of money. Borders are easily negotiated with cash and influence. The average human would be surprised at what still goes on in our so-called civilized society."

"Do you know where this sheik lives?" asked Jennings.

"Yes, indeed. I have been to his palace once before. It is very remote, and very heavily guarded. If, as I suspect, you wish to mount some kind of rescue mission it will not be easy."

"Well," said Jennings, "we've got to try something. We can't just leave her there at the mercy of some oversexed Arab."

"Of course not," Kandinsky agreed. "But we will have to be very careful how we approach the situation."

"Can't you just offer him some money?" said Jennings hopefully.

Kandinsky laughed without humour. "If only it were that simple. Firstly, I cannot let on that I know about Stella as that would put Malik in an awkward position. He does much business in the Middle East and if there is even a whiff of indiscretion then he will no longer be welcome. Secondly, it is not really about the money. The sheik has more than enough of that. He will see a beautiful girl like Stella as a prized possession, and if she is putting up as much resistance as I suspect then he will see it as a challenge to break her. When you reach a certain wealth it is no longer enough to own material things, you must also own people's souls. Unfortunately, I know this from experience." He paused with a look of regret. "Anyway," he continued, "that is why we cannot bargain with him."

"But you can get us in there I assume," said Grady.

"Yes, I think I may be able to. The sheik and I got on well enough, and he did say that I was always welcome. But we shall have to think of a good reason. I do not think he will believe I was 'just passing by'."

"No," chuckled Jennings. "Probably not."

Two of Kandinsky's unfeasibly beautiful waitresses entered the room carrying starters for the table – braised wood pigeon with bacon and cabbage. After tearing his eyes away from the girls Grady took a deep smell of his plate and began to devour its contents.

"What about Pat Cronin?" asked Stratton. "Have you spoken

to him?"

"Yes, I have," said Kandinsky. "And it is not looking good. Word is spreading throughout the Muslim world about their redeemer – the Mahdi as you called him. And in Rome they are preparing their own man as we speak. Cronin predicts that within a week both will have announced themselves to the entire world. And then…Well, we shall see."

"Within a week," said Stratton, thinking aloud. "That doesn't give us much time to stop them."

"I think it is too late for that," said Kandinsky, between mouthfuls. "We have reached the point where their unveiling to the world is inevitable. I feel our only hope is to discredit them by giving the world the truth."

Stratton washed some pigeon down with a little red wine. "I don't think the world will believe the truth," he said. "We can scream until we're blue in the face, but it's going to do nothing against the wave of fanaticism that will accompany these new religious icons."

"We could always shoot the fuckers," said Grady.

"I think that would just make things worse," said Stratton. "The outrage would be catastrophic. And besides, it's not in keeping with what we're trying to achieve. We want an end to violence, we don't want to encourage it."

"It was just an idea," said Grady. "And much as I admire your pacifistic stance, there's no way this is all going to end without some kind of violence. I'm telling you now – if it comes to a choice of 'kill or be killed' then to me it's a no-brainer."

Stratton smiled. "Fair enough. It's all hypothetical at the moment anyway. We can't do anything while we're twenty thousand leagues under the sea. I need to get to Rome and meet up with Pat Cronin."

"What about Stella?!" Jennings said sharply. "Surely we've got to try and rescue her first."

"I said 'I' need to get to Rome. That doesn't mean that

everyone else has to come too."

"So you're not going to help get her back?"

Stratton sighed. "If I don't get to Rome, then rescuing her might well be futile. I need to find out exactly what's going on. You and Grady are more than capable of getting her out of there with Arman's help."

"Of course," said Kandinsky. "You must go to Cronin's aid."

After a long and delicious dinner Grady and Jennings went back to their respective rooms to get some sleep. Stratton joined Kandinsky for a nightcap at the bar in the recreation room.

"I am not used to seeing you drink," the big Russian observed.

"No," said Stratton. "And as of tomorrow I won't be. I just felt like having a few before the shit starts."

"I do not blame you," said Kandinsky. "I feel that we are approaching the point of no return. I have felt it for a long time now."

Stratton drank his cognac down in one and nodded to the barman for another. "Yes, the point of no return," he echoed. "Destruction or salvation? Which will we choose? Is it human nature to self-destruct?"

Kandinsky swirled his drink pensively. "Sometimes it is very hard not to self-destruct. It is often the easier path. At certain junctures in life oblivion can seem like a blissful release compared to the constant trials of existence. I have been down the darkest ways, and it is only through great force of will that I have survived. Not everybody is fortunate enough to be endowed with such strength." He looked across to Stratton. "I hope you do not think I am boasting, it is merely a fact."

"No, I don't think you're boasting Arman. You're not an arrogant man. You're just very aware of your own strengths and weaknesses, and by looking inside yourself you've developed a strong insight into others as well. Too many people spend their lives picking holes in others' personalities without taking a good hard look at themselves first. Searching inside and admitting your own shortcomings is a painful process."

"Yes," Kandinsky agreed. "But a necessary one if you wish to move forward." He signalled the barman to replenish his drink. "So, you wish to get to Rome as soon as possible?"

"Yes."

"Then I shall have my private jet meet us when we dock in Aden. You will go straight to the Vatican, and we shall endeavour to rescue Stella."

"Thanks," said Stratton. "You'll be doing me a great favour. I just hope I can be of some use. My body's all over the place at the moment – one minute I feel invincible, the next I feel drained. Majami did a fantastic job on me in the jungle, but even he can't stop the will of the universe." He shrugged philosophically. "But I accepted the limitations when I came back, and I'll just have to live with the consequences."

"I do not envy you," said Kandinsky. "Having your health attached to the minds of the human race cannot be pleasant. There are some very dark people out there, men and women with hearts of sheer blackness and hatred. Anger and fear, and greed and jealousy spread like bacteria. They are subtle and insidious."

"You're not wrong Arman. But I've got to believe that as a race we're essentially good, and that faced with a final choice we'll come through and take the right path, however hard it might prove. It's my belief that whatever darkness overtakes a person there's always a light inside that will never go out. A light that's been there since the beginning and can never be truly extinguished no matter how hard the wind of time blows. It will always be there, like a diamond waiting to be discovered in the coalface. If I didn't believe it then I wouldn't have agreed to come back."

Kandinsky took a long puff on his cigar. "I am glad that you have so much faith, my friend. As for myself, I would like to think as you do, but I have seen far more of the darker side of humanity than you, and I am quite sure that some lights have gone out for ever. I do hope that I am wrong."

"Your light never went out, did it?" said Stratton.

"No, not totally," admitted Kandinsky. "But I am one of the lucky few. And the destruction I caused in the meantime may never be eradicated."

"Oh well," said Stratton, raising his glass. "Let's forget about it for the moment. Here's to lights that never go out!"

"Indeed," Kandinsky enthused. "To lights that never go out!"

Chapter 25

Jonathan Ayres turned off the television and leant back into the deep sofa with a sigh. There was no news as yet, but it was only a matter of time before the media got into a frenzy over the coming of the Mahdi. He hated to think what it would be like when their reports gained substance as the 'Hand of Allah' started performing miracles in front of the camera. Time was heavily of the essence and they were left with very little to get Christiano ready for his grand unveiling.

Ayres lit up a cigarette and took a swig of scotch. He wondered how many non-Muslims would be converted before he and Vittori could unleash their own 'Messiah'. With the modern world being as suspicious as it was he guessed that most educated people would consider the Mahdi to be some kind of street magician until they witnessed his efforts with their own eyes. And this, together with the West's acquired fear of anything Islamic, led him to believe that any major religious shift would be a long time coming. But he also knew from years in politics that it was dangerous to predict the mood of the public, and that ultimately anything could happen – so it was wise to get Christiano out there as soon as was viable.

He blew an impressive chain of smoke rings and contemplated, raising a toast to his late friend Henry Mulholland. It was a shame that Yoshima had killed him because Henry probably knew nothing about the box at all. It was also a shame that Augustus Jeremy's plan had failed, precipitating a disastrous course of events that had nearly cost him everything. But that was all behind him now, soon Christiano would be hailed as the second coming, and quietly pulling his strings with the real power would be the Pope, Vittori, and of course the new leader of the free world – Jonathan Ayres.

Chapter 26

Stella gazed out of the barred window at the setting sun. Judging from its position she guessed the time to be roughly eight o'clock. The sound of music and laughter drifted across from the other side of the palace, exacerbating her feeling of isolation. The sheik had invited her to join him at his little party, but she had politely declined, citing a headache as her excuse. He had been most disappointed, but a heartfelt apology and an assurance that she would make an appearance at his next gathering seemed to lift his mood. Of course, if he knew the real reason for her absence then he might not have been so forgiving.

Turning away from the window she paced about the room, rehearsing the plan of action in her mind. She would have to be quick and she would have to be brutal. She had only one shot at escape, and if she fucked it up tonight the sheik would have her so heavily guarded she wouldn't be able to pee without his say so.

As the servant knocked on the door her heart started to thump. He entered with a tray of food and shuffled over to the table to lay it down. Stella paced casually across and positioned herself at his unsuspecting back. She lifted her arm and brought her hand down swiftly in a chopping motion, stiffening it at the point of impact for maximum power, the blow hitting the back of his neck with such force that he dropped to the floor without a sound.

Without stopping for breath she picked up the fork from her dinner tray and glided silently across to the open door. She could see nothing of the guard except for the butt of his AK-47 hovering at the side of the jamb. After watching the CCTV camera turn away she steadied herself and shot out into the corridor, at the same time swinging her fork-laden hand round into the general direction of the guard's face. There was a loud scream and his hands shot up to shield his eyes. Now in front of him, Stella removed the fork and stabbed at the side of his neck aiming for his jugular vein. The bewildered guard moved his hands across but could do nothing to stem the spurting blood. His knees buckled and he slipped to the ground, his life fading with every shallow, stuttering inhalation.

For a moment Stella stood there in a daze. The sight of the dead guard's mangled features was almost too much. That she could do something so hideous made her want to throw up. But just as she felt her stomach begin to retch she remembered where she was and the task in hand.

First she leapt up and disconnected the camera, and then hoisted the bloodied AK-47 from the guard's shoulder and set off down the long corridor with caution. The sheik and his household may have been partying in another wing but it didn't mean the rest of the palace was totally unguarded. She knew a patrol could be along at any minute.

Stopping only to avoid the glare of the cameras she made her way stealthily through the maze of passages. Luck appeared to be on her side as she navigated one hallway after another without encounter. Within a matter of minutes she was standing at a door that led to the front courtyard where the sheik's guests had parked their vehicles. She opened it just enough to get a good look at the terrain.

To her right the main entrance to the palace was guarded by two of the sheik's men, both armed with the same weapon as herself. In front of them was a team of valets, taking it in turns to park the guests' cars. To her left was a set of open metal gates that led out into the desert and freedom. These too were flanked by a couple of armed guards.

She pulled the door to, grounded herself, and visualized her next move. Then, after a few steadying breaths, she opened it again and slipped out into the makeshift car park, ducking in behind a new Ferrari 453. Peering cautiously over the bonnet she began watching the valets. As she hoped, they were parking the cars in meticulous order, giving her the opportunity to make a pre-emptive strike.

Staying low she made her way through the rows of luxury vehicles, all the while keeping a close eye on the two sets of guards. The intense lighting made her feel conspicuous, but through a mixture of stealth and a general lack of interest from security she made it across the courtyard without incident.

Positioning herself behind a 4x4 she waited for the row in front of her to fill up. Another three cars and she would be ready to make her move. She focused all her attention and ran through the manoeuvre in her head: whack the valet; take the keys; race through the gates – three simple steps to secure her escape. A pulse of joy seared through her body as she thought about seeing the outside world once more. But just as this went through her mind, a cry from the palace doors caused her heart to stop dead. The gate guards turned round to see what the commotion was about, and she suddenly felt naked. Panicking that she had exposed the tip of her gun, or left a foot sticking out, she huddled up tighter, praying silently and hardly daring to breathe. The voices grew louder and closer, until she was sure that any moment she would see a rifle pointing round the side of the 4x4 forcing her to her feet and back inside the palace. She checked the safety was off on her weapon and braced herself for the inevitable.

Whatever had disturbed the guards, though, it wasn't Stella. The voices were nearly upon her when they abruptly softened and started to drift away. She looked up to the sky in thanks and continued to wait patiently for the row of cars to fill up.

It wasn't long before her moment arrived.

The valet backed a white Mercedes expertly into the space in front of the 4x4 and quickly opened the door to get out. Before he had a chance to expose more than his left foot, Stella was on him. Crouching next to the unfortunate attendant she thrust the butt of her gun sideways into his face with her full weight. His head jerked back and to the side, and then flopped down limply on his chest. Thankful that he had succumbed quickly Stella grabbed his arm and dragged him out onto the grass. Then, watching for hostile eyes, she leapt into the car and started it up.

Taking it slowly, so as not to draw attention, she casually navigated her way through the grid of automobiles, stifling her desire to put pedal to metal. She didn't know how long it had been since she'd disconnected the camera, but she felt sure that if security hadn't checked it out already it would only be a matter of minutes.

As she rounded the last row of cars and turned to face the gates she shuddered with a nervous chill and unconsciously slowed to a near standstill. With liberty just a hundred or so yards away, panic began to overtake her, planting doubts in every corner of her brain. She closed her eyes and made a silent pact with God, promising that if he got her out of there then she would be a good girl for the rest of her life, and devote it to helping others. The Lord was apparently out to lunch, because as she opened her eyes once more a loud shout emanated from the direction of the empty space she'd left. She looked across to see one of the valets leaping up and down and pointing to ground. Within seconds the whole courtyard was in uproar and the guards on maximum alert.

Stella did the only thing she could, and that was floor the accelerator. With wheels churning and tyres smoking she made for the gate. The guards turned to face the speeding car and let fly a heavy salvo from their weapons. Stella instinctively ducked behind the steering wheel. The bullets, however, ricocheted off the armoured windshield, leaving her unharmed and careering towards freedom. The heavy gunfire continued.

As she approached the gates the guards leapt aside, and before she had time to think she was through and away. It was then that she sat up and realized that the headlights had been shot out. Spearing into an unfamiliar blackness she had no choice other than to slow down. But before she could react the gunfire began again in earnest. She heard a loud pop from the back of the car and found herself in a desperate fight with the steering wheel; a fight which she had no chance of winning.

The car lurched heavily to the right, the front end dropping off an unseen ledge, and then flipped into the air. Stella gripped the wheel as she drifted in a weightlessness that seemed to last for ever. And then came the first impact; so severe she thought her spine was going to skewer her brain. After that the world became a dizzying mass of noise and disorienting twists, until eventually there was silence.

Chapter 27

Jennings sprang up and gasped for air in the darkness, gripped by the terror that comes of changing worlds too quickly. For a while he sat motionless, unable to make sense of where he was or what was happening. And then, as his consciousness finally synchronized with his body, he remembered.

Reaching to his left he pulled the switch on the bedside lamp and blinked in the sudden light. He picked up a half bottle of *Evian* and drained it in an attempt to quench his unnatural thirst. Still too hot to think straight he went to the sink and doused his head in cold water until he finally regained his composure.

The dream had been vivid. Stella; the gunfire; the crash – it was all so real. He could still feel every last bump and jolt as the car turned over and over, crunching and smashing its way to a flattened standstill. He paced about the room stretching his arms and legs to remove the stiffness then picked up the phone.

Two minutes later a rather merry and twinkly-eyed Stratton knocked on the door and entered Jennings' quarters. "What's up, mate?" he asked cheerily. "You sounded a bit put out."

"I am," said Jennings. "Well, not so much put out as disturbed. I've had a bad dream."

Stratton was about to make a comment about calling Jennings' mother but decided against it. Instead he took a more sensitive tact. "What was it about?" he asked sympathetically. "You look really shaken up?"

Jennings described what he'd seen.

"That doesn't sound good," said Stratton, pouring a couple of brandies from the mini-bar. He handed one to Jennings and sat down next to him on the bed. "Do you reckon she survived?"

Jennings swigged a hefty measure from his tumbler. "I'm not sure - but I don't know that she didn't."

"What does your gut tell you?"

"It tells me that she's hurt and we've got to get to her as soon as possible."

"You're probably right," said Stratton. "But it's going to be at least another 24 hours before we get to Yemen. Until then you're just going to have to keep calm. I know it's difficult, but there's fuck all you can do about it at the moment."

Jennings shook his head. "This is an absolute fucking nightmare," he said, getting up and pacing anxiously. "I'm all over the place. My mind just won't stay still. It's like billions of little explosives going off every second."

"Your eyes have been opened mate," said Stratton. "And you're still getting used to the light."

"I guess so, but knowing it doesn't help. I need to be out there doing something to help her, not sitting about here twiddling my fingers. I just feel so fucking useless and helpless." He kicked the side of the bed in frustration.

"Careful there," said Stratton. "You're not going to be any use to her with a broken foot."

Jennings gave Stratton an angry glance and then, with the tension building up to a crescendo inside, he began to laugh. "Sorry, mate," he said. "You must think I'm a real twat."

"Not at all," said Stratton. "You just need to clear your mind and get some sleep. Lie down on the bed and close your eyes."

Jennings put down his drink and did as his friend suggested.

"Now," said Stratton. "I'm going to put my hand on your forehead, and I want you to count slowly down from ten."

Jennings felt Stratton's warm hand on his brow and began to count. He was out before he reached six.

Chapter 28

Sophia Zola had not been able to walk since the age of ten. A car accident had left her paralyzed from the waist down for fourteen years. And although she was quite used to her disability and living a happy and fulfilled life, there was still a part of her that longed to roam free, unencumbered by wheels and ramps. The doctors, of course, had told her that this would never happen, but with technology and medicine moving on at a barely believable pace, and the advent of stem-cell research, she had not given up hope that one day she might walk again.

Sophia's mother and father were staunch Catholics, and they were also very wealthy and influential. They went to, and occasionally hosted, the best parties in Rome and were personal friends with His Holiness the Pope. They doted on their daughter and had spent fortunes sending her to the best medical centres in the world. There was nothing they wouldn't do to see their daughter back on her feet once more. So when Cardinal Vittori called and said that he may have found someone to help Sophia, there was no delay in arranging a meeting.

As Christiano walked into the Zola's mansion he was immediately taken aback by its splendour. Working at the Vatican he was used to architectural grandeur, but he had no idea that a private residence could be quite so ornate. He looked around the entrance hall admiring the statues and artwork, and wondered how anyone could possibly afford such luxury.

Daniel Zola appeared from one of the many doorways and strode across to greet Vittori and his young friend. Zola was a young-looking sixty with black and silver hair and a healthy tan. He was dressed casually in jeans, a white silk shirt and a pair of Gucci loafers, and exuded the quiet confidence of the super-rich.

"Fabio!" exclaimed Zola, holding out a manicured hand. "It is so good to see you. It has been too long."

"Indeed it has, Daniel," said Vittori smiling. "I hope I am

finding you well."

"Yes, yes," said Zola. "I am good, very good. And, might I say, since your phone call – rather excited." He looked at Christiano. "Is this the young man you said may be able to help us?"

"Yes," Vittori nodded. "This is Christiano, a special young man – a very special young man."

Christiano went red and shuffled awkwardly at the cardinal's praise.

Daniel Zola offered him his hand. "It is good to meet you Christiano. You are very welcome here."

"Thank you, sir."

Zola laughed kindly. "There's no need to call me 'sir', Christiano. Call me Daniel."

He led them across the hall and into a huge space which Christiano guessed must be a living room. With sprawling leather settees and a selection of sumptuous armchairs it was nothing like his own, but even with the chandeliers and oil paintings it still had the feel of a family area – just a little bit bigger than normal.

As they entered, a glamorous flame-haired lady left the central settee and walked over to greet them. She was so beautiful that Christiano felt almost unable to speak.

"This is my wife Maria," said Zola.

Vittori greeted her as an old friend. Christiano smiled meekly and tried to mumble a hello.

"And this is my daughter Sophia," said Zola, gesturing to young woman who had just pulled up beside him in a wheel-chair.

Christiano was once again lost for words. If the mother was stunning then Sophia was indescribable. As she looked up at him with her dazzling emerald green eyes, he felt as if his heart was thumping out of his chest on a stalk like a cartoon character.

"Hello," she said softly. "It's good to meet you."

Christiano nodded and replied with a falsetto "hi".

Zola invited them to sit down, and the group spent the next half hour catching up over coffee. Christiano felt a little alienated by the conversation, but the Zola's being perfect hosts made every effort to include him wherever they could, and the occasional reassuring glance from Sophia went a long way to putting him at his ease. By the time the talk turned to himself he was feeling quite at home.

"So, Christiano," said Zola. "I believe that you can help my daughter."

Christiano looked across to Vittori, who nodded encouragingly.

"Yes, sir…I mean Daniel, I would very much like to try."

"And how do you propose to do this? Where is your clinic? What methods do you employ?"

Christiano once again looked to Vittori for help.

"Christiano has no clinic," said the cardinal. "You will not find him registered anywhere. He is no doctor or scientist. He is a healer, Daniel."

"A healer?" said Zola, his face tightening. "You have brought me a faith-healer, Fabio? What do you take me for exactly? My daughter is paralyzed from the waist down. She needs a specialist, not some charlatan wafting incense and waving crystals in her face." He stood up and glared at Vittori. "I thought we were friends."

Vittori kept his calm. "Please, Daniel," he said. "Do not get excited. We are friends, very good friends, and you should know that I would not bring false hope into your house. Christiano here is no charlatan, and he does not seek any financial reward for his powers. He is here with the full blessing of the Vatican. I have witnessed his gifts for myself, and I can assure you that if anyone can heal Sophia then it is him."

Zola sat back down and contemplated Vittori's words. "I am sorry, Fabio," he said. "I should not doubt your intentions. But I have been given false hope once too often to be anything other than sceptical. Not a week goes by without some quack or other trying to get money out of me, and I am becoming tired of it. Very tired."

"There is no need to apologize," said Vittori. "You have every right to question Christiano's credentials. But please, reserve your judgement until you have seen the results."

"Yes, father," said Sophia, joining the conversation. "Please let Christiano at least try to help. He can't make me any worse now, can he?"

"No, of course not," said Zola. He turned to address Christiano. "I am very sorry if I have made you feel uncomfortable. If there is anything you can do for my daughter, then please go ahead. Will you be needing a quiet room to examine her?"

"I think it might be best," said Christiano, pleased that the confrontation was over with, but still very apprehensive.

Zola led them across the hallway to the large private gym, and then into a smaller ante-room that housed a couple of massage tables. With Christiano's assistance he lifted Sophia up onto one of them, where she lay face down with her head to the side.

Although Christiano had performed Reiki before, this was his first attempt since learning the three hundred odd symbols that Vittori had supplied him with. He was still unsure within himself as to whether or not they would work, and he felt uncomfortable being thrown in at the deep end.

"Would you like to be left alone?" Zola asked, sensing his apprehension.

Christiano was about to say 'yes' when Vittori spoke for him. "That is not necessary – is it, Christiano?"

Christiano stalled briefly, then replied, "No, of course not." He felt uneasy with everybody watching, but didn't want to displease the cardinal.

He took a deep breath and began his preparations. First he lit a few of the aromatic candles that adorned a shelf in front of the table, then washed his hands in the small sink at the side of the room. After drying them he closed his eyes and drew the master symbol in his head three times, and then did the same with the power symbol. A surge of energy passed through his body. Opening his eyes once more he stepped across and let his hands hover a few inches above Sophia's lower spine. A blast of cold air indicated that he was in the right place. He told her to close her eyes and relax, then rubbed his palms together to get the power flowing.

Vittori looked on in nervous silence with Zola and his wife.

Now completely focused and unaware of anything else around him, Christiano placed his right hand on the affected area and lay his left on top. He closed his eyes and invoked the master and power symbols once more, together with the secret one he had memorized that targeted the lower spine. At once the cold changed to a blinding heat. He wanted to whip his hands away, but they were glued to the spot. Beneath him Sophia started to tremble. Wave upon wave pulsed through Christiano's soul: waves of joy, and waves of light. The intensity was such that tears welled in his eyes and streaked down his cheeks. He was flying; touching the sky; touching God.

Beneath him Sophia was still trembling. From the moment Christiano laid his hand on her, and she had felt that exquisite warmth charging through her upper body, she knew that something amazing was about to happen. The warmth had been supplemented by a tingling in her lower back, a sensation which grew until she could almost feel her nerve endings reattaching themselves under her skin. Now, as life thrust itself back into her, she too was overwhelmed to the point of crying.

Christiano arched his back in ecstasy and let out a gasp. His head fell forward in exhaustion.

Daniel Zola had been transfixed as soon as he saw the tiny cloud form above Christiano's hands. Even from a distance he could tell that something strange was occurring. Maria had grabbed his hand for reassurance, her grip tightening as the haze above their daughter thickened and sparked blue flame. As Christiano reached a crescendo, a subtle chill passed through them, followed by a soothing heat. It was only when he finally bowed his head that they started to breathe once more.

Christiano stood still, tired and disoriented. Vittori walked over and put a reassuring hand on his shoulder. "You are alright, Christiano," he said. "Everything is alright. Just breathe slowly."

Christiano did as the cardinal suggested and gradually regained control. He opened his eyes and looked down at Sophia. "Are you okay?" he asked.

Sophia turned her gaze upwards. "I think so," she said dreamily. Without thinking she flipped over and pulled herself to a sitting position on the edge of the table, swinging her legs idly.

A stunned silence engulfed the room.

"What is it?" said Sophia, sensing everybody's eyes on her.

"Your legs," said her mother.

Sophia looked down and it hit her. She started to cry.

Unable to contain his joy, Daniel Zola leapt across and hugged his daughter. Rivulets of tears cascaded down his face. "Thank you," he wept. "Thank you so much."

Maria embraced her family. "Who are you?" she asked Christiano through her tears.

"He is the Messiah," said Vittori. "He has returned to save us."

Maria looked at him earnestly. "Is this true? Are you the Messiah?"

Christiano felt the universe swell through him again. "Yes," he said. "I am."

Chapter 29

Tariq opened the curtains and watched the sun rising in the east. He thought about the Mahdi. The fever of the meeting at the mosque had worn off, and in the cold morning light he wondered if any of it was really true. Sure, the Imam had told them all that the Mahdi was real, and he'd even done his little dance to prove it, but Tariq wasn't about to leap headlong into anything without first checking it out logically. Having spent his teenage years studying street magic he knew very well not to trust all that you see. Although he did feel guilty for questioning the integrity of a man he'd known since childhood.

He turned his gaze back to the bed and smiled. Jenna was sleeping peacefully, her beautiful face a picture of serenity, her long chestnut hair tousled across the pillow. Being with her felt so right. Just occupying the same space as her made him feel alive like he'd never done before. He got back into bed and kissed her lightly on the lips. She stirred and lazily reciprocated, stretching her arms around him.

"Morning, you," she said drowsily. "What's the time?"

"Seven o'clock."

"Why are you up so early? It's Saturday."

"I know, but the sun was coming through and it woke me."

She grinned and pulled him close. "Oh well, seeing as we're both awake..."

A while later, as Jenna smoked a post-coital cigarette, Tariq went to the kitchen to make some coffee. Once again he started to think about the Mahdi. If he had come to dispense justice on the world, where exactly did he, Tariq, stand. The Koran was open to many interpretations, perhaps nearly as many as there were Muslims. What would the Mahdi's stance be? Would he preach hard-line fundamentalism? Or would he spread a message of peace and forgiveness? What would his opinion be of Tariq and Jenna?

It occurred to Tariq that even if the Mahdi was the genuine article, his presence on earth was going to pose awkward questions for the whole of humanity. If, for instance, he said that mixed-race relationships were wrong, then that would be it for Tariq and Jenna. There would be no argument, no more interpretations, Allah would have spoken. If he said that all women had to cover their faces in public, then that's what they'd have to do. The more he thought about it the more he realized that a legitimate Mahdi had licence to impose any laws or restrictions that he saw fit.

Tariq stirred some milk into his coffee and took a sip. He had been brought up to be a good Muslim, but recently his adherence to the faith had been lacklustre to say the least. He had even been neglecting the recitation of his *salat* (prayer to Mecca). Some days he recited it just once or twice, compared to the mandatory five times. It wasn't that he didn't believe in God anymore, he just didn't believe that Allah was going to strike him down for missing a few prayers here and there. He wondered what the Mahdi would make of it.

Tired of contemplating, he went back to the bedroom. Jenna sat up and took her mug of coffee. "You're the best," she said. "Stay as long as you like."

"Would you like me to make some breakfast?" he asked.

"Breakfast as well? Yeah, I'd love some. Scrambled eggs and bacon would be great. If you don't mind cooking the bacon that is?"

"It'll be fine," he laughed.

Jenna looked up at him with beaming eyes. "You know what Taz? I think I love you."

Tariq gazed into her eyes and knew that he felt the same. He hoped that nothing would change it.

Chapter 30

From the comfort of Kandinsky's Lear Jet Stratton gazed down at the world below and smiled. He hadn't been in a plane for a long time and had almost forgotten the serenity of altitude. As they climbed steadily over Yemen and then out over the sea he felt a calm that had recently been alien to him. The higher one went, he thought, the less significant everything seemed, much like the path to enlightenment.

The beautiful stewardess broke into his thoughts. "Can I get you anything to drink?" she asked.

Stratton swivelled the large leather seat round to face her. "Please," he said. "I'll have some still mineral water."

"Would you like some food as well?"

"What have you got?"

She reached to the side of the seat and produced a small menu. Stratton scanned it quickly and ordered some smoked salmon and scrambled eggs. He had half a mind to get some champagne as well, but knew it would be unwise at this particular juncture. From now on in he was going to need his wits about him every minute of every day.

He watched the girl walk up to the galley and briefly wondered whether she was on the menu as well. It was the first time in months that sex had even crossed his mind. After spending so long with his head in the ether, the physical realities of being human had escaped him. Today seemed different, however. He guessed that the world as a whole was feeling pretty good about itself, because from the moment he had woken his body had been pumped full of energy. The universe was flowing through him like a torrent. A gush of goodwill had sprung from the depths of despond. Were people finally uniting in harmony? He wanted to think so, but instinct told him that the current state was probably temporary and that he should enjoy it while it lasted.

By the time the girl returned with his food he'd shaken off his ardour and was watching the news on the giant plasma screen. Any day now he was expecting the news to break of either a second coming, or a Muslim redeemer. Fortunately there was still no sign of movement from either camp. The headline story was yet another summit on global warming, with the same old people giving the same old soundbites. After five minutes he decided to change channels and watch a movie instead. He finished his food quickly and settled back into his seat, flicking off his thought switch and resting his brain for the long road ahead.

Chapter 31

The desert appeared to go on forever. Jennings stared out on the expanse of empty sand and felt an overwhelming sense of loneliness. As the miles clicked by his thoughts grew deeper and darker, until the isolation began to claw at his heart.

"What's up with you?" said Grady, who was sat next to him in the back of the 4X4. "Are you starting to think again? Didn't Stratton warn you about that?"

Jennings turned away from the window. "Yes, I know," he sighed. "It's difficult to keep your spirits up in this godforsaken wilderness though. Why would anyone choose to live out here?"

"Beats me," said Grady.

"Wait until you see the palace," said Kandinsky, craning back from the passenger seat. "Then you will maybe change your mind."

The palace was as impressive as Kandinsky had said it would be. As they approached, Jennings looked up in awe at the domed towers and felt like he'd been transported back in time to a magical age. It wasn't long, though, before the imagery was spoilt by the sight of uniformed guards with AK-47s slung over their shoulders.

"He doesn't take any chances then?" said Grady

"No," said Kandinsky. "He does not."

Jennings sighed. "Looks like we've got our work cut out then."

They pulled up outside the front gates and, after a lengthy security check, were finally let in. They drove round the courtyard and parked outside the main doors where the sheik was waiting to greet them.

"Arman!" he shouted enthusiastically. "It is so good to see you again."

Kandinsky strode up the white stone steps and grasped the sheik's hand firmly. "Hello, Farouk, it has been too long."

"Indeed it has," the sheik replied. "But no matter, you are here now and most, most welcome." He looked down at Grady and Jennings.

"My bodyguards," said Kandinsky.

The sheik gave Jennings the once over.

Kandinsky leant forward conspiratorially. "He may not look like much, but he is deadly," he whispered. "Ex-SAS."

The sheik nodded approvingly and gave Jennings a respectful glance.

The inside of the palace was much as Jennings expected, with a cavernous entrance hall from which sprang long white decorous corridors. He guessed there were hundreds of separate rooms spread over three or four floors. Even if Stella was still alive it was not going to be easy to locate her.

They were shown to their quarters personally by the sheik. Jennings and Grady being given a room right next to Kandinsky's on the second floor. As they walked through the never-ending passages, Jennings nosed about as much as he could without arousing suspicion. There was, however, no sign of anything strange or sinister.

The sheik left them to settle in and freshen up. "Make yourselves at home," he said. "Feel free to have a look around the palace – there is much beautiful artwork to be seen everywhere."

After sweeping the room for bugs, Jennings sat down on the edge of one of the beds. "It doesn't sound like he's hiding anything," he said to Grady. "He wouldn't be giving us free rein over the place if he was."

"No," said Grady. "But I don't expect the invitation extends to us poking our noses in every room."

"I guess not. But there's no harm in having a little wander about to see what's what."

They both showered and changed, and then joined Kandinsky in the adjoining suite. He agreed that an initial tour of the palace was a good idea, but warned them not to be too intrusive. The sheik could be easily offended. "And remember," he said. "The corridors are monitored by CCTV cameras, so our every move is going to be watched and logged. Just act casually and look interested in the artwork."

Grady felt like saying something about teaching his grandma to suck eggs, but refrained as he knew Kandinsky meant no offence.

Jennings looked at his watch. "Come on then," he urged. "Let's get going. We've only got a couple of hours before dinner."

In other circumstances they would have split up, but for appearances sake they stuck together, Kandinsky leading the way and the other two tagging along dutifully in their role as minders. The sheik had not exaggerated the extent of his personal collection, and round every corner there was always something new and amazing to stop them in their tracks. It wasn't long before all three of them had almost forgotten the task in hand.

"How rich is this guy exactly?" said Grady.

"I have no idea," said Kandinsky. "But he makes me look like a beggar. And not many people do that." He stopped to admire a painting of a wheat field.

"Is that an original?" gasped Jennings, looking at the signature.

"I believe so," said Kandinsky. "I do not imagine that he would have reproductions lining his walls."

"But a Van Gogh in the hallway? Surely you'd have it somewhere more protected?"

"This whole palace is protected," Kandinsky answered. "And besides, I expect it is alarmed from behind."

They continued to amble around for another hour, taking in the third and fourth floors before descending to ground level. There was nothing out of place, and nothing that indicated anybody being held against their will. The only people they encountered were housemaids and the occasional guard doing a routine patrol.

"Well, it looks like we're out of luck," said Jennings despondently, as they finished their circuit of the ground floor.

"Maybe," said Kandinsky. "But maybe not." He pointed ahead to some tape hung across the entrance to one of the corridors. Behind it was a ladder and a few paint pots. "It appears that there is somewhere we cannot go."

"Only because they're decorating," said Jennings. "There's nothing suspicious about that."

Kandinsky walked up to the tape. "These walls do not look like they need painting to me," he said. "And look, there are two guards down there outside one of the rooms."

"Maybe it's the sheik's master bedroom," ventured Grady.

"Perhaps," said Kandinsky. "But I have a feeling it is not."

Jennings closed his eyes and cleared his mind. "She's in there," he said. "I can sense it."

"Yeah, okay Skywalker" said Grady. "But whether she is or not we'd better get going, those guards are staring right at us."

Chapter 32

The world was dark and dizzy. The last thing Stella remembered was the car flipping and tumbling down an unseen embankment. Without thinking she opened her eyes weakly and tried to focus. The first thing she saw was a drip feeding into her arm. The thought that she might be in a public hospital caused a brief wave of happiness, but it was soon replaced by despair as her eyes cleared and she realized she was back in her room in the palace.

"How are you feeling?" said a voice beside her.

She turned her head to see a bearded Yemeni smiling at her. She let out a muted groan.

"You will probably be a bit woozy I expect," he said. "You are very lucky not to have broken any bones."

Stella stared blankly at him. "Who are you?" she whispered.

"My name is Nuri. I am the sheik's personal physician. He will be most pleased that you are conscious once more."

Stella grunted and turned away. Her body started to ache. Nuri stated that she hadn't broken anything, but the way she felt she wasn't so sure. As her consciousness grew the pain increased. Even moving the tips of her fingers induced an agonized grimace.

"I can give you some more morphine if you like," said Nuri.

Stella wanted to say no, but wasn't in a position to do so. "Yes please," she croaked.

Nuri administered the morphine and Stella drifted away on a fluffy cloud. Perhaps it wasn't all bad, she thought. There were definitely worse places to be in the world. Maybe spending the rest of her life in the lap of luxury would suit her. She could buy anything she wanted, from the finest clothes and jewellery, to the fastest cars and the most exquisite food. What would she be going back to in England? A life of dreary days and cold nights, scrimping and saving just to get by. On top of that there was no guarantee that anyone had survived the jungle except for her. She could very well be the only one left. What fun would life be without any friends to share it with? The sheik might be a bit rough around the edges but with a little moulding he might be made sufferable. She fell into a deep sleep and dreamt of her new life as a princess.

Chapter 33

It was midnight in the palace, and Jennings and Grady were busy assembling their weapons. The gate guards had taken their guns earlier, but Kandinsky had anticipated this and equipped them both with hidden pistols. A large plastic pen and an innocent-looking aftershave container slotted together neatly to form a compressed-air shooter. Silent and accurate, they were modified to fire high-strength tranquilizer darts at distances of up to two hundred yards.

"We never had these in Special Branch," said Jennings.

"No?" said Grady. "Plastic guns have been around for ages. Except they usually fire bullets, not these pussy darts."

"You know why we're using them Grady."

"Yeah, I know – no killing, no violence. But if you think we're getting out of here without hurting anyone, then you're living in dreamland, brother."

"Maybe," Jennings agreed. "But we've got to try."

The connecting door opened and Kandinsky walked in. "Are you all set?" he asked.

"I guess so," said Jennings. "I just hope we can pull it off."

"So do I," said Grady. "If we don't we're toast."

They went through the plan one last time. Kandinsky was going to make his way to the 4x4 on the pretence that he had left some important medication in the glove compartment. Meanwhile Jennings and Grady would stalk their way down to the closed-off corridor, going from blind spot to blind spot in the CCTV. Once there the aim was to disable the two guards and get Stella out as quickly as possible, rendezvousing with Kandinsky out in the courtyard. It was fraught with flaws and pitfalls but it was the only way forward.

"What if she isn't there?" said Grady.

"Then we'll follow the plan, and just escape without her," said Jennings. "But she is there, so don't worry."

Kandinsky looked at his watch. "Right then," he said. "I am going. We meet in the courtyard in exactly twenty minutes."

Grady and Jennings both checked their timepieces and nodded.

Once they heard the main door to Kandinsky's suite shut they were up and out of the room. The camera opposite followed the big Russian as he walked towards the stairs. Grady took a quick look around and led Jennings in the other direction.

The passageways were unnervingly quiet and they crept softly along, painfully aware that one misplaced footstep would echo loudly and give them away to any guard in the vicinity. Jennings could feel tiny trickles of sweat running into his eyes. He wiped them with a handkerchief before they started to sting. Grady, who'd been in similar situations throughout his working life, kept calm and concentrated, his pulse barely rising above normal.

At the far stairwell Grady stopped and thrust his hand back to halt Jennings. Down below two guards were deep in conversation. Grady poked his head around and watched them. Although he couldn't understand a word they were saying, it appeared from their body language that the talk was of a friendly rather than professional nature. It briefly crossed his mind to put a dart in each of them, but decided the risk of alarm was too great. Instead, he and Jennings waited like statues, willing the guards to finish socializing and go their separate ways.

After an eternity the chatter finally stopped, replaced by disappearing footsteps. Once all was quiet again Grady led them down the stairs and onto the ground floor. They moved swiftly along the dimly lit passageways arriving at the closed-off corridor without any further encounters. They could just make out the shapes of two guards outside the farthest door.

"Fucking hell," Jennings whispered. "It's further than I thought. I'm not sure I can hit at this range."

"Don't worry," Grady whispered back. "You'll be fine. You

take the nearest one and I'll take the other. Okay?"

Jennings nodded and pulled out his weapon.

Grady moved across to the other side of the passage to get an angle for his shot.

On a muted count of three they both fired into the gloom. Jennings saw his target's hand fly up to his neck and then watched as he dropped to the floor. Grady's guard duplicated the movement.

"See," said Grady. "I told you it'd be fine."

They raced down the corridor and Grady leapt up and yanked the cord from the CCTV camera. Jennings opened the door and burst into the room. The lights were on and the first thing he saw was Stella lying on a glorious, sweeping bed with a drip connected to her arm. Next to her a man shot out of his chair and started shouting in Arabic. Without thinking Jennings lunged and pinned him to the ground, silencing him with a hand over his mouth.

"Be quiet!" he ordered. "Stop struggling and you won't come to any harm."

The man immediately relaxed and let himself go limp. Jennings got up and pulled him to his feet.

"Please do not hurt me," said the man. "I am only a doctor. I do not wish to cause you any trouble."

"Good," said Grady, entering the room with his gun raised. "Now tell us – what's the score with her?" He gestured towards Stella.

"She has extremely bad bruising and maybe some internal injuries. She is heavily sedated."

Grady rolled his eyes. "That's all we need. Haven't you got anything to sharpen her up a bit – maybe an adrenaline shot or something?"

The doctor shook his head. "I am afraid not," he said. "And anyway it would be most dangerous."

Jennings gazed at Stella and felt his heart stir. She looked so happy and peaceful that moving her was the last thing he wanted to do. And with her bruising and internal injuries, would rescuing her do more harm than good? He briefly wrestled with his conscience before deciding that there was no way he could leave her at the mercy of the sheik.

"What are you waiting for?" said Grady, sensing Jennings' apprehension. "Wake the girl up and let's go man. Time's ticking away here."

Jennings went to the bed and shook her arm gently. "Stella," he said quietly, so as not to startle her. "Stella, wake up."

Stella remained motionless.

"For God's sake man!" Grady hollered. "Stop fucking about and give her a good shove."

Jennings shook her again, this time more harshly. "Stella!" he said urgently. "Stella. Wake up!"

Stella opened her eyes and smiled dreamily. "What is it?" she croaked. "What's going on?"

"We're here to rescue you."

Stella eyed him drowsily. "Tommy, is that you?"

"Yes, it's me. Now pull yourself together, we've got to get a move on."

Stella pulled the covers up to her neck. "But I don't want to go anywhere. I'm going to marry the sheik and live like a princess for ever and ever."

"Oh, for fuck's sake," muttered Jennings.

Grady strode over to the bed and attempted to take charge of the situation. "Listen, Stella," he said firmly. "We've risked everything to come and get you out of here, so I suggest you get your pampered little ass out of that bed and come with us like the man said."

"But I don't want to. I want to stay here."

"Right," said Grady. He pulled the tube from her arm, removed the bed sheets, and lifted her out onto his shoulder.

"Ooh, Gravy, you're so strong."

Grady gave Jennings an earnest glance. "Come on, let's get going," he said. "You take the lead. I'll carry this bundle of fluff."

Jennings quickly tied the doctor's hand to a bedpost, and then headed out into the corridor. Grady followed close behind with Stella swinging from his shoulder. They jogged through the palace making a beeline for the side door that led to the front courtyard. Fortune appeared to be smiling on them, and as they drew closer to their exit point Jennings began to pick up the pace even more.

"Hold on a second," gasped Grady.

Jennings stopped and turned back. "Sorry, mate," he said. "I forgot. Do you want me to carry her the rest of the way?"

"No," said Grady proudly. "Just slow down a little bit."

Jennings carried on and rounded the corner into the next passage, then stopped in his tracks. The sheik was walking towards them with one of his bodyguard's in tow. There was no time to turn back.

Chapter 34

The Lear Jet touched down lightly and taxied round to the large hangar where Pat Cronin was waiting by a black limousine. Stratton deplaned and walked over to meet him. Cronin looked worn out; his bespectacled eyes heavy and bloodshot, and his face craggy and pale. It was as if he'd been up all night administering the last rites to an entire congregation.

Stratton smiled and shook the priest's hand. "Good to see you, Pat. How's it going? Or shouldn't I ask?"

Cronin grunted a laugh. "It could be worse," he said. "But not a lot. Everything's happening a little too quickly. I don't even know what day it is."

"Nor do I," said Stratton. "But who cares."

They hopped into the limousine and Cronin instructed the driver to take them to the Vatican. Stratton picked a mineral water out of the mini-fridge and made himself comfortable. "You seem quite sprightly for someone with a snapped Achilles," he said.

"Yes, I am. It was practice for this 'Messiah' of ours," said Cronin. "I'm really glad you're here, Stratton. I'm at my wit's end with all this. I'm supposed to be Desayer's assistant, but I feel more like his carer at the moment. I don't know if it's old age or what, but just recently he seems to have lost all power to make a decision."

"I don't think it's got anything to do with old age," said Stratton. "This situation is enough to confuse the best of men. There's no real way of knowing what to do."

Cronin nodded. "You're right. Of course you are. I guess I'm being too harsh. It's just that I'm so used to him having all the answers that I feel frustrated without them."

"You'll probably feel better now you've spoken to someone about it," said Stratton. "It doesn't matter who you are or what your background is, it's not easy carrying a burden on your own." He leant towards Cronin. "This might help you out as well."

"What?"

"Close your eyes and take some steady breaths."

Cronin did as he was told. After a couple of breaths he felt Stratton's palm on his forehead. It was warm and comforting. Within seconds he sensed a change in his body. The tightness in his chest began to drain away, like somebody had opened a sluice-gate. It rushed through his abdomen and then down through his legs and off into the ether. He flopped back into the leather seat and sighed loudly. "Wow!" he said, opening his eyes. "What the hell was that?"

"Just a little remedy for stress. Do you feel better?"

"Much," said Cronin. "I didn't realize how wound up I'd become."

Stratton picked another bottle of mineral water from the fridge and handed it to Cronin. "Here, drink some of this, you'll probably feel thirsty."

Cronin drank half the bottle straight down. He wiped his lips then finished the rest. In front of him the driver's partition started to whirr down. "What is it, Gino?" he asked.

"It is the radio, Father. I thought you might want to listen. Something is happening."

Cronin reached over and switched the radio on.

"…the scenes here in St Peter's square are quite phenomenal. Since the news broke fifteen minutes ago people have been arriving in their swarms. The whole of Rome has come to a standstill. The faithful are gathering waiting for their first glimpse of him. In all my years as a reporter I've never felt such a sense of occasion and anticipation. There's an expectant hush that's almost indescribable. We're all wondering the same thing – can it possibly be true?…Wait a minute – I think something's happening. The Pope has come to the balcony. He's getting ready to speak…"

Cronin and Stratton leant forward tensely.

"...has arrived. It is a time in the history of mankind, when we must all come together to eradicate the evil that pervades our world. The evil of violence; the evil of greed; the evil of adultery and deviance. As a society we have too easily let ourselves drift into sin. It is now, into this cauldron of depravity, that someone has returned to us. He came two thousand years ago to show us the error of our ways, and there could be no more opportune time for him to come again. He is here to bind us once more, to make the world as one again...I give you – THE MESSIAH..."

The radio roared with cacophonous cheers. Stratton looked to Cronin, and Cronin to Stratton. The storm had begun.

Chapter 35

For a brief moment the sheik didn't register what he was seeing. Then it suddenly dawned on him. But what were Kandinsky's bodyguards doing with his prized possession?

Jennings and Grady kept still and waited for him to speak. There was no getting away from the fact that they'd been caught bang to rights. No explanation in the world was going to get them out of this one.

"What exactly do you think you are doing?" the sheik said calmly.

The bodyguard unlatched the safety on his weapon and trained it between Jennings and Grady who immediately put their hands up.

"Where is your boss?" the sheik asked. "Does he know about this?"

Jennings' mind went blank. Sweat poured into his eyes.

"Well?" pressed the sheik.

A few smart lines went through Grady's head, but the wild look in the guard's eyes helped stay his tongue. He'd been around long enough to spot a trigger-happy lunatic when he saw one.

"I see," said the sheik. "It matters not. We will soon get to the bottom of this little charade." He turned to the guard and barked some orders in Arabic. The guard reached for his headset and hollered into it.

Grady's shoulder was starting to ache, the weight of Stella becoming more pronounced with his inertia. He shuffled awkwardly trying to get her into a more comfortable position without alarming the guard. As he did so he felt her fidgeting clumsily at his waistband. He was about to whisper to her to knock it off when he realized what she was doing, and in that instant he felt the first signs of panic. She was going to get them all killed.

"Turn around," she whispered to him.

Grady ignored her and continued staring face front. The last thing he wanted to do was give the wild-eyed guard an excuse to pop them.

"Turn around," she repeated, this time slightly louder.

Grady weighed up the situation and his options. It was pretty much certain that once back-up arrived for the guard they were finished. There would either be a painful death or, even worse, a painful imprisonment. If they were to have any chance he had to act now. "Fuck it," he mumbled, and swung round while the guard was still occupied on his headset. In the corner of his eye he saw Stella's pistol-laden hand whip out and fire.

The guard felt the sting in his neck and instinctively reached up. Within seconds he was on the floor.

Jennings, who had been caught by surprise, recovered his wits and pulled his own pistol from behind and shot the flustered sheik. "Come on!" he urged Grady. "Let's get moving."

Grady thought about letting Stella down, but there wasn't time to see if she was okay to walk, so he gritted his teeth and followed Jennings. They swerved round the lifeless sheik and his guard and sprinted off down the corridor.

After reaching the exit they stopped briefly to gather themselves. Jennings opened the door and peered out into the courtyard. Kandinsky wasn't there. He checked his watch and discovered that despite their interrupted progress they were still two minutes ahead of schedule. "We're early," he said.

"Great," said Grady. "So we've got to hang around here waiting to be caught." He lowered Stella to her feet keeping her steady with a firm grip. "Are you okay to walk?" he asked.

Stella gave him a daft grin and slurred, "I think sho Gravy."

"It's Grady. G-R-A-D-Y."

He let go of her arms. She dropped to the ground.

"Fuck!" said Grady. "How the hell did she manage to shoot that guard."

"Just pick her up," said Jennings. "Kandinsky's driving across to us now. It's only another few yards and you can dump her on the backseat of the Jeep."

Grady muttered something beyond Jennings' hearing and stooped to pick up his charge.

Two guards appeared at the end of the corridor and rushed towards them. Jennings shot out of the door followed closely by Grady. Kandinsky was making his way slowly round the edge of the courtyard. Jennings sprinted for the Jeep. The cries of the guards seemed to draw nearer and were echoed by another group who had appeared at the main door. As they began to fire Kandinsky sped up. Jennings dived for the cover of the Jeep and whipped the door open throwing himself onto the backseat. Grady hoisted Stella into the moving vehicle and then leapt in after her. "I'm too fucking old for this!" he hollered, slamming the door behind him.

Kandinsky put his foot down and circled the courtyard, going past the gates and round again, the armoured plating and glass standing up well to the barrage of bullets. After a couple of circuits he slowed once more and Grady jumped out into the cover of a clump of bushes fifty yards from the main gates.

"Let's just hope he can get them open," said Jennings.

Grady waited for ten seconds and then took a tentative look. The guards' fire was still concentrated on the Jeep and they appeared to have missed him. He turned to face the gate, where he noticed the two sentries were also engaged, giving him time and space to prepare his shots.

He loaded the pistol with two darts and aimed at the furthest sentry. The shot was a beauty and hit the target right on the side of the neck. Before his partner could react Grady let the other dart fly and once again bulls-eyed the mark. He surveyed the area once more before breaking his cover and running for the gate.

By now the whole courtyard was lit up like a football match, leaving Grady exposed and vulnerable. He was barely halfway to the gate when shots began to pepper the wall behind him. Digging deeper than he ever thought possible he picked up his pace and surged forward, his eyes almost popping with the strain. The bullets continued to clip at his heels.

A mighty leap from fifteen feet propelled him into the open gatehouse. Crashing against a wall he lost his footing and fell to the ground in a momentary daze. He shook his head and sprang back up, scanning the large control panel for the gate mechanism. The buttons were labelled in Arabic. He cursed loudly and began pressing each one in turn, hoping that he'd get lucky sooner rather than later. Shots started to rattle the booth.

"Look!" shouted Jennings. "The gates are opening!"

Kandinsky changed course and made directly for the exit.

Jennings watched as a group of four guards ran along the far wall heading for the gatehouse. "We'll never get there in time! They're going to cut him off!"

Kandinsky swerved slightly and hit the accelerator hard to try and block their route. The Jeep roared and the guards ran faster.

For Jennings the next few seconds were a blur. He looked on helplessly as they headed towards an inevitable collision with both the guards and the wall. As they reached the point of no return he instinctively raised his arms and ducked his head, bracing himself for a brutal impact. There was a screech and a skid, and then a sideways jolt which threw him across into the door. Outside, the guards clattered into the back of the Jeep.

Regaining control, Kandinsky let off the handbrake and thrust forward to the gatehouse where Grady was waiting beside the door. He jumped in, landing on top of Jennings and Stella. "That was some manoeuvre man!" he yelled.

Behind them the shooting started again in earnest. But it was too late. Kandinsky engaged the engine and the Jeep screamed off into the night.

Chapter 36

Stratton was struck by a wave of euphoria. The elated cries of the crowd in St Peter's square pulsed through him like a jet of pure joy. His back arched in an ecstatic spasm, and his chest burst upwards filling his lungs with limitless life. He drew in the atmosphere hungrily, as if he'd just discovered how to breathe after years of suffocation.

Cronin looked on incredulously, unsure what to make of the sudden outburst, wondering if his friend was having a fit, and whether he should do something to help. His quandary was eased when Stratton suddenly relaxed and re-entered the physical plane once more.

"Are you alright?" asked Cronin. "What happened?"

"I can feel their happiness," said Stratton. "It gives me strength."

Cronin's brow furrowed. "I'm not sure I understand."

Stratton took a long drink of water. "No, I guess you wouldn't yet. I haven't told you about it."

"About what?"

"My link to the world. Basically, if the world feels good then so do I. If it's angry and poisonous, then all my power leaves me. I'm like a spiritual barometer."

"Christ!" said Cronin. "That's amazing!"

"It wasn't a few weeks ago I can assure you. This is great, but the downside is really steep."

The limousine ground to a halt. The driver turned round and said, "I'm sorry, Father, but we can't go any further – the whole city's in gridlock."

Cronin lowered his window and looked out into the street. It was mayhem. The sound of horns and sirens was incredible as droves of people abandoned their cars and headed into the heart of the city on foot. "This is a nightmare," he said, turning to Stratton. "It's going to take us ages to get anywhere with all these people about. Even the pavements are gummed with bodies."

"Let's wait for a bit," Stratton suggested. "There's not a lot we can do at the moment anyway. The cat's already out of the bag."

Cronin shrugged. "I guess you're right."

A wild man approached the car and started gabbling at Cronin through the open window. "Father!" he shouted. "Is it true? Has the Messiah really returned to us?"

"I couldn't say," said Cronin. "I've only just heard the news myself."

"But surely it must be true. The Pope himself has declared it."

"Well then – there's your answer."

The man kissed Cronin on the cheek and disappeared into the crowd. Cronin closed the window before anyone else decided to seek a professional opinion on the matter.

"I think you're going to be very much in demand over the next few days," said Stratton with a grin.

"Tell me about it," said Cronin. "I wanted to tell him that the whole thing was a sham, but he was so full of it all that there didn't seem to be any point. He wasn't going to listen to anything I said other than 'yes, it's true'. Any contradiction would have just led to an argument. I don't know what he was asking me for anyway – he'd obviously made up his mind already."

"I guess he just wanted it reaffirming by someone in the know," said Stratton. "More than that, he wanted to share the moment with you. Perhaps he sensed that you weren't as happy as you should have been at the news."

"Well, if he sensed that then at least he wasn't totally gone."

"What about Desayer?" asked Stratton. "I'm surprised he hasn't been in touch about this. Wouldn't he have phoned you before the Pope made his statement?"

"Oh fuck!" said Cronin. "I've had my phone switched off all morning. I was getting fed up with him ringing me every five minutes." He pulled the phone out of his pocket and started it up. "Twenty missed calls. I'll bet he's been having kittens." He speed-dialled the cardinal.

Stratton relaxed back in his seat, listening to Cronin's fumbling excuses and trying not to laugh. The power was still gushing through him and he was finding it difficult to take anything too seriously. His brain knew that the situation warranted his earnest attention, but his body and soul were quite happy to go with the immediate flow.

Five minutes later Cronin hung up the phone and sighed.

"I take it he's not best pleased then?" said Stratton.

"No," said Cronin. "Not really. He's been trying to get hold of me for about four hours. Vittori called him in early this morning and informed him about the imminent announcement. The Vatican press office leaked it to every news agency in the world about half an hour before the Pope made his speech. So I guess nearly everyone on the face of the earth must have heard about it by now. Desayer wants us to meet him in his chambers as soon as possible."

"I suppose we ought to get going then," said Stratton.

Out in the street the horn honking had almost stopped, but chaos still reigned. Cronin barged his way through the crowds, excusing himself by telling people he was on official Vatican business. Stratton followed close behind tingling with the buzz of the masses. He pictured similar scenes all over the globe, with businesspeople throwing aside their corporate shackles, offices and call centres devoid of life, factories brought to an abrupt standstill, empty schools and colleges. At this moment in time, he thought, the whole world could very well be one giant street party. From New York to Beijing and from London to Sydney, people might be celebrating like never before. This was a fanciful notion of course, considering the amount of non-Catholics on the planet, but it heartened him to think that something could unite people on such a large scale, even though the premise was fundamentally false.

It took them a good two hours to reach the Vatican and

another fifty minutes to get into the building. By the time they arrived at Desayer's chambers Cronin was exhausted. Stratton, however, was still fresh and brimming with enthusiasm.

Desayer welcomed them gravely. "It is good to meet you at last," he said to Stratton. "I am sorry it is in such circumstances."

Stratton shook the cardinal's hand and sat down next to Cronin.

Desayer poured coffee for each of them and settled in his chair on the opposite side of the desk. "It has been a long and busy day," he mused. "And I fear this is only just the start."

"It was all a bit sudden," said Cronin.

"Yes," said the cardinal. "It caught me by surprise as well, and I am supposed to be part of this conspiracy. As I told you before, I was summoned very early this morning to a meeting with Vittori and the Pope. They told me they had received word that the Muslims were about to officially reveal the Mahdi, and that we had to act quickly. We gathered all the resident cardinals and informed them of Christiano's coming. There was a lot of disbelief as you can imagine, but the three of us were most persuasive, and by the time he appeared they had more or less accepted our word. After he had cured Cardinal Botti's sciatica and Cardinal Stein's damaged knee – both in seconds – there was no further doubt."

"So this guy's good then?" said Stratton.

"Yes," said Desayer. "He is very good. He knows how to use every symbol on the box."

Stratton thought for a moment. "And I guess we can assume that the 'Mahdi' does too," he said. "Although I'm surprised that they've taken so long to unveil him."

"They probably thought they had all the time in the world," said Cronin. "They wouldn't have known that the Catholic Church had Christiano lying in wait. But it won't be long before they counter-strike. It wouldn't surprise me if they make an announcement before the day is out."

Desayer nodded sagely in agreement. "I fear you are right, Father. They will have been shaken by the news, but not destroyed. They are safe in the knowledge that they have a legitimate miracle worker of their own to show the world. They will make their claim and then do everything they can to discredit Christiano. For all they know he could be a charlatan. They will not be aware that he has access to exactly the same information as the Mahdi."

Stratton sighed. "I think it's inevitable now," he said. "The world is going to have two redeemers and there's nothing we can do to stop it. Our mission's changed from prevention to cure."

"Yes," said Cronin. "But what exactly can we do?"

Stratton shook his head and stared out into the dusk. "I don't know Pat. I just don't know."

Desayer's desk phone trilled ominously. He listened intently, his face growing paler by the second. He hung up and faced Stratton and Cronin. "That was Vittori. The Muslim's have made their announcement. The war has begun."

Chapter 37

Jenna grabbed a handful of popcorn and topped up her glass of wine. Tariq had popped out to the local shop to get her some chocolate, cigarettes and another bottle of chardonnay. They had spent the whole day slobbing about watching DVDs. She was supposed to be going out with a couple of old school friends, but was having such a chilled-out time that she had cancelled by text at the last minute and stayed in her pyjamas. After all the hours she'd put in at work over the week she just wanted to curl up on the sofa in the arms of her man. She was just about to get up and change discs when a breathless Tariq burst through the front door.

"What's up?" she said, taken aback.

"Turn on the TV," gasped Tariq.

Jenna switched from the DVD to BBC One. Early-evening programming had been interrupted by the news. Tariq sat down and they watched in stunned silence as the day's events gradually became clear.

"Christ," said Jenna, breaking her fragmented thoughts. "What the hell is going on? This is surreal. I feel like I've walked into a parallel universe. I can't get my head around it."

Tariq shook his head. "It's fucked up," he said. "Totally fucked up."

Jenna took a large mouthful of wine and reached for her cigarettes. She lit one and had a couple of heavy drags. The news was still trying to bury its way into her head. "I mean – is it good? Is it bad? What's going to happen?"

"It's good I guess," said Tariq. "That's if it's all true. Think about it – God has sent us two messengers. All our questions are going to be answered. That can't be bad can it?"

Jenna got up and paced about the room taking frequent agitated puffs on her cigarette. It had been a long time since she'd thought about God. Having attended a Roman Catholic secondary school the whole concept had become repetitive, stale, and not a little hypocritical. After leaving she'd put the whole religion thing firmly behind her and concentrated on more earthly pursuits. Now it was coming back to haunt her like some kind of divine vengeance.

"Are you okay?" asked Tariq.

Jenna stubbed out her cigarette, gulped some wine, then lit another. "I don't know," she said. "I'm confused. I don't know what's going on. My head just can't cope with it all."

"I didn't think you were particularly religious."

"I'm not," she scowled. "I left all that shit behind me years ago, when I left school."

"What do you mean, left it behind?"

"We had fucking religion shoved down our throats every bloody day. Fucking priests and nuns telling us how to live good, honest lives. Making us pray and sing to some imaginary all-seeing being. Every day there was some bloody guilt trip or other. Telling me I was no good, that I'd go to hell if I didn't change my ways. I wasn't even one of the bad kids." Hands shaking, she took long draw on her cigarette. "And then there was the hypocrisy of the whole thing. These priests telling us what and what not to do, and the whole time they're abusing their power and touching up our classmates. There were a couple of lads in my form – really good kids – who I don't think will ever get over what was done to them. It's going to stay with them for life."

Tariq hung his head, not really knowing what to say.

Jenna sensed his awkwardness. "Sorry sweetie," she said. "It's not your fault. It just makes me mad thinking about it all." She sat back down and gave him a hug.

"I read about it in the local paper a few years ago," said Tariq. "It made me feel awful. The priest in question had been doing it for years."

"Yeah," said Jenna, wiping a small tear from her eye. "The

thing was, we never really knew anything about it at the time – if we had, maybe we could have done something." She looked away and began sobbing. "I guess we knew though, deep down, that something was up. Maybe we were just too scared to say anything."

Tariq put an arm around her. "It's not your fault. The priest was in the wrong, not you."

"I know, but it doesn't stop me feeling guilty."

They sat quietly for a while, Tariq holding her gently to him. He'd never seen her like this before. Throughout their time together she had never once broken down about anything. It was one of the things he loved about her, the fact that she could face the world and its trials without overreacting. And this made the moment all the more poignant. Whereas previously he may have been slightly in awe of her, now, in the midst of her trauma, he felt suddenly protective. It was as if one illusion had been shattered, only to be replaced by something even more wondrous. A layer of beautiful vulnerability, an imperfection that somehow completed her flawlessness.

After a while Jenna pulled away and kissed Tariq softly on the lips. "Thank you," she said. "I'm sorry to go off on one."

"Don't worry about it. You'd have to be inhuman not to be affected by something like that."

Jenna reached for her wine. "Yeah, I guess so. But sometimes I don't want to be human."

Left briefly alone to his thoughts, Tariq began to try and make sense of what was happening. He'd expected the Mahdi to make himself known, but the appearance of this Catholic Messiah had taken him completely by surprise. He wanted to believe that they were both genuine, or at least the Mahdi, but a voice inside told him that something was not quite right.

Jenna echoed his thoughts. "It seems very strange," she said. "I mean, apart from the whole thing being surreal. It's weird that the Muslim's produced their redeemer hours after the Catholic's had announced the 'second coming'. It's almost as if they were doing it in retaliation."

"What are you suggesting?" said Tariq.

"Nothing…I don't know. It's all too confusing."

"Listen," said Tariq. "If you think the Mahdi's just a made-up reaction, then you're wrong. I've got a bit of a confession to make – I already knew about the Mahdi before they announced him."

"What? But how?"

"We were called to a meeting in the mosque the other day. The Imam told us that the Mahdi had surfaced in Mecca. He told us that he was the real thing, that he was a great healer. The Imam has been crippled nearly all of his adult life and I witnessed him dancing about like a little child."

"Why didn't you tell me any of this?" Jenna asked. "I mean, didn't you think the appearance of a miracle worker was interesting or important enough to bother me with?"

"I couldn't tell you. We were sworn to secrecy. We were not permitted to talk about it until he had proclaimed himself to the world. It was the will of Allah – I couldn't go against it."

"Fine," said Jenna, lighting yet another cigarette.

"Listen," said Tariq. "I wasn't even sure what to make of it myself. Yes, I saw the Imam leaping about, but it could have been a trick. How could I tell you about something that may not even have been true? And besides, I'm a man of my word – I made a promise not to say anything and I didn't. It would be the same if you told me something in confidence – not even the Mahdi would get it out of me."

Jenna paused and then smiled. "I know. I shouldn't have questioned you. You're a man of integrity, and I love you for it." She stubbed out her half-finished cigarette. "Come on," she said, getting off the sofa and holding out her hand. "My brain's exploding. I need you to make love to me."

Chapter 38

Kandinsky drove vigilantly through the night, constantly alert to the threat of repercussions. They had taken a great risk, and had gotten away with it so far, but he knew that the sheik was not a man to give up lightly. He was also a man with any amount of money and power at his disposal. It wasn't difficult to imagine him being able to instigate an air search, or sending the Yemeni army out after them. The road to the harbour was possibly fraught with more danger than their escape from the palace.

Grady had moved into the passenger seat. He was exhausted, but the buzz of the rescue was keeping him from sleep. He felt alive like he hadn't done for a good while. Although his years in intelligence had provided him with many delicate, life-threatening situations, it had been a long time since he'd been shot at with such ferocity. In fact, the last incident he remembered was back in his days with the Marines. There was no other feeling like it though. The rush of adrenaline that accompanied dodging a frenzy of fire couldn't be matched. Forget bungee jumping and sky diving, this was life at the extreme. An inch, maybe only a millimetre, between living and dying.

Jennings sat on the backseat with Stella's head in his lap. He stroked her hair lightly and watched her sleep. Like Grady he was tired but unable to switch off. The joy of seeing Stella again was overwhelming. Weeks of heartache and worry were suddenly washed away by the mere fact that she was alive and near him once more. She looked so beautiful in the muted light that it brought a tear to his eye. He took a deep breath of her distinctive scent and let it inhabit his being. Closing his eyes he held it there, and finally drifted into a warm sleep

Despite Kandinsky's fears they reached the harbour without attack. He guessed that the sheik must have been rendered unconscious all night by the powerful tranquilizer, and therefore unable to issue a strike-force.

Once on board the submarine they took Stella straight to Dr Vashista who gave her a thorough examination. "I cannot be one hundred per cent certain," he said. "But she is not showing any signs of internal injury. She appears to be just very badly bruised. She is going to hurt for the next few days though."

"Excuse me," Stella chirped from the examination table. "I am here you know." The morphine had all but worn off and she was starting to feel the effects of her accident.

"How could we forget," said Grady.

Jennings took her hand and gave it a reassuring squeeze.

Vashista gave her another quick check, and then fed her some codeine tablets for the pain. He produced a wheelchair from under the table and Jennings pushed her to her quarters. After fluffing her pillows he helped her up onto the bed.

"Are you going to be alright?" he asked.

"I guess so," she said. "Once these painkillers kick in properly I should be okay. I'd rather have had some morphine though."

"I bet you would. But you heard Dr Vashista – he didn't think it was a good idea. You don't want to get hooked on the stuff do you?"

"I don't know – I can think of worse things." She braved a smile. "I haven't thanked you yet have I?"

"What for?"

"For coming to rescue me. If you guys hadn't turned up I could have been stuck there forever."

"I thought that's what you wanted," Jennings grinned. "You didn't seem very keen on leaving when we turned up. You were all for staying there and becoming a princess."

"Did I say that?" she frowned. "I suppose I did. It was the morphine. Dr Vashista's probably right – I really shouldn't have any more of it. Although being a princess wouldn't be too bad – as long as you've got the right prince." She looked at him briefly then turned away.

"I'm sure you'll find one," he said. "You won't be short of

offers."

Stella switched on the television screen and flicked through the music files, choosing *Radiohead's – The Bends* to soothe her battered mind. "Where's Stratton then?" she asked. "Is he still alive?"

Jennings thought for a moment trying to find a suitable explanation.

"Well?" Stella pressed.

"Yes, he's still alive. He's gone to Rome to help out Pat Cronin. It's all kicked off since you were captured." He paused. "But anyway, I'll tell you all about it later when you've rested a bit."

"I'm already rested," she said obstinately. "I want to know what's going on. I want to know why Stratton didn't come to get me."

Jennings sat down on the edge of the bed and touched her hand lightly. Stella whipped it away and said, "Just tell me."

"He thought that it was more important that he went to Rome. Like I said, a lot has happened in the last few weeks. Basically it's like this – both the Muslims and the Catholics have access to the symbols, and they're both about to unleash a Messiah into the world. Each one will have miraculous healing powers, and each one will be considered real. And you know what's going to happen don't you? Each religion will try and debunk the other until it's all out war. Stratton's the only one with the same knowledge as these fake redeemers, so he's got to be out there helping to calm the whole situation."

Stella chewed on it for a while. "How long did it take you to rescue me?" she asked.

"I don't know," Jennings shrugged. "Maybe about eighteen hours all told."

"Well then. Would eighteen hours have really made that much difference to him? He could have made sure I was alright before he went off trying to save the fucking world."

"Listen Stella, he was in a difficult situation. He couldn't delay any longer. There was no need for him to come with us to get you, and he had the utmost faith in our ability to get the job done. He had to look at the bigger picture and make a decision…Of course, if you're really that bothered we can take you back there and get Stratton to rescue you single-handed." He got off the bed and went to the drinks cabinet for some whisky.

"I'm sorry," said Stella after a brief silence. "I wasn't having a go at you. I was just being silly and selfish. Of course Stratton had to look at the bigger picture. And I'm really grateful that you came for me."

Jennings poured some whisky into a glass tumbler and sat back down next to her. "No, I'm sorry," he said. "I shouldn't have made that last comment. I understand why you're upset. But I don't think his decision had anything to do with the way he feels about you. He was just trying to do the right thing. It doesn't mean he doesn't love you."

Stella sipped at a glass of water. "I know," she said. "It would have just been nice to see him, that's all. But you know what? I'm really glad that you're alright. The last time I saw you, you were lifeless, hanging upside-down from a tree – it made me sick. In fact I didn't know what had happened to anybody. For all I knew you were all dead. And where does Grady fit into all this? He was hanging next to you. Where did he suddenly appear from?"

She listened intently as Jennings related all that had happened since they split up in the jungle. When he'd finished she was beginning to feel sleepy once more.

"Well," she yawned. "You've certainly been busy. I feel like I've had it easy."

"Not at all," said Jennings. "I'd rather have been in my situation than yours. At least I haven't been held captive. You can't put a price on freedom."

Stella lay her head down and closed her eyes. "Still, you've been through a lot. I'm just pleased you're still alive. When I thought you might be dead…" Her sentence trailed off as she drifted into sleep.

Jennings watched her while he finished his whisky. Then he kissed her on the forehead and returned to his cabin for a much-needed rest.

Chapter 39

Jenna carefully pulled back the duvet and slipped out of bed. She reached for her cigarettes in the dim filtered street-light and tip-toed across the room. As she opened the door Tariq's head stirred slightly in the hall light, and then settled back down into a peaceful slumber. She looked at him briefly and smiled, and then closed the door and went to the living room.

She had been trying to get to sleep for what seemed like an eternity, but every time she neared dropping off another thought would enter her mind and start a new train. At first it was merely annoying, but now her head was throbbing, her eyes were stinging, and her throat was sticky and dry.

She lit a cigarette and sat down on the sofa. There was still a half-full glass of chardonnay on the table and she took a couple of swigs from it. The room felt cold and ominous. She shivered and huddled up, stretching her nightshirt tight over her legs.

The reality of the day's events had crept up on her subtly. At first she hadn't really known what to make of it, and then it had all been too much. Making love to Tariq had calmed her for a while, but once he had fallen asleep the voices in her head began to clamour once more. Years of dammed emotions had been released; at first a steady trickle, and then a spurt, a gush, and finally a shattering burst. The resulting torrent eddied inside her head, her disparate thoughts flashing in the foam like irretrievable flotsam and jetsam; the pressure stabbing like keen knives in her temple. She began to cry.

The tears flowed and felt good, releasing the build-up of emotion. She wiped her eyes with the sleeve of her nightshirt and smoked the rest of her cigarette.

After clearing herself up with a Kleenex she went to the front window and looked out over the orange glow of the town. It was 3.00am, around the time that the clubs would be starting to empty. She wondered whether there was anybody out tonight, or whether the earth-shattering news had prompted people to stay in and think about their lives and where they were headed. In her heart she knew that nothing would stop the die-hards from their Saturday night revelry. There would be many a drunken conversation about God and religion, but it would all be a garbled mass of slurred words and alcohol-fuelled ideals. Inevitably it would end up in physical violence, maybe escalating to a full-blown riot. She imagined the scene down the high street, with police attempting to control hundreds of incensed piss-heads who were so smashed and wound up they'd forgotten what they were angry about in the first place. Then she glanced across at the glass on the table and thought about the damage it was doing to her own logic.

Tariq walked into the room in his boxer shorts. "What's up?" he asked.

"Nothing," she said. "Go back to bed, I'll be with you in a minute."

"I'm up now," he yawned. "You don't look so good. You look like you've been crying."

Jenna shrugged. "Just a little," she said. "It's nothing major, just me being silly. I'm overtired and emotional. I'll be okay once I get some sleep."

"Do you want me to get you a cup of tea or anything?" he asked.

She smiled. "That'd be great. Are you sure you don't mind?"

"Of course not. I'll just go and put a T-shirt on, it's a bit cold in here."

Jenna closed the curtains and turned up the thermostat, then sat back down. Although she hadn't wanted to wake Tariq she was pleased he was up. The living room was large and lonely in the dead of night, and her thoughts seemed to echo in the silence. Left on her own she would probably drive herself to distraction.

A few minutes later Tariq appeared with two cups of tea. He set them on the table before sitting down and giving her a hug.

"So tell me," he said. "What's going on? Are you still thinking about the news?"

"Of course I am. Aren't you?"

"Yeah, I can't stop thinking about it. I managed to cut it out and doze off for a while, but then I started dreaming and woke up."

"What were you dreaming about?"

"I don't know really, I can't remember it that well. It was more like images than anything specific. Whatever it was though, it wasn't good."

Jenna leant forward and picked up her tea. She blew on it and took a couple of sips. "That's perfect," she said. "Just what I need. You're the best." She lit a cigarette. "It's just so weird. I feel like I'm in some sort of parallel universe where the rules no longer apply. When I woke up this morning I knew exactly who I was, what I thought, and where I was going. Now it's all been turned upside-down. I don't feel I know who I am anymore. Or even what I am. Suddenly I'm in this world where God or Allah or whatever he is actually exists. What if I'm living my life totally wrongly? What if the priests and nuns at school were right about everything?"

"We don't even know if these people are genuine yet," said Tariq. "And even if they are – do you really think that God would condone priests abusing young boys? It wouldn't make sense."

"God's can condone what they like," she said. "They're gods, that's the essence of their being."

"I suppose so. But my heart tells me that peace and under-standing are the messages of the true God."

Jenna rubbed her tired eyes. "Well, I hope you're right. I don't think I could bear to live in a world ruled by priests or imams, telling me I've got to do what they say or I'll be banished to hell for all eternity. We're well on our way to building a free world, this whole thing could take us back to the Dark Ages."

"I don't know about the Dark Ages," said Tariq. "But I think you're right – it could set us back. I've been worrying about the same things. I don't want to be suddenly subjected to ridiculous and unjust laws. I like my life the way it is. I like my freedom of choice. I don't want to be told I can't do things that make me happy." He leaned across and kissed her. "And most of all I don't want to lose you."

Jenna touched his face softly. "What makes you think you're going to lose me?"

"I don't know. I've just got a bad feeling about the whole thing. I guess I'm worried that the Mahdi might say that you can't be with a non-Muslim. Like you said – there's so many things they could do. It's strange really; when I first heard about it in the mosque I was on a real high and got carried away with everyone else, but the more I've thought about it the more it seems like a bad thing. I mean, do we really need divine intervention – can't we just work it out for ourselves."

"You know what," said Jenna. "You're absolutely right. But what can we do? They're here now and I doubt if they're going away any time soon. Let's just promise each other that we'll stick together no matter what. Promise?"

"Promise."

Chapter 40

Arman Kandinsky sat at his private bar swilling cognac round a balloon glass. He was tired but not yet ready for sleep. He was pleased with the outcome of their mission into Yemen, but the news he had received back on the submarine was not so good. Overnight the world had changed. In the space of a matter of hours mankind had been 'blessed' by two messengers from God. Right now people were celebrating a new era in the history of humanity. Part of him wished that he could join in the blind hysteria. But a stronger part was glad that he knew the reality of the situation.

After inhaling the vapour deeply he took a large sip of cognac. He lit a cigar and pulled a photo from his breast pocket. It was a picture he kept on his person at all times. Faded by time and creased by handling, it portrayed a young woman and her daughter. The girl was on a horse and the woman held the reins. They were both dark-haired and beautiful, the daughter a miniature version of her mother. Their wide smiles lit up the paddock around them. It was the girl's sixth birthday. Kandinsky gazed solemnly at them through cigar smoke. For a while he remained motionless, then in the corner of his eye he noticed a figure approach the bar. It was Grady.

"Mind if I join you?"

"I would be glad," said Kandinsky. "What would you like to drink?"

"I'll have whatever you're having," he said.

Kandinsky motioned the barman to fetch another cognac, and carefully folded the photograph and put it back in his pocket.

"Who are they?" asked Grady.

"People from the past," said Kandinsky emphatically. "They are dead now."

Grady took the hint and said no more about it. He accepted a cigar and sat quietly next to his host. He had managed to force a couple of hours' sleep, but his head was still a mass of energy. His thoughts had turned back to Brooke and their unborn child. The buzz of the rescue had gone, replaced by worry and guilt. If one of those bullets had connected with a vital area it would have left a mother and child alone.

"We did well, yes?" said Kandinsky, breaking the silence.

"Sorry?" said Grady.

"The rescue. It went well, did it not?"

"Yeah. We got her out of there, and nobody got permanently damaged, so we did do well. Personally I had my doubts that it would work. But I was glad to be wrong."

Kandinsky nodded sagely. "But what now?" he sighed. "What can we do to stop the madness that is sweeping the world? Already I fear it is too late."

Grady sipped at his drink. He'd heard the news at the same time as Kandinsky, but hadn't really thought about it too much. Having spent so much time isolated from what he considered the civilized world, it was beginning to seem almost irrelevant. "I don't know what to make of it if I'm being honest," he said. "It's all like a dream to me at the moment. For the last month I've either been stuck in the jungle or on this submarine – I'm finding it difficult to comprehend the world at large. All I'm really thinking about is my pregnant wife."

"That is a fair comment. It is good that you think about your wife. There is nothing as important. But this situation is going to affect everybody, including your family. It would not surprise me if the world was at war within the week."

Grady puffed on his cigar. "You could be right. But like you said – what can we do? The whole world's going to be caught up in this mess in some way or another. But ultimately it's going to turn into a straight fight between the Muslim's and the Christians, with the winner taking control. I'd bet on the Christian's myself – I'm not sure of the exact figures, but I think they outnumber Muslim's roughly two to one."

"Yes, you are correct. But I am not sure if it is really a game of numbers in that respect. The two sides only account for half the world's population between them. It is what the other religions choose to do that will ultimately sway the tide. Our one hope is that Stratton can do something to force opinion away from the two false Messiahs."

"He'll have his work cut out," said Grady. "It's not easy appealing in the face of religious fanaticism. If it was down to me we'd get a sniper to pick them both off. Although, no doubt that would just make martyrs out of them."

"Yes," said Kandinsky. "Absolutely. It is a problem without answer. I feel we will just have to wait and see what happens over the next few days and react accordingly. Meanwhile I think we should head for Rome to meet up with Stratton."

"Probably the best move," said Grady. "But once we get there I think I'm going to head back to the States. If there is going to be trouble I want to be there to protect my family."

"Of course," said Kandinsky. "You must look after them." He retrieved the photograph from his pocket once more and laid it on the bar in front of them. "This was my family. My wife and my daughter."

"They're beautiful."

"Yes, they were. I loved them more than anything."

Kandinsky's face remained impassive, but Grady caught a slight welling in his eyes. He wanted to ask the Russian what had happened, but was unsure of the reaction he might get. Instead he fell silent and ruminated over his cognac, waiting for his host to change the conversation.

"They were murdered," Kandinsky said without fanfare. "Murdered by a competitor of mine. It was my fault. I had grown powerful, but I had also become clumsy and greedy. I was also taking too much cocaine. My judgement had become clouded and paranoid." He sipped some cognac and puffed on his cigar. "I started to treat my employees very badly, and that was the biggest mistake I ever made. I would accuse them of disloyalty and hit them on a whim. I became a tyrant and a bully, and I suppose it was only a matter of time before one of them turned against me. It was contrary to everything I believed in. I had built my empire on discipline and loyalty and respect for my people – once I had lost that it was inevitable that I should suffer a fall."

He sighed and continued. "Anyway, one of my men decided that enough was enough and he crossed over to the other side. He helped my main rival, a man called Kolinsky, penetrate security and enter my house with a small army of men. They shot everyone they came across – including my wife and daughter. I was down in the basement games-room when they attacked, off my head on cocaine and brandy. I heard the gunfire, but by the time I reacted it was too late. I raced up to my daughter's bedroom and found them both lying there, just feet from the safety of the panic room I had installed. Then, I do not know…"

Grady watched Kandinsky swirl his cognac. The story hung awkwardly in his head. The big man was plainly suffering inside, and probably had been for years. It wasn't in his nature to feel sympathy for ruthless killers, but there was something inherently tragic about Kandinsky that caused him to think. The man wasn't after pity, but that in a way made Grady warm to him all the more. Perhaps it was because he saw a part of himself. He wanted to say something, but couldn't find the words.

"Anatol found me the next day: lying in the panic room with Maria and Natalia by my side. I had been shot four times in the back and was barely alive, but he got me treatment and I pulled through. Although sometimes I wish that I had gone with them." He winced, then after a brief silence affected a laugh. "But that is enough of my woe, the past does not matter. We must look to the future now – dark as it is."

Chapter 41

When Stella woke from her long sleep it took her a while to remember where she was. Once her brain kicked in she leant over and switched on the light. She blinked furiously and then pulled herself up to a sitting position. The manoeuvre was uncomfortable in the extreme. The painkillers had worn off and the tiniest movement was accompanied by a stabbing sensation. She reached for her tablets and swigged a couple down with some mineral water. Feeling hungry she phoned the galley and asked for them to bring some breakfast. She then called Jennings who came over almost immediately.

"Morning," he chirped as he came through the door. "How are you feeling?"

"I've been better. But I've just had a couple of those codeine, so hopefully they'll do the trick."

"You certainly look a lot better."

"So do you," she said. "Have you had anything to eat yet?"

"Yeah, I had some breakfast in my room. What about you?"

"I've just ordered some. You can sit with me while I eat."

"Thanks very much," laughed Jennings. "I feel very privileged."

Stella smiled. "I didn't mean it like that. I just meant that it would be nice if you sat with me, that's all."

Jennings pulled up a chair. Stella was glad of his company. She still felt guilty for the way she'd spoken to him the day before. He'd gone out of his way to rescue her and all she'd done was ply him with questions about Stratton. She put a lot of it down to the trauma, but there was no real excuse for taking him for granted in such a cruel way.

"I haven't really thanked you properly," she said.

"What for?" asked Jennings.

"For coming to get me."

"You thanked me last night."

"I guess so," she said. "But I was a bit of a mess and I don't think I said enough. I feel like I was really ungrateful. But I'm not you know. It means a lot that you risked your life for me."

"Grady and Kandinsky did as well."

"I know and I really appreciate it. But I don't think anyone would have come if it hadn't been for you." She reached out and squeezed his hand.

Jennings looked into her eyes and felt himself melting. In that instant he knew that he loved her far beyond the confines of his physical world. A wave of calm swept over him, followed by a beautiful sadness. His eyes began to water. "I'm sure somebody would have come," he said, looking away. "Stratton would have made sure of it."

"Maybe," said Stella. "But it's academic really. You were the one who actually came." She smiled softly and squeezed his hand again.

Jennings felt a sudden dryness in his throat. He reached for Stella's mineral water and took a few sips. He'd waited for ever for Stella to look at him like she was at this moment, but now that the time had come he felt overwhelmed and confused. Part of him wanted to believe that she'd finally fallen for him, but another, stronger part, told him not to misread the signals. He kept the bottle to his lips until he regained a thread of control.

"You wouldn't have heard," he said, changing the subject, "but both the Catholics and the Muslims have announced their redeemers. It happened yesterday apparently."

"That's not good is it?" said Stella. "What's the reaction been like?"

"As far as I can tell from the news reports it's ranged from euphoria to shock. I don't think anyone quite knows what to make of it yet, it's too soon to tell. I think the world's in a state of complete and utter confusion. But whatever happens when the dust settles I don't think it's going to be pretty."

"No, I don't suppose it is," Stella said thoughtfully. "Has

Stratton actually got a plan?"

"I don't know," said Jennings. "You can never tell with him can you? I don't think he went to Rome with anything specific in mind, but equally he might already have the whole thing sorted in his head."

"And what are we going to do?" she asked.

"Again, I don't know. I think Kandinsky wants to meet up with Stratton in Rome, so I guess we'll be heading there. It doesn't really matter to me anymore – I've got no home to go back to so I'll just go with the flow."

"You'll get back there one day," she said. "The truth has to come out sometime. You know you've done nothing wrong."

"I know, and you're probably right." He looked away ruefully. "The problem is, the way things are headed, I'm not so sure that we're going to have anything to go back to."

Chapter 42

Ali Hussein couldn't believe how his life had changed. In a matter of weeks he had gone from crippled errand boy to fully-functioning disciple. From the day the Master had healed him in the market square he had been on a rollercoaster of joy. His previous existence was now but a hollow thought, confined to the depths of indistinct memory. He had been propelled into a world of wonder, where every day was a new and exciting opportunity to learn and become closer to Allah.

The Master was everything that Ali expected him to be: kindly; knowledgeable; wise; and in possession of a patience far beyond the realms of human capacity. However many questions Ali asked, and however long it took him to grasp even the simplest concept, the Master would remain untouched and persist slowly until it had all sunk in. There was no doubt in Ali's mind that he was truly the Mahdi.

The day had been hectic to say the least and Ali was glad to at last have a little time to himself. They had spent the afternoon in Islamabad where the Master had addressed a large gathering at the cricket ground. He had worked his way through a huge procession of the frail and sick, curing everything from limps to blindness. Some people even stood in line pretending to have ailments just so that they could feel the touch of Allah. The television cameras and paparazzi had been in their face all day too, but not once had the Master complained or lost his temper. He had dutifully continued to heal and had even made jokes with the surrounding media circus, answering all their questions with the calm and wit of a seasoned politician. Now that evening was drawing into night they were guests at the presidential palace.

Ali stretched back in the sumptuous red leather chair and closed his eyes. The Master was in the next room performing his daily meditation, and would not be calling on him for at least another half hour. He thought about his mother and wondered what she was doing and whether she was unhappy that he had left so suddenly. He had called her every day and she had sounded pleased and exceptionally proud that he was doing something so important, but he still worried that she would be lonely without him, her only child. He hoped that Farouk was stopping by each day to check on her as he said he would.

A little later Ali woke. He blinked a couple of times and then started from the chair, concerned as to how long he had been asleep. He took his position as the Master's aide extremely seriously and was anxious not to disappoint. The clock on the mantelpiece indicated that he'd been out for just twenty minutes. He went to the table and picked up a mineral water.

Ten minutes later the Master appeared from his room. Even after his long day he was still glowing with energy. His eyes sparkled like stars and his aura glimmered with gold. As young as the morning dew, and as old as mountains. Ageless. Ali gazed up in awe and then bowed his head in reverence.

"Are you rested my young friend?" the Mahdi asked.

"Yes, Master, thank you."

"Good. Then I think it is time for us to eat."

As a rule it was Ali's job to prepare meals for the Mahdi, but on this occasion, as they were guests of the President of Pakistan, their food was made in the palace kitchen and brought to them by servants. Ali felt awkward at being waited upon, but the Mahdi reassured him that it was alright: "You have served me well, young Ali," he said. "You have worked hard and long. Do not deny yourself an experience by layering it with needless guilt. Sit down, enjoy the food, and relax while you can. There is a long road ahead of us and much work to be done."

They said their prayers and began to eat. The table was filled with a miniature banquet of fruits, spiced meat dishes, rice, and vegetables. Ali threw aside his misgivings and dug in hungrily, savouring every mouthful in respect for Allah. He had never starved at his mother's house, but food had not been available in quite such abundance, and he considered the meal to be a rare treat.

"You have quite an appetite," the Mahdi commented. "It is good to see. You are honouring Allah's bounty."

When they were finished and the plates had been cleared, they moved to the comfortable lounge chairs and rested while their food settled. The Mahdi shut his eyes and meditated for a while. When he opened them again Ali took the opportunity to ask a question that had been on his mind. "Master," he said. "How is it that you retain such energy even after a long day? Surely the healing of all those people must tire you out."

The Mahdi smiled. "On the contrary young Ali, the more people that I heal, the more energy I have. Allah replenishes and adds extra for each good deed done. It is the same throughout life."

Ali thought for a moment. "But Master, I know of people who do good things and have very bad things happen to them."

"Yes, this is true, but the bad things are an external force. The good deed is rewarded with the internal energy to combat these misfortunes. Sometimes the kindest people are subjected to the harshest situations, but this is just Allah's test of worthiness. The closer to him you get, the more difficult your tasks become. You have been tested all your young life, but you have persevered in the face of hardship, and you have been rewarded with a place at Allah's side."

"But I haven't really done anything," said Ali.

"Have you not? Perhaps it feels as if you have not, but in the eyes of Allah and of other people you are an example to behold. You were born with a great disability, and yet you have never complained or bemoaned your lot in life. Every trial and tribulation has been met with resolution, determination, and most importantly – a kind word for all. Nobody else has suffered your turmoil, only you. You are an example of all that is good in Allah's world."

Ali felt himself blush. The Master's words were almost too much for him to take in.

"Do not be embarrassed by my words," said the Mahdi. "You should hold your head high." He laughed kindly. "But of course, you are too modest for that – and that is what makes you so special in the eyes of Allah." He leant over and placed his hand on Ali's head. "Bless you Ali, child of Allah."

Ali felt a pulse of light flow through his body. And it truly was as if Allah himself had come down and touched him. He opened his eyes and felt like he was seeing the world for the first time.

The Mahdi smiled broadly. "You are now a part of Allah," he said. "You are an extension of his will. Your touch will help to heal the world."

Ali felt a tingling in his hands. He placed his palms together and found that they were burning with heat. As they connected he shuddered with power. His eyes welled with tears.

"Do not be afraid," said the Mahdi. "You may feel overwhelmed, but you have not been given more than you can cope with. Take a few slow, deep breaths and ground yourself."

Ali did as he was told, inhaling deeply from the pit of his stomach and concentrating his mind. After a few minutes the confusion disappeared.

"How do you feel now?" asked the Mahdi.

Ali broke into a grin that he thought would never end. "I feel light, like I could float away at any moment. But everything is clear, so very clear. I don't know, it feels like I've been dreaming and just woken up. It's beautiful."

"Yes it is beautiful. This whole world is filled with beauty, you only have to open your eyes to see it. I hope that one day the whole world will be able to see as you do. That is Allah's intention."

"But can you not just touch people as you did to me, then they would be able to see wouldn't they?"

"You have earned the right to see, Ali. It is not as simple as just touching somebody and making it happen. If I had done the same thing to somebody else it may well have destroyed them inside. You accepted the power because you are pure of heart and soul. A person must be ready to accept the light before he or she can receive it. It takes years of discipline and searching of the soul to arrive at the correct point. Every piece of debris must be cleared. For most the journey is too hard. But the way is open to everyone who seeks it."

"But I have done none of the things you say," said Ali.

"Have you not?" said the Mahdi. "I disagree. You may not have known it, but you have been on the path all your life. You have resisted bitterness and self-pity and chosen the way of the wise, letting love and laughter into your life. It may seem like nothing to you, but it is far more difficult than you think. If you can bear extreme misfortune and still allow kindness to flow, then you are truly blessed." He paused to think. "Imagine your soul to be like a tube that streams light. Hatred and fear, and jealousy and greed and laziness, are all potential blockages. They float around in the tube distorting the light outwards and causing it to damage the lining. Only when this emotional waste is cleared can the light take its true path. Imagine what the blast of pure light that I gave to you would have done to someone with any of these obstructions. It would have obliterated the tube and taken them apart completely."

Ali fell silent, taking in all that the Master had said. Once it had settled in his mind he continued to question his teacher. "You say that my touch can help heal the world. Have I got the same abilities as you now?"

"No, not yet. You still have a lifetime of learning ahead of you. You will not be able to heal as I do, but your touch will soothe and help repair the injured and broken. As your understanding of Allah grows, so will your power. But that is in the future, you must concentrate on what is happening now. We have a whole world to change."

"What about this Messiah from the West?" Ali asked. "What are we to do about him?"

The Mahdi looked at him curiously. "We do not have to do anything, Ali. He is obviously a work of propaganda. The Catholic Church must have heard of my coming and made an attempt to deflect the world's attention. You must understand how this will affect them. Their way is not the way of Allah. Now that Allah has sent me they are scared. They know that it is only a matter of time before their false religion crumbles beneath them. Do not worry, Ali, once this Messiah fails to prove his divinity their two millennia of lies will be exposed. It is not up to us to hasten his downfall. All you need to know is that I am real, and you do know that – do you not?"

"Yes, of course, Master."

"Good. Never forget that you are one of Allah's chosen few." He looked at the clock. "I think I shall retire to my room for the evening. I have much to think about, and there is much for Allah to tell me." He rose from his seat. "Goodnight, Ali."

Ali bade him a goodnight and sat for a while in quiet and blissful contemplation. The divine power was still coursing through him, making him lighter and happier than he ever thought possible. The revelation of this previously hidden world was almost too much to bear. The excitement inside mounted until he could no longer keep still. Without thinking, he sprang from his chair and decided to go for a walk.

The guards outside the door took little notice of him as he left the suite and wandered off along the vast corridor. He glided to the end and then floated down two flights of stairs to the ground floor. Once there he made his way to a side exit and out into the open. He breathed in the air and laughed. From around the corner he heard the sound of cheering and went to investigate.

The street outside the main entrance to the palace was packed with people. The road was blocked with bodies, and traffic was at a standstill. Ali made his way to the back of the multitude to find out what was happening. Before long it became apparent that the crowd was shouting for the Mahdi to make an appearance. They chanted his name in unison, raising their hands to punctuate each repetition. Palace security was out in force, holding the masses back with a mixture of yelling and strategically aimed machine-guns.

Ali looked on in awe, almost swept away by the sheer magnitude of the crowd's energy. He knew that the Mahdi would not be coming out again that evening, and wondered how long it would take for the people to disperse. From their fervour he guessed that it wouldn't be any time soon. Perhaps they would stay all through the night in the hope of glimpsing the Master in the morning. It suddenly hit him how much his coming meant. People the world over were lost and confused and needed something to bind them. There were so many different sects and sub-sects to all religions that it was becoming difficult to know what was right or wrong any more. The Qur'an was open to so many diverse interpretations that it was almost impossible for anyone to give a definitive answer. It was time to put a stop to the uncertainty and unite the people as one.

Ali closed his eyes and a vision came to him. A picture of a world in harmony. An image of man helping man regardless of race or colour or religion. It seemed so close and real that he could almost touch it. The Mahdi had arrived to make it happen. He was here to lead the peoples of the world out of the spiritual wasteland.

Ali looked to the skies and spread his arms wide, offering himself to Allah and the universe. The crowd's cheers rushed through him. For a brief moment the whole meaning of existence became clear.

Chapter 43

It was night-time in Rome. Christiano looked out on the sea of candles in St Peter's square and wondered if he should make one last appearance. The resolute crowd was showing no sign of dissipating, and he felt that it was his duty not to let them down. They had stopped calling for him a few hours back, but he knew that they were hoping for another blessing. They had been there for over thirty-six hours now, keeping a constant vigil just to catch even the occasional glimpse of their saviour.

Since his unveiling he had been kept busy with a constant stream of the sick, disabled, and terminally ill. First it had been the Romans, then the rest of the country, and by the time he was into the second day people were flying in from as far as America and Australia. They had all come wanting a miracle. They had not been disappointed. It amazed Christiano that he was able to keep going through it all. He'd expected to be tired, but the more people he treated the more energized he became. Now that the queue had gone and there were no genuine cases left to help, he felt a little empty and deflated.

"Are you okay, Christiano?" asked Vittori from his desk across the room.

"Yes, I am fine. I was just wondering whether I should go to the balcony again. The people are waiting."

"Let them wait," said Vittori. "It is nearly midnight. They cannot expect you to be on call twenty-four hours a day."

"Why not?" said Christiano. "God never sleeps does he?"

"Perhaps not. But you will have to. You cannot continue to heal people if you are too tired to do so. You may not think it at the moment, but if you do not get some rest then you will hit a wall."

Christiano sighed. "You may be right, but I just want to go and do something. I'm not sure I can sleep knowing that all these people are out there waiting for me."

"Come and sit down," Vittori said, gesturing to a seat. "Have some water with me. Or have a goblet of wine – it might help you to relax."

Christiano sat down opposite the cardinal and poured himself a glass of water. "I don't think wine would be a good idea," he said. "I want to keep myself clear."

"Your choice," said Vittori. "I just want you to calm down a bit that's all. We have a long road ahead of us and you need to keep yourself fresh. We must travel the world if we are to prove your existence to everyone. In a few days we leave for America."

"America?"

"Yes."

"But this is the home of our faith, why do we have to leave?"

"Because we cannot expect everybody in the world to come here. You must be seen to travel everywhere. I have arranged a tour. We go to America first because it is the most influential country in the world."

Christiano slumped in his chair. He had been expecting to leave Rome at some point, but not quite so soon.

"Do you have a problem with America?" asked Vittori, sensing his apprehension.

"No, of course not. I just like it here, that's all. This is my home. This is where I feel I belong. There's so many people in the city that still need my help. There's so many people in Italy that still need my help."

"Of course there are," said Vittori. "And you will be back here to help all of them. But there are over seven billion people out there who need your help as well. The Messiah doesn't solely belong to Rome or Italy, he belongs to all the people of the earth. You may think of yourself as a local boy, but you are not, you are a symbol of worldwide unity. The vast majority of the world's population cannot afford to fly to Rome, are you suggesting they should be denied seeing you because they are poor?"

"No, Your Eminence. I just wanted to stay a bit longer to build up my confidence. But if you think it is best to leave then I will of course do as you say." He bowed his head.

Vittori sipped at his wine and studied his young charge. The last two days had been hard on the boy. He might not have felt tired, but the signs were beginning to show. His eyes were red and underlined with tiny bags, his shoulders were starting to sag, and his voice was becoming husky and cracked. Another thing that Vittori had noticed was a lack of respect creeping into Christiano's manner. His previous deference to the cardinal had been replaced by an uncomfortable familiarity. He could sense the sprouting of the seeds of revolt. Whether this was down to tiredness he did not know, but he did know that it needed to be quashed before it got out of hand.

"I think you are quite ready for a journey Christiano. If you were not I would not ask you to go. I think the problem lies in the fact that you have never really been away from Rome. Perhaps you are worried about becoming homesick? It would be only natural. I cannot see why you would need to build up any more confidence – think of all the people you have already cured."

Christiano nodded. "Yes, you are right. And perhaps I am slightly scared of travelling. I have never left Italy before."

"Think of it as an adventure. You will see so much more of the world."

"Yes, of course," said Christiano. "But do you think I could perhaps take someone with me?"

"Who?" asked Vittori. "Your mother?"

"Er, no," mumbled Christiano. "It is a friend of mine."

Vittori sensed a hidden agenda. "What sort of friend?"

"I thought perhaps Sophia could join us, Your Eminence. You know – Sophia Zola?"

Vittori sighed. "Yes, I know Sophia Zola. I had no idea you two were friends though. You only met her a few days ago."

"Yes, but we have been communicating online, and she has come to see me a couple of times."

Vittori clenched his fists under the desk. He had given Christiano far too much leeway. He should have been locked away and guarded 24/7. But he had trusted the boy, and had not thought to question all his movements. "I didn't realize you had been socializing when you should have been resting," he said. "I allowed you that computer because I thought you were using it to relax in between studying."

"I was," said Christiano. "Chatting to Sophia relaxes me."

"Maybe," said Vittori. "But I did not give you permission to have guests in your room."

"You didn't say I couldn't."

Vittori made an effort to calm down. "No, Christiano, I did not say you could not have guests. But I thought that you would have had enough sense to know that your position is not conducive to fraternizing with the general public. You are supposed to be the Messiah."

"Even Jesus was allowed friends. And besides, what's wrong with Sophia – I thought you were a family friend."

"I am, and there is nothing wrong with Sophia. She is a charming young lady who has been through a lot. I am just uncomfortable with your interest in her. She is a distraction that you could do without. I do not want your mind straying from the job in hand. And remember, you are supposed to be pure – we do not want the media speculating on whether or not you are romantically linked with somebody. That will not do at all."

Christiano crossed his arms sulkily. "Look," he said. "We are just friends. I don't see why she can't come with us as part of the entourage. Nobody's going to say anything if she's hidden amongst another hundred or so people. I'm not sure I want to go anywhere without her."

Vittori boiled inside. The boy was getting way above his station. The problem was he needed him, and Christiano knew it. One of the reasons Vittori had been happy to choose Christiano for the role of Messiah was his lack of female attachment. He was the perfect option: a devout young man who lived with his mother. But now Sophia Zola had appeared on the scene things were different. She was an unforeseen complication that needed dealing with immediately.

"Listen, Christiano," Vittori said kindly. "I appreciate that you have obviously struck up a rapport with Sophia, but for the time being I really need you to concentrate on what you are doing. There will be plenty of time to see her once we come back to Rome. And you can still contact her via email while you are away. I am sure she will understand the situation."

"Will she?"

"Yes, of course she will. Please, Christiano, it is important that you listen to me on this matter." He looked his young charge in the eye. "What would your grandmother have said?" Vittori knew it was a low blow, but he was at his wit's end and needed some leverage.

At the mention of his grandmother Christiano flinched. He saw the stern look in Vittori's eye and decided that he may have taken his plight too far. "I am sorry, Your Eminence," he said lowering his gaze. "Perhaps I am tired after all."

"Yes, I think you are," said Vittori. "And so am I. It is not a good time to discuss such things. We will talk again tomorrow when we are both more refreshed."

Christiano yawned and stretched his arms. "I think I shall go to bed now. But perhaps I should go out and make another appearance first. Maybe just for a couple of minutes."

Vittori slammed his palm on the desk causing Christiano to shrink in his chair. "No!" he commanded. "I told you – they can wait until morning." He softened his tone. "Look, Christiano, I know your intentions are good, but you must let me make the decisions. If you keep going out there then your appearances will lose their effect. The less they see you, the more they will want to see you. I have arranged a schedule and I expect you to stick to it. Now, do you think you can accept that?"

Christiano felt suddenly worn and deflated. "Yes, Your Eminence."

He said goodnight and left for his quarters.

Chapter 44

Stratton watched the crowd keeping vigil with their candles and shook his head. Already he felt the world slipping away into a terminal coma. Before long there would be no turning back. But what were people supposed to think? As far as they knew Christiano was the real deal. He could heal all their ailments, and he spoke eloquently with reason and compassion. His speeches may have been written for him, but he certainly knew how to work an audience.

Stratton rubbed his eyes and turned away from the window. He slipped his fingers under the dog collar and tried to loosen it. The disguise was uncomfortable both physically and mentally, but it was necessary to keep him from standing out.

Cronin and Desayer were sitting at opposite sides of the desk deep in thought. The three of them had been discussing their options for the last two days, but as yet had come up with nothing. However they looked at it there didn't seem to be any feasible way of stemming the tide.

"Any sign of the Messiah?" asked Cronin.

"No," said Stratton. "I think he's probably called it a night."

"Yes," said Desayer. "I think you are right. Vittori told me earlier today that he was worried about overexposure. I expect he has sent Christiano to bed."

Stratton sat down next to Cronin and poured himself a glass of water. His head hurt with thinking. His body, though, was still charged with energy. Whatever his opinion about the aims of the Church, there was an awful lot of good feeling circulating the globe. But he was only too aware that this was a honeymoon period.

"Perhaps it's time that we retired as well," suggested Cronin. "There doesn't seem to be a lot happening at the moment."

"You're probably right," agreed Stratton. "I reckon everything's about done for the evening. There's no point staying up all night if we don't have to."

They said their goodnights to Desayer and left for Cronin's quarters. The corridor's were unusually busy for the late hour and Stratton felt uneasy with the amount of traffic. He moved along with his head down, letting Cronin guide the way.

"You're a bit paranoid aren't you?" said Cronin. "I don't think anybody's going to recognize you here."

"Maybe not, but I don't want to take the risk. If I'm seen then that's your cover blown, and Desayer's."

"You're hardly an international figure."

"No," said Stratton, "I'm not. But think about it – if Vittori had people doing research on the box, my name could have come up at any time. And it's not difficult to find pictures of people in this day and age, is it?"

"Point taken," said Cronin. "I must be getting a bit lax."

They rounded a corner. Stratton looked up and then straight back down again. He inched closer to the priest.

"What's up?" whispered Cronin.

"Just keep moving."

Cronin nodded politely to the men who walked past them.

"What was all that about?" he asked, opening the door to his room.

Stratton walked in and pulled off his collar. "Don't you know who that was?"

"Sure, that was Jonathan Ayres, the British Prime Minister. What's the problem? Is he a friend of yours?"

"No, I've never met him in my life. But I'll bet he's seen a photo of me."

"Why's that?"

"Because it will have been in the report on the murder of his best friend, Henry Mulholland. I was heavily involved in the whole case, remember?"

"I'd forgotten about that. But you would just have been a face in a file. I doubt whether he'd have given you more than a second's thought. He would have been happy that the killer had been found and would have got on with more important things – like running the country."

Stratton sat down on the spare bed. "What's he doing here anyway?"

"He's been in Rome for the last week. Came over for a conference with the Italian Prime Minister. He's often at the Vatican visiting the Pope. He's a devout Catholic – I thought you'd know that."

"Well yeah, I knew, but I didn't realize he was over here so often. Does he know Cardinal Vittori?"

"He might do, I don't really know."

"I thought you'd been keeping an eye on things over here, and investigating all the cardinals and their associates."

"As far as I could," said Cronin defensively. "You can't keep tabs on everybody all of the time. And besides, our prime concern was not to be found out ourselves. It's difficult watching out for people when you're under the microscope yourself."

Realizing he'd caused offence Stratton backtracked. "Sorry Pat, I didn't mean to question your capabilities. I'm just finding his presence here uncomfortable. I'm not sure why. He gives me the creeps."

"Do you think he's in on the whole thing?" asked Cronin.

"I'm not sure," said Stratton. "But the more I think about it the more suspicious I'm getting. Firstly he was Henry Mulholland's best friend, which should put him out of the frame of course, but he's a politician and let's face it – they don't have real friends. To me it means that he was close enough to know about Henry's family history. And secondly there was all this business with Jennings. He seems to think there was some internal plot to kill the Prime Minister, but if there was surely they would have succeeded by now? I'm more inclined to think that it was all a smokescreen for some other plan they had going. Bottom line is – I don't trust the guy."

Cronin poured himself a whiskey and sat down at his small writing desk. "You could be right," he said. "It might all be coincidence of course, but I'm with you in the fact that I don't trust him. Then again I don't trust any politicians."

Stratton laughed. "You and the rest of the world," he said.

"Yeah," said Cronin, sipping thoughtfully at his whiskey. His eyes lit up in sudden revelation. "But what if you were a politician with the backing of the Messiah – the Son of God? What then?"

"Exactly," said Stratton. "I can hear his brain working now: Jonathan Ayres – divinely approved leader of the free world. God's politician. He's certainly got in here a lot quicker than the American President."

"Like a rat up a drainpipe."

Stratton lay down on the bed and closed his eyes in meditation.

Cronin swirled the remainder of his drink round the tumbler. "What did you want to do with your life before all this?" he asked.

"What do you mean?"

"I mean, before you discovered the symbols, before you discovered Reiki. Maybe when you were a kid. What was your ambition? What was your dream? What did you want to be when you grew up?"

Stratton broke into a smile. "Wow! That's a question. I'd almost forgotten I was a child." He paused. "I wanted to be a lot of things I guess. I suppose it depended on what I was into at the time. I remember at one point desperately wanting to be a snooker player, then later on in my teens I really wanted to compete at the Olympics. That all went to pot when I discovered drinking though, that's when I lost all of my goals. What about you? What did you want to be?"

"When I was a kid I always wanted to be a rugby player," said Cronin. "I wanted to play for Ireland at the World Cup and in the

Six Nations. I used to dream of winning the Grand Slam as captain."

"What happened?"

"I don't know. I think I fell out of love with the game in my teens. I started getting more into books and poetry. I wanted to become the next James Joyce, although I think that might have been overestimating my ability. I would have been happy to be popular like Roddy Doyle."

"Give me *The Commitments* over *Ulysses* any day," said Stratton. "What happened to the writing then?"

"Life happened," said Cronin. "I left home and joined the army and that was that. I didn't look back. I've started putting pen to paper again recently, but nothing solid, just a few bits and pieces."

"Dreams fallen by the wayside," Stratton mused. "The world's just full of them. I guess we all wish we could go back and start afresh, and hold on to them longer."

"Don't we just," agreed Cronin. "I think if I had my chance again I'd take rugby a bit more seriously."

"What about the writing?"

"There's too much thought involved. It's thinking that stops people doing what they want to do. Thinking about conse-quences, thinking about not fitting in. There was something joyous and carefree about my love of rugby. I looked at it with a child's wonder. I'd love to go back and look at things again through those eyes. Without the misery, without the knowledge. I think I've come to know too much. Don't you ever want to forget what you know? Don't you ever long for the day when the world was just the world, as plain and simple as you saw it – a miracle in itself without all these unseen powers? Sometimes I feel that as a race we've become so self-aware that it cripples us."

"I agree with you. But I think that it's all part of a circle. We become self-aware and then spend the rest of our lives learning why we shouldn't be. There's a line from *T.S.Eliot's Little Gidding* that sums it up quite nicely – 'We shall not cease from our explo-ration. And the end of all our exploring will be to arrive where we started and know the place for the first time.'"

Cronin pondered the lines for a moment. "Nice words. I haven't really read a lot of Eliot."

"Me neither," said Stratton. "I just heard the quote somewhere and took an instant liking to it. Like all the best poetry it's simple and profound."

Cronin looked at his watch. "I think it's time to get some rest," he said. He swigged down the rest of his whiskey. "I'll see you in the morning."

Stratton didn't reply. His mind was already far away, searching the universe for an answer he might never find.

Chapter 45

The euphoria had died down and the streets were somewhat subdued. The town seemed to be suffering from a religious hangover. At least that's what Jenna thought as she made her way to work on Monday morning. Heads were drooped and eyes were pointed sharply at the pavement. It may not have been different to any other start of the week, but there was something in the air that made her anxious. An underlying atmosphere of fear that had taken hold of people's frayed minds. At any moment she expected the sinister silence to boil over into murderous mayhem.

Her weekend had been troubled. After the emotional Saturday evening with Tariq she had gone to her parents' house for Sunday lunch. They had been to church in the morning and had spent the afternoon eulogizing about the Messiah and how he was going to save the earth from the evil that pervaded it. Father Malone had told the congregation that he was truly the Son of God and that the day of reckoning was nigh, and that any false redeemer would have to kneel before him and subject themselves to his will. Already she could feel the animosity towards Islam building. She had decided it was not the best time to mention her burgeoning relationship with Tariq. The visit had been painful, but she had switched herself off and escaped with her sanity relatively intact.

Tariq too had spent the day with his mother and father. He had phoned her in the evening and they had talked for over two hours. His parents were of similar mind to her own but on the opposite side of the fence. They had rattled on about the false Messiah and how the Catholic Church was trying to fool the world with its wicked lies. They were sure that he would be exposed soon and have to account to the Mahdi and Allah.

Jenna strode into work, pleased to find some sanctuary from the outside world. "Morning Pami," she chirped to the receptionist. "How was your weekend?"

Her greeting was rebuffed with an icy stare.

"What's wrong with you?" she asked.

Pami stared for a while longer and then, as if suddenly remembering her manners, she gave a frosty "good morning". Jenna shrugged and went through to the office. She knew where the animosity was coming from, but was surprised at its force. Pami was a Muslim, but also open-minded, and they had been on good terms for a number of years. She was taken aback by the overnight change in relations.

She switched on her computer, made some coffee, and then sat down at her desk. Her boss, Bunty Singh, wasn't due for another hour and she took the opportunity to log on to Facebook and catch up with the latest gossip. Unsurprisingly most of the chat was about the revelatory weekend. Everybody had an opinion about what had happened, and most of it was ill-thought-out nonsense. There were calls from the hard-line white contingent to get rid of the "rag-'eads", and there were calls from Islam to "kill the lying infidels". Her inner circle of friends weren't much better informed, but at least their ramblings were focused on the positive side. They were in awe of the whole thing with plenty of "OMGs" and "WTFs" thrown into the mix. She flicked through hoping to find a posting about something normal like boys or drinking.

Singh arrived early and was in sombre mood. He attempted a friendly greeting but it was lost in his world-weary eyes and drawn face.

"Not a good weekend then?" said Jenna.

"No," said Singh. "Not a good weekend at all. Not good for anybody as far as I can see. The world's gone absolutely crazy."

"Tell me about it."

Singh hung up his coat and went to pour a coffee. "I took Alice to the pub for lunch yesterday afternoon, and the amount of abuse I got you just wouldn't believe. It wasn't too bad at first, but then this group of idiots came in and saw me and started making comments about Pakis and Islam and how we should all be deported."

"Didn't you explain that you were a Sikh?"

"I didn't get a chance. It's absolutely ridiculous. The amount of ignorance in this town is unbelievable. The worst thing was that they weren't exactly thugs – just normal blokes out for a Sunday afternoon drink."

Jenna laughed. "I suppose it depends on what you define as normal. So – did they threaten you?"

"Not outwardly, but it was implied. I think they were trying to justify their actions on religious grounds. Although I doubt if any of them had been inside a church in their life."

"That's the thing isn't it," said Jenna. "Every idiot in the town is going to jump on the Catholic bandwagon. They've got a figurehead now, and a cause to fight for. Their lives and hatred have suddenly gained purpose."

Singh shook his head. "I just don't understand the sudden surge of animosity. It's not like these leaders have incited any hatred."

"No, but they've said enough to make people think about it. Neither side has condemned the other as yet, but it's hanging in the air between the lines. And besides, do you really think the pricks in this town need to be told outright? They've seen the news – a white guy proclaiming to be the Son of God, and an Asian claiming more or less the same thing – what do you think is going through their heads? With all that's happened this century - with 9/11 and 7/7 - what do you expect? To them this is just another threat to their liberty. They couldn't give a shit about the religious side of things, it's just an excuse to protect their interests."

Singh sat down opposite Jenna. "It just all seems so crass," he said. "I thought we were living in a more enlightened age."

"You might be, Bunty, and so might your friends. But you're

from London and you have a slightly broader view of the world. I've grown up in this town remember, and I know exactly what the people here are like. Most of them are alright, and it's certainly better than it used to be, but there's still a large element of small-minded wankers. The problem is that the good people of the town are a silent majority."

Singh nodded. "Yes, I suppose that I have too much faith in humanity."

"I thought you would have lost that long ago in this business. I mean, look at all the people you have to represent in court."

"If I didn't have faith then I couldn't represent them. If you don't give people a chance then you will never combat fear and ignorance."

Jenna was just about to speak when a loud smash burst through from the front of the building. It was followed by a scream. Bunty Singh leapt from his chair and tore out into reception. Jenna followed him.

The front window was destroyed, and the dark green carpet was covered in shattered glass. Pami was cowering behind her desk in tears. Jenna went to comfort her. Bunty surveyed the mess open-mouthed. Without thinking about evidence he picked up the large brick from the floor beneath him and unwrapped the message tied to it. It simply said: MUSLIM SCUM.

A stray shard of glass had hit Pami in the head and she was bleeding from her right temple. Jenna mopped the cut with a tissue and went to the cupboard to find the first-aid kit. She returned swiftly and set about cleaning the wound more thoroughly, picking out slivers of window with a pair of tweezers.

"Thank you," said Pami, when Jenna had finished. "I don't deserve your sympathy though."

"Don't be stupid," said Jenna. "Of course you do." She turned to her boss who was absentmindedly picking glass off the floor. "What did the note say?" she asked.

He was about to answer when his partner Robert Harris walked through the door. "What the hell's happened here?"

"Someone chucked a brick through the window," said Jenna.

"What the hell for?" barked Harris. "Did you see who it was?"

"No, but they'll be on the CCTV," she said.

"Have you called the police yet?"

Jenna shook her head. She picked up the phone and dialled the local station. She watched as Singh dropped the pieces of glass and put his head in his hands. He looked broken, and this was just the start.

Chapter 46

Stella hobbled her way to the submarine's dining room with Jennings obliging as a prop. She was still in pain, but felt that the sooner she got back on her feet the sooner she would make a recovery. She'd worked hard to get herself fit at the palace, and didn't want the effort going to waste by lying in bed for days on end. Also, she didn't want the men making plans without her.

"Are you sure about this?" said Jennings. "I mean, it'd be a lot easier having some food brought to you in your room."

"I'm fine," she said. "Stop fussing. I need to be up and about. I'm not going to get better slobbing about in bed am I?"

"That's not what the doctor said is it? He told you complete bed rest for at least three days."

"Doctors don't know everything. Sometimes the patient knows best. It's my body after all."

Jennings knew better than to continue the argument.

They entered the dining room and he helped her into a chair and sat down next to her. The waitress brought them some water. Kandinsky and Grady arrived moments later.

"It is good to see you up and about," said Kandinsky. "Although I thought that Dr Vashista had told you to stay in bed."

"I was bored. I felt like some company."

"And of course you do not want us making plans behind your back," Kandinsky grinned.

Jennings and Grady stifled a laugh.

Stella felt her insides burning, but instead of biting she brushed his comment aside with a simple, "Whatever."

The food as ever was excellent with a delicious bisque to start, followed by lamb cutlets, and a raspberry pavlova for pudding. Jennings wondered if it might be possible to forget about everything else and just spend the rest of his days floating around under the sea in luxury. He had everything he wanted right now:

good food, good drink, and of course the woman he loved sitting next to him. As he sat there with a full belly and a comfortable smile, helping to save the world seemed like an awful lot of trouble.

After dinner Kandinsky lit a cigar and started to discuss their immediate future. "Tomorrow we will leave the submarine and take a launch up the Tiber to Rome," he said to Jennings. "I have spoken to Pat Cronin and we will meet him and Stratton at the Parco dei Principi tomorrow."

"Fair enough," said Jennings. "But ultimately what are we going to achieve? The Vatican already has the symbols, and the whole world already knows about the Messiah."

"I do not know what we can achieve," admitted Kandinsky. "But there are only a few of us who know the truth, and therefore only a few of us who can stop this madness. I promised Desayer and Cronin a long time ago that I would help them as far as was possible, and I see no reason to go back on my word. Even if we are fighting a futile battle I am honour bound to do what I can."

"Of course," said a suitably guilty Jennings. "And I'll do the same."

"What about me?" said Stella. "Am I invited to this little get-together?"

"I had not thought you would be well enough to travel," said Kandinsky. "But I suppose there is no way of stopping you now. If you do not come with us you will probably try and swim to Rome."

Jennings laughed. Stella punched him on the arm.

"What about you, Grady?" said Jennings. "You've been pretty quiet. What do you think about it all?"

"I don't know. But I do know that things are looking bad, and that I'm needed back home. If anything does happen I want to be there with my family. Brooke needs me right now."

"So you're going back to the States?"

"Yes, buddy, I am."

Jennings felt suddenly deflated. He understood Grady's need to go home – in the same position he'd be doing the same thing – but for all his faults he'd grown used to having him around. "I guess you've got to do what you've got to do," he said.

There was brief silence, then Stella yawned. "I think I need some sleep ," she said.

"Do you want some help back to your room?" asked Jennings.

"Sure."

They said goodnight and made their way slowly back to Stella's quarters.

"Never mind," she said. "You've still got me."

"What do you mean?"

"I know you're upset about Grady going back home."

"Not really," said Jennings. "He's a good man and he's helped us a lot, but we'll get by without him."

Stella shook her head. Whatever she said there was no way Jennings was going to admit to anything. She could tell he was depressed though, it was only his male pride holding it in.

Jennings opened the door to her room and helped her in and onto the bed. "I'll see you in the morning," he said. "Have a good sleep."

"Aren't you going to stay for a while?"

Jennings shrugged. "I thought you were tired."

"I am a bit, but you can sit with me for a few minutes can't you? And I thought maybe you could try out your healing hands on me."

"My healing hands?"

"Yeah. I thought you said that monk attuned you when you were in the jungle."

"He did," said Jennings. "But I hadn't really thought about having healing hands. I'm not too sure if I've got that kind of power. To be honest the effects feel like they've worn off a bit now."

"There's no harm in giving it a try though, is there?"

"No, I suppose not. It's just—"

"Just what?"

"Nothing. Let's give it a go." Jennings had been about to question the wisdom of treating someone he was desperately in love with, but realized that saying anything would only implicate himself even further. He wasn't worried about doing her any harm, he just felt that the whole thing might be too emotional for him to deal with. Breaking down in front of her was the last thing he wanted to do.

Stella lay down across the bed with her arms by her side and closed her eyes. Jennings tried to remember what Stratton had told him about the ritual of Reiki. First he went to the dressing table and lit a couple of candles. Then, after turning the light off, he washed his hands thoroughly in the sink. He looked at Stella in the flickering flames and smiled. He was about to get started when he remembered that soft music was an aid. After flicking through the screen menu quickly he decided on a little Mozart.

"Are you still there?" asked Stella.

"Yeah, sorry," he said. "I'm just going to put some music on. It'll help you to relax."

"I'll be asleep by the time you get to me at this rate."

Jennings selected the music and then washed his hands again. He rubbed them to get the energy flowing and then placed them on Stella's forehead, fingers facing downwards over her eyes. Stratton had told him that he could hold his hands above the patient and the treatment would still work, but as it was his first go Jennings decided that contact might be best until he got the hang of things.

There was no initial spark of electricity as he laid his hands on her, just a gentle feeling of calm. Her skin felt slightly cold. He closed his eyes and concentrated on the flow of energy from his crown through to his palms. At first he could feel nothing, and he wondered if he was actually doing anything at all. But gradually he began to sense a charge channelling through, and his hands started to heat up. Within a couple of minutes he was lost in another world. The music seemed to be playing inside him.

After a while he moved his hands to Stella's crown and stayed there until instinct told him to move on. He continued like this down her body, channelling energy into each chakra until he felt the urge to move on again. He felt light like never before, as if his body was made of air. And although he was aware of Stella beneath him, he was no longer conscious of who she was or what he felt for her. Time and space blended into one as he lost himself in the moment.

Eventually he felt the impulse to stop and he slowly opened his eyes and withdrew his hands from Stella's body. The room was bathed in a heavenly haze and her face emitted a golden glow that rose at least two inches from her skin. He blinked a number of times to make sure it wasn't a trick of the light. His palms were still throbbing with heat, and when he placed them together he felt a shiver run through his spine, as if he'd just completed an electrical circuit. The sensation was so intense he felt like bursting into tears.

He stood there soaking in the atmosphere for almost ten minutes, before switching on the lights and blowing out the candles. Stella didn't move or make a sound. He bent over and kissed her lightly on the forehead then left the room, killing the lights once more and leaving it in peaceful darkness. He went back to his quarters and slept without thought.

Chapter 47

Jonathan Ayres looked out across the river to St Peter's Basilica, its illuminated dome dominating the skyline. A whisky in one hand and a cigarette in the other, he smiled and let the warm evening air brush his face. He pictured the scene in the square with the faithful eagerly awaiting another glimpse of their Messiah. Everything so far had gone to plan. Soon the whole Christian world would be behind them. He took one last drag of his cigarette and stubbed it out in the marble ashtray.

Inside the suite his bodyguards, Andrew Stone and Bob Davis, were watching the football on television. It wasn't his idea of a good night in, but he liked to defer to them occasionally just to keep them sweet. They knew far too much about him and his dealings to make enemies of.

"Is it nearly over yet?" he asked as he walked back in from the balcony.

"Just about boss," said Davis. "We're into injury time now."

"What's the score?" he asked, pretending to give a shit.

"0-0," said Davis.

"Fascinating," Ayres muttered under his breath.

The game finished and Stone and Davis went out onto the balcony for a post-match cigarette. Ayres reclaimed the sofa and switched over to the satellite news channel. He was less than impressed to find the initial reports focusing on the Mahdi and his appearances in Islamabad. They needed to get Christiano out into the world soon or they would lose momentum.

The telephone rang and Ayres picked up. It was the guard at reception announcing the arrival of Casper Fox, one of the Home Secretary's army of staff who never seemed to do anything but plant obstacles in his way. He said to bring him up.

Fox was in his late twenties with dark hair. He had an innocent-looking boyish face that disguised an ambitious, calculating mind. Fox by name, fox by nature. He was the type of sharp youngster that Ayres admired, but he was also a bloody nuisance if he wasn't on your side. And at the moment Ayres sensed they were almost certainly in opposite camps.

"Ah, Casper! How good to see you!" he said ebulliently, showing the young civil servant into the suite. "How are you doing? Did you have a good flight?"

Fox laid his briefcase on the dining table and sat down in one of the chairs. "It was alright, but it was bloody nightmare getting a ticket. Is there nobody in the world who doesn't want to come to Rome right now? We had to put pressure on BA to free up a couple of seats."

"Yes," said Ayres. "It's certainly popular. But can you blame people? It's not every day that the Son of God returns to earth, is it?"

Fox cast a dubious glance at the Prime Minister. "If indeed he is the Son of God, sir."

"You have your doubts?"

"Let's just say I'm keeping an open mind about the whole thing. I'll reserve judgement until I meet him myself."

"And what if I told you that he was the real thing? Would you not believe me?"

"I'd believe that you believe it, Prime Minister. But you're a devout Catholic and I'm not. You have far more reason to believe than I do. I'm an atheist, so it's going to take a hell of a lot more than your say so to convince me of his divine provenance. No offence, of course."

"None taken, Casper. We're all entitled to an opinion. Although I think that anybody who's been to the Vatican over the last few days would disagree with your scepticism. Anyway, I'm being terribly rude, can I get you a drink?"

"A mineral water would be great thanks."

Ayres plucked a bottle of *Evian* from the fridge and handed it to Fox. "There you go, old chap. If you want anything stronger let me know."

Fox opened the bottle and glugged half of it down. "That's better," he said, wiping his lips. "Now, let's get down to business."

Ayres sat down at the table opposite Fox. He didn't like the young man's arrogant attitude one little bit. But it was the same with most of the civil service. They had very little respect for political position because they knew it was really themselves who ran the country. They were generally polite, but there was always a lingering air of disdain, particularly if you weren't playing ball.

"So, what can I do for you, Casper?" he said with as much charm as he could muster.

"Well, Prime Minister, it's like this, to put it simply – we need you back in Britain."

"And you came all the way here to tell me that?"

"The Home Secretary has phoned you repeatedly today and you have not answered any of his calls."

"I've been busy, Casper. It's obviously not a national emergency otherwise he would have used the appropriate channels and got through."

"No, it's not a national emergency, well at least not yet. But it's certainly heading that way if you ask me."

"What do you mean?"

Fox took another gulp of water. "To put it mildly, the people of Britain are showing signs of unrest. Since the two religions announced their respective 'saviours' on Saturday there have been incidents all over the country. The ignorant element of the British public have used the news as an excuse to unleash what are essentially racist attacks. You know how sensitive things are already with the war on terror, this has just pushed people over the edge."

"But surely these are just isolated incidents," Ayres countered. "I haven't seen anything on the news."

"You wouldn't, would you?" said Fox. "All the airtime's being

taken up with these ridiculous religious claims. And besides, all
that's happened so far has been fairly localized and not really
worthy of national or international coverage. But all these little
episodes add up and the police are getting very nervous about
the whole thing. Every constabulary in the country is on alert."

Ayres took a sip of whisky. "But surely people should be
celebrating the coming of the Messiah," he said.

"Maybe in your little world they are, Jonathan," said Fox.
"Perhaps here in Rome, at the heart of the Catholic Church,
everything's nice and rosy. But we live in a country of cultural
diversity. Do you really think that having the world's two major
religions at loggerheads is good for the British public?"

"We are not at loggerheads," Ayres emphasised.

"Really?" Fox questioned. "I beg to differ. Both sides have, to
all intents and purposes, denounced the other as a fake. Nobody's
started a slanging match, but the accusation is pretty much
implied in everything either camp says. Are you telling me that
you think the Muslim's have a legitimate 'saviour' just like you."

"Of course they don't," said Ayres. "Their claims are prepos-
terous. Let's not forget that they only made the announcement in
retaliation to the Catholic Church's."

Fox sighed. "Listen, Jonathan, I really don't want to get into an
argument about who pulled whose hair first. The point I'm
making is that the situation is far more tense in Britain than most
other countries. We need you to come back home immediately
and make a statement to the British public. They need to hear a
strong leader telling them not to panic and that everything's
going to be okay."

"What exactly am I supposed to say. I'm not going to betray
my beliefs just to appease the public."

"Why not? You've done it most of your political career," Fox
said disparagingly.

Ayres boiled over and slammed his fist on the table, causing
his whisky to spill. "How dare you speak to me like that you

jumped up little fuck. Are you forgetting who the fuck I am. I am the fucking Prime Minister of Great Britain, and don't you fucking forget it!"

Fox didn't flinch. "I know exactly who you are, Jonathan. Or who you purport to be at least. And I know exactly who I am. I'm a civil servant and it makes no odds to me whose name is on the door of number 10. Governments will come and go over my working life, but I won't. I'll still be in Downing Street when you're a long-faded memory consigned to the history books of incompetence."

Ayres grabbed his fallen glass and went to the drinks cabinet. He poured himself another whisky. Fox was under his skin, but he wasn't going to give him the satisfaction of another outburst. He took a large gulp and returned to the table. "Listen, Casper," he said. "This bickering is getting us nowhere. I really do appreciate what you're saying about the situation back home, but I'm not sure you appreciate the importance of the situation over here. This is all about power and Britain's position in the new world order. Nothing will ever be the same again now that the Messiah has returned. The Church will wield more power than you can possibly imagine. Whether you like it or not politics is going to be governed by religion. I'm in an extremely good position over here as far as the Vatican is concerned and I don't intend to relinquish my influence just because a few yokels are too ignorant to distinguish between race and religion. The American President is here as well you know. Do you really want me to come back and let him grab all the attention? I think we've lost enough standing in the world over the last hundred years, without giving any more ground when we don't need to."

Fox yawned. "Look, Jonathan," he said. "If you don't come back there's every chance you won't have a country to lead. I don't know if you're aware of this, but there's also a certain leadership challenge to attend to. Brian Carrick is gaining support by the day. You're not going to stamp out his threat by swanning about in Rome. Like I said, it doesn't really make any difference to me who's running the country. But even I know that a change of leader at this juncture is not what the nation needs. You seem to think that I'm here as your enemy, when really I'm trying to help you."

"Carrick's full of hot air," said Ayres. "If the party want to get behind him then good luck to them. In a few weeks' time, once Christiano has been established as the Son of God, no-one will want to be voting for anybody but me. Mark my words, Casper – if I play this right over her then we're going to become a superpower. In fact, make that an ultrapower."

"There's too many ifs for my liking Jonathan, and the Home Secretary feels the same. What if Christiano is exposed to be exactly what he is – a street magician? What happens then? I'll tell you what happens – Britain becomes a laughing stock, and you become its chief jester."

Ayres gave the young man an icy stare. "Listen to me, Casper," he said. "I didn't get to my position by being a fool. If I thought for one minute that Christiano was a street magician then I wouldn't even contemplate the course of action I'm taking. But I've been there Casper. I've seen him with my own eyes. I've witnessed the blind seeing again; I've witnessed the paralysed walk out of their wheelchairs without even a limp. Healing people is no cheap trick. I'd like to see David Blaine try it."

Fox grunted and shook his head. "You're just seeing what you want to see, Jonathan. You're blinded by faith."

"If you think that then why don't you come over to the Vatican with me right now? I'll prove to you that he's no charlatan."

"It wouldn't work," said Fox. "The Vatican isn't a controlled environment. They could be up to any amount of trickery there. The only way that man could prove anything to me is if he came over to Britain, and in a controlled environment healed someone I knew to be genuinely disabled. That might go a little way to convincing me."

"He will be coming to Britain at some point, just not straight away."

"Well then, Jonathan, I guess this conversation is finished. You're obviously not going to see sense, so there's no point in me carrying on. But remember – if you don't come back with me then the consequences for you and the country will be dire."

"They'll be even more dire if I leave here now. I've made a decision, Casper, and I'm sticking to it. You might think you have all the answers, but you're certainly not God. So I suggest you go back and carry on as normal. If it keeps you happy I'll make a statement to the British public reassuring them of my intentions, and calling for calm."

"I don't really think that's going to help. You're already making a statement by being over here. You're saying that Catholicism is right and Islam is wrong. That isn't the sort of message you want to be sending a multicultural society. Can't you see what's happening?"

"The message I will be sending is one of peace and harmony. That is the Catholic way. That is the message of the Messiah. It can in no way be construed as inflammatory."

Fox sighed in defeat and picked up his briefcase. "I'm going to get some food downstairs and then I'm going back home. I've warned you what's going to happen, but if you refuse to listen then that's your lookout. There's nothing more I can do here."

Ayres patted him on the back. "Everything will be fine," he said. "You guys are just worrying too much. I'll be back in a couple of days when I've finished here."

Fox shrugged. "Whatever. But don't be surprised if you have nothing to come back to."

Chapter 48

Jennings stepped onto the dock and stretched his legs. It was a beautiful, cloudless morning, and the temperature was already into the seventies. He took off his baseball cap and wiped his brow with his sleeve, resisting the urge to fiddle with the false beard that was driving his skin mad. The disguise was probably slightly over the top, but he knew that he was still on Interpol's most wanted list and didn't want to take any more risks than he needed.

Stella was also incognito, but only with a baseball cap and sunglasses. Her body had made a remarkable recovery overnight, and although the pain hadn't entirely gone, she was able to walk around unaided. She looked up to the sky and basked in the freedom of the sun.

Kandinsky led them off the dock and onto the streets of Rome. The deserted cars had finally been reclaimed by their owners and the traffic was back to normal. The hustle and bustle of the city was a shock to Jennings' system. He'd spent so long away from civilization that the onslaught of horns and human voices took him by surprise. It was like stepping out of an isolation tank into a bar full of drunks.

"Are you alright?" asked Stella.

Jennings took a deep breath. "Yeah, I'll be okay. It's just a bit much. My head's not used to all this noise and activity."

"I know what you mean. I'm suffering from sensory overload myself. It's like being woken from a peaceful dream. How I managed in London all these years I'll never know. When you see things from a different perspective it makes you wonder."

They moved quickly and were soon out of the urban sprawl, and into the relative tranquillity of the Villa Borghese with its lush, verdant gardens and peaceful walkways.

"This is more like it," said Jennings. "I'm not sure I could have stood any more of that noise."

"Yeah, it's beautiful isn't it," said Stella. "I came here once on a school trip. I always wanted to come back. Pity about the circumstances though."

The Parco dei Principi Grand Hotel and Spa was situated towards the edge of the Villa Borghese. It was a byword for five-star luxury and outstanding cuisine. Kandinsky was on excellent terms with the owners and stayed there whenever he was in the city. He had rung the manager the night before and arranged to occupy his favourite suite.

Jennings opened the glass doors and stepped out onto the balcony. The view was nothing short of stunning, with St Peter's Basilica forming a proud and majestic focal point in the most historic of cities. He breathed in the warm air and smiled.

Grady came to join him. "It looks much better from up here doesn't it?" he said. "Without the noise and pollution it's almost beautiful."

"It is," Jennings agreed. "What time's your plane?"

"Seven o'clock this evening. Kandinsky's arranged for a limo to take me to the airport."

"It's alright for some."

"Yeah, it's good. I can't wait to see Brooke again. I've really missed her."

"Ah, you old softie," said Jennings giving him a friendly dig.

"You're not angry with me then?" said Grady.

"No, of course I'm not angry. I'd do the same thing in your position. You've got to look after your family, mate. And besides you're probably more of a hindrance than a help anyway."

"Fuck you," laughed Grady.

A little later Kandinsky called room service for lunch and ordered enough for Stratton and Cronin as well. He and Stella joined the other two at the balcony table.

"What time are they supposed to be here?" asked Jennings.

"About half past twelve," said Kandinsky.

Jennings looked back to the clock in the suite. "It's quarter to one now."

Kandinsky shrugged. "It was not an exact time. And besides, the traffic is murder in the city at this time of day."

"I guess so," said Jennings, none too convinced. He'd had an odd feeling in his stomach all morning. Every time he thought about Stratton a shadow fell over his soul. He hadn't said anything to the others for fear of causing needless worry, but as the time ticked by his sense of dread became greater. Kandinsky was right about the traffic of course, but surely Cronin would have taken that into account.

"I'm sure they'll be here in a minute," said Stella, perceiving Jennings' concern. "Try and relax."

The food arrived at one o'clock and they ate outside on the balcony. Jennings picked at some pasta and salad, but his appetite was waning by the minute.

"If it makes you feel better I will give Father Cronin a call," said Kandinsky. He picked up his mobile and speed-dialled the priest's number. Two seconds later he hung up. "It's gone straight to answerphone. I'll try the phone I gave Stratton." Once again the call failed.

At quarter to two Kandinsky phoned Cronin's direct line at the Vatican. There was no answer. He then tried Cardinal Desayer. Again there was no answer. He started to think that Jennings' worries might be justified.

"What should we do?" asked Stella.

"There's not a lot we can do," said Grady. "We're just going to have to wait for them to turn up."

Jennings stared blankly out across the city. "You can wait all you want," he said. "They're not coming. Something's happened."

Chapter 49

Stratton opened his eyes and tried to focus. The world was one big blur and his head a spongy mass of fuzz. The last thing he remembered was drifting off to sleep. What he did know was that he was no longer in the same place. He was sitting on a cold, hard chair with his legs fastened tight, and his hands uncomfortably knotted behind his back. He shook his head to try and restore some vision, but his eyes continued to see nothing but hazy, swirling grey.

He began to hear whispering voices. They grew louder until eventually he could make out a couple of English accents. He mumbled a groggy "Hello". There was no answer, and the voices fell silent.

A while later he heard a door open. Another person entered. After a brief exchange with the whisperers, footsteps approached Stratton's chair. He opened his eyes once more and tried to get some clarity. This time, instead of a grey mess, he could make out the shape of a person standing in front of him.

"Awake at last," said a man's voice. It was familiar but Stratton couldn't quite place it. "I thought you were going to sleep forever. Perhaps we were a little heavy-handed with your dosage. You can't be too careful with people who rise from the dead though." He held Stratton's head back and tipped some water into his mouth. "Have a drink, it'll help you come round."

Stratton gulped at the water and shook his head again. The man's face began to take shape in front of him. It was Jonathan Ayres. Stratton blinked heavily to make sure he wasn't seeing things.

"Surprised?" said Ayres.

"Not really," said Stratton. "I always thought you were a snake. I never voted for you."

"Never mind, millions did."

"Can I have some more water please?" asked Stratton.

Ayres obliged and he took a long drink. His eyesight was returning to normal and he surveyed his surroundings. He was sat in a corner of what appeared to be a shed. It was about twenty feet by ten feet, with corrugated walls and a concrete floor. It was lit by a single bulb on the far wall where two men were seated at a shabby table. They were both large and wearing suits, and Stratton assumed they were part of Ayres' security detail. Possibly the pair who had framed Jennings. To his left Pat Cronin was bound to a chair and still out for the count.

"Feeling better?" asked Ayres.

"Yeah," said Stratton. "I feel like I could run a marathon."

"You've still got a sense of humour. That's a good sign."

"What exactly do you want?" said Stratton.

"Good question," said Ayres. "For a start I want to keep you out of the way. We're at a critical point, and the last thing the Church needs is someone like you coming along and spoiling the party."

"Why haven't you killed me then?"

"Because I suspect that might be easier said than done. You're a bit of an enigma as far as we're concerned. I wasn't even sure if we'd be able to drug you. Also, I need you alive for a while longer to draw out any conspirators of yours who might want to put their oar in."

"I don't have any conspirators."

"That's not strictly true is it? You have the esteemed father here. And also, I suspect, the late Cardinal Desayer."

At the word 'late' Stratton's head dropped.

"Yes," said Ayres. "I'm afraid he had a heart attack in his sleep last night. It's a tragedy, but he was quite old. Still, he will be honoured by His Holiness for his services to the Church."

"People might wonder why your Messiah couldn't bring him back to life," said Stratton.

"Why would he bring him back to life? He has gone to serve in the Kingdom of God now."

"Whatever," Stratton snorted.

Ayres took a sip of water for himself. "And of course there's the small matter of your little friend Jennings. I can't have him running loose with all that he knows."

"Jennings?" said Stratton shaking his head in ignorance.

"Don't even go there," said Ayres. "I know a lot more than you think. He couldn't have disappeared without help and neither could you. You're all in it together with that Stella girl and this pseudo priest." He pointed at Cronin. "It's all worked out quite nicely really. We've had our eye on Desayer and his stooge for a long time, and now they've brought us a decent prize."

"Who is we exactly?" asked Stratton.

"Just a group of the faithful who want to keep Jesus' message clear and true. We can't have everyone going around being a Messiah now, can we? There would be anarchy across the globe."

"Clear and true?" said Stratton. "That's a fucking joke. It's called lying and keeping people in the dark. But that's what you do for a living isn't it?"

"People need to be led Stratton, you're an intelligent guy, you should understand that. And what I'm doing is no different from what you're trying to do is it? I mean, you're not about to unleash this great knowledge on the world are you? You're trying to keep it as secret as we are. So let's not be hypocritical about this."

"Don't try and turn this around Ayres. My intentions are completely different. This knowledge has to be kept secret because it's dangerous. As a race we're just not capable of utilizing it safely yet. But that doesn't mean that people should be kept in the dark as to its origins. What you're doing is pretending that Christiano's something he's not just to gain power. And the Muslims are doing exactly the same thing. I'm quite prepared to let the world know exactly where Jesus' power came from, and I intend to do so. I've got documentary evidence from St Thomas. People need to know that they can attain the spiritual heights of Buddha and Jesus."

"No Stratton, people need to know that they must obey God and his word. That is the only way to keep them in check. What we're doing is encouraging unity in mankind."

"What you're doing is starting World War III," said Stratton. "You and the Muslim's are dividing the world. As if things weren't bad enough before all this. How do you think this is going to end? With everybody saying 'live and let live'? No. It's going to end with man killing man over two very big lies."

Ayres gestured indifference. "I suppose there may be some conflict, but there's far more of us than there are of them. Christianity is the biggest religion in the world. We've got followers all over the globe. We've got the mightiest nations behind us. If you think a few countries in the Middle East are going to overcome us then you're living in cloud-cuckoo-land."

"It's not about who wins is it?" said Stratton. "It's about the devastation and loss of life."

"Casualties will be minimal I'm sure. Once this Mahdi has been exposed then they will have no choice but to accept Christiano as God's messenger on earth."

"Really? And how exactly are you going to expose him?"

"By killing him of course."

"You'll just make him a martyr."

"No. We'll be showing the world that he has no connection to God or Allah whatsoever. The true Messiah cannot be killed."

"A bit like Jesus?"

"No, this is different," said Ayres. "Jesus sacrificed himself. The new Messiah will not." He looked at his watch. "Anyway, time is pressing. I've got a meeting with the Pope. I'll be back later. If you want a drink of water, just ask my friends over there." He gestured to the men at the table. "If you're really nice to them they might even feed you some bread."

"You're too kind," said Stratton. He watched Ayres leave and then closed his eyes, his head groggy and exhausted from talking.

Chapter 50

Jennings paced up and down the suite wearing out the soft, gold carpet. It was 4.30pm and there was still no sign of Stratton or Cronin. Grady and Stella were sat in the vanilla and green living area, and Kandinsky was out on the balcony making more calls.

"Will you stop pacing about and come and sit down," said Grady. "I'm getting hypnotized watching you go up and down."

"Well don't look then," said Jennings.

"Grady's right," said Stella. "Come and have a rest. Sip some water, take some deep breaths – that sort of thing. It's what you'd be telling us to do."

"I think better when I'm on the go."

Stella rolled her eyes and left him alone.

Kandinsky came in from the balcony. His face didn't inspire hope. "I am afraid I have some bad news," he said grimly. "Apparently Cardinal Desayer is dead."

"What?!" said Jennings. "What happened?"

"He died in his sleep last night. Apparently he had a heart attack. The priest who answered his phone said that it was very peaceful."

"What priest? Why wasn't Cronin answering?" said Jennings. "He was the cardinal's assistant."

Kandinsky put a large hand on Jennings' shoulder. "Calm down," he said. "Come and sit for a while."

This time Jennings did as he was told.

Kandinsky continued his breakdown of the telephone conversation. "The priest I spoke to did not know the whereabouts of Father Cronin, but suggested that he was probably busy with funeral arrangements and the like. He said that he would get Cronin to call me back as soon as he was located. I know it is unsatisfactory, but I am afraid there is nothing we can do but wait."

"Busy with funeral arrangements," said Jennings. "What a

crock of shit. There's no way that Cronin and Stratton wouldn't have let us know what was going on."

"Of course not," said Kandinsky. "But like I said – there is nothing we can do. We cannot go storming into the Vatican making accusations."

Jennings got back up and went outside to the balcony for some fresh air. He closed his eyes and took some long, deep breaths from his diaphragm, just like Stratton had taught him. He had no idea why he was so edgy. Certainly the situation was bad, but he'd been through a lot worse and survived. His brain was telling him that his reaction was unhealthy, but his body was having none of it. Every time he tried to keep still and calm an internal force would take hold, agitating him and compelling him to move.

Stella came out and stood next to him, putting her hand on his arm. "What's gotten into you?" she asked. "You're a right jack-in-the-box today."

"I don't know. I just can't keep still. There's this whole load of energy flowing through me and I can't control it. If I'm still for more than half a minute I feel like I'm going to explode."

"Do you think it's got anything to do with the Reiki you gave me last night?" she asked.

Jennings thought for a moment. "I suppose it might," he said. "The problem is that Stratton's not here to help. He'd be able to tell me exactly why I'm like this. He'd probably be able to calm me down as well. I just wish we knew what was going on. I can't stand all this waiting around."

Stella gently stroked his back. She wanted to say something comforting, but it would have been a lie. She knew as well as Jennings that something was wrong. As a result of his treatment her senses were heightened like never before. She had woken up feeling alert and in tune, as if she'd been wired into a grid. She felt closer to Jennings than ever.

They stood in silence for a while, gazing out onto the city.

Stella's touch was soothing and Jennings finally began to relax. He wanted to grab her and hold her tight and never let her go. He was still playing with the idea when Grady joined them.

"Right then," he said. "I'm off."

"So soon?" said Jennings.

"Yeah. The limo's waiting for me downstairs. It's almost five now and the traffic's bad so I need to make a move. I just came to say so long."

"Well, I suppose if you really have to go," said Jennings.

"I do," said Grady. "I know that things aren't great, but I've already stayed away too long. There's a point where you've got to think about what's really important."

"I know, mate. You've got to do what you've got to do." He held out his hand. "Thanks for saving my life – again."

Grady took his hand and drew him in for a hug. "Not a problem, buddy. Not a problem."

After he'd gone Jennings sat down at the balcony table and looked sadly up at the sky.

"Are you alright?" asked Stella.

"Yeah, I'm fine. I just…I'm fine."

"You've still got me," she said. "I might not be as handsome as Grady, but I'll do my best."

Jennings laughed. "Very funny. I've just got used to having him around, that's all. He's a decent bloke, once you've got through all the macho bullshit anyway."

"Yeah, he's alright," Stella agreed. "Although I never though I'd say it. Let's not forget that he was quite happy to leave us to burn in hell last year at the cottage."

"You know what," said Jennings. "I'd completely forgotten about that. It doesn't seem like the same person though."

Inside the suite Kandinsky's phone rang. Stella and Jennings jumped out of their seats and listened at the balcony door, trying to get a handle on who the caller was and what they were saying. But Kandinsky's face and tone remained impassive. After a two minute conversation he hung up.

"Who was that? What's happening?" said Jennings excitedly.

"That was the priest I spoke to earlier – a Father Panduro. He said that he has located Father Cronin and that he has passed on a message for us to meet him at the Vatican later this evening."

"Well that doesn't sound suspicious, does it?"

"Of course it does," said Kandinsky. "But I do not feel we have any choice other than to accept the invitation. What else can we do?"

"Nothing I guess," said Jennings. "But if we go to the Vatican we're playing right into their hands."

"And if we don't we could be waiting here forever," said Stella. "If we go we'll at least find out what's happened to them."

"We will," said Jennings. "But walking into a trap may not be the best way forward. If we go then they've got all of us in one neat little package. There'll be no-one left who knows the truth."

"I thought you wanted to find out what'd happened to them?" said Stella.

"I do. But I'm trying to think objectively like Stratton now. Would he want us going in there blind?"

"Perhaps not," said Kandinsky. "But there is no doubt that they have been found out, and are either dead or being held captive. We have to do what we can. If that means putting ourselves in danger then so be it. Without Stratton the whole cause is lost. None of us can compete with the power at the Church's disposal."

Jennings sat down on the settee. He knew that Kandinsky was right, but he also knew that going to the Vatican was suicidal. Once they were through the doors it was pretty much a foregone conclusion that nobody would hear from them again. And what could they achieve even if they weren't captured? Nobody wanted to say it out loud, but the chances that either Stratton or Cronin was still alive were slim, bordering on non-existent. What was the point in risking everything just to satisfy their curiosity?

He racked his brains for a solution. A few moments later an idea came. "I'll go on my own," he said.

"What?" said Stella.

"I said I'll go on my own. There's no point us all walking into the lions' den, is there? If we all get caught then the truth is going to be lost."

"No it won't," said Stella. "Grady will still be around."

"Grady's got his own problems," said Jennings. "And besides, by the time he got round to saying anything it would be too late. He'd be one voice lost in a multitude."

"You are right," said Kandinsky. "And I think your plan is a good one. There is one small change that we should make though – it is I who should go to the Vatican. They know my name and are expecting me. And, no offence Jennings, but I am far more likely to come out alive than yourself."

Jennings looked up at the giant Russian and knew the truth in his words. If anyone was going to survive it was him.

Seeing that his statement had hit home Kandinsky continued. "I will get my people up here and have them inject a transmitter under my skin. Then you will be able to track my every move. I will also let them know that in my absence Jennings here speaks for me. Then if anything happens you will still have a huge network at your disposal."

"But without you…" Stella started.

Kandinsky held up his hand. "There is nothing more to discuss," he said. "I have spoken."

Chapter 51

It was almost an hour after Pat Cronin came round that his senses finally returned to something resembling normality. His head was still throbbing, but he could see and hear, and that was a good start. Next to him Stratton was either asleep or dead, he couldn't tell which. He called to the men at the table and asked them to bring him some more water. The bigger of the two wandered over with a bottle and put it to Cronin's lips. He glugged down as much as his weakened system could hold.

When he was done the man rejoined his companion at the table and carried on their game of cards. They had talked between themselves, but had said nothing to Cronin apart from offering him water and bread. He had tried to engage them in conversation without success. All he could tell was that they were English and professional.

Beside him Stratton stirred and opened his eyes. Cronin was hit by a wave of relief. "I thought you might be dead," he said.

"No," said Stratton. "Well, not yet anyway. Although from what I remember death's a lot more pleasant than this."

"Any idea where we are?" asked Cronin. "I've tried speaking to Tweedledum and Tweedledee over there, but they're not the most communicative."

"I've got no idea where we are," said Stratton. "But I do know we're here as guests of the Church and the British Prime Minister. We had a little visit from him when you were still out for the count. I'm afraid we've been found out."

"How much do they know?"

"Just about everything. They've been onto your boss, the cardinal, for ages apparently. I guess they were waiting to see if he turned anything up before they did. It wouldn't surprise me if they've had him watched for years. Probably bugged his chambers and his phones. I can't imagine there's a lot they don't know about."

"Fuck it!" said Cronin. "We were so careful. I've lost count of the amount of times I've swept that place for bugs. But I guess with all the money at their disposal they can always keep ahead of the game. Technology just moves on far too quickly."

"Yeah, it does," agreed Stratton. "There's no way you could have kept on top of it. In this day and age if somebody wants to keep tabs on you there's no way to stop them."

"So where is the cardinal?" asked Cronin.

Stratton fell silent.

"What?" pressed Cronin. "What's happened?"

"He's dead," said Stratton. "They killed him."

Cronin bowed his head.

Stratton continued. "For what it's worth I don't think he suffered. The official line is that he had a heart attack in his sleep, and it's probably not far from the truth. A quick injection I expect."

"It doesn't make me feel any better," said Cronin. "I was responsible for him. He paid me to look after things. I should have been more alert to the danger."

"You couldn't have stopped them."

"I could have at least tried. I should have been more cautious. I mean, what sort of fool allows himself to be drugged in his sleep?"

"I've been asking myself the same question," said Stratton. "But we've both been caught napping and there's fuck all we can do about it."

Chapter 52

The sun was setting and the streetlights were starting to flicker on. Tariq walked down the Middleton Road with his hands in his pockets and his shoulders hunched nervously, his face covered by a hood. The traffic was unusually sparse and the air was heavy with intent. He hadn't wanted to leave the house, but when Jenna had called him his heart had been unable to refuse. There was no gauntlet he wouldn't run just to see her heavenly face.

He passed the deserted Co-op and turned left at the traffic lights, looking nervously across to the railway bridge as he did so. A lone car came towards him and trundled past eerily like a mechanized tumbleweed. There were no pedestrians and there was no sound of trains. He'd never known the town this quiet. The silence of the streets unnerved him.

The Causeway seemed equally destitute, with the exception that every now and then he could see shadows of human life projected through light curtains. It gave him some comfort to know that he was not entirely alone, but at the same time made him feel more isolated. He proceeded cautiously, his eyes and ears alert to every tiny movement or sound.

Halfway down he stopped and turned. His ears had detected what he thought were footsteps. He peered into the orange dusk, but could see nothing except for parked cars and houses. After a brief wait to make certain, he carried on and upped his pace. The footsteps sounded again, this time more hurried. Once more he halted to check, and once more he saw nothing.

He was only a hundred yards from Jenna's flat when he finally saw them: a group of five sprinting towards him noiselessly, their faces covered by scarves. By the time he had a chance to react they were almost upon him. Without thought he sprang away down the path. He had never been the fastest of runners, but fear and adrenaline spurred him on with a rapidity that he would have previously considered impossible.

As he approached the flats it occurred to him that he would have no chance of opening the communal door before his pursuers bore down. He had no choice but to bypass his destination and carry on running. With no more than a rapid glance he hurtled past Jenna's building and off into the darkening evening. He couldn't hear the gang behind, but he could sense them and they weren't losing ground. He made a decision to swerve into the small park and head back through to the main road.

The park was cloaked in near blackness. The one lamp in the centre had blown, and the only light to guide him was that shining through from the Middleton Road a hundred yards ahead. It was here that the relentless effort began to tell and he started to tire. He gritted his teeth and tried to force one last thrust to propel him through the darkness. Behind him the gang prepared to strike.

The next thing Tariq knew he was tumbling forward in an uncontrollable dive. He'd been tripped from behind. He blindly held out his hands to break the fall. Hitting the path at speed he rolled forward and sideways onto the grass. Before he could get his bearings the kicks started to fly in. Cradling his head in his arms he curled himself into a ball and tried to weather the storm.

The blows were fast and vicious and pointed, and came from every conceivable angle. The pain of the constant barrage to his kidneys and back quickly became unbearable. He started to scream loudly, but this only encouraged his tormentors to rain down harder. Boots penetrated his defences and hammered into his face. The beating continued mercilessly until he thought he was going to pass out. Then, with a solitary word the blows ceased.

"Enough," said a gruff voice.

Tariq didn't move. He could feel them stood around him, watching and waiting. He heard one of them clear his throat loudly and hawk a pool of spit. It landed on Tariq's temple and dribbled through his fingers into his eye.

"Muslim scum," said the same gruff voice as before.

It was at least five minutes before Tariq dared to move. He thought he had heard the gang leave, but wanted to make certain. During this time he just lay there in silence dreading the start of another attack. Eventually, convinced that he was on his own, he lowered his guard and sprawled out on the grass taking in shallow gasps of air. The taste of blood swamped his mouth and his two front teeth wobbled in battered gums. His steamrollered body ached with every breath.

Reaching tentatively into his trouser pocket, he withdrew his mobile phone and held it up in front of his watery eyes. The screen was blurry, but he managed to find the right buttons to speed-dial Jenna. He put the phone to his ear and waited.

"Hello honey," said a comforting voice. "I've been wondering where you were."

Tariq tried to rasp a reply, but his throat was clogged with blood.

"Hello," Jenna repeated. "Hello? Tariq?"

Tariq cleared his throat weakly and spat out some blood. "Park," he whispered. "Park."

The phone slid from his hand and he blacked out.

Chapter 53

Arman Kandinsky strode purposefully up to the large arched gates and entered into a brief discussion with one of the Swiss Guards on sentry duty. He stated his name and announced that he had an appointment with Father Cronin. The guard had a brief gawp at Kandinsky's size and then radioed control. After a swift conversation the gate opened and he escorted the Russian in. He led him across a large courtyard and then through a double oak door. Inside the building Kandinsky followed his guide down a maze of imposing corridors. He looked around as they walked, impressed but not overawed by the artwork and architecture. It was striking, but not half as inspiring as the Winter Palace in Saint Petersburg, he thought. He did, however, very much like the guard's multicoloured livery. The red, yellow and blue striped uniform could easily have been over-the-top kitsch, but the tone and blend was such that it exuded imperious grandeur. A reminder of a lost age.

The guard showed Kandinsky into Cronin's office and asked him to wait while he located the priest. Kandinsky sat down and drummed his fingers on the desk, knowing full well that the last person who'd be arriving was Cronin. He patted his waistband, reassuring himself that if trouble emerged then he at least had his tranquilizer gun to take a few down.

It was only a few minutes before a priest – who wasn't Cronin – arrived.

"Hello," he said holding out a hand. "I'm Father Panduro. You must be Mr Kandinsky."

Kandinsky stood up and shook the outstretched hand firmly.

Panduro looked up and smiled, trying to hide his fear. "I'm afraid Father Cronin is unavoidably delayed," he said. "He shouldn't be longer than ten minutes though. I'll make you a coffee if you like."

"That would be lovely," said Kandinsky.

Panduro put the kettle on and fumbled about in the cupboard for some coffee mugs. "I'm afraid it's been all go around here lately, as you can probably imagine. Our whole world's been turned upside down by the appearance of Christiano. After some trying years, suddenly overnight we're popular again."

"I expect you are," said Kandinsky, only half listening.

"There didn't seem to be a lot of room for faith in this modern society," Panduro continued. "People were more interested in worshipping footballers and pop stars than God. Congregations had dwindled to almost nothing in some areas of the world. The only way to fill a church would have been to have Madonna or Beyonce perform. Of course, that's all turned on its head now."

Kandinsky watched Panduro's hands carefully as he spooned in the coffee granules.

"Would you like milk and sugar, Mr Kandinsky?"

"No, thank you. Black will be fine."

Panduro poured the boiling water and stirred. Kandinsky's eyes didn't leave the mug. The priest handed him his drink and sat down in Cronin's chair opposite. Kandinsky sniffed the coffee and placed the mug on the desk.

"Yes, exciting times," said Panduro. "Exciting times. Of course I never dreamt in a million years that something like this would happen, well not in my lifetime. I knew that God would return to us eventually, but maybe not quite so soon. Although if you think about it, we've come to a point as a society where we probably need his guidance more than ever. What do you think?"

Kandinsky stared at Panduro impassively. By the sound of his prattling the priest was nervous and trying to buy time. What concerned him more, however, were the contents of his drink. He hadn't noticed anything suspicious in its making, but that in no way meant that it was safe to imbibe.

"Well?" said Panduro.

"I am not sure what to think," said Kandinsky. "Everything has happened very quickly. And let us not forget that the Mahdi has appeared for Islam. It seems very strange that two saviours have appeared at the same time, no?"

"Let us not forget that Christiano appeared first," said Panduro. "The only suspicious thing is that the Muslims announced this 'Mahdi' a few hours later. It was patently just an attempt to deflect attention. There is no substance to their claims. I'm sure the world will see him for what he is sooner or later. Probably sooner."

Kandinsky looked at his watch. "How long did you say Father Cronin was going to be?"

"He'll be here imminently," said Panduro. "Like I said, we're all rather busy at the moment. And what with the unfortunate death of Cardinal Desayer, I'm afraid Father Cronin has more on his plate than most. Have a drink and relax, he'll be here soon."

Kandinsky watched Panduro sip some coffee, but decided to stay away from his own. The room fell briefly silent.

"So, Mr Kandinsky, what is your line of work, if you don't mind me asking?"

"I am a businessman."

"Really? What sort of business?"

"I have many businesses," he said bluntly.

Panduro realized that the conversation was going nowhere and began once again to talk about the Church. He carried on waffling until eventually Kandinsky could stand it no longer. "Father," he said firmly, holding his palm up. "That is enough. Where is Father Cronin? I really must speak to him."

Panduro feigned indignation. "Well really, Mr Kandinsky, I told you – he'll be here shortly."

Kandinsky shook his head. "Do not lie to me, Father. I am not a fool, and you should not treat me like one. We both know what is going on here. So I ask you once again – where is Father Cronin? What have you done with him?"

"I really don't know what you're—"

Before Panduro could finish his sentence Kandinsky left his

chair and reached over the desk. He wrapped an enormous hand around the priest's throat. He had promised himself not to use violence, but the conversation was going nowhere fast. "I ask you once again – where is Father Cronin?" Panduro said nothing. Kandinsky increased his grip. "Where?" he growled.

Panduro's eyes shot to his left. Kandinsky let go his grip and whipped round about face. In front of him, just three feet away, were two Swiss Guards, each brandishing an Uzi. Before they could react he'd bridged the distance between them and slammed their heads together with his massive palms. They fell to the floor.

Kandinsky closed the office door and locked it. "Nice try," he said to the terrified Panduro. "But you will have to do a lot more to get the better of Arman Kandinsky. Now, where is Father Cronin?"

"You can't escape you know," said Panduro. "This room's being monitored by CCTV. There'll be more guards here in seconds."

"Bring them on," said Kandinsky. "They still have to get into the room. That gives me plenty of time alone with you, my friend." He stepped towards Panduro with intent.

"Alright! Alright!" Panduro yammered. "They took him a couple of days ago. I don't know where. Listen, I'm just a priest, I don't really know anything about all this. I'm just doing what I'm told."

"Oh yes," said Kandinsky. "I am sure you are very innocent in all this." He stepped across the window and sized up his escape options. They were about seven metres up and the drop onto concrete looked less than inviting.

His thoughts were interrupted by shouting and banging at the office door. The guards were trying to break their way in. For a moment it occurred to Kandinsky to pick up one of the Uzis and shoot them through the wood, but he remembered his talks with Stratton and made the choice not to. Instead he pulled the dart-gun from his waistband and positioned himself at the side of the door. He figured that if there were only another couple of guards he might have a chance to put them out. It could buy him a little more time with which to question the reticent Father Panduro. There was no question of leaving without more information about Cronin and Stratton.

It only took ten seconds for the guards to break through. Three of them stormed in at once, giving Kandinsky little time. He shot the first one in the neck, but before he could aim again the whole room was swarming with bright uniforms. He thought briefly about making a fight of it, but with so many guns trained on him he had no choice but to surrender. He dropped his weapon and lifted his arms above his head.

Father Panduro stepped from behind the desk and walked over to his new hostage. In his hand was a syringe. He dragged one of Kandinsky's arms down and injected him. The last thing Kandinsky heard was "Goodnight".

Chapter 54

When Tariq finally came round he was still lying on the grass in the dimly-lit park. A voice was calling his name from afar. His eyes felt like they had been glued shut, but he managed to open them just enough to get a glimpse of the outline of Jenna's face.

"Tariq," she said, her voice growing closer. "Can you hear me?"

Tariq nodded.

"I've called 999. The police and ambulance will be here soon. I love you." She touched his face softly and bent down and kissed him on the forehead.

Tariq closed his eyes, the effort of keeping them open being too much. It didn't matter anyway, he knew Jenna was with him and that was enough. The pain, if anything, had got worse, and even breathing caused him agony. Every time he drew air into his lungs, his chest and back protested with a swathe of stabbing needles. The world around seemed distant.

Jenna looked down at her stricken love through watery eyes. His call had almost sent her into shock, only necessity had held her nerves together. She instinctively knew the park he meant and had slipped on a pair of trainers and run down there. She should have phoned the police before she left the flat of course, but she had been so preoccupied that the thought hadn't registered. When she'd found him lying there, she had at first feared he was dead. A quick feel for his pulse had allayed that fear, although it was faint and decidedly weak. It was only then that she'd called the emergency services. She cursed herself for being so negligent. If he didn't make it, she didn't know what she'd do.

Jenna had never been on a first-aid course, but she'd seen enough episodes of *ER* and *Casualty* to know that talking to the patient was a great help. She squeezed Tariq's hand gently and tried to think of something to say. "Help will be here soon," she started, reassuringly. "I think I can hear the sirens now. Please try and keep awake, I don't know what I'd do if anything happened. We've got such a lot of things to do together."

Tariq tried to force a smile. He wanted to hold on but his spirit was fading quickly. The last thing he heard was the sound of sirens.

Chapter 55

Jennings and Stella watched the screen intently over the operator's shoulder. The dot indicating Kandinsky's position had been static inside the Vatican for over half an hour. In the absence of a telephone call they had to assume that he had been waylaid.

"This is ridiculous," said Jennings. "I knew he shouldn't have gone in there alone. He's wasted himself for nothing."

"We don't know that for certain," said Stella. "We'll have to wait and see what happens. Just because he hasn't moved doesn't mean he's dead. He may just be talking."

Jennings turned away from the screen. He appreciated Stella's optimism, but felt it was probably misplaced. And with Kandinsky out of commission it left just the two of them. He wasn't sure if he was ready for the responsibility.

He was just about to pour himself a coffee when there was a knock on the door of the suite. He strode over and looked through the eyeglass. He was met with a familiar sight that warmed his heart.

Opening the door he gave a broad smile. "Grady!" he said. "You're back. What's happened?"

Grady stepped in and shut the door behind him. "I changed my mind. I knew that you'd be lost without me, and I just couldn't put you through it."

Jennings laughed. "But seriously," he said. "What's going on?"

Grady looked affronted. "That *is* what's going on, buddy. I was in the departure lounge watching the news and it hit me that I needed to stay."

"But what about Brooke and the bump?"

"Brooke was the one who convinced me to stay," said Grady. "I called her from the airport. She knows all about what's happening over here and she said that you guys needed me more than she did. Things haven't kicked off over there like they have in Europe. The Muslim community's proportionally much smaller so there's not so much of a conflict of interest." He paused briefly, a sad look crossing his face. "Anyway, I'm here now, so get me up to speed on what's happening."

"Are you sure you're alright mate?"

"I'll be fine. I just miss her, that's all."

Jennings poured some coffees and then joined Stella and Grady in the living area. The return of his friend had lifted a huge weight from his shoulders.

"So come on – what's happening then?" said Grady.

Jennings handed him a coffee and sat down next to Stella. "Kandinsky's gone to the Vatican to find out what's going on," he said.

"That was a good idea," said Grady. "Straight into the lions' den."

"There wasn't much choice," said Stella. "It was either that or sit around here doing nothing. He spoke to a priest claiming to have a message from Father Cronin. We knew it was a trap, but we didn't have anything else to go on. He's got a transmitter under his skin so we're tracking him with that."

"We'll be tracking him all the way to the morgue," said Grady.

Stella shook her head and sighed. "You certainly know how to lift people's spirits."

"Sorry," said Grady. "I'm tired and I'm not thinking. There probably wasn't anything else you could do. And if Kandinsky was happy to be the fall guy then I guess it was the best option. I just don't like this whole situation, I feel like we're too exposed. They seem to be calling all the shots."

Jennings nodded. "I know how you feel. The problem is we've got no idea exactly how much they know."

Grady glugged a large mouthful of coffee, trying to stimulate his brain into gear. "We have to assume they know everything," he said. "There's no point sitting around thinking we're safe. They may have been watching Desayer and Cronin for years, and if that's the case they're going to have all the information they need. Those two might think they've been careful, but if an organization as powerful as the Vatican wants to keep tabs on you then there's not much you can keep secret. They'll have listened to every phone call, read every email, bugged their offices and their quarters. Nothing is safe nowadays. You can't have a piss without someone somewhere in the world knowing." He paused. "Sorry if I'm being too cynical."

"No, you're right," said Jennings. "They probably do know everything, and we've been pretty foolish thinking anything else. The question is now though – what can we do?"

"Much as I don't like it," said Grady, "I think we're going to have to sit here and wait until we've got something to go on. It's possible they know about us, but if they knew where we were they'd have been here by now. Let's just see if Kandinsky makes it out of there before we start panicking."

Jennings finished his coffee and went out to the balcony once more. The sun was setting and the city was bathed in a rich orange glow. The air was starting to cool, but it was fresh and invigorating. He was about to smile when he looked across to St Peter's Basilica and felt a shudder run down his spine. It was still an imposing sight, but whereas earlier it had filled him with wonder, it now imbued him with a sense of unease. In the soft evening light the dome appeared to crackle with a sinister scarlet hue. As he focused more intensely the aura grew larger, saturating the whole of Rome with a flood of deep red. Jennings felt himself being swept away on a tide of evil, strangled and stifled by the terrible onslaught of power. His throat constricted and he began to struggle for air. Choking and spluttering he fell to his knees and tried to cry for help.

Stella glanced out to see what Jennings was up to and saw him flailing on the ground. Racing to the balcony she knelt down, put an arm round his shoulder, and tried to steady him. "He can't breathe!" she yelled at Grady, who had followed her out.

"Do you know the Heimlich Manoeuvre?" asked Grady. Stella nodded. "Well use that then. Sounds like he's choking on something."

Stella went to move her arms around Jennings' ribcage but he shook his head violently. "No," he spluttered. "No." And then, after a few more coughs, "I'll be alright."

He nudged Stella gently aside and continued to hack away until the fit finally faded. He spat a small pool of saliva onto the floor and took some deep breaths.

"Are you okay?" asked Grady.

Jennings nodded. "Yeah, I'll be fine. I just had a bit of a turn, that's all."

"A *bit* of a turn," said Grady, raising an eyebrow.

"I told you, I'll be just fine. Stop fussing."

"No problem, buddy. I'll just go and finish my coffee." He went back inside leaving Jennings and Stella alone.

"That was a bit rude," said Stella. "He's only trying to help you know."

"I know. I just don't want a lot of fuss. I'll apologize."

"So what happened then?" she pressed. "It looked like more than 'just a bit of a turn' from where we were standing."

Jennings pulled himself up onto one of the chairs. "I don't really know what happened," he said. "I was looking out over the skyline and I suddenly felt like I was being suffocated. The whole city turned red in front of my eyes. It started from over there." He pointed to the Basilica. "Whatever's going on in the Vatican, it's going to be disastrous for everybody."

"So you had a vision?"

"I suppose so. I'm not sure what to call it. It's more of a feeling than anything else. I've been opened up to something I don't really understand. I'm sensitized to everything around me."

Stella looked and saw the confusion in his eyes. She wanted to help, but didn't know how. She was about to reach out and touch him when Grady's voice carried through from the suite.

"You'd better come in, you guys," he hollered. "Kandinsky's on the move."

Chapter 56

Inside the Vatican two of the Swiss Guard guided a hospital trolley down a corridor. On top, covered by a white sheet, was the body of an extremely large man. Christiano stepped out of his room and watched them go by, wondering what had happened and why he hadn't been sent for.

"Excuse me," he said.

The guards paid no attention.

"Excuse me," he repeated. This time louder.

The guard at the rear stopped and turned around. "What?" he said sharply.

Unfazed by the guard's tone Christiano pressed on. "What has happened to this man?"

"He's dead."

"How?"

"I don't know," the guard grunted. "You'll have to ask Cardinal Vittori, we're just moving the body that's all." He turned to face the front and moved on.

Christiano watched them down the hall with a scowl and then made his way to the gate to pick up Sophia. He had been in a good mood, but the guard's rudeness had got under his skin. Who the hell did he think he was talking to him like that? He was the Messiah, not some errand boy. His rage built up as he walked, and by the time he reached the entrance he was determined to have the guard in question removed from his duties. It was only when he saw Sophia that he calmed down, her beauty dissipating his anger like a summer breeze.

"Are you okay?" she asked.

"Yes, I'm fine. In fact now that you're here I'm more than fine." He smiled and took her arm and led her back through the building.

Christiano's quarters consisted of a spacious living room, a bedroom and a bathroom. It was light and airy with a mixture of antique furniture and modern appliances. He had a fridge full of soft drinks and snacks, and if he wanted anything substantial to eat all he had to do was phone down to the kitchens. In fact, whatever he wanted was only a phone call away.

Tonight he had ordered a special meal. He was leaving for New York in the morning and wanted to make his last evening with Sophia a memorable one. After a vast amount of cajoling and blackmail Vittori had finally agreed that he could invite her for dinner, on the condition that she was gone by eleven o'clock at the latest. Christiano had said she would be, but wasn't going to be watching the clock on the cardinal's account.

Sophia sat down at the table and Christiano poured her a glass of wine. She sipped at it and then took a larger mouthful. "Wow! This is good," she said. "What is it?"

"It's from the cardinal's private estate in Tuscany," said Christiano pouring himself a glass. "I managed to persuade him to let me have a bottle. It is very special to him"

"I can see why," said Sophia. "Although I thought he would have been honoured to give you a bottle – even a case."

"Perhaps," said Christiano. "But I don't like to take advantage. It's not why I'm here."

"Of course not," said Sophia. "I didn't mean to imply anything."

"I know you didn't, and there is no need to explain yourself to me. You can say anything you like." He smiled at her and then looked away shyly.

After some antipasti of olives, cheese and bread, the waiter brought in beluga caviar and toast. Christiano opened a bottle of Cristal and poured a glass for Sophia.

"Are you not going to have any?" she asked.

"No, not tonight," he said. "We have to be away early in the morning. And besides I am not a great drinker, a glass of wine will be enough for me."

Sophia layered some caviar onto her toast and took a bite,

washing it down with some champagne. "You didn't have to go to all this trouble you know," she said. "I would have been happy with a carbonara and some bread. This all seems a bit grand."

"I just wanted to spoil you."

Sophia took his hand. "I think you've spoilt me enough already. You've given me the greatest gift that anyone could. I don't think you realize how much it means for me just to be able to walk again. All this stuff," she gestured to the food and drink on the table, "it means nothing really. It looks lovely and tastes divine, but it's just show. I might come from a very rich family, but I haven't been brought up to worship money or anything it buys. I like being with you because you give me something that money can't buy."

"I know," said Christiano. "But I wanted to make this special for you, as a man should for a woman. I wanted to make it romantic. I am flesh and blood just like everyone else you know. I may have amazing powers, but I am still only a man."

"You're not just a man," she said. "You're the Messiah. But it's very flattering that you still want to impress me. I shall enjoy the meal in the spirit that is meant and try to forget who you are."

"Like I said, I am just a man."

After a main course of sea bass and a dessert of panna cotta they left the table and sat down in the living area. Sophia watched Christiano as he poured the coffees, and felt warm in her heart. She still couldn't quite believe what was happening, and regularly had to take a step back and think about the situation logically. Ever since the day she met him her life had been a blur. One minute she was a lonely soul confined to a wheelchair, and the next she was running about in ecstasy, her heart exploding with hope. The miracle of movement had been enough to cope with, but the arrival of the Messiah had been something else.

And yet for all his divine qualities, there was something incredibly human about him. When they saw each other or chatted online the conversation was very rarely about God and humanity, it mainly revolved around mundane things like music and film and television, or sport and hobbies. It was really just like a regular friendship. Of course, it was slightly more than a friendship, there was no denying it. Even when she had first seen him, before she knew who or what he was, she had been instantly attracted to him. It wasn't just his dark good looks, or his deep brown eyes, that had moved her, it was also his shyness and vulnerability. He had seemed very much like a boy masquerading in a man's body, and even knowing what she did now he still had the innocence that brought out her protective instinct. Part of her wished that he wasn't the Son of God.

"I wish you could come with me," said Christiano, gazing at her over the top of his coffee cup.

"I wish I could too," she said. "But you're going to be really busy, and I guess I'd just get in the way."

"You could never be in the way. It's just that Cardinal Vittori feels that I would be better off without any distractions. I don't think you are a distraction, I think you are good for me. You help me to relax. You help me to think straight. You treat me like a normal person."

"Because that's how I see you most of the time. Sometimes it's a bit weird of course – when I think about it, and when I see you on the television – but generally you're just Christiano."

"And that is who I am at heart, who I feel like. I am not this Messiah that people see."

"But you are," she said. "You are him as well."

Christiano hung his head. "Am I?" he said. "Am I really? I can certainly heal people, but is that enough? I don't have any real answers. I cannot tell them what is right and what is wrong. It's like they expect me to lay God's laws down for them, and I really don't think I can."

"But surely God must talk to you," she said. "He must tell you what his purpose is."

Christiano looked into her eyes and desperately wanted to tell her the truth, but the voice of Vittori and the position of the Church suddenly came back to him and he realized that he was saying too much. "It is not as simple as that. Even I do not know the whole picture or his ultimate intention. He speaks to me in many ways, but it is not even for the Son to know the Father's mind wholly. I am but one extension of his will." He sipped at his coffee, secretly pleased with his ambiguous explanation.

Sophia nodded as if understanding. "Does he speak to you all the time?"

"No," said Christiano shaking his head. "But he is with me all the time. As he is with you and the rest of humanity. He only talks to me when the need arises."

"Has he spoken about me? What does he think about me?"

Christiano smiled. "He thinks you are the most beautiful thing he ever created." He paused and looked at her. "And so does his son."

Sophia blushed and looked away. "You're teasing me."

"No, I am not. If you could see the world through my eyes then you would know that I'm not." He reached out and caressed her cheek, the warmth of his hand making her shudder.

She turned back and stared into his eyes, feeling an irresistible urge to draw his lips to her own. They held each other's gaze briefly before moving together for a tentative kiss. Sophia felt her whole body tingle. The kiss grew more passionate until its intensity forced her to pull away.

"Are you okay?" asked Christiano. "I am sorry if I have offended you."

Sophia smiled and shook her head. "No, you haven't offended me at all. It was beautiful." She felt herself starting to cry. She wrapped her arms around his neck and hugged him.

The embrace continued, neither of them wanting to let go.

"I really want you to come with me," said Christiano.

"I know," she said. "And I really want to come too."

They pulled apart and gazed at each other once more.

"Perhaps you should have another word with Cardinal Vittori," said Sophia, clutching his hand.

"I could do," said Christiano. "But I think his mind is made up. I've tried everything in my power to persuade him, but he just won't budge."

"You don't have to do everything he says do you? I mean, who exactly is the Messiah here?"

Christiano thought for a moment, debating how to phrase his answer. "I am the Messiah," he said. "But I am here to serve, not to command. Cardinal Vittori has guided me well so far and I must trust in his judgement. There is a lot more at stake here than our feelings alone. I think we must respect his decision, however hard it might be."

Sophia kissed him. "You're right of course," she said. "I was just being selfish. There is a whole world out there that needs you. And we can still keep in touch can't we?"

"Of course we can. Every day. And it will not be long before I am back. And who knows, if things go well Vittori might relent and you will be able to join me." He smiled at her and she kissed him once more.

Savouring the touch and taste of her lips he wished that the moment would never end. But he knew that it had to. He also knew it was down to Vittori. Sophia's words started ringing in his ears. In a way she was right – who exactly was the Messiah here?

Chapter 57

Stella and Jennings went back inside the suite and joined Grady and the operator, who were in front of the screen scrutinizing a detailed map of Rome. The red dot indicating Kandinsky had left the Vatican and was on the move straight down the Via della Conciliazone.

"Is he in a car or is he walking?" asked Jennings.

"It is difficult to tell," said the operator. "He is moving slowly, but it may just be the traffic." He studied the screen for another thirty seconds. "The movement is very staccato, so I would suggest he is in a vehicle."

After a while the dot gathered pace and turned left, following the river and finding its way onto the Lungotevere dei Mellini.

Jennings watched the map intently and said, "He could be coming back here I guess. He's headed in the right direction."

"Perhaps," said Grady. He paused and then pointed. "No, look – he's missed the bridge, they've gone straight on to Michelangelo."

Jennings saw that Grady was right and resigned himself to the fact that Kandinsky was headed elsewhere. The dot moved onwards up the river road passing bridge after bridge, each one taking it further away from the Villa Borghese.

"Shouldn't we get out there and start to follow him?" said Stella.

"Let's just wait a bit," said Grady. "See how it pans out. He's not that far away yet. Only a couple of miles. If they start to head out of the city then we'll have to do something. There's no point tailing them and making them suspicious. We know exactly where he is. Nobody's getting away."

The dot eventually ground to a halt on the Lungotevere della Vittoria. From there it moved into a mass of trees by the river. After that it remained motionless.

"Right then," said Grady. "I'm guessing that's where he's

going to stay. I don't like it though, it's too secluded. Ideal place to bury somebody."

"Or chuck them in the river," said Stella.

"Exactly," Grady agreed.

"Well," said Jennings, "there's only one way to find out isn't there? What are we waiting for?"

Grady put his hand on the computer operator's shoulder. "Okay then, buddy," he said. "What have we got in the way of men and firepower?"

"We've got the two guys outside the door, and I can probably get four more from the submarine up here, but that will take maybe a couple of hours. As far as weapons are concerned – I've got some handguns in the box and a couple of tranquilizer pistols."

"What sort of handguns?"

"Browning 9mm."

"They'll do."

"Excuse me," said Jennings. "But aren't you forgetting something, Grady?"

"What's that?"

"The fact that we're not supposed to be killing anybody."

Grady raised an eyebrow. "If you think I'm going on another rescue mission armed solely with those dart-guns then think again. This time we're going to use proper weaponry. If people get shot then so be it."

"But—"

"But nothing. I nearly got killed last time and that was only escaping. This time we're on the attack and we need guns."

"Fair enough," said Jennings. "You carry one if you like. I'm sticking with the tranquilizers. I made a promise to Stratton and I'm going to keep it."

"That promise won't be worth shit if you're both dead," muttered Grady. "Anyway, let's get on. We can't afford to wait for back up, so it'll just be the three of us. We'll leave the door guards where they are to protect our man here." He gestured to the operator. "Have you got any more transmitters?" he asked. The operator nodded. "Right then, we'll each have one."

"What? Under the skin?" said Jennings.

"Yes, under the skin. We don't know what's going to happen, do we?"

Grady phoned reception and arranged to borrow one of the hotel's fleet of cars. Jennings and Stella had their transmitters injected, a little put out and taken aback, but secretly pleased that Grady had taken charge of the situation.

"Okay then," said Grady, rubbing his arm after the implant. "Let's get going." He turned to the operator. "Get those four guys from the submarine up here, and keep an eye on us. If you don't hear from us before they arrive then send reinforcements."

They left the suite and headed down the corridor to the lift, Grady in front flanked by Stella and Jennings. Stella tapped the dart-gun in her jacket and felt the adrenalin starting to pump. She was back in the field and, despite the danger, enjoying it. Jennings cleared his mind and focused on the job ahead.

They stepped into the lift and asked the boy to take them to the parking level. Outside, a few rooms down, two men in suits watched the doors slide shut and nodded to each other.

Grady acquired a set of keys from the parking attendant and led his team through the underground garage to the complimentary vehicle. It was quiet and their footsteps echoed off the concrete, bouncing around the featureless white walls. Jennings began to get edgy, his senses telling him to stay alert.

"What's wrong with you?" asked Stella. "We haven't even got to the car yet."

"Nothing's wrong. This place is a little spooky that's all." He stopped and took a good look around.

Stella shrugged and carried on after Grady.

Although he could see nothing Jennings' sense of unease continued to grow, his head darting from side to side as he walked. The other two were now about ten yards ahead with the gap increasing all the time. He heard a noise behind him and spun round. He looked down the row of cars, but there was no sign of movement.

"Come on, jumpy boy," shouted Grady. "Stop fucking about and get a move on."

Jennings took one last look behind. Perhaps he was being paranoid. Maybe there was nothing there. He sighed and turned back to follow his friends.

The car was a black Lexus. Grady unlocked it with the key fob and went to the driver's door. Stella bagged 'shotgun' and Jennings was left with the backseat, which didn't bother him too much as it gave him plenty of room in which to sprawl out.

Grady started the car swiftly and was moving before Jennings had a chance to shut the back door. "Hold on there Lewis fucking Hamilton!" he shouted.

Grady ignored the comment and sped off between the rows of cars.

They had only gone twenty yards when there was a bang and then a loud pop from the front right tyre. Grady fought with the steering wheel, but the explosion had happened so quickly and unexpectedly that he couldn't regain control. With the car still accelerating they spun and went sidelong into a concrete pillar. Jennings, who hadn't bothered with a seatbelt, was flung sideways hard towards the door, his head and shoulders crashing against the window. Stella was thrown towards Grady who hit the driver's door hard. Their airbags failed to deploy.

"Fuck!" yelled Grady, reorienting himself. "What the fuck was that?"

Before Stella or Jennings could answer there was a tap at the passenger window. Stella looked across to see a gun pointing directly at her head.

"Hands where I can see them," said a voice from outside.

Stella raised her arms just enough to satisfy the request. Grady weighed up his options and thought about reaching for his weapon. Although this idea was quickly set aside when a second gunman appeared at his own window.

"Right then," said the voice. "Everybody out of the car. And no sudden movements."

Jennings opened the back door and stepped out onto the concrete. He looked up to face the gunman and froze. It was his former colleague, Bob Davis.

"Hello, Jennings. How very nice to see you. I knew we'd get you sooner or later."

"Davis! You fucking slime!"

"There's no need to be like that is there."

Jennings looked across to Grady who was standing against the car with his hands on the roof. He saw the man behind him and shook his head. "And Stone as well," he said. "You don't get one without the other."

"You know these clowns?" said Grady.

"I certainly do. They're the bastards who framed me for Appleby's murder. Although what the hell they're doing here…"

"That's enough chatter," said Davis. He walked forward and carefully patted Jennings down, finding his gun easily. He eyed it curiously. "What the fuck is this?"

"A tranquilizer gun," said Jennings.

"Ooh, very nice. A bit girly for my line of work though."

Stone and Davis confiscated their weapons and marched them through the car park, heading towards the poorly lit back corner. Jennings didn't need any magical premonitions to tell him what was coming next. He looked back to see if the attendant had become curious about the noise yet.

"There's nobody coming mate," said Davis, reading Jennings' mind. "He's having a nice little sleep."

Before any of them had time to think they were lined up against the wall in a darkened recess.

"Don't do this, Bob," said Jennings. "You don't know what's

at stake here."

"He's right," said Grady. "And we can get you money. Lot's of it." Money, he thought, the big persuader.

"Save your breath," said Davis. "Your time's run out."

Jennings looked across to Stone. "Come on, Andy," he pleaded. "Don't do this."

Stone didn't flicker. "I'm sorry Jennings," he said, and raised his gun.

Chapter 58

Stratton watched in amusement as the two Swiss Guards attempted to lift Kandinsky off the trolley and onto the chair. Eventually, after several comic tries, they enlisted the help of the two burly suits, who were unimpressed at having to leave their card game. Between the four of them, huffing and puffing, they lowered the Russian's enormous frame into place and tied him fast. The Swiss Guard departed and left the captives in the hands of Jonathan Ayres' henchmen.

"Another one down," Stratton said to Cronin.

"And three to go," said the priest. "And the way it's going I don't fancy their chances for much longer. How the hell did Kandinsky manage to get himself caught?"

"Search me. I'm hoping it's part of some great master plan – and that any minute now the cavalry are going to come in and save us."

Cronin gave a grim laugh and said, "I suppose we can always hope."

Stratton called for some water. The chief suit laid down his cards and tutted, and then wandered over with a litre bottle. Stratton drank over half of it and thanked his captor. He had no idea what the immediate future held, but he could feel his strength gradually waning, and the water was the only thing keeping him from a state of permanent fatigue. It may just have been the after-effects of being drugged, but something told him it ran a lot deeper.

"How are you feeling?" asked Cronin.

"Not too bad, maybe a little bit tired. How about you?"

"The same. I'm much better than I was though. I don't know what they gave us but it certainly messed with my head. I don't envy Kandinsky when he wakes up." He sighed. "I still can't believe they killed Desayer."

"I told you before, there's nothing you could have done about it," said Stratton. "There's no point beating yourself up."

"There's nothing else to do though is there?" said Cronin. "Nothing to do but sit here and think."

Stratton was about to answer when a phone trilled in the corner. The chief suit answered, and after a brief conversation hung up again. He nodded to his partner and they stood and picked up their guns from the table. They released their respective safety-catches and strode silently over to the captives.

"Your little friends have been caught," said the chief suit. "I'm afraid your time's up."

They raised their guns in unison.

Chapter 59

The sun was setting on the tree-filled valley. High up on the mountainside Annie looked out from the veranda and watched the day fade into dusk. She took a sip of her vodka martini and focused on a lone cloud hovering in the pink horizon, trying to form an empathy with its peaceful solitude. The loneliness she understood only too well, but the nebulous calm was alien. She longed to find something, anything, to fill the internal void and rid her struggling heart of the inherent and desperate pain. A tear formed in her eye as the chitter of monkeys echoed through her soul.

She finished her drink and called for the servant to get her another. She pulled a cigarette from the pack and lit it. Smoke and booze: old friends from her teenage years who had forged fresh links. She hadn't gone out of her way to get back in touch, it had just happened. Boredom had been her worst enemy. With Kamal disappearing for days on end there had been nothing much to do, and consequently she had begun to spend her after-noons staring out over the valley with a glass in her hand. At first it had been incredibly relaxing, gathering her thoughts in the peace of the trees, but as the days drew on the drinking had increased until all the hatred and self-loathing of her past had crept its way back inside.

The smoking was a result of chance and curiosity. One evening after eating by herself once more, she had gone to the garden to watch the birds when she noticed the servant, Amir, standing outside the gate with a cigarette. Filled with wine she called him over and asked if she could have a couple of drags. After an initial bout of coughing and a head rush she had quite enjoyed the sensation, and so the descent had begun. She didn't smoke when Kamal was about of course, but she got the feeling that he probably knew. Kamal knew pretty much everything, except the effect his frequent absences were having on her.

Below, through a gap in the trees, she saw the red 4x4 making its way up the track to the house. She smiled and put out her cigarette. It wasn't healthy to rely on someone so heavily, but the thought of spending another evening on her own had been eating away. She asked Amir to empty the ashtray and hide the evidence, then she went to the bathroom to wash away the misery of her self-pitying afternoon.

When she returned Kamal was sitting on the veranda sipping at some tea. She walked up behind him and pecked him on the cheek. "Hello," she said. "I wasn't sure if I was going to see you tonight."

Kamal turned to her and smiled. "I felt that I had been away too long. It is not right leaving you here alone so often."

Annie sat down next to him and reached for her drink. "It's not all that bad," she said. "And I know you've got a lot of work to do in the city. The children there are far more important than me."

"They are neither more important nor less important," said Kamal. "But I will not need to go back for a while. Everything is now set up as I want it and my people will look after things. I only wish that I could do more."

"More?" said Annie. "I think what you've done is amazing. Think of how many lives you're going to change for the better. Those children would be on the streets begging if it wasn't for you. Within a few years most of the girls would have been forced into prostitution."

Kamal nodded. "Yes, I know," he said. "But really it is a drop in the ocean. There are still thousands of children out there who need help."

"You can't save every child in Mumbai you know," said Annie. "You can only do as much as you can, and with the amount of money you've poured into this project I don't think anyone could accuse you of lack of commitment. You should be proud of what you've done."

"Perhaps," said Kamal. "But I have also done enough bad over the years. I do not think it will be cancelled out overnight." He finished his tea and poured another. "Anyway," he continued. "How have you been for the last few days? I hope that Amir is looking after you properly."

"I've been fine and Amir's been great. You should stop fretting." She smiled at him as cheerfully as she could, trying to hide the pain.

"I am concerned, not fretting."

"Well, I'm fine," she said, then took a swig of her drink. "There's bigger things in the world to worry about, or haven't you been watching the news?"

"Yes, I have been watching the news. I have been following it very closely."

"And what do you think?"

"I am not sure what to think at the moment. I find it very strange that the two major world religions have simultaneously announced a messenger from God. They both appear to have some kind of healing gift, but whether it is genuine I do not know. There is no way of telling just by seeing them on television. I would have to have one of them come to the slums and heal a crippled child there to make me into a real believer. At present I am inclined to believe that the whole thing is tricks and propaganda. Something does not seem quite right. What do you make of it?"

Annie shrugged. "Like you, I'm not really sure. I'd like to believe that God has sent a messenger to us, but I lost faith in him a long, long time ago. It's more likely to be a manmade trick if you ask me."

"Perhaps," said Kamal. "And if it is, it is certainly a very dangerous one. Already there are signs of trouble in the city. The Christian and Muslim populations are each making the wrong sort of noises. When the news first spread it was a point of celebration, but now it is turning into a battle with both sides claiming they have been blessed by God and that the other is lying. Mumbai is the wrong city to have such conflicting opinions. Religion is a huge part of people's lives, and I fear it will not be long before the strained atmosphere turns into all-out violence."

"What about the orphanage? What are you going to do if everything does kick off?"

"I have two buses ready to take the children away if needs be. But I hope that it will not come to that. They are in a relatively quiet area, so they should be fairly safe. Or as safe as you can be in these days."

Amir came out to the veranda and let them know that dinner would be ready in ten minutes, asking them whether they wanted to eat where they were or in the dining room. Kamal asked Annie who said they would take their meal outside.

"It's such a beautiful evening," she said. "I don't want to be stuck indoors."

"Of course," said Kamal. "A good choice…And then perhaps your cigarettes will not make the house smell," he added with a grin.

Annie frowned and then laughed. "I should know better than to try and fool you, shouldn't I?"

"If you wish to smoke, then go ahead," he said. "I have nothing at all against it. It is entirely up to you what you do. Although I am unhappy at Amir for tempting you."

"It wasn't anything to do with Amir."

"He is the only person up here apart from you. There is no-one else who could have provided you with them. I am sure that if I ask him he will come clean."

"He was only doing what I asked. He is there to serve me after all."

"Do not worry, I am not going to fire him. He is a very good man, and they are hard to come by. So, anyway, if you would like to smoke then please go ahead."

"Maybe after dinner," she said. She looked up to the blue-grey sky and saw the perfect crescent moon. It reminded her of the summer before when she had sat in the back garden at home with her boy David. She remembered him asking if he could climb up and swing from it. That was his thing, climbing and swinging. She smiled briefly and then felt her eyes welling.

"Is everything alright?" asked Kamal.

Annie rubbed her eyes. "Yeah, everything's fine. I'm just a bit tired, that's all. I've probably had one too many of these vodka martinis."

Kamal nodded. "It is easy to do. I know that Amir makes very good cocktails. They are hard to resist. I think I may even join you in one later."

Amir brought the food to the table and left them to eat. He had prepared a selection of traditional Indian dishes. Annie had not felt hungry, but the mouth-watering smell coming from the colourful platters went a long way to restoring her appetite. She picked at first, and then once she'd got the taste she found herself guzzling down more than she had done in the previous two days put together.

"It is good to see you eating properly," said Kamal.

"How could you not, with all this in front of you?" said Annie. "He's certainly a great cook. Where did you find him?"

"He comes from a local village originally, but I found him in the city. He helped me out of a tight situation, and I helped him get out of a bad way of life."

"Sounds intriguing."

"Not especially," said Kamal. "He stopped me from being mugged, and in return I offered him a job out here."

"You, being mugged?" she said. "I'm amazed that anyone would try."

"Well they did, and there were a fair few of them as well. Too many even for me. I am the best, but even the best can be outnumbered. It is not like the movies out there. If you are attacked by a group who know what they are doing then it does not matter who you are."

After filling herself almost to bursting point Annie sat back in her chair and relaxed with her drink. Kamal carried on eating for a while until he too was more than satisfied. He asked Amir to make them another two martinis and to bring some cigarettes out for Annie. He made this last request with a pointed expression, letting Amir know that he was disappointed with the situation.

With the plates cleared, and the drinks made, Annie lit a cigarette and took a few heavenly post-dinner drags. She was glad that Kamal knew about it because having to hide things from him was difficult in the extreme. He had been so good to her that she felt any deviance was a betrayal of his trust.

"Have you never smoked?" she asked.

"Yes, when I was much younger I dabbled with it a little. But it did not suit my lifestyle. I allow myself to drink, and that is enough I feel. To be honest I never really saw the attraction of cigarettes anyway. They seem to be a crutch for people, and I am loathe to ever need crutches."

Annie watched the smoke rise in front of her. "Sometimes people need crutches," she said. "What happens if you break your leg?"

Kamal smiled. "Good point," he said. "I will let you have that one."

Annie liked to see Kamal smile. It was such a rare occurrence that when it happened it made her glow inside. It wasn't that he was a miserable person, he was just serious, and forever contemplating the world and his position in it. He seemed to analyse everything to the point of complete deconstruction and beyond, picking the bones of his own psyche like a Freudian vulture. The upshot of this was that he not only knew himself very well, but could see into the hearts and minds of others like nobody she'd ever met. It was intimidating and yet at the same time comforting, as you could always rely on him to understand exactly what you were going through. His smile let you know that you were not alone.

She stubbed out her cigarette and took a sip of her drink. Kamal was gazing out into the horizon. She watched his face in the half-light and thought how incredibly handsome he was. She had noticed before of course, but there were times when she looked at him and saw something beyond the physical that set him apart. He had a noble bearing with granite cheekbones and a firm jaw, and his deep-set brown eyes glistened proudly under a stern brow, but on top of all this was an indefinable presence that caused him to appear far more striking than even the sum of his parts. She imagined it was how a king or an emperor of old would have looked: regal and imperious and indomitable and wise.

She felt Kamal's gaze shift back to her and looked away self-consciously. She thought the world of him and knew that he wouldn't ever hurt her or take advantage, but she didn't want him knowing how much she adored him, not for the moment at least. It was too close to everything that had happened for her to take a leap like that and leave herself exposed and emotionally vulnerable again. As this thought went through her head the pain came back and she winced.

"Are you okay?" said Kamal.

Annie covered her mouth and yawned. "Yeah, just a bit tired after all that food."

"You can go to bed if you like. You do not have to stay up on my account. I will be quite happy on my own with the view."

"No, I'm fine," she said. "I'd rather just sit here with you."

"Good. I am pleased. I have missed your company." He looked into her eyes and saw the briefest glimmer of a sparkle. It was something that had understandably been missing ever since fate had drawn them together at the hotel in London. It gave him hope that one day she might free herself of the chains of guilt that bound her every waking hour. Guilt from what she could have done, and most of all the guilt of survival.

"I'm not sure why you've missed my company," said Annie. "I'm hardly the life and soul of the party at the moment."

"It does not matter. Just having someone to sit with is good for me. I have not made many friends in my life. Mainly because of my job, but also because I like to keep a lot back for myself. I do not find it easy to talk to people. You probably know more about me than anyone ever has."

"Is that a good thing?"

"It is," said Kamal. "Perhaps if you had asked me six months ago I would have given a different answer, but I have come to understand things a lot better now. I used to think that having somebody know me was a weakness, and now I see it is not necessarily the case. In fact, if I am honest, I feel like a huge weight has been lifted from my shoulders. I am finding strength in my biggest fear." He paused. "Anyway, I am talking too much. It is probably nonsense."

Annie looked at him with moistened eyes. "It's not nonsense," she said. "Not at all." She leant over and kissed him on the cheek and hugged him. After holding the embrace momentarily she sat back down. "I just wish I could forget about everything. I wish that the pain would go away and that I could start living again."

"I want that for you too," said Kamal. "But it will take time, lots of time. There is no hurry, you must not try and force it. The wounds will heal at their given speed."

"I hope so," she said. "Sometimes I'll sit here and everything will be okay for a while, but then suddenly something will pop into my head and take me right back to where I started. There's so much unfinished business floating around in my head that it hurts to even think sometimes. I didn't even have the chance to say goodbye to them properly. I wasn't at the funeral, and I'll never be able to go back and lay flowers at their graves."

"Do not be so sure," said Kamal. "The truth may well come out one day. You have done nothing wrong, remember that."

"Then why do I feel like I have?! Why do I feel so fucking guilty all the time? Why am I stuck out here, unable to set foot in my own country, while those fucking bastards get away with murdering my family? Tell me that Kamal. Why?!" She burst into tears.

Kamal pulled her close and wrapped his arms around her. "I have no answers," he said. "I wish that I did."

Annie held him tight. "I should have killed him," she sobbed. "I should have killed him."

"No. You should not. The violence had to stop somewhere. It would not have done you any good."

"Wouldn't it?" Annie said, pulling away. "At least justice would have been done. I'd feel a whole lot better than I do now."

"Perhaps in the short term. Over the years it would have eaten away."

"Don't keep telling me that! You're always saying that! I don't believe you anymore. It's just words…" Her voice trailed off into her tears.

Kamal pulled her close once more. "Like I said, I have no answers. But you did the right thing. However hard it was, you did the right thing. I feel it in my heart." He kissed her on the forehead and stroked her hair gently. "There is purpose to everything, but only the universe knows."

Chapter 60

"I'm sorry, Jennings," said Stone, and raised his gun. Next to him Davis did the same, aiming straight between Grady's eyes. Stone lifted his weapon above his head and brought it crashing down on Davis' neck. His partner froze and then fell to the ground. Stone clicked the safety back on his firearm and returned it to its holster.

Jennings looked on wide-eyed, unable to comprehend what he'd just seen.

Stone walked forward. "Like I said, I'm sorry. Sorry for everything."

There was a brief silence as the situation was digested.

Eventually Jennings spoke. "What the fuck is going on, Andy?" he said. "What the *fuck* is going on?"

Stone pulled a set of handcuffs from his jacket pocket and knelt down beside Davis. "We'd better restrain him. He won't be out for long."

Jennings helped Stone manoeuvre Davis' porky frame, and they cuffed his hands behind his back. Stella lit a cigarette and paced around in front of a bemused Grady.

With Davis secure and leant comatose against the wall Jennings again pressed Stone for some answers. "Come on, Andy," he said. "I want to know what's going on. For a start you could tell me what the hell you two are doing here."

Stone approached Stella and asked her for a cigarette. He lit it with shaky hands. "We're here with Ayres," he said. "We've been here for over a week. He's been in talks with the Vatican. I couldn't tell you exactly what's been said because he's been behind closed doors, but I know he's part of this whole Messiah thing."

"Who's he been talking to?" asked Jennings.

"The Pope and some cardinal called Vittori as far as I can make out. He's been very careful not to tell us too much. We take him over to the Vatican and then the Swiss Guard look after him.

I wish I could tell you more."

"What about Stratton?" asked Stella. "And Father Cronin. Do you know anything about them?"

Stone nodded. "Yeah. They're being kept in a little hut by the river. Well, they were. I'm not sure they've got long now. Davis phoned through and told Ayres that we had you, so there's no reason to keep them alive now."

"Fuck!" cursed Jennings. He looked Stone in the eye. "Have you got a car?"

"Yeah, it's at the other side of the garage."

"Well come on then, let's get going!"

After retrieving their weapons, and with Stone in the lead, they ran through the parking level to the car, a silver Mercedes. Stone jumped in and started the engine, waiting only briefly for the rest to get seated before reversing out and wheel-spinning off to the exit.

The night-time traffic was slow but not static and Stone weaved his way in and out with speed and skill.

"Why are you doing this, Andy?" asked Jennings. "I mean, why now? Why couldn't you just have helped me when I needed it back in England?"

Stone shifted down a gear and accelerated round a line of cars, causing the oncoming traffic to swerve. "I don't know. It's complicated. There's no time for it now."

Two minutes later Stone hit the brakes and swung in to a parking bay on a secluded part of the Lungotevere della Vittoria, leaving his headlights on. All four doors opened simultaneously as they sprang out into the night.

"Wait!" Stone ordered. "We'll have to be careful. I've got two men in there and they're no slouches. We can't—"

Before he could finish his sentence a muffled gunshot sounded from the trees in front of them. It was followed quickly by another and another. Jennings' heart leapt into his throat. They were too late.

Chapter 61

"Wait!" said Cronin. "You don't know what you're doing. If you kill us then the whole world's in danger."

The chief suit held his gun steady at Stratton's head. "Really," he said. "Do I look like I give a shit? I've got my orders and that's the way it is." He turned to his partner. "Come on let's get this over with."

Cronin closed his eyes. Stratton smiled at his executioner.

"What the fuck are you grinning at?"

Stratton shook his head. "Nothing."

Unnerved by Stratton's knowing look, the chief suit wavered. It was a hesitation that he would sorely regret.

From nowhere a giant arm came flying through the air knocking the weapons out of the hands of the captors. The startled men staggered back and tried to keep their balance. Before they could reorient themselves a huge mass bore down and pinned them to the ground. They struggled violently but were unable to get the purchase to move.

Cronin looked on in astonishment as Kandinsky held the two men down. The Russian's legs were still tied to the chair but he had somehow managed to free his arms, and he now had a henchman under each of them. He waited until they stopped wriggling and then lifted himself slightly and grabbed their throats, squeezing with just enough pressure to render them unconscious. He ripped off the ropes that bound his legs and clambered to his feet.

"How long have you been awake?" asked Cronin.

"Long enough," said Kandinsky. "It will take more than a little injection to keep me down."

Cronin shook his head in disbelief. "But me and Stratton were out for over twenty-four hours."

"That's true," said Stratton. "But we're a lot lighter than Arman. They should've given him a larger dose. Anyway, let's not sit here arguing about it, let's get these ropes off and get out of here."

Kandinsky knelt down and untied them both swiftly. Stratton was first up and hobbled around trying to get some sensation back into his limbs. The ropes had been so tight that he'd lost almost all feeling in his extremities. Cronin followed him, stumbling about as he regained control of his functions. After clearing their heads as best they could, they tied up their captors and propped them against the far wall.

"Right then," said Stratton. "Let's go."

Kandinsky reached for the door handle, but as he did his legs buckled at the knees. He held himself up and took a couple of long, deep breaths.

"Are you okay?" asked Cronin.

"Yes," said Kandinsky, giving his head a shake. "I will be fine. Just a little faint." He turned the handle and slumped forward again.

"Listen," said Cronin. "If you're still dizzy, sit down for a moment. We can take a bit more time – those guys aren't going anywhere."

"No," said Kandinsky. "We cannot afford to wait. We do not know who is on the other side of the door."

"Exactly," said Cronin. "Which is why we don't want to go out there half-cocked."

Stratton was just about to agree when Kandinsky opened the door, and after a brief look stepped into the night. They followed him out and found themselves surrounded by trees, the only illumination coming from the hut behind. They heard the sound of a car passing about fifty yards to the left. They nodded to each other and headed in the direction of the road.

The trees were dense, blocking off any streetlight and leaving them almost blind. Cronin led the way, with Stratton behind and Kandinsky bringing up the rear. They crept along quietly, stopping every few steps to listen out for dangers.

They had only gone fifteen yards when a barely audible click caused them to swing round and face the hut again. A lone figure stood in the gloom, its arm stretched towards them. They froze.

"Come out with your hands up!" commanded a man's voice.

No-one answered.

The man repeated his command. Again he was met with silence. Another man appeared by his side.

"You two must run," whispered Kandinsky. "On the count of three. One, two, three…"

Before either Stratton or Cronin could stop him Kandinsky was thundering towards the gunmen, his arms outstretched to shield his friends. There was a flurry of shooting, but still he stormed on, oblivious to the bullets peppering his torso. He ran to within three yards and then launched himself into the air and down onto the two helpless shooters, crushing them with his unnatural frame. Stratton and Cronin broke cover and came to his aid.

Stratton raced up and knelt down beside the heap of bodies. The two men were still conscious but groaning under Kandinsky's weight. Their guns had been thrown in the collision and were safely out of reach.

Stratton touched Kandinsky's shoulder. "Arman," he said. "Are you alright?"

There was no answer.

"Arman?!"

Kandinsky moaned and lifted his head. "I am not so good," he croaked. His head dropped back down.

"Come on, Pat," said Stratton. "Let's help him off and get a look at his injuries."

Cronin picked up the guns and tucked them safely away. He then bent down to help Stratton move Kandinsky. They heaved with all the energy they could muster but it was no use, the Russian was just too heavy.

"Fuck it!" said Stratton.

It was then that a number of bodies burst through the trees. Cronin looked up and instinctively drew one of the guns.

"It's us, Pat!" shouted a familiar voice.

Cronin squinted into the gloom and saw Jennings running towards them flanked by Grady and Stella. He sighed with relief and put the weapon away again.

"What's happened?" asked a breathless Jennings.

"We think he's been shot," said Cronin. "But we can't lift him."

With extra leverage from the newcomers they slowly lifted Kandinsky off the two gunmen and lay him on his back in the grass. His eyes were closed and his breathing was shallow. Stratton ripped apart his shirt to get a better look at his wounds. His body was covered with blood and bullet holes.

"Can you do anything?" asked Cronin.

"I'm not sure," said Stratton. "I'll give it a try. I just hope the world's in a good mood."

Kandinsky opened his eyes and lifted his head slightly. "No," he gasped. "Leave me. Let me go." Blood sputtered out of his mouth as he choked.

"We're not leaving you," said Cronin. "You'll make it. Stratton will look after you."

Kandinsky shook his head again. "No," he rattled. He reached down to his pocket and then moved his hand to his chest. He closed his eyes and spoke no more.

"Come on Stratton!" shouted Stella. "Do something!"

Stratton shook his head. "I can't," he said. "He's gone. He wanted to go. I can't save someone who doesn't want to be saved."

They all bowed their heads and fell silent, each with their own thoughts. Grady looked at the battered photograph clutched to the big man's heart. A solitary tear rolled down his cheek.

Chapter 62

The twelve men that made up the council sat behind the crescent-shaped marble table and studied the Mahdi in silence. He had been summoned before them as a matter of routine to review all that had happened in the last two weeks. They were pleased with his progress, but equally wished to keep him from becoming too arrogant with his new power, and so had isolated him in the centre of the room a level lower than themselves to compound their authority. He sat there cross-legged waiting for them to start their questioning.

Eventually a grey-bearded man near the middle of the crescent began to speak. "Welcome, Assam," he said gravely. "We have been following your progress most closely."

"I hope that you are not displeased with my efforts."

"We are not. We are satisfied with the situation thus far. You have done as we asked, and performed your tasks admirably. We do, however, have some concerns about the way we are headed."

The Mahdi gave a single nod, but did not reply.

The grey beard continued. "Wherever you go the crowds have taken you to their hearts, of that there is no doubt. You have proved yourself beyond question to everyone that has seen you, or been healed by your hands. And so the word has spread that you are indeed the genuine redeemer, the Mahdi. Even those who thought the legend fictional are now converted. Throughout the Muslim world there is unshakeable belief that the time has come when the faithful shall be given their just reward by Allah." He paused and looked around the table. "There is also a line of thinking that Allah will at last punish the infidels who have taken his name in vain and kept his children in fear and subjugation. The greedy West who take our lands by force, and the stubborn, cursed Jews who kill our brothers with impunity. These people and other enemies of Islam need to be brought to justice. Do you not agree?"

"I agree that the violence should stop."

"You agree that the violence should stop? That is not the same thing. I am talking about justice."

The Mahdi surveyed the stony faces around the table. There would be no allies for the stance he was about to take. "Perhaps we would be better served by a less vengeful attitude."

The grey beard's eyes flashed with anger. "What!?" he thundered. "Are you trying to tell this council what to do? Are you trying to dictate our doctrine? We had an agreement, Assam. When you were chosen for this task you went in knowing full well what our intentions were. You cannot start changing now."

"The intention was to free Allah's children and to bring his teachings to the world at large."

"Yes, indeed it was. But we cannot free our brothers without rising up against our oppressors. All your speeches are about peace and forgiveness, which is admirable, but our immediate aim is to maintain our standing and to rid this world of those who do not wish to live under Allah's loving laws. It is almost as if you are oblivious to everything else that is going on in the world. We are at war with the West whether you like it or not. And now our enemy the Catholic Church grows mightier by the day. We need to be giving our brothers the strength and the heart to fight."

"No," countered the Mahdi. "We need to be giving our brothers the strength and the heart to lay down their arms. The force of mind and faith to bow before their enemies."

The council murmured angrily. The grey beard echoed their sentiments. "This is madness!" he exclaimed. "We cannot give way to the West! We have lost too much already. They are wicked and will turn our lands into havens of sin and debauchery. Our people will be turned from their faith. The time has come to rise up in force against our dissolute enemies. It is the will of Allah."

"I cannot agree," said the Mahdi. "The will of Allah is to lay down our weapons and talk with our enemies."

"We are not the aggressors here, Assam. We are the victims. The West have brought this war to us. They are the ones who wish to conquer the globe, not us. I agree that the Qur'an demands love and understanding, but it also permits defensive warfare. We will do no more than stand our ground, and once we have driven them away we will stop. This was all agreed."

The Mahdi stood up, raising himself to the council's level. "I did not agree to incite violence in our people. My remit was to promote the true ideals of the Qur'an and Allah. I will continue to do only that." His eyes went from one elder to the next, burning each with the intensity of his focus.

"Come now, Assam," said the grey beard. "Please sit down. There is no point arguing amongst ourselves. We are on the same side – the side of Allah."

"That is to be determined," said the Mahdi. "I fear the council has strayed from the path."

"I understand your concerns, but we have not strayed from any path. The coming of this bogus Christian Messiah means that we must alter our strategy. It is true that in an ideal world we would solve our differences peacefully, but this world of ours is far from ideal."

The Mahdi continued to stand tall. "I will not be swayed on this. There will be no violence on our part. You say that defensive warfare is permitted by the Qur'an, and I do not deny this, but there has as yet been no act of aggression from the Catholic Church or anyone else in the West. And even if there were I am no longer sure if I can condone any form of combat."

"Open your eyes, Assam!" said the grey beard. "Reports are coming through every day about attacks on our brothers in the West. The two mightiest religions on earth are both claiming the high ground – there is no escaping bloodshed. Do you want to see your brothers suffer? Is that your wish?"

"It is not my wish to see anyone suffer, be they Muslim or Christian or Jew or Sikh or whomever. As I said, I do not deny that the Qur'an permits defensive warfare, but my attitude towards this has changed. The power and the energy given to me by the symbols has shown me a new wisdom. There is no room for retaliation in the world of the future, we must do as the prophet Jesus said and: 'if anyone hits you on the right cheek, then offer him the other as well'. This is the way forward for Islam and the world. After all, did not Muhammad himself accede to the demands of the Meccans, enabling him to take the city without bloodshed? That act of surrender empowered him with the true spirit of Allah that flows with inner peace. Islam is 'surrender'."

"We know very well what Islam means thank you, Assam, but it is not meant to be taken literally all the time. You must temper it with common sense. Offering no resistance to a man who is about to kill you will not save your life. The modern world is brutal and we must change with it, we must adapt to our environment."

"The world of Muhammad was far more brutal than ours," countered the Mahdi, "and look what he managed to do. We must go back to this fundamental tenet and lay ourselves bare to our enemies. We must throw down all weapons and engage the power of Allah and the universe. We will come to no harm."

The grey beard slammed his hand down on the table. "Fool!" he yelled. "If you persist with this nonsense we will be destroyed! The Meccans in Muhammad's time may have been brutal but they were also deeply religious and believed in the power of Allah. It was the fear of Allah that stayed their hands. Do you think the West is afraid of God? Their leaders might be making a big show of faith in light of the emergence of the Messiah, but do they really believe? Do you really think the powers that be at the Pentagon are going to be scared of divine intervention? Once they see us back down they will crush us like ants. They will take everything that is holy and desecrate it with their immoral greed. Our people will be led down the path of capitalist evil. We cannot allow this to happen. We *will* not allow this to happen."

"Then we are at an impasse," said the Mahdi. "For too long we have manipulated the Qur'an for our own purpose, justifying our actions with false interpretations. The hatred must stop now. I will not incite our brothers to fight. That is my final word on the matter." He stared firmly and unblinking at the grey beard, who replied thunderously.

"Just who do you think you are?! This council has the final say on all matters – not you! It was us who gave you the knowledge to become what you are, and you will do well to remember that. Without us you would be nothing; a nobody. You took an oath to serve us. Do not break it?"

"I took an oath to serve Allah's purpose not yours."

"This council decides Allah's purpose It is made up of the wisest scholars in the whole of Islam. Are you suggesting that you are somehow more erudite than the twelve of us?"

"I am not suggesting anything," said the Mahdi. "I am merely stating my cause. And I believe it to be just and right."

"Then, as you say, we are at an impasse. I am not sure that we can let you go on. You must return the box and the parchment to us at once."

"And what will that achieve?" asked the Mahdi. "You cannot suddenly produce a new redeemer. The people will not stand for it. You must let me continue with my work. I have united our faith, and we grow stronger by the day. You must trust in the course I am taking."

The grey beard looked to his colleagues for guidance. He knew that removing the Mahdi was unfeasible, but equally he knew that their present course would lead to failure. The council, however, had no immediate answer to the stalemate either and he was forced to let the matter lie.

"I see that we are getting nowhere with this, Assam," he said. "You have commitments to keep, and so we must let you go and keep them. But do not think that we are happy with the situation. There will come a time in the forthcoming weeks when we will have to make a stand, and I trust that when that time comes you will do what is best. In the meantime, think very carefully about what we have said."

The Mahdi bowed to the council and left. The grey beard sat in silence meditating with his peers. As they had feared, Assam was already way beyond their control. The situation needed to be remedied, and soon.

Chapter 63

Grady wiped his cheek and cleared his throat. "We'd better be getting out of here," he said.

"I agree," said Stone. "Someone's bound to find Davis soon, and when that happens the whole of Rome will be looking for us."

Stratton looked up suspiciously at the newcomer.

"It's okay," said Jennings. "He's with me. It's a long story. Let's just get a move on."

"What about Kandinsky?" said Stella. "We can't just leave him here."

"And what do you suggest?" asked Stone. "Where exactly are we going to put him?"

"In the boot of the car," she answered.

Stone was about to shoot her idea down when he saw the look on the others' faces. Instead he decided to acquiesce. Between the six of them they carried the body through the trees to the car and folded it neatly into the spacious trunk. Jennings phoned the hotel and told Kandinsky's men to leave and meet them at the docks.

Stone drove cautiously through the city not wanting to attract attention. The enormity of what he was doing began to hit home. He'd crossed a line, there was no turning back. His career in the Met was over. He thought about his wife and daughter and how it would affect them. It would probably mean losing their comfortable life, but that was nothing compared to the harm he'd already caused them. At least this way they might be able to forgive him, and maybe carry on their lives with pride instead of shame.

They reached the docks without interference and carried Kandinsky's body to the waiting launch. The team from the hotel were already there, and within a couple of minutes they were speeding down the Tiber towards the open sea and the submarine. Stella sat next to Stratton at the back of the boat watching the city dwindle. There were a million and one things she wanted to say to him, but they could wait for a more appropriate moment.

"I can't believe he's dead," she said, trying to break the awkward silence. "I thought he was almost indestructible."

"So did I," said Stratton. "Well, as far as anyone's indestructible. But he wanted to go, so there's nothing we could have done."

"I know," she said. "But it's still hard to take. It doesn't seem right his body just lying there. It's like he's created this giant void."

"I didn't think you were that keen on him."

"I wasn't at first. But once I got to know him better he grew on me. And how could I not like someone who put their life on the line to rescue me?"

Stratton felt the last words sticking four inches out of his back*. "Good point," he said. "Are you trying to say something?"

"No," she shrugged. "Why? Should I be?"

"No. Just checking."

The conversation tailed off and the boat was left in silence, the drone of the motor lying heavily over Kandinsky's lifeless body. Jennings felt exhausted and drained of all emotion. Even the sight of Stratton and Stella sitting together failed to bother him. He leant back against the side of the boat and closed his eyes, trying to clear his mind of death.

They reached the submarine safely, and after hoisting Kandinsky up and in they took his body to the medical room where he was put in cold storage, with a view to burying him next to his family in Russia when the chance arose. After paying their last respects, they each went to their quarters to sleep.

Jennings showered and then sat down on his bed with a large

---

* Raymond Chandler – The Long Goodbye.

glass of whisky. His emptiness was complete, and as he looked down into the amber liquid he felt a darkness seep through his soul. He cupped the glass tightly between his hands and started to weep, his tears dripping into the alcohol. He remained motionless until a knock on the door sparked him out of his trance. He wiped his eyes with a towel and went to see who it was. Hovering in the doorway was Andrew Stone.

"Hi, Jennings, I hope I'm not disturbing you," he said apologetically.

Jennings wanted to tell him to go away but the demoralized look on his face pulled heavily at his conscience. "No, Andy, you're not. Come in."

Jennings offered him a whisky, which he accepted, and they sat down, Stone in the chair and Jennings on the edge of the bed.

"So what's on your mind?" asked Jennings.

"Everything," said Stone bluntly. "I feel like I've just woken up from a bad dream." He sipped at his whisky. "Everything I've done, it's just…" He hung his head.

"What exactly have you done?" asked Jennings. "I mean, apart from destroying my entire life."

Stone shook his head. "It's such a bloody mess I don't know where to begin."

"Try the beginning."

Stone swigged down his whisky and poured another. "I guess it all started not long after I was assigned to the Prime Minister. Probably last November, just before all that Mulholland business kicked off. He took me and Davis aside and told us that he wanted us to do some off-duty work for him. It was nothing major he said, just a little project he had on the side. He said he'd pay us well and off the books. We'd both been having problems financially so it was a no-brainer."

"What was the project then?" asked Jennings.

"He wanted us to do some digging around on Henry Mulholland."

"I thought they were best friends."

"Even friends have secrets Jennings, you should know that. Anyway, he wanted us to do some research on him and his father Charles Mulholland. Wanted us to find out anything about their family history that wasn't in the public domain, and any dirt that was around in their files. We didn't find anything, but then a month later Henry was dead. After that he had us checking up on Brennan's investigation. He wanted to know everything that was going on at ground level. He was particularly interested in what you and Stella were up to. He had us tap your phones. He told us to listen out for any talk of a box covered in symbols."

Jennings looked at Stone in disbelief. "Ayres knew about the box?!"

"I guess he must have done. We had no idea what it was about though, we just did what he told us. He seemed to lose interest though after you had it taken at that service station. He said it wasn't important anymore. But then, after that night at Stonehenge when it disappeared, he was absolutely fuming. He sent us out the next day to search the area."

Jennings' mind whirred as he tried to make sense of what he was hearing. If he wasn't mistaken, then reading between the lines there was a definite connection between Ayres, Jeremy and Yoshima. "And what about after that, when you didn't find anything?"

"He was sullen for a few days, but then when Stratton's body was stolen from the mortuary he suddenly perked up again. After Christmas he had us investigating all his known associates – including you and Stella. The problem was manpower though, there were so many of you to keep tabs on that we just couldn't spare the time. We needed more men."

"I see," said Jennings. "And I suppose that's where the assassination attempt came in."

"Yes," said Stone. "Ayres figured that his detail would double at least if there was a major threat to his life, and so we hired someone to make the false hit."

"So I got shot as part of the plan?"

"You didn't get shot did you? You just took a hit in your vest. It all worked out beautifully: no-one got hurt – well, apart from me – and the PM looked under threat. Even better was the fact that everyone thought he was a Muslim, and that Al-Qaeda were behind the attack."

"Well, so far so good," said Jennings.

"Yes. It seemed pretty much perfect. We got our assignment of men, and best of all we got you."

"Me?"

"Yes. Ayres wanted to keep you close, he thought you were the best link to Stella, and therefore Stratton and his mob."

"So you knew Stratton was alive?"

"No, not at all, well at least I didn't. I mean it's not something you would even contemplate is it? My understanding was that we were searching for this box that he wanted. I had no idea what it was all about, but I was getting paid for it so I didn't ask any questions."

"It's a lot of trouble to go to just for a wooden box. Didn't you suspect anything?"

"I knew there was something strange about it from the reports you wrote, but I'm sure you didn't say everything you knew."

"No, I didn't. I kept most of it out to be honest. I told Brennan about it, but he advised me to keep everything normal, just to call it a religious artefact."

"Exactly," said Stone. "And that's what I thought we were looking for – a religious artefact, probably a priceless one. It all fitted in with the visits Ayres was getting from the Vatican."

"So where did it all start to go wrong?"

Stone smiled and shook his head. "When Ayres started to get greedy and paranoid. He decided that he didn't want to pay the hitman and that it was too risky having him alive. He wanted all links to us and him buried. It was an absolute nightmare. I called in a favour from MI6 and together we tracked him down through his network. He was a clever bloke with a load of intermediaries in the pipeline so it wasn't easy, but eventually we traced him to a hotel in London. And that's where we made our first mistake. Or, should I say, where I made the mistake."

"What did you do?" asked Jennings, now totally immersed in Stone's admissions.

"I don't know – and to this day I'll never know. I was tired and stressed and overworked, but there's no real excuse for what happened. Maybe it was the bump in the head I got when the hitman assaulted me at Cheltenham. Anyway, whatever the reason, I made a severe error in judgement. We couldn't mount a big operation and draw attention to ourselves so we had to try and get rid of him quietly. I knew that if we sent one of ours up to his room he'd smell us out immediately. I was in the hotel lobby debating what to do when I saw one of the staff taking room service into a lift. I recognized her face but couldn't put a name to it. It was only on my way out when it suddenly hit me…"

Jennings listened intently, and somewhat flabbergasted, as Stone relayed the story of the child-killer Tracy Tressel and the subsequent fallout.

"What a fucking mess," he said when Stone had finished. "I can't believe you got yourself into such a lot of shit. What the hell were you thinking?"

"Like I said, I really don't know. I made that first mistake and then it just escalated. Before I knew it we were in so deep there was no turning back."

"Oh the tangled web we weave," said Jennings.

"Indeed," said Stone.

Jennings got up and poured himself another whisky. "So, who killed Appleby then? Was it you?"

"No. Davis did it. But I'm just as culpable. I ordered it, just like I ordered the death of Tressel's mother and son. I could have stopped it all, Jennings." He put his head in his hands.

"But why blame me for his death. I thought you wanted to keep me close."

"We did at first, but by that time Ayres decided there was nothing else to get from you. We guessed Appleby had voiced his suspicions to you so we had no choice but to try and get rid of you as well. When you escaped it actually got us out of a hole. Rather than two dead bodies to explain we only had one and a desperate fugitive."

Jennings looked down at his former colleague and sighed. "What happened to you, Andy? This isn't you. You're a family man with values and morals, or at least I thought you were. You're telling me all this stuff, but it's just not registering."

"I know, I know," said Stone. "I can't explain it. It's like I was in a dream – a nightmare. It felt like it was someone else doing it, not me. It was only when Patricia and Jenny were taken that it really hit home. When I thought they were going to die everything caught up with me, I was physically sick. If that hitman hadn't turned up to stop the whole thing…"

"But he did," said Jennings.

"Yes, he did. And he showed me mercy. He said that I had a second chance and that I should take it. That's stayed with me ever since. I couldn't get the words out of my head. And this afternoon when we had you lined up against the wall I knew it was time to put an end to everything – time to do the right thing. It's a bit late I know, but it's something I guess."

"It is late, but better that than never as the saying goes. You've done more than you know today. I can't absolve your sins, Andy, but I can tell you that I'm grateful and there's no hard feelings from me."

Stone looked up at him with pitiful eyes. "Thanks, Jennings," he said. "I'm not sure I deserve it, but thanks."

Jennings finished his drink and left the glass on the side. "It's getting late," he said. "I reckon I ought to hit the hay. And God knows you look like you need some sleep."

"I do," agreed Stone. "These last few days have really fucked my head up, with the advent of this new Messiah and everything. And when I found out Stratton was alive – well, you can imagine. This whole thing gets stranger by the day. I'm not even sure what's real anymore."

Jennings laughed and said, "Join the club." He saw Stone out and flopped onto his bed and fell asleep.

Chapter 64

Ali Hussein finished his last Salat of the day and rose to his feet. It was getting late and there was still no sign of the Mahdi. He rolled up his prayer mat and set it aside, and then went to the kitchen to prepare some food for his master's return. After their recent travels, being back in Mecca seemed like a bit of a let down. It was only for a day of course, but Ali had become used to the excitement of the crowds and without it he felt flat. He hoped there would be no hold-ups and that they would be back on their way the next morning as planned.

As Ali laid out some cold meats and bread he heard the front door open. He looked through the living area and saw the Mahdi enter. He appeared tired and troubled. Ali picked up his tray and took the food to his master.

"Thank you, Ali," he said. "Please sit down and join me. We will eat together – yes?"

Ali nodded and sat down on the opposite side of the wooden table.

The Mahdi broke some bread and chewed on it slowly.

"Is everything alright, Master?" Ali asked. "You look tired."

"I am fine, Ali. I have just had a long afternoon with the elders. We have discussed many things. There is much going on in the world that we need to address."

"Do you mean the Christian Messiah?"

"Yes, among other things. I have had a change of heart with regards to him. I now think that perhaps I was harsh to criticize him and suggest that he was a lie."

"Is he real like you are then?"

"We are all real, Ali. Just as we are all figments." He laughed. "But in answer to your question, then yes – he is just as real, and he represents God just the same as myself. He has the power to heal, and that power cannot come from anywhere else."

"Then why are people saying that he is fake?"

"For the same reason that his followers are suggesting that I am fake. It seems it is not enough for them to be blessed by Allah, they must have power over their fellow man as well. Each side fears the other will take control. But there is no control. We are all Allah's children and should be celebrating this, not arguing over who he loves the most."

"So their God is the same as ours?"

"Yes, he is different only in our minds. Now come, let us eat. There will be time for discussion after dinner."

They ate in silence. Ali tried to clear his mind, but found that it was bursting with things to ask. This was common with the Mahdi, instead of giving a conclusive solution he would answer in such a way that left Ali with more questions than he started with. So when the Mahdi eventually finished and pushed his plate aside Ali was waiting to pounce.

"If we have the same God, then why did he send two of you to earth?" he asked.

"That is a good question," said the Mahdi. "It is because of the way the world has divided itself. If there were just one of us then the other half of the world would not listen. This way our message can be heard by all."

"But what about the Jews and the Sikhs and the other religions? Why have they not been blessed with their own redeemers?"

"Perhaps they will be. I do not know Allah's whole mind, only my part of it. I am only the beginning of this change. I am but one piece in a vast puzzle." He looked out into the night in contemplation.

Ali cleared the table and washed their plates then sat back down. The Mahdi turned his gaze away from the window and smiled. "You are a good boy, Ali. You have served me well these last weeks. You are certainly one of the chosen few."

Ali bowed his head and blushed. "Thank you, Master."

"No, Ali, thank you – for all you have done. You are a shining light of all that is good in Allah's world. If there were more people like you then my task would be so much easier. Unfortunately I find myself up against a world of fear and hatred. I am trying to make myself heard, but I think that my voice may be drowned in the clamour for power."

"What do you mean?"

"I am sorry, Ali, I am thinking aloud. There are many things that you do not know, and are probably better off not knowing. You are a trusting boy and I would not have it any other way. Not everybody is as pure and honest as yourself. Please do not change. Whatever happens to you or whatever happens to me, please do not change."

"I will try not to, Master. But nothing will happen to you will it? You are the Hand of Allah."

"I am indeed, but that does not mean I am invincible. If men do not wish to open their hearts to Allah then I cannot force them. This is a time for choice, for men to decide their path. I am here to show the power of kindness and surrender, but I cannot change those who do not wish to see."

"But surely everybody wishes to see."

"You would think so, but it is not the case unfortunately. People only see that which they want to see; that which suits their purpose at the time. I am trying to open their eyes to the whole panorama, but they only want to look at one small piece." He sighed. "Perhaps they are just not yet capable of stretching their vision."

"Then you must show them how, Master. You must keep going until the whole world can see."

The Mahdi smiled at his young charge. "You are right of course. Forgive my mood please, Ali. It has been a long day, and even I get tired at times. I think it is time for me to meditate and then go to bed. But first I have something to show you, something very important." He rose from his seat and walked across the room to retrieve a small wooden chest from the sideboard. It was an item that Ali kept safe for his master while he was addressing crowds and healing. "Do you know what is in this chest, Ali?"

Ali shook his head. "No, Master. I only know that it is very important to you."

The Mahdi removed his neck chain and with the attached key undid the padlock on the chest. He opened it up and removed a wooden box covered with hundreds of small symbols. For no reason he could fathom Ali felt the hairs on the back of his neck bristle.

"This," said the Mahdi, "is thousands of years old. It is a very important artefact. It holds the key to great power."

He passed the box to Ali who surveyed it with shaking hands.

"It is beautiful, Master. Very beautiful. But what power does it hold?"

"It contains the knowledge to harness the power of Allah."

"The power of Allah?! But nobody except you can do that, Master."

"No, Ali. As I have told you before, we all have the power of Allah within us whether we know it or not. Allah is all around. He flows through the creatures of earth, he flows through the sky and the sea, and he flows through the stars and the planets. He is everywhere and everyone and everything."

As the Mahdi spoke Ali knew his words to be true. He felt a surge of energy rush through the room causing him to shiver with joy. He closed his eyes and lost himself in the unseen world beyond, feeling Allah's warmth flood his soul, and in that instant he understood.

When he opened his eyes again the Mahdi was staring at him with a broad smile. "You feel him do you not?"

"Yes," said Ali. "I do."

"And how does he feel?"

"He feels warm and compassionate and filled with love for all things."

"That is correct. And you can feel that because you yourself are filled with the same pureness. Or should I say that you are not tainted by impurities. It is like I said before about allowing the light to pass through you."

"Yes, I remember," said Ali.

"Then you know that the dark hearts of men cannot allow this light to pass through in its full form. The power of it would destroy their very souls."

"Yes, Master. I understand."

"Good," said the Mahdi. "Then you will understand what I am about to ask of you." His manner became earnest. "I think that my time here may be short-lived, Ali. Things are not turning out exactly as I hoped. There are forces in this world who do not wish to see the light come to its full glory; they would taint it with their own ambition. They do not share my vision of peace. These forces I feel may try and stop me from completing my mission."

"What forces?" said Ali. "Who are these people?"

"It does not matter who they are. You are better off not knowing. All you need to know is that if anything happens to me you should trust only yourself and your instincts. If an ill fate befalls me then I want you to make sure that this box is kept safely hidden. Let nobody near it! Take it far away from greedy hearts and bury it deep. And if you cannot do that then you must destroy it."

"Destroy it!"

"Yes, Ali, destroy it. This knowledge is not yet for mankind. It is too dangerous. It would be better to disappear for ever than be misused for destruction. I want you to promise me that you will protect the secret at all costs."

Ali looked across at his master's stern face and knew that he must do as he was asked. "Yes, Master," he said. "I promise. By the will of Allah, I promise."

"Good. Now I am pleased. It is a great burden for you I know, but I think you are ready for it." He broke into a smile. "But let us not dwell on the subject. The chances are that nothing will happen to me at all, so do not worry yourself with it too much. I just needed to know that the knowledge will be safeguarded."

Ali forced a smile back, but inside he was torn. The brave new world suddenly seemed dark and uncertain.

Chapter 65

Stella dried herself off and put on some blue jeans and a white T-shirt. She had slept long and soundly, and after a hot shower felt refreshed and ready to face the day. Her injuries were now no more than a minor irritation and she moved freely about the room without pain. She was just about to order some breakfast when there was a rap on her door.

"Oh, it's you," she said, opening up and finding Stratton in the doorway.

"Don't sound too excited," he said. "Were you expecting someone else?"

"No, I wasn't expecting anybody. I was just about to order some breakfast."

"Well, don't let me stop you. Can I come in?"

Stella nodded and let him through. He sat down at her dressing-table, and she perched on the edge of the bed.

"So what do you want?" she asked.

"I wanted to see you. We didn't really get a chance to talk yesterday. I wanted to come and see how you were."

"I'm fine, now that you ask. I wasn't sure you were that interested."

Stratton drummed his fingers on the dressing-table. "Of course I'm interested," he said. "I've just been busy doing other things."

Stella snorted and looked away. "Yeah, I understand. You've got a whole world to save haven't you, Mr Big Shot?"

"It's not like that. We decided it was better for me to come to Rome to help out Father Pat. The others were more than capable of getting you out of the palace without me. I mean – you're here aren't you?"

"Yeah, I'm here." She sighed and turned to face him again. "Look, I know that you did what you thought was best, but you can't blame me for being a little upset. I mean – how did you think I'd feel?"

"Like you do, I guess. But like I said – I did what I thought was best for everyone. If I didn't think the others could do it then I would have come and got you myself."

Stella desperately wanted to stay angry, but as she looked into Stratton's eyes she found it impossible. She laughed out of sheer frustration. "Oh well, what's the point?" she said. "Life's just too short."

Stratton got up from the chair and held out his hands. "Come on," he said. "Give me a hug."

Stella got to her feet and embraced him, feeling a torrent of mental exhaustion flooding out into the warmth of his body. She held him close, staying in his arms until the hidden anguish had disappeared. She pulled away slowly and sat back down on the bed.

"How about coming up to the dining room for breakfast?" said Stratton. "I know you were going to have it in here, but the others are meeting up there in a few minutes so we might as well join them."

"Why not," she said. "I'll just get my trainers on."

They walked up to the dining room side by side. Stella thought about reaching for his hand, but something stopped her. Their dynamic was somehow different than before; it wasn't something she could put her finger on or explain, just a subtle shift in emotion that prevented her from letting go.

When they arrived Jennings, Grady and Stone were already seated at the table. At the head, in Kandinsky's place, was his second in command, Gregor Kharkov. Stella had seen him around the sub many times before but had never actually spoken to him. He was around six feet tall with a large face, a square jaw, and dark wavy hair that hung loosely just above his shoulders. His eyes were chocolate brown and they stared curiously under bushy black brows. His face appeared dour, but as they entered he broke into a warm smile.

"Good morning," he said. "I am glad that you are here. Now we can all talk together."

They sat down at the table and the waitress brought them coffee. Jennings chewed on a piece of toast absent-mindedly, trying to gauge Stella and Stratton's body language without looking like he was doing so.

"Yesterday was a very sad day for all of us," said Kharkov. "Arman Kandinsky was a great man, and a great leader of men. And he was a good friend." He bowed his head briefly in remembrance and then addressed the table once more. "But he would not want us to sit around mourning his demise. He would want us to carry on fighting for what was right and that which he believed in. He spoke to me yesterday before he went to the Vatican and said that if anything happened to him then I should help you in every way possible. I will of course honour this request, and therefore you still have the full weight of his empire behind you. In fact, he requested that in his absence I should take my command from Mr Jennings, so I shall defer to any judgement he makes."

Jennings finished a mouthful of toast and washed it down with a sip of coffee. He knew that Kandinsky had given him control of his resources in the interim, but with all that had happened he'd completely forgotten. In the cold light of day, with Kandinsky gone, he felt like a bit of a fraud.

"So what's the plan then, Mr Jennings?" asked Grady with a grin.

"I don't know. It's not like I'm really in charge anyway, Grady. I've got no idea what we should do next. If anyone's going to be making decisions it should be Stratton."

Stratton laced a piece of toast with marmalade. "I'd say it should be more of a team effort. I don't think any of us have a set idea about how to proceed, so let's discuss it and see what we come up with."

"I agree," said Pat Cronin entering the room. "We need to get our heads together."

They ate a leisurely breakfast while Stone filled them in on his side of the tale. Stratton listened with interest, piecing the information together with what he already knew.

"So I guess Ayres must have teamed up with Jeremy," he said. "And I suppose that's where he got a copy of the key to the symbols. He's been stringing everyone along right from the outset. Never trust a politician."

"No," said Jennings. "And certainly not one with links to the Vatican. I feel stupid for not having sussed him out in the first place. I mean, I'm sure the signs were there. What makes me really mad is that I was almost tempted to give myself up to stop the 'conspiracy' against him."

"It's a good job I stopped you then isn't it?" said Grady.

"Yes, mate. I don't suppose you'll ever get bored of being proved right."

"Come on kids, play nice," said Cronin.

Stella washed down the last of her food with a gulp of orange juice and straightened her cutlery. "So what are we going to do now then?" she said. "It seems to me that our options are fairly limited. We've got two extremely large factions going head to head against each other, and neither is going to back down."

"They're not quite going head to head yet," said Jennings.

"Not all over the world, no," said Stella. "But I've been watching the satellite news this morning and certainly back home things are starting to look dodgy. It's not going to be long before the tension breaks. It will have spread all over Europe before you know it."

"I agree," said Stratton. "And I think tensions are a lot worse than any of you think. I can feel it inside. I can feel the world being dragged to and fro. I can the feel fear and confusion. And it's going to get a whole lot worse as well: particularly if Jonathan Ayres and the Vatican succeed with their plan."

"And what's that?" asked Jennings.

"They're going to assassinate the Mahdi."

Jennings' mouth dropped. "Jesus!" he said. "What the hell do they think they're playing at?! That'll start World War III."

"Yeah," said Stratton. "And the rest. Ayres seems to think that by getting rid of the Mahdi and proving he's not divine, that somehow it's going to convince the world to follow Christiano."

"More likely it's going to convince the Muslims to start a holy war," said Grady.

"Exactly," said Stratton. "But these little points don't seem to cross the minds of men in power. No doubt he thinks that all those people in the world who are undecided will suddenly start to believe in Christiano. He's probably already organizing some little stunt to prove his absolute divinity." He turned to Stone. "I don't suppose you know anything do you?"

Stone shook his head. "I'm afraid not. It's always on a need-to-know basis with him – and obviously I didn't need to know. He'll have his friends in the Vatican dealing with it I guess."

"Is there no way of stopping the assassination or warning them?" said Kharkov.

"I wouldn't have thought so," said Cronin, chipping in. "If they're going to do it they'll do it soon, and even if we could get word to the Muslims it wouldn't make any difference. I imagine their security is already as tight as they can make it, and they're hardly likely to stop the Mahdi going out in public on our say so."

"You're right," said Stratton. "There's no way we can stop the assassination. The Vatican has operatives throughout the Islamic world. It's only a question of when."

"So what can we do then?" said Jennings.

Stratton looked round the table and said, "Any ideas welcome."

It was Stella who spoke first. "Well," she started. "It occurs to me that fighting between the two factions is unavoidable. Once the Mahdi is dead all hell is going to break loose. And although I guess it's going to include everybody eventually, the war is essentially between the Catholics and the Muslims. They make up about a third of the world's population between them I believe – one billion Catholics and one and a half billion Muslims. I'm not including all Christians in that number of course – if you take the whole of the Christian faith then that adds another billion or so I think." She looked across to Stratton who nodded in agreement. "Anyway, the point I'm trying to make is that, even if you take a worst case scenario, not everyone in the world is going to be wrapped up in this fight – in fact just about half. So that leaves three and a half billion people with no allegiance. That's three and a half billion potential allies for us."

The table fell briefly silent while they took in her statement.

"Theoretically you're right," said Stratton. "But we'll have to factor in people being converted, although I guess that could be cancelled out by Muslims and Christians who refuse to get caught up in the fervour."

"And how do we reach these potential allies?" asked Grady.

"Well," said Stella. "I suppose we reach people the same way everyone else does – through the media. We use television, radio, the internet – whatever's available."

"And how do we convince them that the religions are lying?"

"We produce a miracle worker of our own. One who tells them exactly where the power comes from."

Stratton shot her a sharp glance.

"Why not?" she said.

"Because I don't want to, that's why not. I'm supposed to be dead, remember?"

"Exactly," said Stella. "You'll trump Christiano easily."

Stratton shook his head. "No. It's not going to happen. People will start treating *me* like some kind of Messiah, and that's what we're trying to get them away from. We're trying to get people to think for themselves. We want them to step away from mass religion, not set up a new one."

"Look, Stratton," she said. "If you've got a better idea then we'll try it. But ultimately these people need to be exposed, and you're the only person who can do it. Think about it – not only can you persuade the rest of the world, you'll probably be able to stop a lot of Muslims and Catholics from getting embroiled in the fight. You can appeal to their fundamental desire for peace. The majority of these people don't want confrontation, it's not in their nature, they just need a legitimate voice of reason to persuade them to stay out of the madness. If you stand up and speak then people will listen."

"Maybe," Stratton admitted. "But you're forgetting that any power I have is dependent on the prevailing mood. If the whole world's already at odds then I'll have no way of proving that I can perform the same feats as Christiano and the Mahdi."

"That's why we have to act now," said Stella. "Before the world does tip over the edge."

"I don't know, Stella. I'm still not convinced that I won't just be starting another religion."

"Oh for fuck's sake, Stratton!" she shouted. "Wake up and smell the fucking coffee! Grow a bloody backbone for Christ's sake! You always come out with some bloody excuse to avoid responsibility. It's been the same ever since I've known you. Every time something means putting yourself out you come up with some bloody clever philosophical excuse not to bloody well do it. It's always 'let people work it out for themselves' or 'it's not really my place to get involved'. Well this time people aren't working it out for themselves and it *is* your place to get involved. I don't care if you are some super-being from the limits of the cosmos, at the moment you're human and that means taking some action to help the rest of us mortals." She exhaled loudly. "Christ, you make me angry sometimes."

The table went deadly silent. Jennings and Grady pulled a grimace at each other. Stella lit a cigarette.

Stratton crossed his arms and puffed his cheeks awkwardly.

"Okay," he said slowly, unsure of how to proceed in the face of Stella's tirade. "I think you might have a point." He looked around the table to see if anyone else was going to speak. It was clear that they weren't. "But this isn't about me avoiding responsibility. This is about logistics and doing the right thing. My power is dwindling already, so even if I wanted to I can't go out there and perform miracles like Christiano and the Mahdi. And if Ayres has his way the Mahdi will probably be dead within the day, and then I'm going to be no use whatsoever. I think in essence your plan was a good one, and with a few tweaks here and there it might have been viable, but the way things are we just can't implement it as you'd like with me as a figurehead."

Stella tutted and took a drag of her cigarette.

"I think you're on the right track though," he said, trying to pacify her. "We need to reach people and let them know that the whole thing is a sham. The question is how we go about it."

"I think it's like Stella said," Cronin pitched in. "We need to somehow get control of the media. We need to petition all the world leaders and try to get them to see sense and put a stop to this. The ones that aren't already in the pocket of either religion that is."

"And how are we supposed to do that?" asked Jennings.

"I expect between us we've got more contacts and influence than we think," Cronin explained. "I know for a fact that Kandinsky was a very good friend of both the Russian President and Prime Minister. Is that right, Gregor?"

Kharkov nodded. "It is true. I will be able to gain the support of Moscow. I will also be able to influence the media, we are friends with major shareholders in a large number of networks throughout the world. Arman knew all the most influential men, including Rupert Murdoch. They were very close and he will be saddened to hear of his demise. I am certain he will want to work against his killers."

"Good," said Cronin. "Well that's a start. What about

America, Grady? Is there any way that we can get through to the President? Surely you must still have some good contacts?"

"I can give it a go," said Grady. "I'm certainly owed a few favours. I can't imagine this situation is sitting well with the Washington power brokers. Religion's the one thing they can't control. And there's nothing they hate more than being out of control."

"What about China?" asked Jennings. "They're the biggest country in the world aren't they? I mean, population wise."

"Yeah, they are," said Stratton. "I imagine they're just watching and waiting at the moment to see what happens. They do have some Christians and Muslims, but their main religions are Buddhism and Taoism. They probably won't get themselves involved unless it's absolutely necessary. I'm guessing the state will put an immediate stop to any infighting. If anything you have to put them down as allies because they aren't going to be encouraging violence."

"Okay then," said Cronin. "Let's leave China out of the equation for the moment." He paused. "The Middle East is obviously going one way only, so there's no point appealing to their better nature. Although I expect the Israeli's will quite happily stand against both sides. Any thoughts on India?"

"India's a tricky one," said Stratton. "I can see all sorts of trouble brewing there. It's so diverse that it'll be impossible for the authorities to control."

"Good point ," said Cronin. "What about Europe?"

"Again, it's diverse, isn't it," said Stratton. "It's predominantly Christian but there's plenty of Muslims. I can see it becoming a real battleground. I'm not sure there's any way for the authorities to get a grip, even if we can persuade them." He sighed. "Anyway, all this is getting away from the main point. I don't think we're going to have that much trouble convincing governments that the Mahdi and Christiano are fakes: like Grady said they'll be only too happy to hear the news if it means retaining control of their population. What we are going to have trouble doing is getting them to rein people in without recourse to violence. As soon as there's a whiff of civil unrest the military will be sent in."

"I don't think there's any way of avoiding military action now," said Grady. "Even if the Mahdi manages to escape being killed I think it's inevitable eventually. But if Stratton's right and it happens today then there's going to be an immediate holy war. And it won't matter how many people we influence – there *will* be bloodshed."

Stratton leant back in his chair and rubbed his eyes. "Maybe you're right," he said. "But we've got to try at least. If we don't then it's going to be Armageddon."

Chapter 66

Jenna sat by Tariq's bedside holding his hand. He had been drifting in and out of consciousness all night, but the medical staff said his condition was stable. She had lied to them and said she was his wife. She knew, however, that the subterfuge wouldn't last and the police would eventually find out and call his family. Once they arrived she knew she would be unwelcome. Until then she would stay by his side and comfort him as best she could.

Tariq opened his eyes and smiled at her. "Still here?" he croaked.

"Of course I am. Where else would I be?"

"What about work?"

"Don't worry about that. I've phoned in and Bunty's fine with it. How are you feeling?"

"Like I've been run over by a train."

She squeezed his hand. "I really thought I'd lost you last night. How could somebody do this to another human being? Do you know who it was?"

Tariq shook his head gingerly. "No. Just some blokes. I guess they were white, from what they were shouting." He coughed loudly. "Have you phoned my parents yet?"

Jenna hung her head. "Not yet," she admitted. "I wanted to stay with you."

"Don't worry about it," he said. "I want you to stay with me as well. They'll only make things worse. Let's wait a while."

"If that's what you want?" she said.

"That's what I want."

Jenna looked up to his battered face. She had had plenty of time to get used to it but it still made her sick inside. Not because it made him unattractive or diminished her feelings, but because it reminded her constantly of the violent and fearful nature of man. That anybody could wish to impart such pain on another human being was quite beyond her. She wondered if his attackers could see him now exactly what they would think. Would they stand by their vicious assault? Or in the cold light of day would they repent of their ignorant, senseless crime? She wanted to believe the latter, but perhaps it was a false hope.

"How long will I have to stay in here?" asked Tariq.

"I don't know," said Jenna. "But I think they'll probably have you out as soon as they possibly can. The doctor said that they'll probably keep you in for today and tonight for observation, but if they're satisfied then you may be able to go home tomorrow. I know it's quite quick, but they're really struggling for beds at the moment. You're not the only person who's been on the wrong end of a beating in the last 24 hours. When I came in with you last night A&E was overrun with people who had been in fights. The town's gone absolutely crazy, and it looks like it's only going to get worse."

"That bad is it?"

"Yeah. It's getting that way all over the country. The government are calling for people to stay calm, but nobody's listening. There aren't enough police to cope with it now. The feeling in the media is that the army are going to be brought in to try and keep some sort of order. It's turning into some kind of surreal nightmare."

Tariq gazed at her through his one good eye. "If I come out tomorrow, can I come and stay with you?"

"Of course you can. As long as your parents don't kick up a fuss."

"I'm sure they will, but it's not their choice. I want to be somewhere where I can get away from all this religious hatred."

Jenna smiled. "So do I."

It was then that Tariq's family walked through into the ward. His father, dressed in a suit, was at the head, followed by his elder brother and then his mother and sister. They rushed over to his bed. Tariq looked to Jenna and she held his hand tight.

"Tariq!" exclaimed his father. "My son! What have they done to you?"

"It's okay, Dad. I am alright," he spluttered.

His father gave him a concerned stare. "You do not sound alright, and you certainly do not look alright. And who is this?" he said, pointing to Jenna.

"This is Jenna," said Tariq. "She's…"

"I'm his girlfriend," said Jenna getting out of her chair. "It's good to meet you at last." She held out her hand.

Tariq's father stood in silent alarm. He took her hand and gave it a half-shake through instinctive politeness. He turned to Tariq with wide, questioning eyes.

"I've been meaning to tell you," Tariq stumbled.

His father regained his composure. "Could you leave us alone for a while please?" he asked Jenna. "We would like to see him as a family."

Jenna's immediate reaction was to stay, but wanting to keep on their right side she decided to leave them as requested. "Sure," she said. "I'll go and grab a coffee."

As she walked through A&E to get to the coffee shop she couldn't believe how busy it had become. There were no chairs left, and many of the sick and injured were either sitting on the carpet or propped up against the wall in the corridor. She hurried along and tried not to take on the air of despondency.

The coffee shop was inevitably busy and she had to wait for over twenty minutes to be served. Once she'd got her drink she went outside to the car park and lit a cigarette. The air was mild but the sky was filled with portentous black cloud. She looked up and felt a shadow grip her heart. She was suddenly isolated and alone. The wind picked up and blew a crumpled can across the empty tarmac. She shivered and huddled her arms close. A siren wailed in the distance.

She finished her cigarette quickly and downed the tepid and tasteless coffee in a couple of gulps. She checked her watch and saw that she'd been away from Tariq for over half an hour. Plenty of time for them to have had their family discussion, she thought. She went back inside through A&E and headed for the ward.

When she arrived back Tariq's family were still by his bed. His father looked up and stared at her suspiciously.

"Why did you not tell us that Tariq had been injured?" he asked.

"I was going to," she said. "But I was so worried about him that I forgot all about it."

"You lied to the police. You told them that you were his wife."

"I wanted to stay with him."

"Nevertheless, you lied."

"Dad! Stop it," said Tariq. "I wanted her here with me as well."

"That is no excuse, Tariq. If she had not lied then the police would have got in touch with us much sooner. If we had not rung ourselves we would never have found out."

"I'm sorry," said Jenna. "I'm very sorry."

Tariq's father gave a dismissive grunt. "It is very easy to be sorry after the event."

Tariq struggled to speak. "Dad, please!" he coughed. "This isn't the time or place."

"These things need to be said, Tariq," he said, getting out of his chair. "This woman obviously does not have your best interests at heart. She is interested in herself, and herself alone. She is like all these so-called 'modern women' from the West – she is greedy, jealous and divisive. Already it appears that she is coming between you and your family. I do not doubt that you were on your way to see her when you were attacked. I had warned you that the streets were dangerous and not to go out, but you disobeyed me. You sloped away like a thief in the night – and for what? For the false promises and wicked allure of a harlot."

Jenna stood there, for a moment too stunned to speak. "Excuse me?" she said.

"I think you ought to apologize, Dad," said Tariq.

"I apologize for nothing. My son is in hospital through no fault of his own. He has been blinded by lust and temptation. He is a good boy; a good Muslim, and you have tainted him."

"Listen to me," said Jenna. "I've done nothing to him. We're in love. Is that so hard for you to stomach? Don't you believe in love? Or do you only believe in control and subjugating women? It's not me who's in the wrong here, it's you and your outdated beliefs. It's the likes of you who've caused all that's happening at the moment. If you were a bit more tolerant then this world wouldn't be in such a mess."

Tariq's father glared at her, his eyes ablaze with fury. "How dare you!?" he roared. "This world is in a state because of Godless people like you. You have no respect for Allah, you have no respect for your fellow humans, and you certainly have no respect for yourself. Our troubles are a direct result of the loose morality of the West."

Jenna was about to reply when a senior nurse came up to calm the situation.

"Excuse me," she said. "Could you possibly keep this down. This is a hospital – not the House of Commons. If you don't keep quiet I'm going to have to ask you all to leave. I'll call security if I have to." She gave them a matronly stare.

"I'm sorry," said Jenna. "You're absolutely right."

Tariq's father mumbled an apology and sat back down.

Tariq gave Jenna an apologetic glance.

"Listen," she said. "I'm going to go home and grab a shower and leave you guys to talk. I'll be back in a couple of hours, Taz." She leant over and kissed him softly on the forehead. "Is there anything you want me to bring you?"

"No thanks, just yourself."

She smiled and left him with his family. Outside the hospital she lit a cigarette and took a number of heavy drags. She hoped that when she returned Tariq's idiot father would be gone.

Chapter 67

The Ataturk Olympics Stadium in Istanbul was packed to capacity. Over 81,000 people were crammed into the stands, and another 40,000 flooded the football pitch. The temperature was 90°F and rising. It was uncomfortable and unsafe in the extreme, but not a soul was heard to complain. They were there for a defining moment in their lives: the moment when they were going to see the Mahdi in the flesh for the very first time. They had watched the television reports and heard all the rumours, and now at last the great redeemer was coming to bless them. Anticipation electrified the air.

At the side of the pitch a large podium had been erected. Behind this was a temporary covered tunnel to allow the Mahdi to appear without obstruction from his followers. It was in here that Ali stood alongside his master waiting for him to take the stand. It had been a busy morning, with an early flight out of Mecca followed by a private audience with the Turkish president. After that they had been swept away to the stadium in a convoy of armoured cars. Ali had not even had time to collect his thoughts properly. He felt tired and confused, and was beginning to wonder whether he was really the right person to assist the Mahdi in his work. Also, the conversation of the night before kept replaying in the back of his mind, and he couldn't help but feel that something awful was going to happen.

"Is everything alright, Ali?" asked the Mahdi.

"Yes, Master, I am just tired. It has been a long morning."

The Mahdi eyed him curiously. "Are you sure? You look most concerned. I am only going out to talk to these people. I have done it many times."

"Yes, Master. But…"

The Mahdi rested his hand on Ali's forehead. "There is a reason for everything, Ali. For good things and bad things. As I have told you many times before – only Allah knows his own purpose. Do not fret over what might come to pass, just enjoy the moment you are in."

Ali forced a smile. "Yes, Master."

"Now," said the Mahdi. "I must go and address the faithful. I will see you in a while."

Ali watched his master ascend the steps to the podium. As he neared the top an air-shattering roar broke out causing Ali to cover his ears. It continued for over a minute until the crowd finally obeyed the Mahdi's appeal for hush.

"Welcome my brothers and sisters!" he started. "Welcome to this magnificent arena! I hope that I have not kept you waiting for too long." He paused to gather himself. "I am here today to talk of many things. I am here to talk about faith, about respect, and about diligence and hard work. I am here to talk about honour, about truth, and about family. But first and foremost I am here to talk about love and peace."

The crowd cheered.

"We are living in a world defined by war and hatred," he continued, "and I am here to tell you of Allah's desire for serenity and harmony. Of his wish to see all men reconciled. There has been much speculation in the media about myself and the Christian Messiah, about which of us represents Allah's true intent. I hope that today I can prove to you that I am indeed a true messenger of Allah."

The crowd cheered again.

"But I also hope to persuade you that I am not the only messenger he has sent. I wish to tell you…" His voice stopped abruptly and he slumped forward onto the rostrum and then down to the floor. The crowd fell silent. Blood began to stream from a dark hole in his temple. The two guards either side of the podium leapt across to help. They checked his body for vital signs and then picked him up and carried him down the steps away from the crowd who began to vocalize their disarray.

In the tunnel the guards laid the Mahdi down and called the

medics over to see to him. Ali watched as they tried to save his life.

"There's nothing we can do," said one. "We have to get him to a hospital."

Ali knew in his heart that his master was past saving. He knelt down by his body to say a prayer, but was lifted out of the way. He watched helplessly as the medics stretchered the Mahdi out of the panic-ridden stadium. Before long he was alone in the tunnel. The crowd continued to bay.

When he'd finally gotten over the initial shock, his first instinct was to chase after the entourage and get a lift to the hospital. He cursed himself for being so pathetic and set off through the building. He negotiated the maze of corridors swiftly and made it to the exit just as they lifted the Mahdi into an air-ambulance. He was going to make a run for it and hop aboard when something stopped him. A voice inside his head told him to slow down and think. The Mahdi was dead, of that there was no doubt. The hospital would not be able to save him, and he would not be coming back. This meant that Ali had a task to perform. He remembered his master's words of the previous night, and decided that he must return to the hotel immediately. He needed to retrieve the box before anyone else could get their hands on it.

Chapter 68

Stratton lay on his bed meditating. The enormity of their task was almost suffocating and he needed time alone to recharge his failing batteries. Their discussion had been animated and informative, but nevertheless inconclusive. However he looked at it there was no real way of stemming the already powerful tide. Their only option was to carry on regardless and hope that a solution presented itself naturally. He blocked all thought from his mind and drifted off into the ether.

Minutes or maybe hours later his peace was disturbed by a distant tapping. The noise grew until he could ignore it no longer. He opened his eyes and grounded himself back in the room, and then said loudly, "Come in, it's not locked."

Jennings opened the door and stepped inside. "Hi, mate," he said. "Hope I'm not disturbing you."

Stratton swung his legs over the side of the bed and sat on the edge. "No, mate, don't worry about it. I was just having a little meditation. I needed to get away for a while. My head was starting to hurt."

Jennings nodded. "You and me both," he said. "It's difficult to get any sort of grip on the situation. Everything seems to have been taken out of our hands."

"Pretty much," agreed Stratton. "But sometimes that's a good thing. If you've got no decision to make then you can't make a wrong one. Sometimes the universe forces you into the right place at the right time without you realizing it. Remember – we're only little pieces in an infinite jigsaw."

Jennings went to the fridge and pulled out two bottles of mineral water. He handed one to Stratton and then sat down and had a long drink.

"Stella was a bit harsh on you, don't you think?" he said, after quenching his thirst.

"Maybe," said Stratton. "Maybe not. I guess she had a point in a way. I have tended to shirk responsibility in the past. But it's not as easy as accepting responsibility or not. It's difficult to decide when to intervene in something and when to let nature take it's course. Like I said, we're only tiny pieces of the jigsaw and we don't always know where we're supposed to fit. If I take action on something am I doing the work of the universe or am I trying to force a piece in where it's not wanted?"

"I think that sometimes you think too much," said Jennings. "There's no real answer once you start delving too deep, is there?"

"No, you're right, there isn't. There's only more questions. But wouldn't it be boring if there weren't?" He smiled and took a sip of water. "How are you feeling at the moment anyway? How's your attunement settled in?"

"I haven't really thought about it for a while to be honest, so I guess I'm used to it now. Although, I did try a bit of healing on Stella the other night, and that was an experience. I really felt the power flowing through me. I think I got just as much out of it as she did actually."

"Yeah, that's how it works if you're doing it properly – it should be an exchange of energies. I'm glad you've started to put your talent to good use anyway. I might ask you to have a go on me soon if things get much worse."

"Are you really not good then?"

"Not great, no. I felt fantastic a few days ago when the whole world was rejoicing at the second coming, but now the reality's set in I just feel tired most of the time. I'm certainly no good for healing anybody at the moment, I'm having enough trouble keeping myself alive. I just hope we can start to turn things around. But I've got a feeling they're going to get worse before they get better – if you'll excuse the cliché." He smiled grimly and then suddenly clutched his side in pain.

"Are you alright?" asked Jennings.

Stratton shook his head and gasped, falling sideways onto the bed. Jennings jumped out of his chair and went to his aid. He manoeuvred his hands around and tried to place them on Stratton's ribcage. But as soon as he made contact a rush of electricity shot through his body and sent him flying backwards to the floor. He pulled himself up on his elbows and shook his head to clear it. Stratton continued to hold his side.

Jennings got to his feet and approached the bed once again.

"No!" yelled Stratton. "Don't! I'll be alright."

Jennings sat down and took a drink of water. He watched as Stratton slowly regained control of his body and eventually sat up. "Are you okay?"

Stratton nodded. "Yes, mate. Just about anyway."

"What happened?"

"I don't know. I just got this really bad pain in my side – like a stitch but ten times worse."

"Well," said Jennings, "whatever it was it sent me halfway across the room. I thought I'd been hit with a sledgehammer."

"Yeah, sorry about that. I should have warned you." He grabbed his bottle of water and took a long drink. "I think something's happened," he said.

"Like what?"

"I don't know. Something bad."

Just then Stella burst into the room. "It's the Mahdi!" she gasped. "He's been shot!"

Chapter 69

Ali walked casually into the Ciragan Palace Kempinski Hotel and headed for the stairs. He looked around nonchalantly as he walked, but inside he was racked with anxiety. His palms perspired and his throat was dry. Every person that caught his eye was a potential enemy. Every step he took a potential giveaway. He felt alone and exposed. He smiled politely at the girl on the reception desk and continued on his way.

He negotiated the stairs quickly and strode off down the long corridor to the complimentary suite that he and the Mahdi were to have shared. The air was cloying and humid and the walls closed in on him as he walked. By the time he reached the door his breathing was laboured and his clothes moistened with sweat. He took one last look down the hallway and entered the suite.

Closing the door behind him he took a couple of deep breaths in an attempt to relax. The Mahdi's death had shaken him to the centre of his soul. An hour ago his world had been full of optimism and life, and now it was empty and devoid of all hope. He hung his head and slumped back against the door.

He remained impassive until a wave of electricity suddenly jolted through his spine, freeing his body of its temporary paralysis and causing him to stand to attention like a scolded soldier. In less than a second he was alert and wired to the world once more. The Mahdi's voice whirled around his head, urging him to hasten.

Without any further thought he rushed to the corner of the room and removed the portrait of the sultan from the wall, revealing the safe behind. He closed his eyes and tried to remember the eight-digit code that the Mahdi had taught him only a few hours before. The first four digits were 4154, of that he was pretty certain; the last four, however, were proving elusive. He had never had a good memory for numbers, and indeed had never had the need to recall so many at one time. The harder he tried, the more jumbled the figures became. Eventually his head hurt so much he thought it may explode with the pressure.

Just as he was about to lose it completely the Mahdi's voice came to him once again, telling him to relax and clear his mind. As soon as he did the whole sequence of numbers popped into his head: 41542389. He typed them into the keypad and pressed the 'Enter' button. The safe clicked open and he reached in and pulled out the box in its hessian sack.

With his heart drumming he left the suite and entered the corridor once more. He had no idea where he was going, but instinctively knew he had to get out of the hotel as quickly as he could. He was about to make for the ground floor when a group of the Mahdi's security guards appeared at the top of the stairs. For a brief moment he froze with panic, and then with no other choice he walked the opposite way. He looked back and knew that he had been seen.

His footsteps got faster until he was almost at a run. He had no idea if there was another way down to the ground floor, but he had to keep moving forward. Behind, he heard the guards shouting at him to stop. He reached the end of the hallway and, after a quick look both ways, turned right.

After another twenty yards he came to a fire exit. He swung it open and leapt down the flight of steps to the floor below. Without looking back he burst through the bottom door and sped off down another long corridor. Ahead he saw another fire exit. He hoped it would lead him out of the building.

With the guards closing down on him he thrust through the exit into the open air. With no time to get his bearings, he jinked to the right and hared towards what he thought would be the city streets. He knew once he was there he would have a good chance of losing his pursuers in the complex maze of alleys and bazaars.

Having been crippled since birth Ali had never run before in his life, but somehow he managed to keep going. With abrasive lungs and weakening legs he sprinted through the hotel gardens and out onto the main road. Weaving through the heavy traffic he crossed over and into a narrow street. The guards fell back, their ungainly frames unable to match Ali's agility.

Gleaning hope from the distance he had put between himself and those chasing, he found a second wind. He ran and ducked and dodged down a succession of slender passageways until he felt sure that he'd lost them. Then, cradling the box in his arms, he flopped down in a doorway and tried to catch his breath. Never in his life had he felt so exhausted. For two or three minutes he didn't move. Then, as his composure slowly returned, he lifted his head and peered out from the recess. He looked up and down the street but could see no-one. Clambering to his feet, and without any fixed idea, he moved on calmly and headed deeper into the city.

He felt in his pocket to check he still had the money the Mahdi had given him. It was a sizeable amount and would certainly enable him to get far from Istanbul. But where was he going to go? He certainly couldn't take the box back to Mecca. He had to take it someplace out of the way. Someplace where nobody would find it – hopefully for hundreds, maybe thousands of years. The problem was that the only place he knew was Mecca. He'd been there all his life in the same house on the same street. He knew nothing really of the world outside the city walls. He decided that he would go to the station and just get aboard the first train out of Istanbul and take it from there. The longer he tarried, the more chance there was of getting caught.

He wandered through the empty backstreets looking out for someone to ask for directions to the nearest train station. After a couple of minutes he came upon a woman with a young child in tow and she gave him the information he needed. He went over the route in his head a number of times and then moved along.

The streets grew gradually busier allowing Ali to feel slightly more comfortable and anonymous. He slowed his pace and tried to blend in with the locals, attempting to give the appearance of one who had lived there forever. Like this he covered the distance to the station safely and without sign of the guards.

He was about to climb the station steps when he took one last look around. His heart lurched in horror as he saw two guards running directly towards him from the right. He flew up the steps and into the main building, his eyes darting frantically looking for a means of escape. Behind him the guards entered the station.

With nowhere to hide Ali began to run blindly towards the platforms, shoving bodies out of his way as he went. The guards were hot on his heels and gaining with every stride. There was no way he could reach a train without getting caught. The only hope he had was to try and lose them some other way. He ran to an empty platform and jumped down onto the tracks hoping that the guards would think twice about following. The move didn't deter them. They leapt down straight after him and continued to close. Ali scrambled back up onto the platform and ran back into the station.

By now the chase had drawn the attention of the police. Three uniformed men appeared at the main entrance and started to move towards Ali. He swerved in and out of the crowd and made a run for the side exit. But before he could reach it two more policemen came into view and blocked his way. He was fast becoming cornered. In a last desperate attempt to escape he launched himself sideways and into the middle of a large group of students who were checking the timetables. He ducked down and ploughed through them stealthily, keeping as low as he could.

At the edge of the crowd he poked his head out warily. After looking left and right he saw no sign of either the guards or the police. The main entrance was now directly in front of him. Without stopping to think he ran for the doors. Behind him the police hollered as they caught sight of him once more. With one last spurt he crashed through the doors and out into the open air. His elation was short-lived. Coming towards him from the street were two more guards. He looked around for possible escape routes, but there were none. This time he was trapped.

With nowhere to left to go the Mahdi's words came flooding back to him. Whatever happened he could not let them get hold of the box. As the net closed he had one last, desperate idea. He hesitated for a moment, uncertain whether what he was about to do was right. And then, knowing that he no longer had a choice, he shot to his left towards a kebab-seller. The man shouted as he approached but Ali wasn't listening. He pushed the man out of the way and flung the grille off the top of the flaming brazier, scattering bits of meat everywhere. Then, pausing only for a split second, he dumped the hessian sack and the box deep into the heart of the fire.

Within seconds the police and the guards were upon him. They grabbed him roughly and restrained his arms, but Ali didn't put up a fight. He just stood and watched mournfully as the flames licked higher and higher. His task was complete. The knowledge was gone forever.

Chapter 70

Inside the Plaza Hotel, New York, Cardinal Vittori switched off the television and reclined thoughtfully in his armchair. The scenes in Istanbul had been terrifying, and the enormity of what they had just done was beginning to strike home. He closed his eyes and said a small prayer for the people in the stadium.

The plan had been Ayres' for the most part, and although Vittori had agreed to it, it had been with a certain amount of reluctance. Of course he wanted what was best for the Church, but the resulting storm had worried him from the outset, and the reaction from the crowd in Istanbul had only increased his fears. They were, without doubt, headed for trouble on an unimaginable scale.

Christiano came out of his room and sat down opposite his mentor. He had seen the news report and his face was fraught with concern. "It is terrible, Your Eminence."

"Yes, Christiano, it *is* terrible."

"But who would do such a thing? Who would want to kill him?"

Vittori shook his head. "I am not sure. There are many crazed people in this world, and many dangerous ones too. There are also many dangerous governments. It is possible that his assassination was ordered by one of these. It is well-known that his coming has upset the Israelis. Their situation in the Middle East is becoming increasingly precarious. It would not surprise me in the least if they had a hand in this."

"But what if it wasn't the Israelis? What if it was someone else? Like you say, there are a lot of crazed and dangerous people in this world. It worries me."

"You do not need to worry, Christiano. You are very well-protected."

"So was the Mahdi," said Christiano. "And look what happened. What if the same people want to get rid of me as well?

Or maybe someone else will try? I no longer feel comfortable about my appearance this evening."

Vittori leant forward and laid his hand on Christiano's knee. "Come, come, Christiano. There is no need for fear. Nobody will be able to do anything to you. We will have the best security possible. The Americans are meticulous in all aspects of counter-terrorism. There will be no place safer than Yankee Stadium this evening."

"I am still not happy with the situation. They cannot watch everybody all of the time."

"You would be surprised what they can do," said Vittori. "But I nevertheless appreciate your concerns. Of course, if you wish to pull out of this evening's appearance then I will understand. And I am sure that the people will understand too. But you have to ask yourself – would the Son of God be afraid of showing himself in public, even in these circumstances?"

Christiano was about to answer when the door to the suite clicked open and Jonathan Ayres walked in. "Have you heard the news?" he asked, grabbing a chair.

Vittori nodded solemnly.

"Awful business," said Ayres. "Absolutely awful." He shook his head. "But there you go. That's the kind of world we live in at the moment. That's what we're here to change. Isn't it, Christiano?"

"Of course."

"You're not frightened, are you?" asked Ayres.

"A little," admitted Christiano. "But I know that I must not let it affect me. I cannot show my fear to the people or else they will lose faith in me."

"Exactly," said Ayres. "You must show the world how strong you are and that you fear nothing. Your strength will be their strength. And really there is no reason for you to be afraid anyway."

"I know," said Christiano. "Cardinal Vittori has assured me

that my security is the best. The Americans will protect me well."

"Yes, they will," said Ayres. "But that is not the only reason for you to feel safe is it?"

"What do you mean?"

"Your divine powers of course. Surely the Son of God cannot be harmed if he doesn't want to be?"

"I have the power to heal. Not the power to stop bullets."

"Well, that's not entirely true, is it?"

"What do you mean?"

"I mean that you do have that power, but perhaps you don't realize it. I believe that amongst the symbols there is one that you can use for protection. It is signified on the key as a picture of a man with – how should I put it – a force-field around him: he's repelling an attack from a warrior. Do you know the picture I mean?"

"Yes, of course," said Christiano. "But I have not tried to use it. I wasn't really sure exactly what it did. I guessed that it was some kind of protection against a physical attack, but I have had no cause to try it out."

"Well then," said Ayres. "Let's do it now. I'll try and punch you, and you use the symbol."

Vittori frowned. "Are you sure about this, Jonathan?"

"Yes, yes, Fabio. Don't worry about it. I'll just start off with a gentle tap to the shoulder or something like that, and then build it up from there. I'm not going to give him a right hook straight away. It's the only way we're going to be able to test it out. Is it alright with you, Christiano?"

Christiano looked uncertain. "I suppose so," he said.

"Good. Let's give it a go. Let me know when you're ready."

They stood up and faced each other. Christiano concentrated on the relevant symbol and gave Ayres a nod to indicate his readiness. Ayres threw a tentative tap towards Christiano's shoulder. Then another, this time slightly harder.

"Well?" he asked.

"I cannot feel anything so far."

"Can I get a little rougher?"

Christiano nodded and Ayres began again, throwing more weight behind his punches. He continued to up the pressure until he was hammering away with full body-blows and hooks and jabs to the face. Christiano stood motionless.

After a while Ayres stopped. "Well," he said breathlessly. "I guess we can safely say that it definitely works. I used to be a bit of a boxer at Oxford you know." He poured himself a glass of water and sat back down. "Well, Fabio, what do you think?"

"Very impressive, Jonathan. But a few punches is not a bullet. This defence was designed way before firearms were even thought of. At best it will work against swords and knives."

"I agree," said Christiano.

"I appreciate that," said Ayres. "But my guess is that the field will stop anything physical – be it bullet, arrow or whatever. And anyway it's all hypothetical really. Like I said, the Americans have got extremely tight security so nobody will get through. This was only to try and set Christiano's mind slightly more at ease. I do suggest that you use it before you go on stage though. Just to be sure in yourself."

"I will," said Christiano.

Ayres sipped at his water. "Good," he said. "We shall all feel more comfortable now. This is a highly important address you're making tonight, Christiano, and you certainly mustn't be seen to be afraid. Remember, above all else these people think that you're the Son of God. They expect a voice of calm and reason amongst all the madness that is going on. They need to see that you are in control."

"I understand what is expected of me," said Christiano. He got out of his seat. "I think I will go and rest for the afternoon, and perhaps get some sleep. I am still a little jet-lagged."

"Good idea," said Ayres. "We'll see you later on."

Christiano went to his room.

When he was out of earshot Vittori turned to Ayres and said, "Well, Jonathan, I really hope that you know what you're doing. If anything happens to him then we are finished."

"You worry too much, Fabio," said Ayres. "This time tomorrow Christiano will be very much alive, and the whole world will be in awe of the new Messiah." He sat back and allowed himself a broad smile.

Chapter 71

Jenna stepped out of her flat and shut the door behind her. She felt slightly better after a shower and a bite to eat, but the long sleepless night still weighed heavily. She decided that she would spend another couple of hours at the hospital, but return home at around eight to get some much-needed shuteye. She felt that Tariq was over the worst now and that her constant presence was no longer required. It would also sit well with his family if she left them alone for some extra private time.

After making doubly sure she had her car keys, she descended the stairs and exited the main entrance, making her way to the residents' car park. She looked up at the overcast sky and wondered if she should go back for her umbrella, but then remembered that it was already in the boot of the car. She hurried along into the wind, her hair cascading behind.

The car park was silent and grey. The wind eddied and blew the first spots of rain into her tired face. A sudden fear overtook her, causing her to cast her eye suspiciously around, watching out for an as-yet-unseen enemy. There was nobody there, but the tingle in her spine told her to move forward as quickly as she could. She shuddered against the breeze and started to jog. She squeezed the key fob and disabled the car alarm, the orange lights blinking brightly in the gloom.

Once inside she slammed the door and locked herself in and started the car. The rain started to hammer down and she flicked on the wipers. She was safe and yet she still felt exposed. She engaged the headlights and set off slowly for the road. It was then that she noticed a group of people assembling at the exit to the car park. She beeped her horn for them to get out of the way.

As she drew closer she started to make out their faces. It was a gathering of young Asian men. Probably a similar age to Tariq, she thought. Instead of moving out of the way they stood their ground and stared through the windscreen. She beeped her horn again, revved the engine, and inched the car forward with intent. This time the group parted and let her through, but not without a number of minatory glares as she passed.

The rain continued to beat down. She turned onto the Causeway and accelerated slowly, watching the group of youths disappear into the background. She was unsure as to their purpose, but whatever it was they had made her more than uncomfortable. There was menace in the air, mirroring the darkness of the sky, and her nerves told her to stay vigilant.

She switched the radio on to try and soothe her fear. She listened in disbelief as she learnt of the Mahdi's assassination for the first time. A chill spread through her body as the implications of his death hit home. Already the Muslims were laying the blame firmly at the door of the Catholic Church, and already the backlash had begun, with rioting reported in a number of major cities, including London. She had no doubt that even more trouble would hit Banbury soon, and that the gang she had just passed were only one of many readying themselves for violence.

The rush-hour traffic was quieter than normal but still provided Jenna with a sense of security. Once she reached it the pressure that had been growing inside started to dissipate slightly. The isolation of the back streets replaced by the relative safety of numbers. She couldn't remember being so pleased to be one of the faceless masses. She turned off the news and put on the CD player, and relaxed into some *Keane*.

Her peace was, however, short-lived. As she passed Morrisons' petrol station a large missile flew out from the left and hit the car in front. She peered out into the rain to see where it had come from, and saw a large gang of Muslims appear from the side street. There were over thirty of them and they were all chanting something in Arabic. They began to pelt the traffic with stones and bricks. All sense was lost as the road descended into mayhem, with drivers mounting the pavement and taking any available gap to get away from the destructive mob. Jenna swerved to her right into the oncoming traffic and then weaved across to the far verge. She had almost made it when something hit her backend and sent the car into an uncontrollable spin. She wrestled desperately with the steering-wheel, but to no avail. The car rotated 360° and crashed into a low wall.

The blow reverberated through her entire body, and for a moment she was completely disoriented. Outside the traffic began to pile up. Gathering herself as best she could she unbuckled her seat-belt and tried to open the driver-side door. She pushed with all her strength but it wouldn't budge. In desperation, with claustrophobia setting in, she jumped across to the passenger seat and pulled vigorously at the door-handle. The door did not move. Feeling herself becoming almost hysterical she took a couple of slow breaths and attempted to think. A few seconds later her stupidity hit her full in the face. She flicked off the lock and opened the door.

By now the road was packed with stationary vehicles, most of them smashed or dented. Jenna was surrounded and only just managed to squeeze herself out. She reached inside for her handbag, and without looking back, began to run away from the burgeoning riot. Behind her the shouting grew louder, heavily punctuated by the sound of breaking glass.

She ran quickly up the street, thankful that she'd worn trainers and not heels. The traffic backed up beside her with horns blaring and irate men shouting blindly out of wound-down windows, but her only interest was to get as far away as possible.

Eventually, almost half a mile later, her body could take no more and she had to stop. By this time she was halfway up Hightown Road and well away from the trouble. She dropped her handbag onto a patch of grass and then flopped down beside it, gasping for breath with her head cradled on her knees. The rain beat down on the back of her neck. The world she knew had changed forever.

Chapter 72

Stratton sat in front of the huge television screen in the bar with Jennings and Stella. He watched intently as events around the world unfolded. The Mahdi's assassination had brought about exactly the fear and confusion he and the others had expected. Incensed Muslims all over the globe were taking to the streets, in emphatic displays of anger against the people they believed responsible for the death of their beloved saviour: the West and the Catholic Church. The hatred was escalating to unparalleled levels, and already the military had been deployed in heated troublespots.

"This is unreal," said Jennings.

"If only it were," said Stratton. "And this is only the start of it." He winced and grabbed his left side.

"Are you okay?"

"Just about. I'm starting to feel it now though."

"Is there anything I can do?"

Stratton shook his head. "I don't think so. I would ask you to channel some energy into me, but after what happened earlier on I don't think it would be a good idea. It'd probably send you flying again. The best way to help is to keep calm and don't get caught up in everything that's happening. It'll help counteract all the negative energy. If you can summon up a few cheerful thoughts I expect it'll be even better."

"I'll have a go," said Jennings unconvincingly.

Grady walked in to join them. "How's it going?" he asked. "Any break in the storm?"

"No," said Jennings. "What about you? Have you had any luck with the US government?"

Grady sat down in an armchair. "I've spoken to a few people, and the one thing I do know is that everyone's scared. The whole thing's becoming unmanageable. Internally, the atmosphere in the States isn't too bad, but relations with the Middle East are at an all-time low, as you can imagine. There's a very real concern that before too long this is going to turn nuclear. The Iranians have already made threats."

"Surely they haven't got enough firepower to be a real concern?" said Stella. "Their capability's nothing compared to the States."

"Maybe not," said Grady. "But they've got enough to hurt. And if they start gaining allies elsewhere then who knows what could happen. The whole world's on a knife-edge at the moment. Nobody knows which way anyone else is going to turn."

"So have you told anyone what's really going on?" asked Jennings.

"I've told people as much as I can without sounding like a lunatic. I've had to tread a bit carefully, because they're not going to let us through to the main men if they think we're off our heads. But having said that, I think they'll be prepared to believe anything that gives them back the advantage over the Church. At the moment they're having to pander to their every request. Take tonight for instance: they've had to second top men from all the various agencies just to police Yankee Stadium for this appearance by the Messiah."

"That's still going ahead then is it?" said Stratton.

"Yeah," said Grady. "They tried to get them to cancel it, but apparently the Church won't be swayed. They said that Christiano isn't afraid to face his people and has to make a stand. They said that as he is God's one true messenger there's no way that he could come to any harm. Of course, they still want all the security in place, so I guess they're not that confident in his abilities. What do you make of it?"

"I'm not sure," said Stratton. "But there's bound to be more to it than meets the eye. They're up to something – I just don't know what."

Chapter 73

Yankee Stadium in the Bronx, New York is home to the New York Yankees baseball team. It opened in 2009 across the street from the old stadium which it replaced. The Vatican had looked at other arenas, but its iconic status made it the perfect venue for Christiano to begin his tour of the States. If there was one thing that united America it was baseball.

Christiano stood nervously in the wings. The stands were filled to capacity, as was the field in front of the stage. He had memorized the speech that Vittori and Ayres had written with him, but the sight of such a large and intense audience gave him goose bumps. In front of his home crowd, using his own language, he had been fairly confident, but now he felt well beyond his comfort zone. His English was very good, but he hadn't used it a lot since his school days.

"Are you nearly ready?" asked Vittori. "The crowd are getting somewhat restless."

"I think so," said Christiano. "I just hope they understand me."

Jonathan Ayres patted him on the back. "Of course they will," he said. "Just speak like you did when we rehearsed: it was beautiful English – crystal clear. And if you get stuck just look at the autocue."

"I will do my best."

"And remember," said Ayres. "Don't worry about a thing, you're perfectly safe."

Christiano took a deep breath and then walked out onto the stage. The noise that greeted him was unlike anything he had ever heard or even imagined. The stage shook with the applause, and his ears felt like they were going to implode. He looked out onto the ocean of bodies and for a brief moment thought about turning back. Then the energy grabbed him. It hit his chest like a bolt of lightning. They were here for him. They were all here for him. Forgetting his anxiety he raised his hand and walked boldly to the rostrum. For a while he stood there, soaking up the wild atmosphere with hunger; then he motioned for silence. The masses obeyed his command.

"Good evening, New York!" he started. "It is an honour for me to be here."

The people cheered.

"Thank you!" he said. "Thank you very much. As I said, it is a great honour for me to be here in America, especially in the famed Yankee Stadium. I am a great lover of sport and the way it brings people together. Whether it is baseball, or soccer, or basketball, or football, it unifies people all over the world whatever their faith. At its best and most profound it takes us out of our everyday lives and teaches us meaning. Among many things it shows us the importance of teamwork, it shows us the importance of good grace, it shows us the importance of practice and hard work, and it shows us the importance of belief. These are all attributes that we require to live happy and fruitful lives."

He paused briefly and looked around the stadium, and then glanced at the autocue.

"But I am not here today to talk at length about sport. On another day perhaps I might, but not today. Today is a very sad day for us all, not just the Muslim faith. I am talking about the shooting earlier today of the man they called the Mahdi. There have been many accusations thrown, including a suggestion that the Catholic Church was somehow involved. This, I can assure you, is a lie. The Catholic Church deplores any act of violence, and is as saddened at the news as the rest of the world. This is not only an act against Islam, it is an act against God himself. It does not matter if this man was indeed who he claimed to be or not, the killing of another human being cannot be justified in any way."

He paused again, this time to sip some water. He was about to carry on when a movement at the corner of the stage caught his eye. A dark, bearded man, dressed in loose cream trousers and shirt appeared from the shadows. In his hand he held a gun. Christiano froze and then looked around for help – had nobody seen this intruder?

The man moved into view and towards the rostrum. Christiano began to panic. He knew the man was going to shoot and there was nothing he could do to stop him. Time slowed down. Christiano closed his eyes and drew the protection sign in his head. He heard a gunshot; then another. He felt nothing. Opening his eyes he saw the man being wrestled to the ground by two agents. He looked down at his body to see if he had been injured. There was no blood, but on the floor beneath him were two crumpled lumps of metal. He eyed them curiously.

The world suddenly returned to real time. The crowd was in uproar and government agents piled onto the stage. One of them came up and grabbed his arm.

"Are you okay, sir?"

Christiano stared at him blankly for a moment, then said, "Yes, I am fine thank you."

The agent noticed the mangled bullets on the floor and gave his charge an inquisitive look. Only then did the magnitude of what had just happened hit home. An overwhelming pulse of empowerment rose through Christiano's entirety. "Do not worry about me," he said. "I am the Messiah – nothing can harm me." The words echoed in his head: *"Nothing can harm me."*

Christiano regained control of himself quickly and ordered all agents off the stage. He picked up the bullets and approached the rostrum and began to speak, urging the crowd to calm themselves. His voice was rich and commanding, and soon the whole stadium was surrounded by hush.

"Thank you," he said. "I understand your concerns, but really there is no need. As you can see I am unharmed." He held out his palm and showed it to the camera linked to the giant screens dotted around the stadium. "These are the bullets that were fired at me." The crowd gasped. He drew himself up and spread his arms wide. "If any of you doubted before, then doubt no longer! I am the true Messiah!"

In the wings Ayres and Vittori smiled at each other. The plan had worked perfectly.

Chapter 74

Jennings watched the live feed open-mouthed as Christiano opened his palms and displayed the crumpled metal. His disbelief continued as the "True Messiah" reinforced his divinity to the spellbound crowd. Beside him, Grady, Stella and Cronin were equally dumbfounded. Even Stratton appeared bemused.

"What the hell?!" said Jennings. "I just don't believe it. How the hell did he manage that? It must be some sort of trick."

"It's got to be," agreed Stella. "There's no way anyone can stop bullets." She turned to Stratton. "What do you think?"

Stratton gave a non-committal shrug. "I'm not sure what to think at the moment. I'd like to take a look back at it before I make any sort of judgement. It could be a trick, but then again he might have really done it. If you remember, I managed to stop Yoshima hurting you by using the symbols."

"I know," said Stella. "But stopping a bullet's completely different to stopping someone kicking you."

"Maybe. But the principal's still the same. The shield isn't made of anything tangible so there's no way we can know what sort of force it can take. For all we know it may be able to stop cannonballs or even missiles. Don't ever underestimate the power of the universe."

Jennings grabbed the remote control for the big screen and rewound the picture to the point just before the shooter appeared from the side of the stage.

"Look," said Stratton. "Just as he picks up his water he looks to the side. Watch his face – he's just as surprised as anyone else that someone's invaded the stage."

Jennings paused the film. "I agree," he said. "Unless he's a brilliant actor then he's genuinely startled. He's not really sure what to do." He let the footage run again.

"There you go," said Stratton. "He's closing his eyes and drawing the symbol in his head."

"How exactly do you know that he's drawing a symbol in his head?" asked Grady. "It looks to me as if he's just scared and closing his eyes to pray to God."

"He could be, but my instincts tell me otherwise. He's concentrating hard. Praying is just a spur of the moment thing, it doesn't require much concentration at all."

They watched the footage through another couple of times, pausing and slowing it down at relevant points, but still couldn't tell for certain what exactly had gone on.

"If only we could slow it down enough to see the bullets," said Cronin.

"We probably could," said Jennings. "The machine's capable, it's just the camera was too far away. We wouldn't be able to zoom in close enough."

"It doesn't look as if we'll need to," said Grady pointing at the screen.

The live broadcast had stopped and the CBS news team were now discussing the event in detail. They were showing slowed down and magnified footage from a camera positioned directly on the stage. The picture followed the path of the first bullet as it left the gun and headed towards Christiano. They watched in silence as the projectile stopped and crumpled in mid-air about an inch from Christiano's head, and fell harmlessly to the floor. The second shot followed a different course but ended with the same result.

"Well there's our answer," said Stratton. "The camera never lies, as they say."

"Except when it's lying," said Grady. "That doesn't prove a thing. You can do pretty much anything with special effects nowadays."

"I don't know, Grady. It looks realistic enough to me," said Jennings. "They'd have had to have worked bloody quickly to manufacture these images in the time since the shooting – even in this day and age. I think you're clutching at straws."

"Perhaps," admitted Grady. "But someone's got to keep a reality check on all this."

"Fuck reality," said Stella. "This is beyond any reality that we're used to. The parameters are changing every day. I agree with Jennings – there's no way they could have doctored the image so quickly. And the pictures are from CBS anyway – not the Catholic Church."

"And who's to say that CBS aren't in cahoots with the Catholic Church?" said Grady.

"No-one," said Stella. "But I think it's unlikely. I think we've just got to accept that this guy has mastered the symbols and can do pretty much anything. Convincing people that he isn't the Son of God is going to be nigh on impossible."

"And so is getting rid of him," said Grady. "I think this guy's here to stay."

Chapter 75

Night drew in and the rain continued to fall. Jenna stood underneath a tree in the hospital gardens smoking a cigarette. The car park was full and ambulances seemed to be arriving every few minutes. She looked on with detachment as people helped their injured loved ones through the doors, and paramedics wheeled in trolley after laden trolley. How far the rioting had spread she didn't know, but from the amount of traffic in and out of A&E she guessed the police had been unable to contain it. And how long before it reached the hospital itself? How long before the patients began fighting amongst each other? The atmosphere on Tariq's ward was already beyond tense. One misplaced word and the place could erupt.

With these thoughts travelling through her mind she stubbed out her cigarette and went back inside the building. The formerly long, bleak corridors were now hives of activity as overworked medical staff attempted to go about their business while fending off enquiries from distraught visitors. Bedside manner had long gone, replaced by stern looks and curt and efficient statements. Jenna tried to ignore the desperation in the air, but it was infectious, and by the time she got back to Tariq's bed her spirit was beginning to fail. When she saw he wasn't there it almost broke. Lying in his place was a young girl of about twelve with a bandaged head and a plastered arm. At her side were a couple of tearful parents.

"Excuse me," said Jenna. "Where's the man who was in this bed?"

The father shook his head. "I'm sorry. I don't know."

Jenna looked around the room and spotted a nurse conversing with a doctor. She walked over and interrupted the conversation. "Excuse me, but where is the man who was in that bed?"

"We've discharged him," said the doctor. "We needed the bed

for the little girl. Her injuries are far more severe."

Jenna opened her mouth to say something, but the doctor was already giving the nurse instructions about another patient. Too tired to argue she left and made her way down the corridor, shuffling slowly with her head down. She had only gone a few yards when something bumped into the back of her legs. She turned round to find Tariq behind her in a wheelchair.

"Aren't you going to wait for me?" he said.

Jenna forgot her troubles briefly and smiled. "I didn't know where you were. The doctor just said that they'd discharged you. I couldn't believe it, I'd only been gone for half an hour."

"Yeah, well they work quickly in here. They're discharging anyone who can move a couple of feet at the moment. They just haven't got enough beds. The doctor seemed happy enough to let me go though. He doesn't think I'm in any great danger. I just need a lot of rest."

Jenna shook her head. "I don't believe this. I don't think you're in any state to be going anywhere."

"Listen," said Tariq. "I honestly don't feel that bad. He's given me a couple of liquid morphine capsules to take home as well. That girl they brought in needs the bed far more than I do, I'm sure. She's got really bad head injuries."

"Where are your family?" asked Jenna.

"They're still here somewhere. My dad went to find out if the roads are clear yet so he can take us back home."

"I thought you were going to stay with me."

"I want to, but he's trying to organize everything and it's difficult to talk to him when he's got a head on. I think he'll be alright about it to be honest – he's probably got enough on his plate trying to look after the rest of the family. He'll be glad if you take me off his hands."

"If you say so," said Jenna, unconvinced. "Anyway, the way it is in the town, we'll be lucky to get you anywhere. God knows what's happened to my car, and I doubt whether there're any taxis running."

"Come on," said Tariq, wheeling past her. "Let's go and find my dad and see what's going on."

Jenna followed him down the corridor wondering what exactly they were going to do. It was all very well the doctor discharging him – but where were they supposed to go? And how were they supposed to get there? The emergency services were obviously still able to manoeuvre about the streets, but did that viability extend to civilians as well? She soon had her answer when they caught up with Tariq's father near the entrance to A&E.

"What's happening then, Dad?"

Tariq's father gave them a disconsolate look. "It is not good I am afraid. I have just spoken to a policeman and he says that the centre of town has been closed off to all traffic except ambulances. There is only limited access anyway, as most of the roads are still blocked with abandoned cars."

"What about the rest of the town?" asked Jenna. "Is there any way of getting around the outside?"

"It is possible I think, but it is not wise. There is still a lot of trouble, and any journey will be dangerous. The police cannot guarantee our safety. Their advice to everyone at the moment is to stay put."

"So we're stuck here for the night then?" said Jenna.

"I do not think there is any other option. The military are coming in with emergency bedding and food supplies so it may not be too bad."

"Not too bad?" said Jenna. "It couldn't get much worse. "

Tariq took her hand. "We'll be okay, Jen. It's only one night. By tomorrow they'll have calmed everything down I'm sure. Then we'll be able to go home."

Jenna forced a smile but her senses told her this was only the beginning of the nightmare.

Chapter 76

Jonathan Ayres laid the phone back into its cradle and sighed. The news from back home was not good and had brought him roughly down to earth after the elation of the afternoon's success. He knew, of course, that trouble had been brewing for a while, but he assumed that it would be a minor storm, and over almost as soon as it had begun. And even though Casper Fox had warned him, he never thought that the situation would really escalate to the point where the military had to be deployed. Yet, that was exactly the juncture they had reached.

Ayres leant forward and cupped his face in his hands. He was suddenly very tired. It was eight o'clock in the evening New York time, but as he'd started the day in Italy, for him it was two in the morning. He decided that he would have a light supper and then go straight to bed. He was wondering what to order when Vittori burst into the suite unannounced.

"Hello, Fabio," Ayres said wearily. "What can I do for you?"

Vittori stormed over and stood over the PM with fire in his eyes. "Did you really think I wouldn't find out?!" he shouted.

"What, Fabio? Find out what?"

"About the bullets of course."

"What about them?"

"They were real, Jonathan. The bullets were real," he growled.

Ayres rose from his seat and held up his hands defensively. "Listen, Fabio. Let's not get too worked up about this. Why don't you take a seat and calm down."

"Calm down! You promised me that everything was in hand. You assured me that Christiano would not be in any danger."

"I did promise you that, and I kept my word. Christiano's still alive isn't he?"

"That's not the point is it, Jonathan? The point is that he could have very well been killed. The plan was to fire blanks and then get the agent to drop some crushed shells on the floor. In none of our conversations did you ever mention live ammunition."

"Okay, okay, I might have taken a bit of a risk, and I'm really sorry. But it's all worked out hasn't it? Come on Fabio, let's sit down and talk about it. I'll pour us some drinks."

Vittori reluctantly took a chair and waited while Ayres got them each a brandy.

"Listen, Fabio," said Ayres, handing the cardinal a glass and sitting down in the chair next to him, "I really am very sorry for all the subterfuge, but I really didn't think you'd go along with the plan if I told you the truth."

Vittori sipped some brandy to calm his temper. "Of course I wouldn't have gone along with it, Jonathan – it was an absolutely ridiculous plan. So many things could have gone wrong. For a start we had no idea how strong the protective shield was. It might have been okay against a few punches but we hadn't tested it out against weaponry – not even a knife."

"True," said Ayres. "But I figured that any power higher than man would certainly be able to stop something man-made."

"Even so, Jonathan – what if Christiano had just frozen? What if he had not had the wherewithal to protect himself with the symbol?"

"Come on, Fabio – I think I'd drummed it into him enough in the afternoon. And just before he went on, I reminded him about it again. He knew exactly what to do if anything happened. Can't we just put this behind us and move on? I mean, everything's worked out perfectly hasn't it?"

Vittori shook his head and sighed. "It has worked out, Jonathan, but I am still not happy. The fact that you decided to go behind my back does not please me. And it certainly does not please His Holiness. We are supposed to be in this together, Jonathan. We are supposed to discuss everything before we act. That is how it has been from the start. There is no room for individuality in this, it is far too dangerous. None of us should have too much power – it was agreed years ago."

"I made the decision for all of us, Fabio – can't you see that? And look at how far forward we are now. Thanks to that camera on the stage the whole world knows that Christiano can stop bullets with his mind. We didn't need to resort to trickery, the whole thing is there in glorious Technicolor! No-one can question his divinity now, can they? And think of the confidence he's going to gain from this: if we'd staged it then I'm sure he would have sussed us out. This way he actually believes in himself. I never did this for myself, Fabio, I did it for the Church as a whole, and I stand by my actions."

"Okay, Jonathan, I believe you. But from now on we must discuss everything before any action is taken. No more secrets. Do you agree?"

"Of course, Fabio."

"Good," said Vittori. "Because if we do not work collectively then this whole situation is liable to come crashing down around us. Although I get the feeling that it already is."

"What do you mean?" said Ayres.

"You know exactly what I mean, Jonathan. You must have watched the news at some point today. And you must still be in contact with your cabinet back home. The world is in turmoil, Jonathan."

"Well, there are a few troublespots I agree, but nothing that can't be rectified now the Messiah has proven himself."

"I would like to believe that, Jonathan, I really would. But I am not sure if the situation has gone too far already. There was plenty of trouble even before the Mahdi was killed. Now it is much, much worse."

"We knew it was going to get worse before it got better," said Ayres.

"Perhaps," ceded Vittori. "But I did not envisage it being quite as bad as this. Nations all around the world are having to call in their militaries just to keep some semblance of order. Look at your own country, Jonathan – it is one of the worst affected. How can you be happy with your people in so much turmoil."

"I'm not happy about it, far from it in fact. But it will all settle down once everyone gets behind Christiano. I'm sure of it."

"I do hope you are right. But you must forgive me for not sharing your optimism. It seems to me that nobody is listening anymore. The people of the world are too caught up in their own prejudices to heed anything that Christiano has to say. Nobody is watching television, they are all out in the streets venting their frustrations against each other. Fear and anger have swept the globe. Even here in God-loving America there are signs of discord. We have unleashed something which we cannot contain."

"I think you're being far too negative, Fabio. All major changes are accompanied by hardship and heartache. The world will come out of this a much safer and stronger place. For the first time in history mankind will be unified. And they will be unified under the Church. That was our aim in the first place, and I have seen nothing so far to persuade me that it will not be attained. You knew what we were getting into when we began all this, Fabio – you knew there would be violence, and you knew there would be death – please don't get cold feet now."

"I have not got 'cold feet' as you put it. I am merely stating the facts as they are and voicing my concerns. It helps me to assimilate the situation as a whole. And even if I did have doubts there is no turning back now."

"Exactly," said Ayres. "We've got to see it through to the end, whatever happens."

Vittori finished his brandy and offered his glass to Ayres for another. His initial ire had gone and he was starting to think clearly again. He sipped at his refill thoughtfully and relaxed.

"Have you spoken much to Christiano since the shooting?" asked Ayres.

"Not really," said Vittori. "He was very quiet about the whole thing. Understandable I suppose. He did seem very pleased with himself though. I think you are right that it has boosted his confidence."

"Yes, I'm certain it has. You could tell that immediately. The way he strode up to the microphone and held out those bullets was pure theatre. For a moment he even had me convinced he was the Son of God."

"Yes," agreed Vittori. "I must admit to thinking the same thing. I just hope that he does not become uncontrollable."

"He won't," said Ayres. "We know too much about him. It's easy enough for us to pull the plug on him whenever we want to anyway. Still, it's probably worth having a chat to him in the morning, just to see where he's at. In fact, we could call him in now if you want."

"No, I do not think so. I am too tired. I need a good night's sleep to refresh my brain cells. And besides, I think he has done enough today, let us leave him to his own devices."

"Yes, but what are his own devices? Is he going to be chatting to that Zola girl online all night?"

"I do not think so," said Vittori. "Not tonight anyway. He seemed very keen to get to his room and study the symbols. This afternoon's success seems to have fuelled his interest once again. I am very pleased because it saves me having to force him into it. It has been very difficult getting him to sit there and concentrate I can tell you."

"Surely he knows them all off by heart by now?"

"It is not that easy, Jonathan – remember, there are over three hundred for him to remember. He obviously knows the ones he uses the most very well, but there are some that he has not had the occasion to implement yet. He needs to keep these fresh in his mind. Surely you do not want to see him fail his followers?"

"No, of course not. I'm just worried about the knowledge. What if something happens to it while he's studying. What if he spills something on it, or sets fire to it? What then? Perhaps we ought to make some copies just to be on the safe side."

"No, Jonathan, we agreed that it would not be a good idea. The papers are perfectly safe. Christiano is well aware that he has to keep a clear desk when working. And when he is finished they are sealed in the security case. The only person that needs to look at them is Christiano."

"Yes, I know," said Ayres. "But however safe you think things are there's always a situation round the corner to prove you wrong."

Vittori held up his hand. "This is not open for discussion, Jonathan. The committee, yourself included, agreed that the knowledge should not be made available to anyone except for the person we eventually chose. The risks of any of us having too much power outweigh the consequences of losing the symbols. You know that if we made copies the temptation to steal and use the knowledge would be great. This way we know exactly where it is at any given time."

"I suppose you're probably right," said Ayres. "I just like to have a contingency plan, that's all."

Vittori glanced at the clock and swiftly finished his brandy. "I think I shall retire for the evening, my friend. It has been an extremely long day, and I am not getting any younger." He rose from his chair and wished Ayres a goodnight.

Ayres watched the cardinal leave, ordered room service, and went to the balcony for a cigarette. It had been a good day, but a doubt still lingered in his mind. As he looked down onto the bustling city he wondered if Vittori was right and that Christiano might indeed become uncontrollable. He began to feel uneasy about letting him have so much power.

Chapter 77

For Jenna the night had passed slowly, in fits of half-sleep on a rough army camp-bed. Tariq, who was in the adjacent bunk, had drifted off almost immediately, leaving her alone to wrestle with her fears. She had got up a couple of times for a cigarette and chatted to her fellow smokers, but nothing had managed to calm her enough to allow more than a ten-minute doze. The constant toing and froing of the military had not helped either. Every five minutes there seemed to be an order barked or a pair of heavy boots tramping past the foot of her bed. That, coupled with the seemingly never-ending wail of sirens, had put an end to any ideas she had of a good night's rest.

Tariq stirred and opened his eyes and looked across to her. "Morning," he yawned. "What time is it?"

"Just gone seven," said Jenna. "How do you feel?"

"A bit sore, but my head's a lot better. The sleep's definitely done me some good."

"Lucky you," she muttered.

"What was that?"

"Nothing," said Jenna. "Sorry, I'm just a bit crabby this morning. I didn't get the best night's sleep. It's been a bit chaotic in here."

"I'll bet it has," said Tariq. "It's lucky I had that morphine otherwise I don't think I'd have got off either."

"Yeah. Perhaps I should have had some as well."

Tariq sat up and drank from a bottle of mineral water. "Where's my dad?"

"He's in the tent next door with the rest of your family. I don't think he's had much sleep either. I bumped into him when I went for a cigarette a couple of hours ago. I don't think he trusted people not to steal his belongings while he was asleep."

Tariq laughed. "That doesn't surprise me. He sees everybody as a potential thief."

"I don't think it helped that they were put next to a couple of shaven-headed white blokes," said Jenna.

"I'm surprised he didn't ask to be put in a Muslim-only tent," said Tariq.

"I think if there was any possibility then he would have," said Jenna. "But everyone's had to make the best of what's available. It's a bit weird really, it feels like the stories my grandad told me about the Blitz. You know – everyone pulling together and all that."

"Everyone except my dad of course. Although he's been speaking to you, so that's a good sign."

"I don't think he's got much choice. But to be fair he's certainly made an effort, just like everyone else. I think it's dawning on people exactly how stupid this whole thing is. When you see somebody injured it doesn't matter what race or religion they are, you still feel sympathy."

"I'm sure there's some that don't. But you're right about this place – there's definitely a communal atmosphere. Although I don't suppose it's as friendly on the streets. Is there any news about what's happening?"

"I haven't had a chance to ask anybody yet, they've all been too busy. I'm going to have a cigarette, so I'll see if I can find a friendly soldier on the way. Do you want anything?"

"I'd love something to eat. Something soft though, I don't think my teeth could manage anything else." He gave her a gap-toothed grin.

"I'll see what I can do. I expect they'll have some soup or stew or something. I'll see you in a bit."

Jenna wandered out of the tent and across the grass to the area that had become 'smokers' corner'. A few people she had met overnight were there, as well as a young soldier who looked as if he had been awake for a week. She sidled up to him and asked for a light even though she didn't need one. He obliged and she started to make small talk, eventually steering the conversation round to the outside world.

"So then," she said. "Any idea what's been happening outside in the town? Or can't you tell me?"

"I can tell you," he said. "I can sum it up in two words – 'fucking nightmare'."

"That bad is it?"

"Yeah, it is. It's unreal. I've been out on patrol all night, and I can tell you it's not pretty. I did a tour of Afghanistan a couple of years back and I felt safer there than I do here. There's just gangs, gangs, and more fucking gangs – excuse my French. There's no reason for them, they're just out there looking for trouble. As soon as they see anyone in authority they start to attack."

"But surely they haven't got guns? Not in a town like this."

"You'd be surprised. But it's not their firepower it's their numbers. And we're under strict orders not to shoot anyone unless it's absolutely necessary. It's all about containment at the moment. We've let off a few warning rounds, but it doesn't seem to stop them. Just makes them keener to have a go. The problem is we're spread too thin. It's happening all over the country and we don't have enough men to cover it. We're getting sent out in pairs to control gangs of a hundred or more, it's fucking ridiculous. I never thought I'd see the day where Britain came to this."

"I guess it's happening all over the world," said Jenna.

"I think it is," he agreed. "But I'm just saying that I never expected to be doing this here, in the country I love. What the fuck has happened to people? It's like they've been infected with anger."

"Religion happened," said Jenna. "But that was just a catalyst I guess. It's not all about that any more. It's about everything – race, poverty, jealousy, fear – this country's been simmering with rage for years. And now the dam's burst it's all come flooding out. The forgotten people have suddenly found a purpose."

The soldier shrugged. "I don't know anything about that, but

I do know that it's fucking scary. The fact that it's your own people makes it worse. It's difficult having to turn on the guys you've spent years defending."

Jenna finished her cigarette and asked the soldier if there was any food available. He pointed her towards a tent on the other side of the one she had slept in. She wished him good luck and went to find something for herself and Tariq to eat.

Chapter 78

Stratton woke in a sweat. He could feel the fever running through his body. He leapt from the bed and threw himself into the bathroom, just making it to the toilet bowl before he began throwing up. He knelt there for a good five minutes, convulsing hard with his eyes watering, until he finally felt the last drops leave his stomach. After flushing away the vomit and rinsing out his mouth, he went back and sat against the bed with his head bowed. He remained static until Stella appeared over half an hour later.

"Are you alright?" she asked, walking into the room and finding him half-naked and bent double.

"Not really," he said, glancing up. "But I suppose it could be worse."

"You look awful."

"Thanks."

"Do you need a hand getting up?"

"No, I'll be fine." He pulled himself up and sat on the bed and grabbed a bottle of mineral water from the cabinet. "You're up a bit early aren't you?" he said.

"Not really," said Stella. "It's about 8am GMT. I'd say you were up a bit late."

"I suppose so. I've lost all track of time to be honest." He opened the bottle and took some water on board.

Stella sat down at the desk. "I take it you haven't watched any news reports this morning then?"

Stratton shook his head. "No, but the way I'm feeling it's obviously not good."

"You're right there. Europe's turned into a battle zone and the Middle East is waging a holy war on America and the West."

"What's happening back home? Have they got that under control yet?"

"No, it's getting worse. The whole of the UK's under martial law."

"It doesn't surprise me," said Stratton. "It was only a matter of time before everything exploded."

"It's ridiculous," said Stella. "Why can't people see what's happening, and where it's all headed? Why can't they just say 'enough's enough'."

"Because it's not that easy now. They're right in the middle of it all. Violence and hatred are like a chain reaction. It's easy enough for us here on board the submarine, we're not being constantly exposed to it. We can sit here and look at everything dispassionately. Out there on the streets it's all about survival – and people will do almost anything to survive. Their lives are being threatened and the only way to deal with that for the majority of people is to fight back. It's just human instinct. I'm not sure if there is any way back now."

"So we just give up?! Is that it?"

"No, we don't give up," he said. "We never give up." He put down his water and lay on the bed and closed his eyes. "I'm just tired. Very, very tired."

He drifted off and said no more.

Chapter 79

Ayres woke refreshed. He ordered his breakfast and showered and then phoned his wife to see how she and the children were holding up. He knew that it must be a strain for them without him around, but he knew that his wife at least understood the importance of what he was doing, even though she had no idea of the whole story. He allayed her fears about the state of the country and assured her that everything was under control. Then, after a brief but happy talk with his kids, he hung up and started to plan the day ahead.

Breakfast arrived at 8am sharp and consisted of pancakes and bacon and eggs. He ate with a good appetite and then settled down with a cup of strong black coffee. Two minutes later Vittori came to join him.

"Good morning, Fabio. I hope you feel suitably revitalized."

"I do not feel too bad, but I am still trying to adjust to the time."

"Sit down," said Ayres. "I'll pour you a coffee. Will you want some brandy in it? Or is it too early?"

"It is never too early," said Vittori. "And besides, I am still on Italian time."

Ayres made Vittori's drink and set it down on the table in front of him. "Have you spoken to Christiano this morning?" he asked.

"I have, but only briefly. I have asked him to come and see us as soon as he has breakfasted."

"Good," said Ayres. "How was he? Did he seem any different?"

Vittori paused for a moment. "Perhaps a little. But it is difficult to tell with him, as he has changed so much already. He makes great leaps every day."

Ayres nodded thoughtfully. "Yes, he does."

Twenty minutes later Christiano arrived at Ayres' suite. He

looked fresh and ready and certainly none the worse for his ordeal. In fact, Ayres thought, he appeared more relaxed and confident than ever. He waved away Ayres' offer of a coffee and instead took a bottle of mineral water. He sat down at the table opposite his two mentors.

"You look very well this morning," said Ayres. "You must have had a good sleep."

"Yes, I did," said Christiano vaguely, staring out of the window.

"I thought you might have been a little shaken by yesterday's unpleasantness."

"Not really. I expected something to happen at some point."

"Maybe," said Ayres. "But I feel awful after all the promises I made to you about how good the security was."

"If someone is determined enough they can get in anywhere," said Christiano. "And anyway, it does not matter now. Security is no longer a relevant issue – I cannot be harmed."

"All the same," said Ayres. "I don't think it would be wise to invite people to have a shot at you."

Christiano shrugged nonchalantly and sipped his water. "So," he said. "What can I do for you this morning? Why did you want to see me?"

"We just wanted to check that you were alright really," said Ayres. "The cardinal and I were worried that it might have been all a bit much for you to take in, but I can see that we had no cause for concern. We also wanted to go through your speech for this afternoon in Washington."

"I am not sure if I wish to go to Washington today."

"But you have to," said Ayres. "The President is expecting you. The whole country is expecting you."

"Maybe they are, but I am sure they can wait."

Ayres glanced at Vittori for help.

"Come, Christiano," said the cardinal. "This is all arranged. You cannot let the people down. They might begin to lose faith in you."

"They will not lose faith in me, not after what they witnessed yesterday."

"But your itinerary is set," pleaded Vittori. "The world is in enough confusion already. The people need some sort of consistency in their lives. They need to know that in all this turmoil their Messiah can be relied upon. Please, Christiano, do not let them down."

"Yes," said Christiano. "It would be wrong to let them down, and I do not wish to." He paused. "But in order to comply I have a request of my own."

Ayres sighed. "And what is this request?"

"I want Sophia to accompany me to the White House."

"I'm afraid that's just not possible," said Ayres. "There just isn't the time to arrange it."

"Isn't there?" said Christiano. "Or are you just trying to put me off?"

"Of course not," said Ayres. "I am solely looking at the feasibility of it. We're due there in a couple of hours. We cannot get her here that quickly." Ayres stopped and realized he was becoming flustered. He gathered himself and tried to put his foot down. "And even if we could I do not think it would be a good idea, Christiano. You have a job to do, and a very important one at that. We have been through all this before. You do not need anything distracting you from your task."

Christiano looked Ayres directly in the eye. "Listen, Jonathan, I do not need you to tell me what I can and cannot do. In case you hadn't noticed I can stop bullets with my mind. If I can do that then I think I am perfectly capable of concentrating on my work with Sophia around."

Ayres felt the urge to sigh heavily but resisted. "I'm not questioning your capabilities, Christiano. But you're a young man and it's easy for you to be distracted, especially by a girl as lovely as Miss Zola. I'm sure it would be difficult for anybody to keep their mind on things with her as a companion."

"But I am not just anybody," said Christiano. "The normal rules no longer apply to me. I will not be swayed from my work by Sophia."

"I beg to differ," said Ayres. "The fact that you're asking us to bring her over in itself means that you have already been swayed."

"This is not open for discussion, Jonathan. I want her with me."

Ayres' eyes flashed with anger. "How dare you dictate to us!" he barked. "Don't you realize who you're talking to?! Who do you think put you where you are you arrogant shit?! We gave you the knowledge, don't forget that. We can quite easily send you back to repairing roofs."

"I do not think so," said Christiano calmly. "How would you explain it to the public? You need me. Without me your whole plan comes crashing down."

"Don't overestimate your usefulness," said Ayres coldly.

Christiano stared at him harshly. "And do not overestimate yours."

Ayres felt Christiano's eyes bore into his own. For the first time he was scared of their young protégé. His jaw tensed and his throat began to congeal with fear. His chest tightened. He found himself struggling for breath. His eyes watered with the strain.

"Jonathan?" said Vittori, concerned.

Ayres heard the cardinal but couldn't answer. He tried to, but all that came out was a muted cough as he continued to gasp for air. His face turned white and then a subtle shade of blue.

Vittori leapt out of his chair. "Jonathan?!" he cried.

Ayres clutched his throat and tried once again to breathe. He toppled forward to the floor and knelt there, looking up to Christiano with pleading eyes.

Vittori turned to his young charge. "Christiano! Help him. For

God's sake help him!"

Christiano nodded.

Ayres crashed to the carpet and breathed in rush after rush of air. Vittori reached down to help him up. "Are you alright, Jonathan?" he said, pulling him to his feet.

Ayres nodded and started to even his breaths. "I'll be fine," he wheezed, easing himself back into the chair. "I'll be fine."

Vittori handed him a glass of water. "What happened, Jonathan?"

Ayres sipped at the water slowly and then cast a glance at Christiano. "Perhaps our young Messiah would like to explain?"

Christiano shrugged. "I do not know what happened. Perhaps you have asthma or something like that."

"Don't give me that!" Ayres snapped. "You did this to me! I could feel you."

Vittori gave an incredulous stare. "Is this true, Christiano? Did you do this to him?"

"He has done it to himself. All I want is for Sophia to come over here. The Church is getting quite enough out of this arrangement and I have only asked for one thing. I think it is time you realized just who is in charge."

Chapter 80

It was nearing midday but the overcast sky made it seem like late evening. Paul Smith walked slowly through Banbury's deserted streets with his weapon at the ready, and wondered if life would ever be normal again. The descent from civilized nation into complete anarchy had happened so quickly that he'd hardly had time for it to register. One minute he was enjoying a well-earned leave, the next he was patrolling the streets of his hometown, fearful that any moment he would have to shoot down one of the people he had sworn to protect: maybe even an associate; a friend; or worse still, a family member.

The High Street had seen many changes over the years, but none quite as dramatic as the one that greeted him now. As he looked ahead at the shattered shop windows with their broken displays, and the rubbish- and rubble-strewn parade, his eyes misted over. He had travelled the world and witnessed destruction and barbarism that defied humanity with barely a flicker of emotion, but seeing the place he grew up in reduced to this was almost too much.

"Are you alright, mate?" asked Graham, his fellow patroller.

"Yeah I'm fine," said Paul, wiping the side of his eye. "It's just a but dusty."

"I suppose it is," said Graham with a grin. "Do you think we should put our masks on?"

"Don't be funny, mate."

They moved on up the road cautiously, the emptiness making them nervous. Overhead a helicopter broke the silence, the sound of its rotors briefly giving them company before fading back into the clouds. The wind picked up and began blowing litter across their path. A light rain started to fall.

Just before they reached the town hall their radios crackled to life. It was base command telling them to proceed up to the Bretch Hill estate immediately. They ran back up the High Street and jumped into the waiting Jeep.

"What's going on?" Paul asked the driver.

"What isn't going on," the driver replied. "It's all kicked off up on this estate. The Paki's have gone mental and the white boy's are fighting back. They reckon there's thousands of them involved. It's worse than fucking Beirut."

The Jeep hurtled around the Banbury Cross and up West Bar towards the action. Fearful faces peered out from behind twitching curtains as they went. Paul checked his weapon one last time and lit a cigarette. He only managed four drags before they came to the final roadblock. He threw the unfinished cigarette from the Jeep and then jumped out.

He and Graham hooked up with another six men from their unit and marched up the hill. Terrified citizens ran past them the opposite way, fleeing for their lives. Blood-spattered women and children screamed and pleaded for help. Paul focused his mind, trying to forget where he was.

Soon they came upon the battleground. The main road across the top of the hill was a roaring sea of people and missiles and fire. Petrol bombs had already set nearly half the houses alight. A police officer with a megaphone tried unsuccessfully to appease the situation with some futile words, his voice drowned out by jeers of aggression and the helpless cries of the injured.

Paul's unit let off a volley of warning shots, but it was like a whisper in a thunderstorm. Even those rioters closest to them barely noticed the cracks of gunfire.

"This is ridiculous!" shouted Graham. "We need more men!"

"Tell me about it!" yelled Paul.

They let off another volley of warning shots, and yet again received no acknowledgement. On command they stepped away and awaited further orders.

"Fuck this!" said Graham, watching the riot continue from fifty yards back. "Where the hell are the rest of the police? And where the hell are the rest of our men?"

Second-lieutenant Alan Rigsby lit a cigarette. "There's another incident on the other side of town," he said. "Just as big as this one apparently. They've had to split us between the two. If you ask me we should all deal with one and then move onto the other – we're never going to get anything under control this way. Well, not unless we start…"

His voice tailed off as he side-stepped a flaming bottle. There was no need for him to finish his sentence though. Everyone knew exactly what he was going to say. It was a suggestion that each of them feared more than anything. An order to fire at will on their own people.

Chapter 81

The helicopter banked sharply and Stella got her first glimpse of the White House, a mile away and four hundred feet down. Even in the circumstances she allowed herself a gentle smile. Whatever her views on America and its over-zealous foreign policy, there was no denying that their destination was probably the most iconic and powerful political headquarters in the world, and the fact that she was on her way there as an invited guest gave her a secret tingling of importance. As they drew nearer and descended towards the famous lawn she had to stop herself from appearing too overawed and excitable.

Next to her Stratton was dozing fitfully, seemingly unimpressed by the whole adventure. He hadn't said much at all since breakfast, and she was beginning to wonder how much longer he would last. Unless mankind veered from its present course his outlook was bleak.

The chopper landed softly on the grass and the group disembarked. Grady was out first and Stella followed. Jennings and Cronin guided a weakened Stratton, and Stone jumped off last. They were met by White House Chief-of-Staff Greg Albany, who shook Grady's hand and led them away from the slowing but still-noisy rotors.

"It's good to see you, Scott. It's been a long time," said Albany as they approached the building.

"I know," said Grady. "But it's not like you're any easy man to reach anymore, Greg. I can hardly drop by when I like to visit you."

Albany grinned. "I guess not. But you're here now, and like I said – it's good to see you, old buddy. I just wish it was a better time."

"You and me both."

Inside the White House they were led along a plain white corridor to a room on the left where they were offered coffee and some light food. Greg Albany left them in the hands of a junior aide while he rushed off to meet the President for a short briefing.

"This is alright," said Jennings, munching on a fresh donut. "Coffee and cakes in the White House. If my mother could see me now."

"She'd probably tell you not to speak with your mouth full," said Grady.

Stone sipped his coffee nervously and stared out of the window. He would have been a lot happier staying behind on the submarine, but the others insisted that his standing as Ayres' head of security, and knowledge of the situation would lend much-needed weight to their claims. He had pointed out that he was no longer anything to do with Ayres, and probably considered a traitor, yet his protests had fallen on deaf ears.

Stratton stretched himself out in a leather chair and drank some water in an attempt to stay alert. His body was teetering between sluggish and exhausted. He could feel the world and its people gradually slipping away to the point of no return. Soon the fear and the hatred would have taken hold completely, forcing them towards a sorrowful and desolate destiny. He tried to keep his thoughts light, but the pressure on his mind grew increasingly tense.

Stella put down her coffee and went over to kneel beside his chair. "How are you feeling?" she asked, knowing the answer before she spoke.

"I'll be alright," he said. "How about you? I expect you're made up being here in the White House."

Stella gave a sheepish smile. "You know me too well," she said.

"There's nothing wrong with it," said Stratton. "I'd be pretty excited too if I could manage it."

Ten minutes later Albany returned and they followed him along a number of short corridors to a huge meeting room with white walls, a deep blue carpet, and a large twenty-seat conference table in the middle. Already sat down at the head was James Mackenzie, the first black President of the United States. To his left were a couple of military men, and to his right an empty seat followed by three men in suits. Albany performed some quick introductions and then took the chair next to the President. The newcomers took their places – two one side and four on the other to balance the table.

Jennings tried to digest all the names. He knew who James Mackenzie was of course, and the two military men next to him were both generals – Johnson and Perry. The three suits were the heads of the CIA, NSA and FBI respectively: Bob Tobin, Trent Arthur and Lionel Jones. They all waited quietly for Mackenzie to begin the meeting.

"Well, gentlemen," he started. "I think we should get straight down to it and find out exactly what our friends here have got to say." He opened the folder in front of him and took a cursory glance. "We've had a chance to look through various files relating to this – let's say 'mystical knowledge' – but I'm not sure that we have all the facts. Most of what we have is hearsay and conjecture from a Professor Miles, late of the National Institute for Paranormal Studies. And we have no intelligence whatsoever since a vague report from Mr Grady here at the end of December, saying that the box and its contents had gone missing at Stonehenge. Would you care to fill us in on events since then."

Grady nudged Jennings with his arm. "I think it's probably best if you give them the lowdown on this, buddy."

Jennings looked around the table for help, but none seemed forthcoming so he began to tell the story as he saw it from the point of Grady's last report. At first he stumbled slightly, mindful of the esteemed company he was in. But after a while he began to speak freely, ignoring the stony-faced Americans and recanting events with as much relevant detail as he could. Stone filled in some blanks about the Prime Minister's involvement and between them they drew a clear and current picture for the assembled council, stopping only to answer the occasional question.

When they'd finished President Mackenzie called for coffee and leant back in his chair. "Interesting," he said. "Very interesting. So neither of these guys was sent by God at all."

"No," said Jennings.

"The thing is," Mackenzie continued. "I'm not sure which story is the most unbelievable. I'd just about got used to the fact that Christiano was really the Messiah returned. I've met him and seen him in action and he certainly fits the bill. And for me personally as a Christian, I really wanted it to be true. But now I don't know what to think."

General Perry cleared his throat. "Do you have any real hard evidence of this 'mystical knowledge'? I mean to say – we only have your word about all this. I've seen the footage from yesterday at Yankee Stadium and I've got to say I'm pretty convinced that guy's the Son of God."

"But we've explained how he did that," said Jennings.

"Can you do it?" asked Perry.

"No, I can't," said Jennings. "I don't know the right symbol."

"What about you?" he said to Stratton. "You know all the symbols don't you? Can you do it?"

Stratton shook his head. "Not at the moment," he said. "I'm not feeling too good."

"You're not feeling too good? Well that's an excuse if ever I heard one. If these symbols were real and you did know all of them why would you be feeling unwell. Surely illness should be a thing of the past for you?"

"It's complicated," said Stratton.

Perry raised an eyebrow. "Really? Do enlighten us."

"His power is linked to the human race," said Grady, surprised by what he was saying. "I don't pretend to understand the finer details of it, but basically if we're all at peace then so is he, and if we're at war then he's sick. And at the moment with all that's going on he's sick."

"It all seems very convenient," said Perry. "Christiano's powers don't seem to be index-linked."

"Listen, General," said Grady, starting to lose his cool. "Stratton here is for real, I've seen what he can do myself. I saw this guy die, for Christ's sake. How would you explain his resurrection?"

Perry shrugged. "I can't. But it could have been a trick. It wouldn't be the first time someone had faked their own death."

Grady sighed and tried to calm himself. "With all due respect, General, what exactly are you trying to achieve here? I would have thought what we've said would please you no end. Christiano is a real risk to National Security. You're not going to be able to maintain control of the population with him around. As it stands he's probably the most powerful person in the world right now."

"And that's exactly why we need to keep him on side," said Perry.

"No," said Grady. "What you need to do is take back control of your people. This whole thing is ripping the world apart – can't you see that?"

"I agree with Grady," said Bob Tobin. "We need to discredit this guy and get everybody back to reality. This religion thing's gone far enough."

Perry looked to skies and shook his head. "And how do you suppose we discredit him, Bob? How do you discredit someone who can stop a fucking bullet with his fucking mind?!"

"I don't know, but there must be a way. If we discuss it properly I'm sure we can come up with something. What do you think, Mr President?"

Mackenzie was non-committal. "I don't know, Bob. I think that General Perry has a point. But I also think that you're right about the situation being out of control. If these guys could come up with something more to convince us it might help."

"Scott Grady's word is all I need to convince me," said Tobin. "If he says the guy's using mystical symbols then that's exactly what he's doing. I introduced him to Sharlo Miles last year when I was Deputy Director. I put him on the job for two reasons: one – because he's our best field agent by a long way; and two – because he's nobody's fool. He's the last person that would believe in this shit if it wasn't true."

Mackenzie raised his hand. "Okay, Bob, you've made your point. But even if you're right we still don't have any feasible way of getting rid of Christiano without causing a complete uproar. The American people are behind him one hundred percent. They've probably forgotten I exist, for Christ's sake. Unless you can come up with a decent plan I don't see we have any choice but to go along with him. We've got enough on our plates with the Middle East situation, we don't need our own people turning against us like they have in Europe. Whether he really is the Messiah or not I think at the moment he's our only chance of restoring some kind of peace to the world."

"With all due respect, Mr President," said Tobin. "Do you really think the Muslims are just going to accept him as the one true messenger of God? Their own saviour's just been murdered, Christiano is just inflaming them even more. Perhaps if we get rid of him then there's a chance we can avoid all out war – because that's where we're headed."

"The war's already started, Bob," said Mackenzie. "And a World War is almost inevitable. There's hardly a country on the planet that isn't experiencing at least some trouble. Our sole responsibility is to keep the citizens of the United States safe from harm. We have to protect our nation by whatever means possible. And at this moment in time I think we'd be best served going along with the show."

"I totally agree, Mr President," said Perry. "Our battle is against the Middle East not the Vatican. We need to deal with them swiftly. The Iranians are liable to launch a nuclear attack on us at any time. And I suspect they're not the only ones. Our intelligence tells us that other countries are making deals as well. Soon we could be facing enough firepower to wipe out the Eastern Sea Board, if not the entire United States. I think we need to act before any of these bastard countries get hold of anything bigger than a Roman candle."

Stella, who'd been listening with increasing anger decided to finally speak up. "Excuse me!" she said, getting out of her seat. "But have you not been listening to a word we've said? If you start launching nuclear attacks then you may as well kiss this world goodbye. The only thing you're going to achieve is more bloodshed. You'll bomb them, they'll bomb you, everyone else will join in, and that will be the end. The end of you; the end of me; the end of us all! We've come here to try and avoid all that."

Perry nodded slowly, looking as if he was trying to hold back a grin. "I can see your point, missy," he said. "But we're going to flatten these little states before they can do anything to us. And for once even the Russians agree with us."

Stella's eyes and face turned scarlet. "Who the fuck do you think you're calling 'missy'!?" she growled. "My name is Stella – or did you not catch that when we were introduced? No, I guess you were too busy looking at these, you fucking dinosaur." She thrust her hands under her breasts.

Mackenzie stifled a chuckle and raised his hand. "Okay, okay," he said. "Let's just all calm down. I don't think General Perry meant any disrespect, and I'm sure he's very sorry – right?"

He turned to Perry who nodded and apologized.

"Good," continued Mackenzie. "Now if you would like to sit down, Stella, we can carry on this discussion sensibly. There's no point fighting amongst ourselves. If you've got something to relevant to say then I'm sure we'd all like to hear it."

Humbled slightly by Mackenzie's intervention Stella apologized for her outburst and sat down. She took a deep breath and tried to gather her thoughts. "The thing is, Mr President," she began, "we think it's still possible to stop this violence. We think it's possible to avoid unnecessary action. It's just going to take a big leap of faith from all parties concerned. You're going to have resist using any sort of force."

"What is this?" grumbled Perry. "Stop wasting our time."

Mackenzie put his hand up to silence the general and nodded at Stella to continue.

"A war at this point is quite possibly going to destroy the planet. The whole human race is being slowly eaten away by fear and anger and hate. The only way to stop it is for everyone to be brave and lay down their weapons."

Perry interrupted once more. "For Christ's sake, Mr President, this is ridiculous! This is exactly the sort of liberalist bullshit that will get us destroyed."

"Please, General," said Mackenzie with a firm stare.

"Listen," said Stella, facing General Perry. "I know it sounds crazy and I used to think exactly the same way as you, but look at where it's got us. This is the point of no return in human history, and if we make the wrong decisions now then that's exactly what we will be – history."

"So what exactly are you proposing?" asked Mackenzie. "Are you asking us to engage in some kind of unilateral disarmament?"

"No, I'm just suggesting that as the major superpower if you promote the idea of a truce then maybe others will follow."

"You know what, Stella," said Mackenzie, "I really wish that it was that simple. I wish that we could say 'enough already' and all get along. And if it was me on my own facing another guy with a gun then I'd take the chance and lay down my weapon first. But I'm responsible for hundreds of millions of people and I can't take a chance with their lives. The Muslims are so enraged at the moment that there's no way they're going to listen to anybody. Don't you think we've tried? Don't you think we've had our people negotiating 24/7 with them? The inescapable truth is that they're beyond appeasement. They think that the Christian West is directly responsible for the death of their Mahdi, and nothing is going to dissuade them."

"You're looking at it too logically," said Stratton taking the baton from Stella. "This isn't about the real world anymore, Mr President. This is about the power you can't see. This is about the universal life force. And it's infinitely more potent than all of your nuclear weapons put together. If you wipe out the Middle East then your own destruction won't be far behind I can assure you. Like Stella said – this moment in time is pivotal to mankind. You can either embrace the light or be swallowed by the dark, it's really up to you."

Mackenzie searched Stratton's eyes and then looked away. "You're asking me to do something that my head says is completely contrary to the interests of my people."

"What does your heart say?" asked Stratton. "What does your instinct say?"

"I don't know," said Mackenzie. "Maybe to believe you. I'm just not sure. But it doesn't really matter anyway. I'm here to make cold, calculated decisions, not to risk people's lives on a hunch. Whatever I feel personally about it takes second place. I have to play the percentage call. And at this juncture that percentage is heavily in favour of getting behind Christiano, and also defending my nation from oblivion."

"Exactly, Mr President," said Perry. "I'm sure these people mean well, but as they said themselves – they're not talking about the real world. The cold, harsh reality is that we're one step away from an all-out attack on our major cities, and we have to neutralize the threat."

Stratton shook his head. "You just don't get it do you?"

"No," said Perry. "It's you who doesn't get it."

Mackenzie looked at his watch. "I'm afraid we're going to have to wind this up, ladies and gentlemen. Christiano is arriving in just under fifteen minutes and I need to be there to meet him for the cameras. So if you'll excuse me." He nodded to Greg Albany.

The table stood and watched Mackenzie leave with his Chief-of-Staff. The two generals followed soon after, and then Trent Arthur and Lionel Jones. Only Bob Tobin remained.

"Well, guys," he said, sitting down and pouring himself a coffee, "if it's any consolation I'm on your side. This conflict's only headed one way, and I don't like the direction."

"What can we do though, Bob?" said Grady. "You heard the President – he's already made up his mind. And so has the rest of the world."

"Perhaps," said Tobin. "But it's not over yet, Scott. It's not over yet."

Chapter 82

Christiano turned on the cold tap and doused his face with water. He looked at his reflection in the mirror and rubbed his eyes. The lack of sleep was beginning to catch up with him. He had managed to grab a few hours the night before, but the exhilaration of stopping the bullet had charged him with so much energy it was almost impossible to contain his thoughts. Each time he felt he'd reined them back another revelation would shoot forth, and then another, and then another. His brain had become a continuous sprouting of miniature shoots, with each one forming their own little buds which in turn multiplied again into infinity. At first it had been beautiful, but now it was starting to hurt and he wanted it to stop.

He splashed his face once more and then dried it with a hand towel. He wondered how long he'd been in the rest room and whether it was beginning to look conspicuous. They were waiting for him, he knew that, but he still didn't feel ready to face the world quite yet. The ever-expanding choir in his head was becoming claustrophobic and nothing was making sense. He had temporarily lost the ability to reason. He sat down on the toilet and lay his hands on his mental chakra in an attempt to calm himself.

A while later – perhaps five seconds, maybe five minutes, he didn't know – there was a knock on the door.

"Christiano!" called a female voice. "Are you alright?"

He tried to place the voice, and then it came to him. He remembered that Sophia had arrived from Italy and was waiting with Ayres and President Mackenzie. It concerned him that he had already forgotten.

"Christiano!" she called again.

"I'm okay," he said. "I'll be out in a minute." He stood up and stretched his arms and shook his head vigorously. He walked up to the door and reached for the lock. A sudden bolt of fear whipped through his chest and his hand froze. He couldn't do it. Drawing his hand away he retreated back to the toilet.

Sophia's voice came pulsing through once more. "Christiano!"

He rose again and tried to pull himself together, willing the darkness away from his mind. He unlocked the door and opened it a couple of inches.

"Thank God!" said Sophia. "I thought you'd be in there all day. They're waiting for you in the press room."

Christiano edged the door open a little further but then stopped. "I just need a little longer," he said.

"What's wrong?"

"Nothing," he snapped. "I just need a little longer. The media can wait. They can't dictate when I appear. I'll come when I'm good and ready."

Sophia hung her head and then looked back up at him. Her eyes welled with tears.

Christiano's heart sank. "I'm sorry," he said. "I didn't mean to take it out on you." He opened the door. "Will you come and sit with me for a while?"

Sophia nodded and walked in. Christiano shut the door behind her.

"I am really sorry," he said, drawing her in for a hug. "I don't know what's happening to me. Everything's confused. Everything's a mess."

Sophia held him tight with her head against his chest. "Don't worry," she said. "I'm here for you now. I'll stay as long as you want me to."

Christiano felt Sophia's warmth run through him. He caught a waft of her flower-scented hair and breathed it in like the first fragrance of summer. The pressure on his mind briefly relaxed. He released his embrace and held her face gently in his hands, looking into her deep emerald eyes. He leant forward and kissed her softly on the lips. She reciprocated and then pulled slowly away.

"We shouldn't," she said.

"Why not?"

"Because you have a job to do," she said. "There are billions of people out there waiting for you to talk to them. A whole planet of lost souls waiting for you to lead them to fulfilment."

"That's the point," said Christiano. "I don't know if I can."

"Of course you can. You can do anything you want. You are the Messiah – the Son of God."

Christiano threw his hands up. "Yes, yes," he said. "But I do not feel in control any more. They all want a piece of me: the Church, Jonathan Ayres, and now President Mackenzie. They all want me to say things that will help their cause. They all want me behind them. But is it right? Are they really acting for humanity or just for themselves. It is I who has the power, and yet they constantly tell me what to do and what to say. I need time to think for myself. I need time to decide what I want to do."

Sophia caressed his hand. "If you need time then just take it. I'm sure people will understand. You cannot carry on like this if you are unhappy. But remember the state the world is in. People are looking for direction and if it doesn't come from you then it will come from the politicians and the Church, and they will surely lead us to destruction."

"Perhaps that is our destiny," said Christiano. "Perhaps mankind deserves to be wiped out. I mean, look at the world: it is full of greed and lust and jealousy and hatred."

"Yes, it is," said Sophia. "But it is also full of warmth and compassion and love and kindness. You cannot give up on humanity while these good things still exist."

Christiano felt his brain careering once more. "No…Yes…I don't know. I cannot think." His hands shot up to his forehead. "What is happening? What is happening to the world? Why can they not see as I can see?"

"What do you see?"

"I see everything! And I see nothing! Shapes, colours, stars and voids!" He spread his arms wide. "I can see creation and oblivion! Fire and brimstone! The brightest light and the blackest dark!" He closed his eyes and his body shuddered.

Sophia looked on in fear as his body continued to shake more and more furiously. "Christiano!" she yelled, trying to jolt him back to reality. "Christiano! You're scaring me!"

He juddered one last ground-shaking time, and then hit by an unseen force he was thrust off his feet and back into the door.

Sophia raced over and knelt by his side. "Christiano?" she said with concern. "Christiano."

He opened his eyes and blinked rapidly.

"Are you okay?" she asked.

Christiano nodded. "Yes, I am fine." He sat up and blinked some more to regain focus.

"What happened?"

"I don't know," he said. "I just started to see things."

"What sort of things?"

"I can't explain. I'm not sure if I really understand it all myself." He looked her in the eyes. "But it's beautiful. So, so beautiful. Just like you."

Sophia felt herself blushing. She looked away briefly and then returned his gaze. His eyes were like two multicoloured blazing volcanoes, each one in a constant state of flux. In them she saw the depths of time and the universe. The storm raged creating and destroying indiscriminately. She wanted to look away again, but found herself hypnotized. The maelstrom dragged her forwards, floating and twisting and turning. Soon she was deep inside, lost in a world of waking dreams, overcome by the wonder of the universe, immersed in a beauty so violent it took her breath right away. Suddenly aware of her mortality she began to struggle for air, tumbling open-mouthed in a weightless free fall, her arms grasping wildly in the vacuum. She cried out silently, pleading for mercy to an unseen force. There was no reply except for the muted echoes of her own appeal. Then, just as she felt she could take no more, his eyes faded and the moment passed and she was back in the rest room at the White House. She drew in a huge rush of air.

"Are you alright?" asked Christiano.

Sophia swallowed some more air. "I think so," she said. "I'm not really sure. I need to get out of here. I'm getting claustrophobic." She got to her feet and turned the lock. "Come on," she said. "Come with me, we'll go out together." She held out her hand.

Christiano reluctantly rose to his feet and followed her. Outside the rest room Ayres and Vittori had turned up and were waiting impatiently.

"Thank God," said Ayres. "I thought you were never going to come out. Is everything alright?"

Christiano gave a non-committal shrug.

"Come on," said Ayres. "You've got a press conference to address." He led them down the corridor to the press room where President Mackenzie was waiting behind the curtain. He looked relieved when they finally turned up.

"I thought we'd lost you there," he said. "Mind you, this is a big place. I've been here over three years and I still get lost myself at times."

"I was not lost," said Christiano, curtly. "I wanted some time on my own."

"That's fine," said Mackenzie. "But at least you're here now. Let's get out there and give them what they want."

"I'm not sure if I can," said Christiano.

"What do you mean?" said Mackenzie. "We've planned this already." He turned to Ayres. "What's going on, Jonathan?"

Ayres attempted to assuage the Messiah. "Come on, Christiano," he said kindly. "I know you have some reservations, but it's not all that bad is it? You only need to give them five minutes and then that'll be it for the day. You can relax and have a wander round the White House with Sophia. Or do whatever you like. All we need you to do is this one little thing."

"Yes, Jonathan, it is just one little thing. But it is not my little thing. You want me to go out there and tell the world what *you* want them to hear, not what I want them to hear."

"Well, what do you want them to hear?" asked Ayres.

"I don't know. I have not had enough time to think about it. I need some space to myself."

"Well, how long do you need? Five minutes, an hour?"

"I need longer, much longer. I am going to go back to Rome, to the Vatican. I need to be somewhere familiar."

Mackenzie began to panic. "For Christ's sake, Jonathan! Do something will you. I thought we had this all sorted."

Ayres tried to keep his cool. "Come, Christiano," he said. "I know you're confused, but that is why we have written your speeches for you. You have to trust that we know what is best for the people of the world."

"No, Jonathan, I do not trust that. I have come to realize that you only want what is best for you. You only want that which gives you the most power. It is the same with all of you. I have had enough of being told what to say and what to do. I am the Messiah, I shall keep my own counsel from now on." He took Sophia's hand and started to walk off.

"Listen here, Christiano," said Mackenzie. "You have a responsibility to the people of the United States. You came here to give an address and we expect you to do it. I cannot allow you to leave until you do." He nodded to his Secret Service men who stood in front of Christiano blocking his way.

"I suggest you remove yourselves," said Christiano.

The men didn't move.

"Very well," he said.

Ayres felt his spine tingle with fear. "No!" he yelled.

It was too late. The men were already on their knees choking. Christiano breezed past and turned to face Ayres and Mackenzie.

"I want a helicopter outside on the lawn in five minutes."

"Listen here, Christiano..." Mackenzie started. Before he could finish his sentence he felt what he thought was an electric shock pass through his body and slam him against the wall.

Christiano looked down at him coldly. "Five minutes," he said.

Chapter 83

Stratton coughed heavily and reached for his left side, the momentum taking him from his chair. He lay on the floor of the conference room writhing as the pain took hold once again. Cronin, who was nearest, rushed to his aid, but was fended away by a flailing hand.

"No!" spluttered Stratton. "Keep away!"

Cronin stepped back in confusion.

"It's alright," said Jennings. "The same thing happened yesterday. I tried to help him and got thrown back across the room for my troubles. Give him a minute and he'll be okay."

Cronin was dubious but sat back down and waited with the others for Stratton to regain control. Bob Tobin watched curiously.

Half a minute later Stratton was back on his feet. He returned to his chair and took a drink of water.

"I take it something bad's happened then," said Jennings.

"I guess it must have done," said Stratton. "I've no idea what though."

"Could somebody enlighten me as to what's going on here?" asked Tobin.

"It's like we told you before," said Jennings. "Stratton's well-being is linked to whatever's going on around us. At points when something terrible is happening the pain becomes more acute. It happened yesterday just after the Mahdi was assassinated."

Tobin was about to speak again when Greg Albany burst into the room. "You're still here," he said, catching his breath. "Good. I was worried you might have gone."

"What's up, Greg?" asked Grady.

"It's Christiano. He's attacked the President."

"What?!"

"Behind the press room just now. He took out a couple of Secret Service and then turned on Mackenzie."

"How the hell did he take out two men?" asked Tobin.

"We don't exactly know. They just crumbled in front of him. The President was thrown against the wall. It seemed like he did it with his mind."

"Jesus!" said Grady. "What's happening now then?"

"Christiano's waiting for a chopper to take him to the airbase so that he can get a plane back to Rome. It doesn't look like we can do anything to stop him – unless…" He looked to Stratton.

"I'm not sure what I can do," said Stratton. "I'm not in the best shape at the moment. Perhaps it's best to let him go if that's what he wants."

"And let him get away with assaulting the President?"

"If you have to, yes."

"But we need him to make his speech to the people. We need him to pacify their fears. You know the position we're at. We need him visibly backing the President and his Administration."

"You can't force him to do something he doesn't want to," said Stratton. "I expect that's how this all started in the first place. You're going to have to let him go otherwise the situation will only get worse."

"If we let him go then the situation will definitely get worse," said Albany. "These are troubling times for the United States and people need reassuring. The President's word alone just isn't cutting it. Can't you at least try and talk to him – you're the only one who might be able to understand what he's going through."

"That's rich," said Stella. "Half an hour ago you lot were saying that our claims were a load of rubbish. And now you suddenly believe that we were telling the truth?"

"The decision was nothing to do with me," said Albany. "And it wasn't a slight on the validity of your claims. It was solely a matter of expedience. For what it's worth I believed you from the start – I've been suspicious about these so called 'Messiahs' from the moment they appeared. It always seemed a bit convenient that they turned up at almost exactly the same time. But look, we haven't got time to argue about it, the chopper will be here any minute. Will you try and talk to him?"

Stratton nodded. "I suppose I'd better. But I'm only doing it to try and calm him down. He's dangerous at the moment and that's no good for anybody. I'm not going to try and persuade him to do your dirty work."

"Thanks," said Albany. "Follow me and I'll take you to him."

He led them through the building at speed, fending off questions from passing staff with a dismissive wave of his hand. Jennings walked beside Stratton helping him along as the pace increased. It hadn't surprised Jennings that Christiano had started to display signs of aggression, his own experience of Reiki attunement may not have been on the same scale but it had certainly caused him a few anxious moments when he felt unable to stay in control. Given the wrong circumstances he could see how easy it would be for someone to get carried away with the flow of energy. Sometimes the power was so strong it left you without a will of your own.

Christiano was waiting outside with Sophia. The sky was grey and steadily blackening. Stratton walked across to join them, leaving the others inside. Christiano eyed him with suspicion as he approached.

"Who are you?" he asked with a scowl.

"My name's Stratton. I've come to see if you're alright," he said in bad Italian. He held out his hand. Christiano took it, but flinched at the touch and withdrew.

"Have you really come to see if I'm alright?" he grumbled. "Or are you here to try and keep me here like the others. If you have then I suggest you leave."

"I'm not trying to keep you anywhere. It's none of my concern whether you stay here or not."

"Well, what is your concern then?"

"My concern is you. I know what you are, Christiano, and I know what you are not."

"What is that supposed to mean?"

"You know exactly what it means. It means that I know you are not the Messiah. I know where your power comes from."

Sophia looked at her love questioningly. "What does he mean, Christiano?"

"I don't know what he means. I am the Messiah and no-one should question my divinity."

A soft rain began to fall.

"I'm not here to argue with you, Christiano, I'm here to help you," said Stratton. "I know what the Church have done to you. I know that Vittori and Ayres have given you too much power and tried to corrupt you for their own purpose. And I know that if you carry on the way your going you will destroy yourself, and possibly the world."

"And how do you know all this?"

"I just do."

"That is no answer."

"I haven't got time for the long answer. I'm just here to let you know that you're not alone. I know all about the symbols and I know how to use them too. I know what you're going through. I know about the light and the darkness, and I know about the visions and the confusion. I can help you control your emotions and harness your power properly."

"I do not need help from you or anybody else. I am the one with the knowledge. I am the one with the power. Nobody is going to tell me what to do anymore."

The sound of rotor blades grew loud overhead.

"I don't want to tell you what to do! I just want to help you!" yelled Stratton, trying to be heard over the approaching helicopter.

"Listen to him, Christiano!" Sophia pleaded, her hair flowing in the downdraft. "You don't have to do this alone!"

Christiano hesitated for a moment and then took Sophia's hand and led her towards the waiting chopper. She looked briefly to Stratton and then resigned herself to leaving.

Stratton watched them climb aboard and rise up into the darkness.

Chapter 84

The battle of Bretch Hill raged on. The rioters had been subdued briefly by tear gas, but it hadn't taken them long to regroup and return even more frenzied than before. Paul Smith and his small group had retreated once again and were awaiting fresh orders. He looked up into the ominous sky and felt the hope drain from his soul.

"I think this is it," said Graham.

"What's that? asked Paul.

"Just it. I've got a bad feeling in my bones about this one. It feels like the end of the world." He pointed upwards. "Look at that. I can't even tell what time of day it is anymore. It's permanently black."

"I know what you mean," said Paul. "And the worst thing is that it's silent and still. It feels like there's something massive happening up there, but it's taking an age to brew."

"How can you tell if it's silent with all this noise going on behind us?"

"I can just tell." He pulled out his cigarettes and offered one to Graham.

"Cheers, mate. I don't suppose it matters how much we smoke now, we're not going have time to develop lung cancer."

"No, I guess not," laughed Paul. He drew a flask from his pocket. "How about a little nip of the good stuff?"

"Don't mind if I do."

A hundred yards away the riot continued.

"You'd think they'd have got tired by now," said Graham. "I mean, how long have they been at it? Must be a good four or five hours."

Paul checked his watch. "Yeah, it's getting on for that. Maybe it'll cool off once they get hungry. Perhaps everyone will stop for tea, like in the old days."

Graham swigged at the flask and handed it back to Paul.

"Cheers, mate, that's hit the spot. That'll be it for me though. Need to stay alert."

"Yeah," Paul nodded. "It's going to be a long night." He put the flask back in his pocket and took a lungful of smoke.

Out of the gloom the shadowy figure of Alan Rigsby approached. He drew up quickly and knelt down to speak to his men. "It's bad news, guys, I'm afraid. I've just had the order."

"What?" said Graham. "*The* order."

Rigsby nodded gravely.

The men took one last drag of their cigarettes and threw them to the floor. They checked their weapons and formed a line and marched forward into the warzone.

Chapter 85

Stratton stood in the rain and listened as the helicopter faded into the distance. The look in Christiano's eyes had disturbed him. Whoever he had been before was long departed and all that remained was a fiery torrent of confused energy. He hoped he was wrong, but his gut told him that the young man was probably beyond recall. With a heavy heart he walked back into the White House.

"What happened?" asked Jennings. "Did he try and do anything bad to you?"

"I don't think so," said Stratton. "If he did then it didn't work. I don't think he was interested in hurting anyone else, I think he just wanted to get away."

"He's still dangerous though, isn't he?"

"Yes, he's still dangerous. Very dangerous."

Greg Albany led them back through the numerous corridors to the conference room. President Mackenzie and his small committee were waiting for them at the table. Jonathan Ayres and Cardinal Vittori had joined them.

Jennings took one look at the Prime Minister and flipped. "Ayres! You fucking snake!" he shouted.

He made a lunge for the table, but Grady held him back.

"Not now, buddy. Leave it for another time. We've got bigger fish to fry."

Jennings muttered under his breath then simmered down slowly and took a seat alongside Stella and Stratton. He asked one of the aides to bring him a coffee.

"I take it you didn't have any luck with our young friend then?" said Mackenzie, addressing Stratton.

"No. I'm not sure if there's anything we can do about him. He's been given too much power too soon. His head's exploding with concepts that he can't possibly understand."

"Of course he understands them," said Ayres. "He's the Son of

God – he understands everything."

Mackenzie gave the Prime Minister a harsh look. "I think we all know that Christiano is *not* the Son of God, Jonathan, so let's just cut the bullshit. I think you've done enough lying already."

Ayres opened his mouth and then shut it again.

"Good," said Mackenzie. "Now that we're all agreed, let's decide what we're going to do about him. About this whole fucked-up situation."

"So you agree with us now then do you?" said Stella.

"I didn't disagree with you in the first place," said Mackenzie. "But I have to do what's in the best interest of the country. The circumstances have changed now, and if you might have the good grace to accept my apologies then we can start to address the new position. Is that okay with you?"

Stella nodded.

"Good," said Mackenzie. "Now let's get down to business. Has anybody got any ideas as to how we deal with Christiano? It seems pretty clear that he's going his own way now."

"But which way?" said General Perry. "We've got no idea what he's going to do next. He's a loose cannon, and if you ask me he needs to be taken out of the equation.."

"And how do you suggest we do that, General?" asked Ayres. "Bullets are no good against him."

"No, they're not," admitted Perry. "But I don't think even he could stop a missile." He looked at his watch. "He'll be flying over the Atlantic in about an hour, a long way from our shores. We can pick the plane off then."

"What about the other people on board?" said Vittori. "Sophia is the daughter of a very good friend of mine."

"There may be a few civilian casualties, but that can't be helped I'm afraid, Your Eminence."

"This is not what we want," said Vittori. "Not what we want at all. I do not think that killing Christiano will help our cause in any way whatsoever. It will just make a martyr of him, exactly like the Mahdi. And besides, it is immoral."

"Immoral?" said Perry, eyebrows raised. "Forgive me, Your Eminence, but having heard the full story of what you've done, I don't think you're in any position to take the moral high-ground with us. You and your little gofer here," he waved his hand at Ayres, "haven't exactly been boy scouts have you? We know you had the Mahdi killed, and I suspect that he isn't the only one who's died during this little contrivance of yours. I'm guessing that between the two of you there's more blood on your hands than the rest of us put together."

"I resent that," said Vittori, becoming visibly flustered.

"Well," said Perry. "Resent it or not, it's true. I think you should stop trying to fool everyone with your pious act, because everyone at this table knows what you are."

Vittori bowed his head and fell silent.

"Good," said Perry. "Now that we all know what's what, let's get down to business. Does anyone else object to our shooting the plane down?"

A chorus of yeses echoed round the table.

"Okay," said Perry. "Can somebody enlighten me as to why?"

"For the same reason we don't want you nuking the Middle East or anywhere else," said Stratton. "Because none of this is going to be resolved by killing anybody. We've already stated our case to you, General. The only way to avoid Armageddon is for everybody to just stop the violence. No more aggression and no more retaliation. You need to get this message across to the whole world by whatever means possible. And you need to start everything off by laying down your own weapons."

"We may as well pull our trousers down and ask Johnny Arab to fuck us up the ass with a nuke. There is no way I'm going to allow this country to lay itself open to attack."

"I don't think it's your decision," said Stratton, looking to Mackenzie.

"Listen, General," said Grady. "As a rule I'd be right behind you one hundred percent on this one. But if you'd seen the shit that I have over the last six months then you might think differently. I agree that what he's saying goes against every instinct we have, but if he says that's the way to go, then I think that we should listen. Whether we sense them or not, there's powers in this world," he opened his arms, "in this universe if you will, that are greater than anything mankind could possibly create itself. This isn't a case of logic or military strategy anymore, this all comes down to faith and bravery."

"There's a thin line between bravery and stupidity, Mr Grady."

"Yes, there is, and if you don't listen to Stratton then you've crossed over into stupidity." He turned to Mackenzie. "What do you think, Mr President? Ultimately it's your decision."

Mackenzie shook his head. "I don't know," he said. "I just don't know. I can see where General Perry is coming from on this, and my head, in the role of President, tells me that to survive we've got to act, and act quickly."

Perry nodded his approval.

"But," Mackenzie continued. "There's a part of me as a human being that's telling me to listen to Stratton here. And sometimes even the President has to act as a human being would."

Perry's face dropped. "Mr President, you surely can't even consider taking the course that they're suggesting. We'll all be wiped out within a few days."

"I'm sure you won't, General," said Grady. "You'll be locked safely away in your bunker with the rest of the White House and the Pentagon."

"That's not the point," Perry countered. "This isn't about me, this is about the people of the United States, the people of the free world. We have a duty – no, we're sworn – to protect them, and I'll be damned if I'm going to go back on my word. And I'll be damned if I'll let you go back on yours, Mr President."

Mackenzie stared Perry in the eye. "Have you forgotten who you're talking to, General."

"No, Mr President I haven't, but you seem to be forgetting who you are and what you're here to do. This is a democracy we're defending. Do you think any of the good citizens out there would vote to sit around and let themselves die?"

"Of course they wouldn't, General. But they voted me capable of making the big decisions for them. They have faith in my judgement and I will not let them down." He paused. "And before you go off again, just remember that as yet I have not made any decision. All I'm doing is giving all options their due consideration."

The table went briefly silent while everyone digested all that had been said so far. It was Stratton who started the discussion again. "I can certainly understand your concerns, General," he said. "And if I was in your position I would probably be saying exactly the same thing. But what you have to understand is that this is no longer just about territoriality, or about the United States or the Middle East or China or Russia defending themselves, this is about humanity as a whole. If you take the route that you're suggesting then everyone will die. It'll start off a chain reaction that will destroy the planet. If you choose to stay passive then there's every chance that the others will as well."

"And what if they don't?"

"Then the United States will fall, but humankind will survive."

Perry grunted. "I've never heard such crap in all my life. You expect us to sacrifice ourselves for a bunch of barbarians. What sort of world would it be without us. The whole planet would be back in the Dark Ages within months. Women and children would be terrorized, the civilized society that we've created would be gone forever. Nowhere would be safe."

"I'm sure that your enemies would say similar things about you. But that's the whole point isn't it. Everyone thinks that their way is the best and only way. The attitude is that if you're going to die then the enemy must die too."

"It's a natural reaction," said Perry.

"I know it is," said Stratton. "And look where natural reactions have brought us…This is time for the human race to rise above its primitive urges and act for the higher good. If you lay down your weapons and get blown to smithereens then at least there'll be someone left on the planet? They might not share your beliefs, but they'll be alive – and just maybe they'll learn from your sacrifice. Perhaps the guilt of slaying an unarmed man will finally show them the futility of it all. If nobody lays down their arms then there'll be nobody left to learn anything. Well, not on this planet anyway."

"This is bullshit!" yelled Perry. "I am not going to allow myself and an entire nation to be killed for the small possibility that a few savages might learn a lesson in life!"

"Listen," said Stratton. "I'm not trying to upset you, General, I'm just trying to make a point. The point is that human life is sacred and no-one's life is more important than anybody else's. Just because you think your life is worth more than some lowly Muslim, doesn't make it so. Just because someone doesn't agree with you doesn't make them any less deserving of life than you." He paused. "Look at it this way, as a General it's your job to minimize casualties – am I right?"

"It's one of them."

"Okay then, let's say there were two strategies available to you. One of which saved over half your men, and one of which killed them all. Which one would you choose?"

"The first one obviously."

"Exactly, so would any commander in their right mind. Now take a big leap of imagination and see the universe as a general, and everyone on earth as his men. Which strategy do you think would be most beneficial to him at this present moment – yours or mine? And remember, just like you he doesn't have any favourites – he just has men, and to him like to you it's a numbers game."

"Listen to me you jumped up little shit!" yelled Perry. "You're not going to trick me with your fancy philosophizing. This is the real world, and my job is to defend my country. And you can talk until you're blue in the fucking face – it's not going to change my mind!"

"General!" said Mackenzie. "Please calm down. This is only a discussion. Let the man have his say."

Stratton thanked the President and continued. "I'm sorry, General, I didn't mean to upset you, I just wanted to make a point. But that point is only hypothetical anyway because I don't expect anyone to be bombing anyone else. If you call a ceasefire or a truce then the world will follow, I'm sure of it. Nobody wants to start a nuclear war if they don't have to."

"Well, you certainly don't know the Muslims then," said Perry.

"I don't know all of them personally, no. But do you? Have you really tried to make a truce with them? Or has all the negotiating been on your terms?"

"The things they want are ridiculous," said Perry.

"Ridiculous to you maybe, but not to them. I seem ridiculous to you, but that doesn't make me wrong – or even right, we just have different points of view."

"Okay, I accept that. But they don't want to negotiate anyway. All they want is the destruction of the United States and its allies."

"Gentlemen," said Mackenzie. "I think that's enough. You've both made your points well. But this argument could go on forever. I think it's time I made a decision. General, I appreciate your position, and at any other time I would wholeheartedly agree with you. But you made a point about this being the real world, and that just doesn't hold true anymore. This is no longer the world we knew, this is something new and dangerous, something we don't really understand. We need to adapt to this new understanding or I believe we will indeed be heading into oblivion. We are still the most powerful nation in the world, and as such we have a responsibility to lead from the front. I believe that we should follow Stratton's recommendations and reduce our defence condition to its lowest level."

"But—" Perry started.

Mackenzie put up his hand. "I've made up my mind, General. I'm not just the President of the United States, I'm the leader of the free peoples of the world, and if we can save lives by doing this then I suggest we do it. I don't want to die, but neither do I want to be responsible for the extinction of mankind. This is time for a dramatic leap of faith. My heart tells me so."

Perry stood up. "Are you guys just going to sit there and let him do this?!" he shouted to the table. "You've got to be out of your minds!"

"Enough!" said Mackenzie. "Let's put this to the vote. All those in favour of the peaceful solution raise your hands now."

"We can't include outsiders in this vote, Mr President," said Perry.

"We can, and we will," said Mackenzie. "Have you not listened to a word that's been said General? This is no longer just about the United States."

Only three people kept their hands down: Perry, General Johnson and Trent Arthur from the NSA.

"Well that settles it then," said Mackenzie.

Perry would not give up. "But you can't do this, Mr President! It's totally unconstitutional!"

"General!" Mackenzie ordered. "Please be quiet! The decision has been made. You may not like it, and I certainly understand your reasons, but if you had been taken off your feet by an unseen force then you might think quite differently. I've been on the receiving end of it, so I know. There is no weapon on earth that can match the power I'm talking about. You saw it yourself with the bullet being stopped. We either pacify this power or we die, it's as simple as that."

Stratton felt a huge wave of benign energy pass through his body.

"This is all very well," said Vittori. "But what are we going to do about Christiano? He has more power at his disposal than any country. There is no telling what he might do if left to his own counsel."

"Well, what do you suggest?" asked Mackenzie. "The way I see it there's not much we can do. He doesn't seem to want to listen to reason and we can't use force against him, so where does that leave us?"

"We cannot do nothing," said Vittori. "He is becoming deranged, and the people of the world are hanging on his every word."

"I suppose we could always tell them the truth," said Stratton. "I know it probably won't do any good after that bullet stunt, but we can try. I think the truth is about all we have left to give. Calling off military attacks is just the start, this whole thing needs to be blown wide open. Soldiers can be controlled by orders, but you can't control the population. People around the world are angry and fearful, and they need to be calmed. We've had enough lies and it's time to be open. You and the other leaders need to tell them exactly what's happened, and let them know that the only way forward is a peaceful way. It may take a while to filter down through to everybody, but if nothing's done then a military stand-down won't be worth a bean, the citizens of the world will have wiped themselves out. I believe that's what's already happening in Europe and parts of Asia. And Britain's totally out of control isn't it?" He looked to the Prime Minister for conformation.

"Yes," said Ayres. "It appears so. We seem to have lost control somewhere along the way."

"I wonder why," grunted Stella.

"But it's not just us," said Ayres defensively. "Like Stratton said, it's all over Europe and Asia. The whole world's divided. I'm not sure how feasible it is to reach everybody with words of calm."

"Fuck feasibility," said Stratton. "It's got to be done. And you're going to be the first to act. You've helped get everybody into this bloody mess, and now you're going to help get us out of it."

"I'm not sure it's entirely my fault."

"No-one said it was, but you've played a major part. And now you're going to play a major part in reversing the flow. The first thing you're going to do is stop the military from killing any more civilians – I've seen the reports and it's looking dangerously like carnage over there. So pick up the phone and call them off."

"Who do you think—" Ayres started. His sentence tailed off though when he felt Mackenzie's glare. "Okay, okay. I'll do it." He reached for a phone and dialled London.

"But what about Christiano?" said Vittori. "We have still not come up with a solution for him. What will happen to him? What will happen to the Church?"

"Quite frankly," said Mackenzie, "I don't really care what happens to the Church. You've led the world a merry dance for nearly two millennia now, and I think it's about time you were put out to grass. You and the Muslims have caused all this with your lies. I think the world will be a lot better off without either of you."

"But where will people go for spiritual guidance?"

"I don't know," said Mackenzie. "But at the moment that's the least of our concerns. If we don't have anybody left to guide then it won't matter. As far as Christiano's concerned I don't know. We'll have to do something about him, but it's really not my area of expertise." He looked over to Stratton for help.

Stratton shook his head. "I really don't know what to do about him. All I can do is go to Rome and try to reason with him again. I've got to be honest though – I think he's too far gone to listen to anyone. Although his girlfriend might be a useful ally."

"Okay then," said Mackenzie. "That's sorted. You go to Rome and do whatever you can to contain the situation. Let me know if there's anything you need. In the meantime we're going to have to get busy communicating with the rest of the world." He picked up his telephone and began to dial. "Gentlemen, it's time to start saving the human race."

Chapter 86

Paul Smith jumped into the back of the Jeep and lit a cigarette. The order to withdraw had come not a moment too soon. Fortunately they had been so reluctant to carry out their duty that no shots had been fired before the retreat. He wondered whether he would have been able to do it anyway. He'd spent his short adult life obeying orders and it had become second nature to do as he was told, but the slaughter of your own people was a different matter. It would have taken a heart and mind of steel to carry out that particular command, and he was no longer sure that he possessed either.

He pulled out his flask and took a large mouthful of brandy, and then handed it to Graham, who accepted gratefully.

"Cheers, mate. I really thought that was it back there. I felt sick to be honest."

"You're not the only one, mate. I was a couple of seconds away from puking myself. Thank God they pulled us out of there, that's all I can say. I wonder what's happened to make them do it?"

"Fucked if I know," said Graham. "Whatever it is it's probably political. They wouldn't be doing it unless there was something in it for them."

"You're too cynical, mate. Maybe they decided killing their own people just wasn't right."

"Maybe. But when you've been in the army this long you get to be cynical. I'm surprised you're still so naïve."

"Not naïve," said Paul. "I've just got faith in human nature."

"Still?" laughed Graham. "After all we've seen? You must be fucking mad, mate!"

"Maybe I am. But without it what have I got left? You've got to hang on to something, Graham, otherwise you may as well be dead. We're soldiers, we're not robots."

"But that's exactly what we are mate – robots. We're not paid to think or to have faith in humanity. We're paid to do a job – a fucking horrible job – but just a job. If we started thinking for ourselves then there wouldn't be an army."

"And maybe that wouldn't be such a bad thing," said Paul.

"Oh, for fuck's sake. Don't start getting conchie on me now, buddy."

The Jeep pulled up at the Horton Hospital, and they got out and reported back to their commanding officer. After a short debriefing they went to the tented canteen to get some dinner.

"I can't believe that," said Graham. "A total military stand-down. What the hell's going on? What the hell are they thinking?"

Paul dipped a dry piece of bread into his stew. "Perhaps they've suddenly seen sense," he said. "Maybe they've learnt that war doesn't solve anything."

"What's wrong with you man? I thought you were a fucking soldier."

"I am, but I'm a soldier who's had enough. I've been in this fucking army for five years and I've never once questioned anything. I've killed people without a second thought, and all for what?"

"To protect those that can't protect themselves," said Graham. "We've done what we had to do to restore law and order where it's been lost. We haven't killed without reason, and you know it."

Paul sighed and finished a mouthful of stew. "Maybe you're right. But it doesn't make me feel any better. Christ, I don't know what's wrong with me."

"Lack of sleep, mate, I reckon. Go and grab yourself a couple of hours and you'll be fine."

Paul mopped up his gravy with the last of the bread and drained his mug of tea. He looked up to see a young woman approaching the table trying to catch his eye. He recognized her as the girl he'd met earlier in smokers' corner.

"Hi," she said. "Sorry to bother you, but we met this morning, remember?"

"Yeah, I remember. I didn't catch your name though."

"It's Jenna."

"Well, I'm Paul, and this is Graham."

Graham said hello and gave Paul a sideways glance indicating that his mate was 'in there'.

"Is it alright if I sit down?" she asked. "I just wanted to find out what's going on in the town. Nobody wants to tell us anything."

Paul gestured for her to sit down on the bench next to him. Graham gave him a sly wink.

"Sorry to be a bother," she said.

"It's no problem," said Paul.

"So," said Jenna. "Is it true that the military are standing down? We've just seen the Prime Minister and President Mackenzie say so on TV."

"Yeah, it's true," said Paul. "Well, we've been asked to withdraw anyway. I don't know anything about the Americans. It seems you know more than us about it."

"Only what I saw on the news report. The President made quite a long statement actually. I can't remember all of the details, but the basic gist was that he had evidence that the Catholic Messiah and the Mahdi were both fakes, and that the people of the world needed to take a step back and calm down before we destroy ourselves. He said that with immediate effect all US forces were standing down, and any planned missile strikes were now aborted. He said that the USA had taken these steps to lead the way for a peaceful solution to our current troubles."

"He's fucking mad!" said Graham. "The rag 'eads will be all over them like rash. They'll bomb the fuck out of them!" He shook his head. "And we're part of this fucking lunacy as well are we?"

"I guess so," said Jenna. "The Prime Minister backed up

everything Mackenzie said. And seeing as you've been recalled it must be true."

"I thought it was only a temporary measure," said Graham. "And just a domestic one. I didn't realize we were opening ourselves up to attack from abroad as well. This is fucking insane!"

"Is it?" said Jenna. "Somebody's got to back down haven't they? Or everyone will die. I think this is the best thing that our politicians have ever done."

"Gah!" Graham spat. "That's a typical fucking civilian comment! You don't know what those fuckers are capable of. I tell you something – if you lay down your weapons in front of that lot they'll shoot you down like fucking ducks at a fairground. I've done my tours of Afghanistan and Iraq, love. I know exactly what they're like." He shook his head and sneered disparagingly.

Jenna bowed her head slightly. "I'm sorry," she said. "I really didn't mean to offend you. I know you guys have done amazing things out there, and I think you're terrifically brave. I just want to see an end to it all."

Paul put a hand on her shoulder. "It's alright," he said. "We all want to see an end to it all. We're just a bit tense at the moment." He looked to his colleague for an apology.

"Yeah," said Graham. "We're all a bit on edge, love. Sorry, I didn't mean to get on at you."

"Anyway," said Paul. "You wanted to know what was going on in the town. Well, I can tell you it's not pretty. There's two major battlegrounds – one in Grimsbury and one up Bretch Hill – and it's carnage in both. We don't know the exact numbers, but we reckon there's at least a hundred dead so far. And you can see how many serious injuries we've had up here already. There just aren't enough medical staff to cope anymore. We're going to go back in soon to try and get some more of the injured out. We're hoping that it dies down a bit before then."

"Is that likely?" she asked.

"Probably not. But they've got to tire themselves out sometime haven't they?"

Jenna got up to leave. "Well, thanks for letting me know," she said. "I'd better get some food and get back to the tent. My boyfriend will be getting hungry and wondering what's keeping me. Good luck!"

"Boyfriend eh?" said Graham, when she'd gone. "That's a bit of a shit isn't it mate? I thought you were well in there."

Paul laughed. "That's what you always say, mate. Come on, let's go and have a smoke."

They stood outside in the dimness away from the tents and lit their cigarettes. Paul leant against a wall and looked up to the still, gathering sky through a large, perfectly formed smoke ring he'd just blown. There was no rain as yet, but the closeness in the air suggested it wouldn't be long coming. And there was something else, something he couldn't explain, something that prickled the back of his neck. He swallowed nervously and suddenly wondered if he or the world would ever see another dawn.

Chapter 87

Air Force One began its steady descent towards Rome. Stratton stared out into the blackness and tried to close his mind to the raging pain inside. The President had made a positive step, but it was still only one good gesture in an ocean of ill-feeling. Whether the rest of the world would follow his lead was firmly in the balance. But at least there was hope, and that would remain until all else was lost.

In the chair next to him Pat Cronin was waking from a brief doze. He opened his eyes and stretched and yawned. "Are we nearly there yet?" he asked.

"I think we've just started to descend," said Stratton. "I guess we're about half an hour away. How was your sleep?"

"It could have been longer, but I've shaken off the worst. What about you? Have you managed to get any shuteye?"

"No. I haven't really tried to be honest. I've been too busy thinking about how to approach Christiano. He's in a very delicate state at the moment, and I really don't want to send him over the edge by saying the wrong thing."

"Well, if anyone can help him it's you."

Stratton gave a muted laugh. "I'm not so sure, Pat. My mind's all over the place, just like my body. I've tried every technique I know and I just can't quiet my thoughts. I'm suddenly remembering what it's like to be completely human again, and I'm not sure I like it."

Cronin grabbed a bottle of water from the table and took a drink. "There is one good thing about all this," he said. "I never thought I'd ever get to fly on Air Force One. It's certainly better than Ryan Air." He looked at the empty chairs opposite. "What's happened to the others?" he asked.

"They've gone up to the war room to see what's happening around the world."

"Aren't you interested?"

"Yeah, I am, but there's nothing I can do about it at the moment so I'm concentrating on what I can do."

Cronin relaxed back in his chair. "Do you really think people are going to stop fighting? Do you think that the Muslims will follow Mackenzie's lead?"

"I hope so," said Stratton. "For the sake of the world, I hope so."

The plane banked to the right and far below them the bright lights of Rome came into view for the first time. Stratton fastened his seatbelt and shuffled to get comfortable. He closed his eyes and breathed deeply. The storm was about to break.

Chapter 88

Generals Johnson and Perry were soldiers of the old guard and had over eighty years service between them. They had both fought in Vietnam as junior officers, and had risen through the ranks almost in tandem over the subsequent decades. They had seen administrations come and go, and wars won and lost, but whatever the campaign they had served their country with unimpeachable loyalty and valour. They loved the United States and the values it stood for with a passion bordering on obsession, and they were damn certain that nobody was going to let it be annihilated while they still had life in their respective bodies.

Perry checked the chamber of his ceremonial Colt 45 one last time and tucked it into its holster. Johnson did the same. They nodded silently to each other and walked out into the corridor and headed for the Oval Office.

Secret Service agent Bryn Byers watched casually as the two old Generals came towards him. The President hadn't mentioned they were on their way, but there was nothing suspicious about their presence with all that was happening. He turned to his partner who gave a small shrug.

"Hi, boys," said Perry, with a friendly smile. "How's it going? I guess it's a bit mad with us old-timers in and out all afternoon."

Bryn didn't get a chance to answer. The last thing he remembered was a flash of movement, a sharp pain in the side of his neck, and then a deep blackness.

Perry and Johnson opened the door and dragged the two unconscious agents through and out of sight.

"Not bad for a couple of oldies," said Perry. "These youngsters just don't know their job nowadays."

After securing and gagging the agents they opened the door of the Oval Office and strode in.

Mackenzie looked up from his desk in surprise. "Good evening, Generals," he said. "What can I do for you?"

Perry and Johnson reached for their weapons and pointed them simultaneously.

"It's more what you can do for us, Mr President. Or, more importantly, what you can do for your country."

Mackenzie reached down for his panic button.

"Don't even think about it," said Perry. "Keep your hands up and away from that desk. And don't think your little buddies outside will save you because they're having a little sleep."

"What the hell is this, Perry?!" barked Mackenzie. "What do you think you're doing barging in here? I'm the goddamn President of the United States, for Christ's sake!"

"Well," said Perry. "That's a matter of conjecture if you ask me. I don't know how you can call yourself that after what's happened. To me you're just a weak-minded piece of liberal shit who's letting his country down big-time."

"Listen to me, General," said Mackenzie. "I've made a decision based on what I know, and what I believe to be right – not just for the United States, but for the whole world. If you've got a problem with that, then talk to me about it. There's no need for all this heavy-handed bullshit."

"The time for talking has gone," said Perry. "Now is the time for action. You've made your position very clear, and so have we. The problem is that your position is going to get everyone killed, and we're just not going to allow it."

"And you think holding me at gunpoint is going to make a difference?"

"That's what we're here to find out. If you play ball with us then nobody gets hurt. If not, then…"

"What exactly do you want?" asked Mackenzie.

"It's quite simple, Mr President – we want your security codes for a nuclear strike."

"That's out of the question and you know it. There is no way on earth you're ever going to get those out of me. I don't care if you kill me."

"Listen to me, Mr President. We get no joy out of having to resort to this, but I'm afraid you've left us no option. Unless we take action, within the next couple of hours we are going to be the victims of a large-scale nuclear attack. The Muslims are just watching and waiting to check that we really have stood down. Once they realize we have they're going to come at us like a biblical storm of vengeance. They don't care about peace with us, or sorting things out – they hate us, Mr President, they fucking hate us! The resentment's so deep in them that it can't be removed. As far as they're concerned the only solution is the complete and utter destruction of the West. And that is just not going to happen. Not on my watch."

"I don't believe they will launch, General. I think the years have made you cynical. The days of warfare are over. This is a time for harmony. A time for peace."

"Bullshit!" said Perry. "Absolute bullshit. Your not living in the real world anymore. You need to be declared incompetent. But as we don't have time for that, we have to do what we can. This peace you talk of is all in your head. We're at war, and we need to defend ourselves."

"This is futile," said Mackenzie. "I've already told you that I'm not going to give you my launch codes."

"I think you might do with the right persuasion."

"And what would that be?

"You'll find out soon."

Perry and Johnson took seats opposite the President and kept their guns trained on him. Mackenzie kept still and wondered how long it would be before one of his other aides came calling.

A minute later the door opened and the President's wife and daughter walked in, closely followed by Colonel Sam Matthews with a gun at their backs. The young girl had tears in her eyes. Mackenzie was lost for words.

"So then, Mr President, I think you might want to reconsider giving me those codes," said Perry.

"You wouldn't," said Mackenzie.

"I would, and I will, unless you give me what I want. The safety of the whole nation's at stake here, not just a few people."

Mackenzie looked to his family and then back to Perry. "Listen to me, General, there's no need to bring my family into this. They've done nothing wrong have they? So why hurt them?"

"The people of this country have done nothing wrong either, and yet you seem determined to put them in jeopardy."

Mackenzie sighed. "I can't do it, General. I've made my decision and I will not be bullied into changing it."

"Then I have no choice either," said Perry. "Who goes first? You decide." He moved his gun and aimed it at the girl. "Perhaps your daughter."

Mackenzie searched Perry's eyes for a weakness; a sign of a bluff. But there was nothing, just cold, hard, determined steel. He had to make a choice. And whichever way he went he was going to lose.

Chapter 89

It was nearing midnight and the corridors of the Vatican were cold and silent. Stratton followed Cronin and the two Swiss Guards, with Jennings and Stella close behind, the air thick with fear and uncertainty. Their every footstep clicked like a final countdown. Jennings looked across to Stella and attempted a smile, but it fell apart and his gaze dropped to the floor. He felt her hand gently squeeze his own.

The guards suddenly halted and put their arms out to stop the group from going any further. They raised their weapons. Up ahead the sound of quick and light feet drew closer. A few seconds later the distraught figure of Sophia Zola appeared and ran towards them, sobbing and seeking help.

Cronin pushed in front of the suspicious guards and reached out to comfort her. "Come now," he said, holding her close. "What's happened, my child?"

"It's Christiano!" she bawled. "He's going crazy! I don't know what to do!"

"Don't worry," said Cronin. "It'll be alright. We've come to help him."

It took several minutes, but between them they eventually managed to calm her down and get a full picture. Christiano's state of mind had deteriorated rapidly since Stratton had tried to reason with him at the White House. Unable to cope with the heavy traffic gushing through his brain he had become increasingly irrational and unpredictable.

"He's removed the Pope and taken up residence in his quarters," said Sophia. "Tomorrow he's going to declare himself the new head of the Church. He says they're all cheats and liars and that they need to be exposed for what they really are."

"I can't argue with him there," said Stratton.

"I know," said Sophia. "But he's started to hurt people. I don't know what he did to the Pope, but he's lost all power of speech.

He's almost like a vegetable. And the guards that were protecting him are all lying on the floor. I don't know whether they're dead or alive."

"We must hurry," said one of the guards. "We must stop him before he hurts anyone else." He took the safety off his weapon and made to go.

"There's no point trying to overpower him," said Stratton. "You'll never be able to do it. Whatever you do, he'll turn it against you."

"Then what are we supposed to do?" said the guard.

"We've got to try and talk to him," said Stratton. "We've got to somehow try and get him to start reasoning again. He's lost and confused. He needs our help, not our animosity. Just take us to him and we'll do the rest."

The guard shrugged and led them off towards the Pope's private rooms. In ordinary circumstances he would have paid no attention to the opinion of the interlopers, but not only was he wary of Christiano's power, he was also mindful of the fact that Vittori had given them instructions to do as commanded.

When they reached their destination Christiano was nowhere to be seen. A total of five Swiss Guards were out for the count in various positions, from slumped to spread-eagled. There was relief when their pulses were checked and found, although nothing seemed to be able to wake them. They located the Pope in a small ante-room and although he appeared to be awake they could get no decipherable words from him. He sat on a chair murmuring and repeatedly making the sign of the cross on his chest.

"Will he be okay?" asked Sophia. "Is there nothing you can do for him?"

"I don't know," said Jennings. "Can we do anything, Stratton?"

"I don't think there's anything I can do at the moment," said Stratton. "I've got no power flowing at all. I think he'll be okay though. He might just be in shock."

"So what do we do now?" asked Stella. "Where's Christiano gone?"

One of the guards picked up his radio and made an open call to his remaining team, asking for any sightings of the Messiah. A few seconds later he received a reply. He turned to Cronin with a furrowed brow. "He's in the basilica."

Chapter 90

Grady followed Greg Albany through the door into the waiting room next to the Oval Office. There was no sign of the secretary, but a pair of motionless feet were poking out from behind her desk. Albany peered over to find the two incapacitated Secret Service agents.

"What the fuck is this?" he murmured to himself.

Grady reached down and released the gags and tried to bring the agents round.

"Fuck that," said Albany. "Let's get next door."

Grady looked up a him and shook his head. "We don't know what's going on, Greg. It's best to get some information first."

"We haven't got time for that," said Albany. "Grab their guns – we're going in."

Grady shrugged and removed the agents' weapons and handed one to Albany. They approached the Oval Office carefully. There was no way of hearing anything through the thick soundproofed door, so their only option was to storm in blind. Albany closed his palm over the handle and took a breath. He turned to Grady who gave him the nod. In one lightning movement he dropped the handle and thrust through the door.

Grady held back for an instant taking in the scene, and then followed his friend through. Perry and Johnson shot round and levelled their weapons at the intruders.

"Drop them!" commanded Perry.

Grady and Albany raised their guns and held fast.

"No, General," Albany said flatly. "You drop them."

"Give it up, Greg," said Perry. "You're outnumbered three to one. One word from me and Matthews here goes to work." He nodded towards the Colonel who now had his gun aimed at the President.

"He hasn't got a prayer," said Albany. "He'll be dead before you hit the ground."

"What are you, Greg? Some kind of sharpshooter? This isn't the Wild West you know. The odds are well against you. Surely you don't want to be responsible for the death of your beloved boss here." He gestured to the President.

"Don't listen to him, Greg," said Mackenzie. "Nobody's going to shoot me – they need me alive. They need my launch codes."

"So that's what this is all about," said Albany. He stared at Perry. "Listen, General, nobody is going to launch any missiles today. We've made the decision and it's final."

Perry ignored the comment and turned to Colonel Matthews. "I think perhaps we ought to go back to plan A, Sam."

Matthews switched his aim from the President back to his daughter.

"Now then," said Perry. "Unless you guys want to be responsible for the death of an innocent little girl then I suggest you drop your weapons right now. This has gone on long enough. I need those codes and I need them now."

"It's not going to happen, General," said Albany. "You need to lower your weapons right now or your going to die. And then no-one will be launching anything will they? It needs both your codes to instigate a strike."

"Listen, General," said Grady. "There's no way you can win. In fact there's no way any of us can win. I suggest we all act like the civilized people we are and just lay down our guns. If you don't then my guess is that we're all likely to get hurt or die for no reason."

"We're all going to die anyway thanks to him," said Perry, waving his gun at the President.

"Maybe," said Grady. "But if we are, let's die as a team – not like this. I mean, look at yourself, look at what you've become. Look at this frightened little girl – is that why you joined the army, to bully children? To scare them to the point of tears?"

Perry looked away.

"No," said Grady. "I didn't think so. I know you only want to protect your country and its citizens, but this isn't the way to go about it. Look, I'll lower my weapon first." He let his hand go limp and laid the gun on the President's desk.

"What the fuck do you think you're doing, Grady?!" yelled Albany.

"Making a stand, Greg. Someone's got to give first."

Perry looked at Grady and then to the President and his family. Then he thought about the millions of families across the country. The millions of little girls that were going to die because of Mackenzie's pigheaded stupidity. One little girl to save millions of others – the answer was self-evident. "I'm sorry, Greg," he said, and squeezed his trigger.

Greg Albany felt the savage belt of the Colt in his chest. He dropped his gun and fell to the floor, bloody fingers clutching at his heart.

Grady watched his friend go down and instinctively leapt across the room at Perry. The Colt fired again, but Grady felt nothing as he crashed down on top of the maverick general and pinned him to the ground.

Mackenzie picked Grady's gun off the desk and pointed it at Matthews. "That's enough!" he ordered. "Everyone drop their weapons! No-one else is going to die in here today."

Matthews looked to Johnson who nodded and let his own gun drop.

Mackenzie hugged his wife and daughter. "It's okay," he said. "You're alright now. No-one's going to hurt you."

Just then his phone started to ring. He picked it up and listened briefly before replacing the receiver.

"It's bad news, I'm afraid," he said calmly. "It seems that I've made a big mistake. The Muslims have just launched their first missile."

Chapter 91

The flames continued to flicker in the distance covering the town with a sinister blood-orange. Up above, the first rumble of thunder broke through the thick carpet of cloud and sent a shiver through all that heard it. Trees creaked in the shadows, bending and swaying and heralding doom. Jenna huddled herself against the hastening wind and took one last drag of her cigarette before throwing it to the floor and stamping it out. She looked fearfully to the sky and then hurried across the grass to the tent.

Tariq watched his girlfriend approach down the crowded aisle and smiled to himself. Even in the midst of all the mayhem she shone as a beacon of beauty and hope. His heart soared as her radiance cancelled out the bloody and battered background, and filled it with streams of angelic light. In that moment it hit him that nothing else mattered; that should all their fears come to fruition, he would always have that image of her to wipe away the pain. He'd told her that he loved her before and had meant it, but now the feeling had pierced him more completely than ever, and his previous words and emotions seemed to fall desperately short of the deeper reality he was now experiencing.

As Jenna drew near she noticed a strange look in Tariq's eye. She looked down at him on the camp-bed and gave him a quizzical glance. "What's up?" she said. "Is everything okay?"

Tariq smiled and nodded dreamily. He stood up and held her cheek and gazed deep in her eyes. "I love you," he said. "I love you more than anyone could ever love anything."

Jenna wanted to look away but felt unable. It suddenly occurred to her that she knew exactly what he meant, and that she felt the same. A wave of exquisite joy and pain thrust its way into her soul, and as her eyes welled she felt Tariq's soft lips touch her own and envelop her completely.

For a brief moment everything made sense. And then the world came crashing down around them.

The tent erupted in a maelstrom of chatter and confusion. Patients began leaping fearfully from their beds. Tariq and Jenna broke off their kiss and looked around bewilderedly, trying to get a grasp of what was happening.

A young man thrust past them and Tariq grabbed his arm. "What's going on?!" he shouted above the din.

"They're outside!"

"Who's outside?!"

"Them!" the young man shouted. "The rioters. They're outside the hospital!" He shrugged off Tariq's hand and scurried off out of the tent.

"What shall we do?" asked Jenna.

Tariq shook his head. "I don't know. Maybe it's better to stay in here. I'm not sure leaving the tent's such a good idea."

"But that's what most people are doing."

"I know," said Tariq. "But we're not most people. They're just in a blind panic at the moment. That's not going to do anyone any good. I reckon we should sit tight for a while."

"I don't want to hang around like a sitting duck," said Jenna. "We need to find out exactly what's happening." She grabbed his hand. "Come on, let's go and find someone who knows the score."

They hurried out of the tent together and into the open air. The scene outside was even worse. People ran and scrabbled blindly in the semi-darkness, trying to escape but unsure of which direction the threat lay. Lost children screamed for their parents. Infirm bodies tripped and fell and were crushed under fleeing feet. Jenna scanned frantically for a safe passage, but the sea of hysteria appeared impregnable. She was just about to retreat back inside when she felt a hand upon her shoulder. It was Paul, the soldier.

"Are you guys alright?" he asked.

"I think so," she said. "We don't know what to do though. How do we get out?"

Paul's answer was blunt. "We don't," he said. "The whole place is surrounded."

"But why?" she asked. "What the hell do they want? There's no threat to them in here."

"They want the Muslims. There's been a load of deaths out there today and they're demanding payback."

"But surely there's been deaths on both sides?"

"Yeah, there has. But the white boys want more. They don't think we should be treating Muslims up here in the hospital."

"That's ridiculous!" said Jenna.

"The whole thing's fucking ridiculous," said Paul. "I don't even think they're bothered about the Muslims anymore. It's just any old excuse. Something's got hold of them: it's like a contagious madness."

"Yeah," said Tariq. "It's called hatred."

Paul pulled them back into the tent. "Listen," he said. "If I was you guys I'd wait in here. There's no point trying to go anywhere else."

"What are you going to do?" asked Jenna.

"What I'm told to. I think our stand-down's going to be short-lived. There's no way we can let these fucking idiots destroy the hospital. We're holding them at bay for the moment, but it won't be long before we have to start shooting." He looked out into the fray. "I'd better get going."

Jenna watched him disappear into the melee and felt her heart sink, every cry of the crowd removing a little more hope from the well. Overhead the thunderous sky grew louder, its incessant growl reverberating through her frightened mind. She looked up to the heavens and despaired, seeking guidance from a God that had deserted her long ago. And then, as she stared vacantly into the ether, her soul almost spent, she let out an abrupt laugh. The laugh segued into another, and then another, until she was unable to control her joy. She turned to Tariq. "Come on," she said. "Let's get going."

"Where?" said Tariq, confused by her sudden delirium. "What's wrong with you?"

Jenna took his hand. "There's nothing wrong with me. There's nothing wrong with me at all. Just trust me."

"The soldier told us to wait here."

Jenna laughed once more. "Who cares? Who do you trust more – him or me?"

Tariq looked into her eyes and detected a madness. "I just think we should keep out of the way," he said diplomatically.

Jenna tightened her grip on his hand. "Listen," she urged. "You don't have to be scared. Fuck it! None of us has to be scared! Don't you understand, Taz – nobody has to be scared. That's the answer to all this."

Tariq tried to move away, but she held him tight.

"Look at me, Taz," she pressed. "Look into my eyes and try to understand what I'm saying. We…don't…have…to…be…scared!"

Tariq had seen this look before, not from Jenna, but in the eyes of deranged zealots and unhinged fanatics who had suddenly 'seen the light' and wanted to tell the whole, unsuspecting world about it. He had seen it in the eyes of newly converted Mormons in the street, and Jehovah's Witnesses parking themselves at the front door with their *Watchtower*'s. It was a look that almost exploded from the eye-sockets, showering the recipient with an unbearable luminosity that forced them to recoil in suspicion and fear. It was a look that Tariq never thought he would see in the eyes of the woman he loved.

For a moment he stood there, uncomfortable and unable to speak, his face unconsciously frowning. And then it happened. Their eyes locked together, and in that brief instant he understood. She was right – they didn't have to be scared. This simple understanding sparked a reaction in his brain and rapidly flooded his whole being. For the first time he could remember he felt truly alive, as if his previous existence had been a dull and stagnant dream. His face lit up with new-found awareness.

"You do understand, don't you?!" Jenna screamed excitedly.

Tariq nodded serenely. "Yes, I do."

"Come on then," she said, tugging at his hand. "Follow me."

Tariq had no idea where she was leading him or what she was going to do when they got there, but he no longer cared. The world had opened up in front of his very eyes, and he moved dreamily among the frightened hordes like a heavenly cloud in the eye of a storm.

At the entrance to A&E Paul Smith looked on as the insufficient police presence bravely held back the rioters with shields and batons. With more angry bodies joining the mob by the second he knew that soon their resistance would be broken, and when this happened he knew what he and his team were going to have to do. The stand-down had been a nice dream, but that was all it had been. The cold reality being that the only way to stem the tide of violence was to meet it head on with greater force. He checked his weapon nervously once more, blanked his mind, and got ready to begin the cull.

Within half a minute the police wall had foundered, trampled by an overwhelming surge from the unformed masses. Paul lifted his gun and took aim. The crowd stormed towards them: two hundred yards…one ninety…one eighty. Paul swallowed and expelled his breath and squeezed the trigger. Then he stopped.

Out of nowhere, the girl, Jenna, and her boyfriend had appeared directly in his line of sight, between the guns and the oncoming riot. For a brief moment they stood there motionless, seemingly oblivious to the onset of gunfire around them. And then, inexplicably, they sat down. Paul found himself shouting for them to get out of the way, but they couldn't hear him, no-one could; his voice was lost in the groundswell of battle.

Chapter 92

In the bunker half a mile below the White House, President Mackenzie and his aides watched the screens as they filled up with blips depicting incoming missiles. A total of ten were now headed for the States, all of them targeting major cities. Both New York and Washington DC would soon be reduced to rubble, and the destruction would continue right across to Seattle and Los Angeles on the west coast.

Grady couldn't remember feeling so low. He was way past the point of upset and had descended into numbness. He'd tried phoning Brooke in LA but there had been no answer. It seemed like they would be parted forever, and he hadn't even had a chance to say goodbye. His only hope was that Grant, with all his connections, had access to a nuclear bunker, and had taken Brooke and the baby with him to keep them safe. This thought gave him strength as he clutched his wounded stomach in pain.

In front of him General Perry was still trying to convince Mackenzie to strike back. "Mr President," he said. "If we don't launch soon then these missiles are just going to keep on coming. If we send out some warning shots then I think they'll stop. At least that way we can save some of our people."

Mackenzie shook his head. "No, General. We're not going to retaliate. I made my decision and I'm going to stick to it. I will not be responsible for the entire destruction of mankind: and if we launch then that's what will happen. It won't stop with a couple of missiles, it'll carry on until every last person on the planet has been wiped out. At least this way some people will survive. And maybe they might make a better job of the future than we have of the past. I told you before – my responsibility is the whole world, not just the United States."

Perry threw up his hands. "Christ!" he shouted. "That's it then. We're history. The United States of America is fucking history."

"So are the Greeks and the Romans," said Mackenzie. "Every great civilization falls, but future generations take the lessons and learn from them." He smiled. "I know you think I'm mad, General, and I don't blame you, but this is the right thing to do. This is the way the world is meant to proceed. And the closer we get to our destiny, the more convinced I am that I've done what I'm supposed to."

"You're right," said Perry, "I do think you're mad. And I'm certain I'm not the only one."

Mackenzie continued to smile. "You just don't get it, do you, General? Even with all that you've seen in the last few days, you still don't get it. Forget about everything you think you know because it's no longer relevant. This isn't about common sense or science, or military strategy or politics; this is about something much bigger and deeper. This is about a power so vast it's unimaginable for us to comprehend. We're just a tiny part in a never-ending story. And maybe America's already played it's role. If that's the will of the universe, then so be it."

Perry grabbed Mackenzie's arm and shook him. "You fucking madman!" he yelled. "Don't you understand! We're going to die! We're all going to die!"

Mackenzie laughed, suddenly overcome by a wave of serene understanding. "Of course we are, General. Everybody does, don't they? But there's no need to be frightened. Fear is what's holding us back as a race, fear of what may or may not happen. But things just happen; they just are. There is nothing for us to fear! There's no need for us to be scared!"

Perry stared silently at his Commander-in-Chief, completely lost for words. The man was insane; utterly insane.

Grady's head slumped forward. Blood began to seep through his fingers. He started to drift away. 'There's no need for us to be scared' were the last words he remembered.

Chapter 93

In terms of size St Peter's Basilica is the second largest church in the world. But in terms of sheer beauty, majesty and status, it has no rival. As soon as Jennings set foot inside he let out an involuntary gasp. It was only the third time in his life that he had felt totally insignificant and speechless: the first was when he had first seen Stella; the second was hearing of Stratton's resurrection. But this perhaps topped them both. He looked up and around in the soft light trying to take it all in. He felt like Jack must have after climbing the beanstalk. Everything was on such a large scale it was almost impossible to comprehend. His heart ached with joy.

"Amazing isn't it," said Stella, sensing his awe.

Jennings looked right to the huge statue of St Teresa of Avila and nodded. "It's beautiful," he said. "Completely and utterly, mind-blowingly beautiful. It's just perfect." His eyes brimmed with tears.

"Come on, you two," said Stratton. "Stop mooning. Help us find Christiano." He raced off down the nave towards the centre of the building.

As Stratton approached Bernini's Baldacchino, he realized that he didn't need any help to locate his quarry. Under the ninety-foot, solid bronze canopy, at the papal altar, Christiano was standing in full view with his arms outstretched to the heavens. His eyes were closed and he was talking to himself in Italian. Stratton's knowledge of the language was limited, but he could still make out that Christiano's chants were an appeal to God.

Stratton turned to Sophia who had run up beside him. "What exactly is he saying?" he asked.

"He's asking God for more power," said Sophia. "He's asking the Lord to bless him with the power to right the world. To give him the strength to overcome the foes of righteousness."

"He's mad," said Stratton.

"Can you help him?"

"I don't know. Only if he wants to help himself, I guess."

Sophia ran towards the altar. "Christiano!" she shouted. "Christiano! Stop this – please!"

Christiano carried on oblivious, continuing his petition to the unseen Creator.

Stratton looked at the baldacchino and followed its spiral columns skywards into the dome. His eyes fell upon the inscription along its base: TV ES PTRVS ET SVPER HANC PETRAM AEDIFICABO ECCLESIAM MEAM. TIBI DABO CLAVES REGNI CAELORVM. Stratton remembered the translation in his head - 'You are Peter, and on this rock I will build my church...I will give you the keys to the kingdom of heaven.' As he looked up at the mighty eight-foot-high letters, he suddenly wondered if God really did exist in the form that the Church believed, and whether his own tenets were fundamentally flawed.

He drew his gaze down once again to the altar. Sophia was now next to Christiano, grabbing his shirt and pleading with him to return to the real world. Her cries, however, were falling on deaf ears. He reached one arm out, and without touching her, thrust her across the floor and crashing down into the sunken chapel – the Confessio.

The blow shuddered through Stratton's body. He could feel the whole world descending into chaos. Images of bloodshed and panic shot through his brain. He saw men and women and children being slain. He saw bombs flying through the air, and petrified faces staring blindly at mushroom clouds of dust. Everything he'd ever known and loved was collapsing under the interminable weight of fear and hatred. He dropped to his knees and clutched his ribcage. The ground beneath him started to shake.

Jennings and Stella watched helplessly with Cronin and two

Swiss Guards. The rumbling grew louder until the whole building began to tremble. It came to all of them that they and the world were standing on the edge of oblivion.

Cronin got down on his knees and started to recite the Lord's Prayer. "Our Father, who art in heaven, hallowed be thy name…"

The Swiss Guards joined him.

Stella looked to Jennings. "Perhaps we ought to start praying too."

Jennings saw the fear in her eyes and pulled her close. And as he stood there with her in his arms, everything made sense. He couldn't explain it, but his brain suddenly clicked and the universe opened up in front of him.

He pulled away and held her gaze. "We don't have to pray," he said. "We don't have to be afraid."

Stella furrowed her brow. "What are you talking about?"

"Just trust me, Stella. I love you more than anything or anyone, and I'm telling you – we don't have to be afraid. We don't have to be scared. Do you understand?"

Stella watched as Jennings' eyes dilated and began to shine like mini suns. At first she recoiled, but then she felt his love burst through and finally grasped what he was saying. It was simple; so simple that it made her smile to think how stupid she had been all her life. He was right – there was no need to be scared.

High above them the dome started to crumble. Small pieces of stone fell to the floor. Jennings raced across to the Confessio and hurtled down the stairs. He picked up the unconscious Sophia and carried her back up into the basilica. The debris falling from the roof grew larger by the second. A six-inch piece of masonry shattered by his feet.

"Come on!" shouted Stella. "Let's get out of here!"

Jennings looked round and saw Stratton struggling to get off the floor.

"It's alright!" yelled Stella, above the deafening quake. "I'll go and get him. Just get the girl out!"

Jennings watched her leap to Stratton's aid and then started for the main doors. Cronin and the Swiss Guards were still knelt on the floor praying. "Come on, Pat!" Jennings shouted. "Let's go!"

Cronin looked up solemnly. "No!" he hollered. "We need to pray! Don't you understand? This is the end, Jennings! The end of all things! This is Armageddon!"

Jennings shook his head. "No, Pat! This isn't the end. Not if we don't want it to be. This can be the beginning! We don't need to be afraid any more!"

Cronin held Jennings' bright eyes briefly and saw the truth in the words he'd spoken. A fresh surge of hope pulsed through his heart. He got to his feet and pleaded with the guards to go with them.

Michelangelo's beautiful, iconic dome was disintegrating rapidly. Huge chunks of masonry crashed to the ground like giant grey hailstones. Stella helped Stratton to his feet and looped his arm over her shoulder for support. They moved away slowly towards the nave, Stella checking upwards for danger every couple of steps. Ahead of them she saw the others running through the main doors and out into St Peter's Square.

"You'd better run," said Stratton. "Don't worry about me, I'll get out."

"I'm not going to leave you!" she yelled, forcing him onwards.

A six-foot piece of stonework fell from the roof of the nave and shattered on the floor in front of them. Stella checked herself and manoeuvred round the rubble. Just behind, a statue toppled from its recess and closed off the passage. She looked ahead and saw Jennings running back down the nave. He reached them quickly and took Stratton's other arm. With his assistance they progressed rapidly.

They were almost at the door when yet another piece of

stonework crashed before them. Jennings and Stella clambered over the fragments with Stratton dangling in between. Then, out of the corner of his left eye Jennings sensed something move. He turned quickly to see the statue of St Teresa bearing down with increasing speed. The next thing he knew he was being thrust forward by a strong hand, the momentum forcing him into the clear. He stumbled awkwardly out into the square with Stella beside him. They looked back in unison to see the figure of Stratton trapped underneath the giant sculpture.

Jennings raced back inside the church.

"Get out!" Stratton shouted. "Just get the fuck out!"

"I'm not leaving you!" yelled Jennings, struggling to make himself heard.

Stratton waved his hands towards the door and barked: "Trust me! Just go!" For a brief moment he stared harshly at Jennings, then he smiled and his eyes lit up. "Like you said, 'there's no need to be afraid'!"

Stratton's look told Jennings everything he needed to know. In that instant he realized that he could do no more. He flew back through the doors and out into the square again. He grabbed Stella's hand and pulled her clear of the crumbling basilica.

"What about Stratton!" she screamed. "We've got to help Stratton!"

Jennings shook his head. "No! We need to get clear! There's nothing more we can do for him!"

Stella took one last look back. The doors had slammed shut. She closed her mind and followed Jennings away from the carnage. After two hundred yards they reached Cronin and the guards and stopped and sat down and caught their breath.

"Look!" cried Stella, pointing to the sky above the basilica. "Look up there!"

Jennings couldn't believe what he was seeing. The storm clouds above the dome had parted in an almost perfect circle, letting through a dull grey glow. As they watched, the light grew brighter, and began to filter slowly down to the basilica. The ground beneath them shook ever more violently. Stella gripped Jennings' hand tightly. And then, in an instant, the light hit the tip of the dome and flashed with such a ferocious intensity that it sent them flying backwards into space.

Jennings found himself floating through the air in a sea of pure white. Time appeared to stand still as he hovered between colliding worlds. He wondered if this was what it was like to die, and waited for his life to flash before his eyes. But it never did. There was just a moment of sudden realization, and then blackness as his head smashed against the floor of St Peter's Square.

Chapter 94

Paul watched helplessly as the crowd bore down on Jenna and Tariq. How they had escaped being shot by one of his company he had no idea. There was something about them, though, that filled him with strength. What it was, he didn't know, but watching these two lay down their lives somehow gave him hope. And in the midst of all that was going on he allowed himself a tiny smile. Then he looked up to the sky and saw it.

Far above the furious clamour the clouds had parted. A brightening circle of light shot through and headed downwards. Paul shielded his eyes and followed the beam towards the ground. It touched the top of Tariq and Jenna's heads and then flashed so intensely that it was impossible to avoid its brilliance even with closed eyes.

Paul was thrown back against the hospital wall. His head crashed against the bricks. He slumped to the floor, but remained conscious. As the light died down he opened his eyes and tried to focus.

In the middle of the car park Tariq and Jenna were still sitting there, hand in hand and bathed in white. The rioters had been cast back, and were either lying on the ground or walking around in a stupefied daze. None of them looked remotely like renewing their attack.

To his left Paul became aware of a groaning. He turned to see Graham lifting himself from the floor into a sitting position. "What the fuck was that?" he murmured.

"I don't know," said Paul. "I just don't know…" his voice trailed off.

Graham felt around on the concrete. "I don't believe it," he said.

"What's that?" asked Paul.

"My gun, it's disappeared. I had it in my hands when that thing hit, and now it's just gone." He looked down the line of bewildered soldiers and saw that the entire company had been disarmed. "What's going on mate? What the fuck is going on?!"

Paul rose to his feet and held a hand out for his friend. "Who knows," he said. "But let's just enjoy the peace while it lasts. Come on, we'll go and see if anyone needs help."

They walked slowly across the damp tarmac and breathed in the calming air. The storm had passed and in a few hours a new dawn would be on its way.

Chapter 95

James Mackenzie held his daughter close and stroked her hair. His previous serenity had gradually waned as the missiles drew closer. Now his calm demeanour was only an act to strengthen the spirit of his staff, and to keep his little girl from breaking down in tears. As the enormity of what was about to happen hit home, he wondered what the hell he had been thinking when he decided not to take action against the Muslims. The theory had been sound, but the reality was that he had just consigned himself, and the nation he'd sworn to protect, to certain oblivion. He winced as the clock ticked down towards the first strike on New York City. 10...9...8...7...

...As the clock reached 6 he began to shake. At 5 he felt his stomach turn. 4...3...2...1. The missile disappeared from the screen and he hung his head.

For a few seconds there was silence, and then one of his junior aides began to shout. "I don't believe it! I just don't believe it!" he hollered excitedly.

Mackenzie turned and gave the aide a confused frown. "What are you talking about?"

"They've gone!" he whooped. "Look! They've all gone."

Mackenzie looked at the screen and tried to fathom what was causing the commotion.

The aide grabbed his arm and pointed. "Look, Mr President! Look! The missiles, they've all disappeared!"

Mackenzie inspected the screen once more and realized that the aide was right: it was just a blank map without any blips. He tapped the monitor to check it was working. "Where have they gone?" he asked. "They can't have just vanished into thin air. Someone get New York on the phone and find out if it's still there!"

The room buzzed with activity as operators and military chiefs made calls to posts around the nation, attempting to verify the condition of the attack. It was quickly confirmed that New York was indeed very much still standing, and that all missiles had disappeared completely.

For a while Mackenzie was too stunned to speak. Like the rest of the room he was finding it hard to come to terms with what had just happened. They had witnessed the impossible: a full-blown, bona fide miracle.

General Perry came over and offered his palm. "Well, Mr President," he said. "I guess I owe you an apology. You were right. God dammit, you were right."

Mackenzie smiled and shook his hand. "There's no need to apologize, General. I'm just glad we're all still in one piece."

His daughter tugged at his sleeve. "Does this mean we're going to be okay, Daddy? We're not going to die?"

"No sweetie, we're not going to die, nobody is. Not today."

Chapter 96

When Jennings came to the world seemed particularly dark. A crowd had begun to gather round and were gazing ruefully at the shattered remains of what used to be St Peter's Basilica. He could hear them muttering in Italian, but had no idea what they were saying. He sat up and tried to refocus his vision.

Next to him Stella was still unconscious. He reached across and gave her a small nudge to wake her up. Her eyes fluttered lightly and she lifted her head. "What the hell was that?" she muttered.

"I've got no idea," said Jennings. "But it's laid waste to the basilica. There's hardly anything left of it."

Stella sat up and rubbed her eyes and stared out into the rubble. She started to cry. Jennings put an arm around her shoulder. He wanted to say something but couldn't find any words.

"It's only a building," said a voice from behind. "It's not like anybody's died, is it?"

Jennings whipped his head round, almost ripping his neck from his body. Above him, smiling as if nothing had happened, was the familiar figure of Stratton. A little bit dusty with part-shredded clothes, but definitely Stratton. Jennings opened his mouth wide.

"Did you see the light?" asked Stratton. "It was amazing wasn't it?"

Stella looked back through watery eyes and saw him standing there. She paused for a moment taking it in, and then leapt to her feet and threw her arms around him.

Jennings got up and stretched his legs. "How the hell did you get out?" he asked.

"Through the front doors," said Stratton.

"But I saw them slam shut," said Jennings.

"They did," said Stratton. "But when the light hit they opened again. I was thrown out with the rest of the debris. It was quite cool actually. A bit like flying."

Stella loosened her hug and wiped her eyes. "What about Christiano?" she asked.

Stratton shook his head sadly. "He's gone."

Jennings moved his head from side to side to free his stiff neck. "So what exactly was that light then?" he asked. "Was it God?"

"Perhaps," said Stratton. "If that's the way people want to perceive it. But to me it's just energy. Christiano called on it, but he just couldn't cope with the intensity. He was too twisted inside. Corrupted by his own power."

"Poor bloke," said Jennings.

"Yeah, it's a shame. It wasn't even his fault. If it wasn't for this power-hungry Church then he'd still be alive. Still, I think their days are numbered now."

"You think this is the end for them?"

"Perhaps."

Jennings stared at the flattened basilica. "It's a shame about the building though. It was absolutely beautiful."

"It was," said Stratton. "But it symbolized something that had become rotten to the core. It's foundations were built on fear, and as you said – there's no need to be afraid anymore."

Jennings saw Cronin and Sophia through a gap in the crowd and headed over to see if they were alright. Stratton and Stella stood side by side and watched as the police and fire brigade approached the basilica.

"I wonder if they'll rebuild it," she said.

"I'm not sure they could," said Stratton. "It'd probably be too expensive. It wouldn't be the same anyway."

Stella sighed. "So what do we do now? Is this the end of it all?"

"It is an end. But mostly it's a beginning. It's a time to start again."

"Does that mean for you and me as well?"

"For everyone."

"I meant..."

Stratton turned to her and smiled. "I know what you meant. But I don't think that's what you want anymore, is it?"

"I just thought maybe—"

He took her hand. "We're done now, Stella, you and I. We live in different worlds. I know what you want, and it certainly isn't me. You want to be married, have children, and enjoy a normal life. I can't give you all that anymore. And even if I could, can you honestly say that you'd want me to?" He paused. Stella remained silent. "I think if you delve down deep enough into your heart you'll realize that you've moved on already. The only reason you're confused is because of some misplaced loyalty to me. A history doesn't oblige you to love someone more than another – love doesn't know time."

Stella looked into Stratton's eyes and for the first time in ages her emotions were perfectly clear. He was right, about everything. "Thank you," she said, and kissed him on the cheek.

"Don't mention it. Now, why don't you go and start the rest of your life."

Stella kissed him once again and hugged him. Then she turned and made her way through the crowd.

Jennings watched Pat Cronin accompany Sophia onto the ambulance and then walked out into the square for some fresh air. The crowd was now almost a multitude, and it was becoming impossible to think. His head still hurt from the flash of unbearable light, and the questions kept bouncing through his brain. So many questions. Too many questions. And on top of it all there was Stella. It came to him that in the heat of disaster he had openly declared his love for her. At the time it had seemed the natural thing to do. But now, in the aftermath, it felt like the biggest mistake of his life. What the hell had possessed him to say such a thing? It was abundantly clear that she was in love with Stratton, and that he, Jennings, was just a 'good friend', maybe more like a brother to her than anything else. And even that link would disappear now that he'd opened his big mouth. Everything between them would be stilted and awkward, with Stella feeling uncomfortable around him. Perhaps it would be better if he just disappeared. Perhaps he should just walk out of the square and never look back, like Bogart at the end of *Casablanca*. Determined not to hang around like a lovesick fool, he steeled himself and began to do just that.

After no more than ten paces a hand tapped lightly on his shoulder. "Are you okay?"

Jennings turned to see Stella standing with a concerned look on her face. He gathered himself together. "Yeah, I'm fine," he said. "I thought I might get out of here. I'm getting a bit claustrophobic."

"Weren't you going to let me know?"

"You were busy with Stratton, and I thought it was better just to leave you guys alone. I thought you probably needed a bit of time to yourselves."

"I suppose we did. But we're done now."

Jennings looked into her eyes and felt his heart melting. "Anyway," he said, cutting off his emotions. "You needn't worry, I'll be fine. I'll catch up with you guys tomorrow or something. I'm going to see if they've got any rooms left at the Parco dei Principi."

"Oh, right," said Stella. "Maybe I can come with you. I'm pretty exhausted myself."

Jennings sighed. "Okay. Go and get Stratton and I'll wait here for you."

"Why would I need to get Stratton?"

"I just thought…"

Stella took Jennings' hands in her own and drew him close. "I know what you thought," she whispered. "But maybe you ought to stop thinking. It's not getting us anywhere."

She cupped his neck softly and they kissed for the first time.

Epilogue I

In the two months since what had become known as 'The Day of Miracles', Jennings had hardly had time to sleep. After being completely exonerated of all charges relating to the death of Appleby, he had been rightly reinstated. His life had then been swamped with media interviews, government investigations, internal reports, and general day-to-day mayhem. His testimony had been crucial in bringing legal action against the Prime Minister, and he had also been instrumental in clearing the name of former murderer Tracey Tressel. His influence had even stretched to allowing Andrew Stone immunity for his part in the scandal.

The world as a whole had yet to fully come to terms with what had happened that day. The beams of light that had struck all around the globe were still being talked about and debated by every newspaper, TV and radio station, and internet site on earth. Some said it was God; some said it was Allah; some said it was the universe; and some said it was aliens. But whatever their viewpoint most agreed that it was a message to stop the bloodshed. The lights had only appeared where people had thrown down their weapons.

As Jennings reclined in his first-class seat he wondered whether it really was an end to warfare, or whether the current armistice was just a fleeting reaction. Perhaps when the impact of the miracles had subsided, people might forget and resume their petty grievances against one another. That was something to address in the future, however, because right now all he wanted think about was enjoying a well-earned holiday.

Next to him Stella was sipping a glass of champagne and nibbling a smoked salmon sandwich. Of all the things that were right in his life, she was the most perfect. Ever since that first kiss in St Peter's Square his existence had taken on a whole new meaning. Every day he woke up and pinched himself to check that he wasn't dreaming. It hadn't all been plain sailing as they'd both been busy, but the bond that linked them was such that no amount of time apart could come between them.

"Aren't you going to have any champagne?" she asked him.

"Maybe in a bit," he said. "I'm just enjoying the moment." He smiled and took her hand.

They touched down at LA-X just before midday. After passing easily through customs they were met at the exit by a smart driver holding up a card with Jennings' name on. He led them to a long, blacked-out limousine. Waiting for them in the back was a bottle of Dom Perignon on ice.

"Mr Romano's at the studio right now," said the driver. "He said that you can either meet him there or go straight up to the house."

"I think we'll go to the studio," said Jennings. He turned to Stella who nodded eagerly.

"No problem, sir," said the driver. He rolled up the privacy screen.

Jennings opened the champagne and poured them both a glass. He'd only had a couple of sips on the plane, but now they were in LA he felt like his holiday had really begun. He raised a toast to Grant Romano and his fantastic hospitality.

At the studio they were greeted by Romano's personal assistant and whisked round to the film set on a buggy. The Californian sun blazed down from on high.

The indoor set was alive with technical staff and runners and actors. Jennings recognized a couple of big names hovering in the background waiting to be called for their take. He looked around for Romano and saw him giving instructions to one of the cameramen. Romano turned and saw them and cut his conversation short.

"Jennings!" he said, rushing over to greet them. "It's great to see you, buddy!" He opened his arms and gave him a hug. "And this must be the beautiful Stella. I've heard all about you."

Stella blushed as he kissed her cheek.

"Come on," said Romano. "I've saved you a couple of seats. You'll have a great view of the action."

He led them across the studio floor to a row of chairs at the other side. One of them was marked 'Director' which was obviously Romano's, and there were two empty ones next to it marked 'Executive Producer'. Next to those a man sat holding hands with his heavily pregnant wife. He looked up and smiled. Jennings grinned and strode over to greet him.

"Looking good there, Grady," he said.

Grady stood up and held out his hand. "Likewise, buddy." He pulled him in and slapped him lightly on the shoulder. "It's good to see you."

After being introduced to Grady's wife, Brooke, they sat down and waited for the filming to start. Jennings looked at the set and sensed something familiar about it. It was a room with books covering the walls and an antique desk in the centre. To the left was an old grandfather clock.

"You'll like this," said Grady. "In fact you'll be a big help."

Jennings looked at him with curious eyes. "Me?"

"Yeah, you. You're not just here for a holiday you know. We need your input."

"Why? What's going on?"

"Just wait and see."

Jennings watched the two actors walk onto set. One of them was dressed in a shirt and tie and the other was dressed in black, his head covered by a balaclava. It suddenly dawned on him what was going on and he laughed.

The actors took their positions and an assistant held up the clapperboard and shouted: "The Reiki Man – scene one, take one. Action…"

Epilogue II

Stratton followed his young guide through the light brush. It was early morning and the jungle was cool and still. They had been travelling for just over ten days, and according to the boy they would reach the monks by early evening. Stratton looked forward to seeing Majami again, and taking a long break at the temple.

For a week after the Day of Miracles he had hidden himself away in the Vatican with Pat Cronin. The only other two people who knew he was alive were Stella and Jennings, and he wanted to keep it that way. As far as the rest of the world was concerned, he had died in the collapse of the basilica.

Cronin had decided to stay on in the Vatican and help root out the inherent corruption. Whatever had happened on that fateful day, there were still a large number of people in the world who wanted to remain Catholic, and he felt that left to their own devices the Vatican would build another web of lies. People needed to know the truth, and he was damn sure that Vittori and his fellow conspirators wouldn't give it to them, no matter how badly they had been burned.

On leaving the Vatican Stratton had taken a trip back home to England in Kharkov's submarine. He had missed home and had wanted to spend some time there before heading off to India. After just over a month Kharkov had come back for him.

As the morning drew into afternoon the heat once again became almost intolerable. Stratton and his guide stopped for a while in the shade and ate a small meal. It was then that Stratton had his first surprise. He had just dropped off for a brief nap when he was woken by the guide shaking him vigorously.

"What's wrong?"

"Bagheera!" the boy whispered urgently. "Bagheera!"

Stratton looked to where the boy was pointing and smiled. Trotting towards them across the small clearing was a large black panther.

"It's alright," said Stratton, calming the boy. "There's no need to be frightened." He got to his feet and welcomed his old friend. "Hello, Titan. I was wondering where you'd got to."

The panther stood on his hind legs and nuzzled Stratton's face.

They journeyed the rest of the afternoon together, and arrived at the small temple just before sundown. Majami welcomed him warmly and they sat and talked well into the night.

The next morning Stratton awoke early and joined Majami, Tawhali and another monk for breakfast.

"There is somebody I think you should meet," said Majami, as he poured Stratton some jungle tea.

"Who's that then?"

"The fourth member of our order. He has only recently joined us."

"Doesn't he eat breakfast?" asked Stratton.

"He has already eaten," said Majami. "He is outside meditating. I will take you to him in a while. The villagers called him 'Mardkonmarna' – the man who cannot die."

Stratton finished his breakfast quietly, curious about Majami's keenness for him to meet this other monk. A crazy idea kept popping into his head, returning ever stronger each time he tried to dismiss it.

By the time breakfast was finished and they had washed the plates Stratton was eager to go and find the mystery monk. Majami led him down a series of paths until they reached a small clearing next to a stream. The monk was sitting in the lotus position on a large flat rock. His head was shaved and he wore a white robe. Stratton walked up beside him and sat down on an adjacent rock. The monk opened one eye and glanced across.

"I wondered when you were going to get here," he said.

"I've been busy."

"What, saving the world?"

"Not exactly, it kind of saved itself."

"So, you're no longer needed then?" said the monk.

"I guess not."

"Do you think they'll remember what has happened? Do you think they'll learn from their mistakes?"

"Who knows," said Stratton. "You know the old saying – you can lead a horse to water…"

"What about Stella?" asked the monk. "What's happened to her?"

"She's gone off with Jennings. Best thing really I guess. They love each other more than anything."

The monk nodded sagely. "And what about the knowledge? Did you bring back the box?"

"No, it's been destroyed. And so has the copy the Vatican made. It only exists in my head now."

The monk reached to his side and produced a plain wooden box. "I made this for you," he said. "It just needs the lid doing. Perhaps you'd like to finish it off."

Stratton took the box. It was pretty much exactly the same size as the original, with a secret compartment underneath. Inside he found a small chisel. "Thanks, mate," he said.

"It's not a problem," said the monk. "Just don't fuck it up."

Stratton grinned. "Fuck off, Oggi." He picked up the chisel and started to carve.

The End

Roundfire Books put simply, publish great stories. Whether it's literary or popular, a gentle tale or a pulsating thriller, the connecting theme in all Roundfire fiction titles is that once you pick them up you won't want to put them down.